The
DRACULA
DOSSIER

The

DRACULA
DOSSIER

JAMES REESE

WM

WILLIAM MORROW
An Imprint of HarperCollins*Publishers*

THE DRACULA DOSSIER. Copyright © 2008 by James Reese. All rights reserved. Printed in the United States of America. No part of this book may be used or reproduced in any manner whatsoever without written permission except in the case of brief quotations embodied in critical articles and reviews. For information address HarperCollins Publishers, 10 East 53rd Street, New York, NY 10022.

HarperCollins books may be purchased for educational, business, or sales promotional use. For information please write: Special Markets Department, Harper-Collins Publishers, 10 East 53rd Street, New York, NY 10022.

FIRST EDITION

Designed by Cassandra J. Pappas

Library of Congress Cataloging-in-Publication Data has been applied for.

ISBN 978-0-06-123354-8

08 09 10 11 12 OT/RRD 10 9 8 7 6 5 4 3 2 1

ISBN 978-0-06-171131-2 (international edition)

The
DRACULA
DOSSIER

«Le Comte de Ville»
c/o Massip, Boscardin & Hercé-Morel
Avocats à la Cour de Paris
33 rue Galland
75016 Paris
FRANCE

3 January 2008

Mlle Sarah Durand
Senior Editor
William Morrow & Company
10 East 53rd Street
New York, New York 10022

Mademoiselle Durand:

You do not know me, and you never will.

Anonymity is *all* in this matter, and mine must be assured. I bear a noble name and have led a noble life; I will sully neither by public association with the enclosed *Dossier,* the originals of which, in the hand of the late Abraham (Bram) Stoker, known to the world as the author of *Dracula,* will be forwarded to you by my attorney once my anonymity has been assured and my privacy has proved inviolate.

What you do with the *Dossier* at such time is of no import to me. I want neither recompense nor renown, and I will refuse recognition. Simply, as my days decrease and death draws on, I mean to unburden myself of Stoker's secret. I cannot die with the truth untold, as none alive know what I know.

Stoker's biography—scanty at best—tells of several auctions to which he was party, knowingly or not, and doubtless this dossier passed from his close hoarding on one such occasion. It is likely that occasion was the auction of Stoker's personal papers upon his decease, as he was far too careful, far too circumspect a man, to let the dossier slip from his hands while alive.

On 7 July 1913, Sotheby, Wilkinson & Hodge auctioned off some three hundred–odd items, adding four hundred pounds to Stoker's meagre estate. Among these items were his notes for *Dracula;* other original manuscripts; research volumes concerning sea travel, weather, folklore, Egyptology, history, et cetera; seventeen volumes associated with Walt Whitman; fifty-odd presentation copies inscribed to Stoker by authors of his close association, such as Oscar Wilde, George Bernard Shaw, W. B. Yeats, and Robert Louis Stevenson; and a collection of the actor David Garrick's letters, which Stoker himself had inherited from the estate of his longtime employer, the actor and theatrical impresario Sir Henry Irving.

My research shows that at the Sotheby's auction a Mr. Drake paid £2.2 for Item 182: the eighty-five pages of *Dracula* notes referenced above as well as other related "miscellany." Among this last lot may have been the dossier now in my possession and soon, perhaps, to be in yours: a ragged assemblage of newspaper clippings, correspondence, and notes written, as was Stoker's habit, on whatever paper was at hand—the backs of envelopes, hotel stationery, menus, and any other flat surface capable of holding ink. Most significantly, Stoker's personal journal for the year 1888 was included in the lot as well.

The *Dracula* notes were resold on 25 February 1970 to Philadelphia's Rosenbach Museum and Library, yet the record of that sale makes no mention of "the miscellany" of Item 182. It is my belief that the two lots were separated sometime between Stoker's estate auction and the Rosenbach acquisition; further, I believe that the miscellany was purchased by a relation of mine.

Said relation was a devoted acquirer of all things Dickensian and may have purchased the miscellany—what I have entitled *The Dracula Dossier*—along with an early typescript manuscript of the now-famous novel to which it gave rise, then entitled *The Dead Un-Dead*, which somehow came to be associated with a lot of Dickens's papers in California, circa 1959. These papers I later inherited, and though agents of mine sold both the *Dracula* manuscript and the larger part of the Dickensiana over the years, I held to Stoker's miscellany. I did so for one reason only: an early perusal of the papers showed that some were written, by Stoker, in cipher. These encrypted pages piqued my interest, but I soon supposed that Stoker was simply partial to the espial, as were other sensationalist authors of the nineteenth century. And my supposition seemed confirmed when I later learned that the plot of one of Stoker's lesser novels—these, sadly, are legion, though I refer here to *The Mystery of the Sea*—turns upon the Bilateral Cipher of Francis Bacon, dating to 1605, the construction of which Stoker details in an appendix at the end of the novel, presumably as a reward for those few readers who make it that far.

So it was that, thinking I'd stumbled upon some authorial sport, a parlor game indulged in by Stoker and his writing cronies and nothing more, I let those ciphered pages lie amongst the other, unread pages of the *Dossier* for a long, long while, returning to them only in late years. This time I more than perused the papers. Imagine my surprise, Mlle Durand, in discovering that I had inherited a secret known only to Stoker and several of his intimates—a secret of abiding interest to a far, far wider world.

It all began some few years ago when I lifted the *Dossier* from my personal safe, spurred, if memory serves, by the umpteenth iteration, on celluloid, of Stoker's vampire king. As said, the pages had sat untouched for some time; shame, now, precludes my saying how long. As I riffled the pages, there fell from them a brittle, browned clipping. A partial piece of newsprint. Though all identifiers had been torn away along with much of the body of the article, I can now cite the article as having been published in the New York *Herald* on 11 November 1888. The clipping was of interest in itself—indeed, I well recall the dizziness induced by the headlines—but even more interesting was the marginalia it bore, written, evidently, by Stoker himself.

OFF THE SCENT
Sir Charles Warren's Men Still Unable to Track the Fiend.
VERY NECESSARY RETICENCE.
One of "Jack the Ripper's" Threats Partly Carried Out.

Jack the Ripper. Could it be? thought I. Could the man known to the world only as the author of *Dracula* have had a more than casual concern in the case of Jack the Ripper? The presence of other such clippings seemed to confirm it.

The subhead of the article in question goes on:

WHITECHAPEL'S LATEST.
The Police As Far Off the Scent As the Bloodhounds.

And here—most odd—Stoker had scrawled "Yes," underlining the word so emphatically as to have torn the newsprint. Other such commentary trailed the story's contents, which are:

"The Herald's European edition publishes to-day the following from the Herald's London Bureau, No. 391 Strange, dated 10 November 1888:—

Thirty-six hours have passed since the ghastly discovery in Miller's Court, Dorset Street, and nothing more has become known about the murder or murderer than what was sent to the Herald last night. Neighbors have been fancifully garrulous, absurdly ineffectual arrests have been made, and sensational journals have printed a number of absurd, groundless rumors." And here, in Stoker's hand, even more scrawl-like than usual: "Good *good*."

The story continues: "It is still said 'the police are reticent.' Quite so, and for the best of all reasons—they know nothing. Sir Charles Warren has issued a proclamation offering a pardon to any accomplice, as if so secretive a murderer possessed accomplices." Here, eerily, Stoker has sketched an ill-closed circle—it cannot be ascertained which of the words, "pardon" or "accomplice," was his target—and written, "MUST STOP CAINE." Caine. I did not know the name.

"A story is afloat that the victim"—and reference here is to Mary Kelly, the last victim attributed to Jack the Ripper's reign—"was last seen outside in the morning shortly before the shocking discovery, but medical evidence shows that this was impossible, as from post-mortem signs she had been dead some hours."

And at the end of the last legible line, above the clip's ragged edge, which reads, "The hoaxer, 'Jack the Ripper,' is again at his postal methods," Stoker wrote, "Hope. Hope remains."

Hope? Hope of what? That is the question that led me then, and finally, to train all my resources on Item 128. What I learned in the process is of an interest that cannot be overstated. This I assure you.

I close by saying that what you have in hand is my transcription of the lost miscellany of Item 128, *The Dracula Dossier*. Though I make no claim on creativity, I have arranged the original *Dossier*'s varied contents in such a way as to render them logical, or rather *chrono*logical. Its division into three Epochs is my doing as well. So, too, have I done that research necessary to render sense from pages that were never meant to be read by persons beyond Stoker's small circle. This research I have interposed as footnotes, wherein I identify persons of relevance, some lost to time, others of enduring fame, et cetera. Otherwise I have let Stoker tell his story, his secret.

My Parisian lawyer awaits word from you, Mlle Durand. Settle the issue of my anonymity and *The Dracula Dossier* is yours to publish as you please. To you I will bequeath the originals. To the world we two will bequeath Stoker's secret. In return I ask only that you let me pass from this world *un inconnu*, an unknown. Spare me my name's being associated with these pages, with the Crime of All Time and the devil that did it.

Sincerely,
«Le Comte de Ville»
Witnessed by Nicolas Massip, *avocat*

The First Epoch

THE DAY

BRAM STOKER'S JOURNAL

Monday, 12 March 1888.—Out on the streets, it seemed wise to hide the bloodied knife.

I'd preserved *that* much sense; but just why I'd brought the knife with me, I cannot say. Better to have left it back in the hotel, or to have hidden it in the theatre where last we'd used it. But no, here it was in hand, and reddened, and yes, rather hard to hide: the convex blade bends eight steely inches to its tip, and the hilt is carved in the Nepalese style. Once seen, this knife is *not* to be forgotten.

The hilt protruded from my pocket. I tried to hide it in the hollow of my ruined hand. The blade-tip itself pushed through the pocket's bottom, like a spring shoot eager for the end of this Manhattan winter, the worst in living memory. And so it must have seemed, as I stumbled down Fifth Avenue in the snow, that I would draw the knife, put its blade to purpose on some passerby; but no, no indeed.

Mad? Maybe I was. But the only knives I have known heretofore are of that spring-loaded species common to the stage. The kind that *give* upon contact with actorly flesh, the bashful blade retracting to conceal itself in the hilt. But this knife, my knife, is another type entirely; for Henry will not hear of props upon the stage. *Reality is all,* says he; and his Shylock, when nightly he begs his rightful pound of flesh from Antonio, lays a real blade, lays *this* blade upon his bared chest. Yes: Reality is all.

That: a pound of flesh, as scripted by the bard. This: a gallon of my own gore.

Had the knife sought the All of Me, sought to set the All of Me to running red? Had I sought it myself? No knife knows a will of its own; . . . but can a hand act of its own accord? I ask because, if not . . . Alas, I dare not write the word begged by so rash an act. I shall leave its sinful *S* steaming, unspoken, upon my tongue. I shall not trade ink for blood and name the act here. No. But the blood, yes, all the eager blood, drip drip dripping through the mean tourniquet I'd tied, dripping down to the knife's tip to drip drip drip onto the new-fallen snow of Fifth Avenue: a red trail to betray my wandering way, to betray me as my own hand had a half-hour earlier.

No more scratch now. Let this suffice. My left and penless hand throbs in sympathy with this, my ruined right; and so I close. The blade I have scrubbed of its blood, but the body knows no such ready repair. Nor does the soul. And so what can I do but embrace this pain as my penance?

Whatever did I mean to do? And what will become of me now?

LETTER, BRAM STOKER TO HALL CAINE [1]

19 March 1888

My Dearest Hommy-Beg,[2]

I've much to apprise you of, old friend, as Life's pendulum has swung of late to the bad; for damned I am if the Black Hounds are not hot upon my heels.

I write whilst training to West Point with all the Company,[3] and

---

1. On letterhead of the Brunswick Hotel, Madison Square, Fifth Avenue at 25th St., New York, NY.

2. Means "Little Tommy" in the Manx language; addressee of this and subsequent letters contained in the *Dossier* is Thomas Henry Hall Caine. The careful reader of Stoker's work will recognize "Hommy-Beg" as the dedicatee of *Dracula*. The less careful reader is advised to take greater care.

3. The Lyceum Theatre Company, of London, England.

whilst profiting from the peace afforded me by the Guv'nor's shunning me at present.[4] As the Lyceum herd follows his lead, I am spared having to see to *their* manifold needs as well. Though of course it fell to yours truly to arrange this 8 a.m. special from Madison Square on which we—players, scenery, costumery, &c.—chug toward the military academy. And no mean feat that, may I say, as still New York, as still *all* the eastern seaboard sits snowbound. Indeed, so desperate is the citizenry *to locomote* that some stand at the side of these very rails on which we ride, hailing our train as if it were a hansom cab.

Of course, from the aforementioned herd I exempt dearest Ellen.[5] It is she alone with whom I share this car, hence the rare peace I reference; for E.T. sits staring out over the snowscape, lost to the present save when she slips a treat into the mouth of her Drummie, the treasured terrier upon her lap. A sidelong glance at her impossibly fine profile tells me she "rehearses" at present: no doubt it is Portia she plays within, as it is *The Merchant of Venice* we will play to-night for the assembled cadets.

Alas, though I need not describe to you, Caine, those dank cellars to which the mind and soul do sometimes descend—you've suffered so long your own mullygrubs and glooms—I shall address a few particulars of my own descent. Catharsis, may I call it? Confession? Regardless, I must begin by begging your pardon for the fearful state of this letter. On tour I have even less time to myself than in London, and if I set this letter aside till such time as I can make a fair copy, well, it would be many more days till you heard from your old friend Stoker. So I shall post this in time, saying now *do not mind the stains.*[6]

---

4. Reference here is to Henry Irving. Suffice it to say—here, now—that Henry Irving, Lord of the Lyceum Theatre, was the foremost actor of his day. As he writes, Stoker has been in Irving's employ as Company Manager and informal aide-de-camp for ten-plus years.

5. Ellen Terry, actress; AKA the Lady of the Lyceum, though history whispers that Irving and she were Lord and Lady in other ways as well. As a measure of her (and Irving's) standing, consider this: Amongst the monied women of England, Ellen Terry was second only to Queen Victoria. And Terry earned it all.

6. The first few sheets of the letter do indeed show the referenced stains on the upper left corner.

Yes, they are bloodstains. And yes, it is my blood, *accidentally* shed. So I hope. And so I'd pray, if prayer availed me still.

Surely I must beg pardon, too, of my penmanship. The train knocks this nib about, yes, but this scribble is more attributable to the mummified state of my left hand. It is bandaged and cross-bound from forearm to fingertip. The thumb is splinted so as to help its nearly-severed tendon heal. My four fingers stick out from the white swaddling like spring shoots from snow. And my right hand, my writing hand, seems to suffer in sympathy; hence this horrid scrawl.

The blood, yes; quite a flow came. And I am quite lucky to—

No, no, *no*. What I am is *remiss,* what I am is *rude,* if I do not set my own woes aside for a half-page more and congratulate you, friend, upon publication of *The Deemster.* Are you aware that *Punch* has renamed it *The Boomster?* Surely you are. But you cannot know what I have lately learned from your stateside publisher: the novel has sold some 70,000 copies in its first three weeks of release here. Prodigious indeed! Your Rossetti [7] was right in directing you to become The Bard of Manxland, for such you are now, and I hope as you hold these ill-conditioned sheets you sit with your face to the sea, high and happy in your beloved Greeba, with Mary at your side and Ralph at your knee. [8]

Of course, I shall be glad to hear more about your new story— its aim, its *grip & go*—when next we are both in London; though you quite flatter me in your last letter. Please, no more thank-yous for the slight, slight role I may have played in bringing forth *The Deemster.* Only parts of it were yet crude when I read it in draught, and if my sub-editing helped set those aright, so be it. But *the work,*

Here, and throughout my transcription of the *Dossier's* originals, I italicize where Stoker and his correspondents underscored. To underscore is to unsettle the eye of to-day's reader, or so I find. You, Mlle Durand, will have your own opinion, to which you are welcome.

7. Dante Gabriel Rossssetti, poet-cum-painter; primary amongst the Pre-Raphaelites. Remember the name (if it is not known to you already).

8. Greeba Castle, Caine's home on the Isle of Man. Caine always claimed he was a Manxman, island born and bred, though he was Liverpudlian by birth. One may safely suppose that his domicile upon the island had more to do with its lack of an income tax.
  Mary: Caine's young wife; Ralph: his only slightly younger son.

friend, was all yours. So, too, is the glory and the great fall of coin that has come.

Alas, the blood. The particulars are these:

I had returned to the Brunswick on the day in question—I narrate events of Sunday the 11th instant,[9] little more than one week ago—not long after sun-up, cold to the bone and weary, quite; for Irving had held us all night at the theatre. We play the Star Theatre at present, and he deems the place "deficient" as regards the lighting of the Brocken scene in *Faust.* This was the situation he meant to set aright after that night's run. Poor Harker—a stout young Scot; you'll like him, Caine[10]—poor Harker, I say, lives in fear of being made to repaint all the backdrops, which Henry says do not pass scrutiny in the cooler electric light which reflects off them, rendering flesh pale and lips purple. Electricity versus limelight: this was the topic of *hours* of talk.

When finally I returned to my room, I knew that my respite would be short-lived: I would have but a few hours to sup and sleep, for Irving had let it be known that I was expected back at the Star by noon. "We shall lunch," said he, words which had seemed to me more threat than invitation.

So I made it back to the Brunswick bone-weary, wanting naught but some beef tea and my bed. Into the lobby I came, and toward the stairwell I went—oh, but here comes a bellman in a monkey's suit handing me a banded bundle of Irving's correspondence. And there the man stands in attendance, as if he's provided me something I wanted—*he decidedly had not*—for which provision I might wish to tip him. Lest you set a black mark beside my name in your accounts, Caine, let me say that I would have fished up a coin with still-frozen fingers but for this:

Atop the pile sat a note in Henry's own hand: "See to these straightaway."

---

9. *Webster's;* meaning 2: "the present or current month."

10. Joseph Harker, the Lyceum's newly-hired scene painter and namesake of *Dracula*'s hero, Jonathan Harker.

I was a half-flight past the bellman before I realised I'd excused myself with a curse and no coin; but I feared that the man might find a tear upon my cheek if I did not remove myself from his presence *post-haste*, so frustrated, so tried and troubled was I.

Nothing new in this task of correspondence, of course: in London I sign Irving's name fifty, one hundred times a day to letters of which he knows little or nothing; but on tour the correspondence does not decrease, as one might suppose. On the contrary, it increases, with a flow of invitations to *This That & the Other*, all of which Irving insists be answered immediately. That is, *straightaway*. I knew he'd enquire as to my progress when next we met, and I knew, too—from unfortunate experience—that he'd delved deeply enough into the letters to test me well.

I trudged upstairs. I settled at my makeshift desk. My neck was slack from want of sleep. My head swayed. My eyes were tearful from tiredness and more. Oh, but there was work to be done, and no-one to *see to it* but Stoker.

Now, dealing as I do with reams of Henry's letters, I have of course developed habits. One such is the patent refusal to open an envelope by hand: the resultant flaps and tears and tiny cuts are a torment to me. Yet as my preferred, pearl-handled letter opener wasn't ready to hand, and as I was too tired to search it out, I sought a secondary blade and settled, stupidly, upon the same knife Henry insists upon using onstage as Shylock. It was in my possession, as often it is when our host theatres provide no safer keep; for indeed I value it *highly*. It is a kukri knife of the type used by the Gurkhas when they fought for us in India, and it was gifted to me by Burton himself.[11]

Do you know Burton? I think not; and so let me say, Caine, that men such as he are rare, rare indeed. He is steel itself, and runs through fools like a sword. His talk is legendary; and as he offers it,

---

11. Sir Richard Francis Burton: explorer; translator of the *Arabian Knights*, the *Kama Sutra*, and the Tantric text *Vikram and the Vampire*; and—to judge from the description that follows—a model for Count Dracula.

his upper lip rises to reveal canines gleaming like daggers. The effect is prodigious indeed, and I have remarked it on many well-remembered occasions, not the least of which was that night, two years past, when Irving invited Sir and Lady B. to dine with us after the first night of our *Faust*. This was the night of the knife, which gift was accompanied by the tale of its having once been put to purpose by the giver, Sir B.:

Often, on his journeys to Mecca, Burton has had to pass himself off as a Mohammedan, and carefully so; for the slightest breach of the multitudinous observances of that creed would call attention to his *not belonging,* the mere suspicion of which would warrant instant death at the hands of his hosts. In a moment of forgetfulness, or rather inattention, Burton made some small infraction of rule, whereupon he saw that a lad had noticed and was quietly stealing away. Sir B. faced the situation at once and, coming after his would-be assasin in such a way as not to arouse suspicion, suddenly stuck his knife, now *my* knife, into his heart.

As Burton offered this last detail, Lady B. excused herself from the dining room; whereupon Burton averred that the tale was quite true, and that the telling of said truth had never troubled him from that day to this, the moment at which he was speaking. Said he—and I quote confidently—"The desert has its own laws, and there—supremely of all the East—to kill is a small offence. In any case what could I do? It had to be his life or mine!" Then he went on to say that such explorations as he had embarked on were not to be entered into lightly if one had qualms as to the taking of life. That the explorer in savage places holds, day and night, his life in his hand; and if he is not prepared for every emergency, he should not attempt such adventures.

Meet Burton if ever you may, Caine; but here let me resume my red tale, saying:-

So it was that, with a tool wholly out of scale to the task, I cut the band holding Henry's correspondence and scattered the lot of it upon the desk. Amidst this mass of scribbled supplication and

sycophancy—such was my mood—there stood a silver frame
featuring Florence and our nine-year-old Noel: *la famille,* whom I last
saw some months ago as they stood quayside, waving as the S.S.
Britannic set out to sea with all the Lyceum Co. aboard.

See me, Caine: There I sat at my desk in the Brunswick Hotel,
naught before me but hours of sleep-depriving work to be done
amidst a framed reminder of a family that is far away in every sense.
That Noel is nine I know all too well, for I missed the related
festivities December last, the Company having been summoned to
Sandringham on short notice, Prince Eddy asking, nay *commanding,*
that Irving please the Queen with some bits from the Bard and the
second act of *The Bells,* in which H.I. leaves not a stick of scenery
unchewed. Nine years of life, and Noel, it seems, hardly knows me.
(Tell me differently as regards your Ralph, please.) Indeed, I shall
admit to you, friend Tommy, a certain shame as regards my son: His
English is *accented,* for he has learned it neither from myself nor his
mother but rather a governess come over from Dieppe. Is that not
shaming, Caine? Of course, I might enter a plea of not guilty, or
rather *not present,* and blame the owl's hours I keep at Irving's
insistence, but still there is shame in such filial distancing, whether
the blame be his mother's or mine.

And as for Florence Balcombe Stoker? (I hear your kind inquiry,
Caine.) Well, she is beautiful still, and portraitists clamor to capture
her on canvas—she writes that she has lately sat for Whistler—but
ours has long been what Noel's Mlle Dupont would term *un mariage
blanc,*[12] and whilst we are apart, we conduct said marriage via telegraph
with no appreciable loss of warmth and far fewer *stops.* (A good line,
that. Must take care not to utter it in front of the larcenous Wilde
when next we meet!)

Alas & alack, still I *urged* myself toward work on the night in
question. *Stoker will see to it,* as Henry is wont to say. *Straightaway.*

---

12. Sexless, in other words.

There the letters lay in disarray. Would I sort them, answering by date of receipt, as typically I did, or would I cull from the lot those from persons most prominent? Perhaps I'd finger them, feeling for that thickness which betokens an invitation. I had settled on the latter course of action—lest any RSVPs be overlooked—when, in the course of shuffling the correspondence accordingly, I came upon a letter from the American Secretary of War. This I read first, for it bore upon our present trip:

". . . a pleasure to accept your offer, Mr. Irving, to play for our cadets, . . . an exception to the iron rule of discipline which governs the Military and Naval Academies of the United States," &c. Nothing urgent; no need of reply. And so I set the Secretary's letter aside; but his is the last letter I remember reading, for:

I then picked up another that seemed to bear an ambassadorial seal, but when I made to open the envelope with the kukri—yes: the kukri—well . . .

With a speed and strength for which I cannot account, I sliced deeply the padded area below my left thumb. The force of the up-slashing knife stunned me well before I felt the resultant pain, saw the resultant blood. It was as though the kukri were in a hand *not my own.* Indeed, though I saw the act *as it happened,* I did not realise, or rather did not understand, that I had cut myself until I felt the sting of it, until I saw the skin split and the red fount begin to flow.

And still I sat staring, staring long after another man would have reacted. I stared as the stain spread upon these very pages, then piled before me and ready for "Henry's" responses; oh, but that would be the least of the redness. Soon there'd be blood upon the letters themselves, upon the chair, upon the rug, upon the bed; for yes, quite inexplicably, when finally I stood, it was only to wander about the room like an arrow-struck buck.

I had brought the blade quite close to that blue-green cross-hatching that sits at the wrist, the *locus classicus* for suicides seeking to marry melancholia to sharpened metal. Had that been my intent? Had the Black Hounds finally tree'd me, as it were, such that I saw no other way out of my present predicament? To you, friend—as to no other—I confess that *I do not know.*

When finally I understood that I had cut myself, well . . . I did nothing commonsensical. I did not summon the hotel physician. Neither did I fashion a tourniquet from a neck-tie or towel. No. Instead I took up a bottle of whisky and went to the window. Throwing high the sash—sprays of blood upon the panes, upon the wall—I sat on the sill, left arm extended out over the city. The cold and the cut conspired: I grew woozy, and were I a man as small as yourself, Caine, and had I lost consciousness, I might well have slipped from that sill. But it was then that I roused myself by pouring the whisky over the cut. Oh, the sting of it, Caine! Yet there I sat, watching as the whisky married my blood and rained down red upon the street, freezing as it fell.

The snow that had been all the talk for a half-day past had finally begun to fall. The sky was low and leaden, sunless despite the early hour. The rising wind brought the snow onto the sill, into the room. I lay my split flesh upon the sill. If I thought to stanch the flow with the cold of concrete and snow, I succeeded only in staining the sill. Alas, there I sat a long, long while, watching my out-pulsing blood.

Finally—being shy of blood, as ever I've been—I fell back into the room seeking only to stop its flow. No survival instinct, this: I sought to stop the blood simply because I did not wish to see it any longer.

In the bathroom I swigged the last of the whisky before letting the bottle fall to shatter upon the tiles. Then the mirror and I shared a long moment that no man need describe to another.

Coming from the bathroom, slipping upon the blood-slick tiles, I saw the kukri where it lay upon the table. Red, seeming somehow alive. I cannot recall donning my overcoat, but next thing I knew, I was walking out onto Fifth Avenue into the blowing white with the knife in hand.

Whatever did I mean to do? Did I imagine myself a Mohammedan, searching out some infidel? Or was I myself the infidel deserving of slaughter?

Here I misremember the facts as they passed; and I can report only that I wandered the streets of the city as they went quiet and white. The Manhattanites sought shelter. Storefronts shuttered. Transit fell still. And there I was, wandering through the blowing white and leaving a blood-red wake.

The wound, Caine, was of course quite serious. I know that now. And when finally I returned to the Brunswick some several hours later, the hotel surgeon closed it with eleven stitches whilst impressing upon me how lucky I was, how lucky indeed. But as I wandered through the storm, I must have seemed a madman indeed to any who saw me, who saw the red-state of my ill-wrapped hand or the hilt of the knife it yet held. Oh, I am attached to the kukri, true; but still, to have brought it from the Brunswick with me? Was I intent on mutilating myself the more? Questions, Caine. So many questions to which I did not, *do* not, want the answers.

I wended southwards through the storm, and next I knew it I sat staring out through the greasy windows of a gin house deep in the bowels of the Bowery. There, having drunk away some small part of the pain, I summoned sense enough to tell the publican the tallest of tales as to what had happened. Of the knife in my pocket I made no mention. I paid her, too, for the provision of a none-too-clean pillowcase fetched down from an upstairs room, the type of room that rents in hourly increments. The kindly, cunning publican—too skilled in lying to swallow mine—nursed me nonetheless: she ripped the pillowcase into strips, washed my still-running wound, and wrapped my hand mummy-tight. As the makeshift bandage reddened right away, she impressed upon me the need to see a surgeon. Indeed she denied my request for an upstairs room, doubtless thinking I meant to die within it, and instead sent a boy out onto the snowy streets to summon a fly.

I must have let slip the name of the Brunswick, for soon the aforesaid fly had brought me back to the hotel. Hours had elapsed.

This was attested to by the depth of the snow that had drifted into the room over the bloodied sill. It was mounded now in the room's corners. The carpet was white. And the room itself was, of course, frigid beyond description. Still, I dared not touch the window. I dared not touch anything; for now it seemed I'd returned to a murder site. *Oh, the red of it all!* Only when I knew, *knew,* that all the red was mine, only then did I summon the hotel surgeon, first breaking a window-pane with a boot: another story to concoct. (Which stories, which lies, Caine, comprise the sum total of the creativity I've engaged in of late.)

While awaiting the surgeon, I sat at the desk on which Henry's letters were strewn. I was tired, Caine, *mortally* tired. I cannot say that I was yet myself, not at all. On the subject of Self, however, I can report that through heavy lids I saw an envelope addressed to me. The hand was somehow familiar. *Could it be?* I stared at the letter, which seemed to gleam now like stream-bed gold, and I dared to hope, dared to dream, that it might be from him, from Whitman.[13]

And indeed it was: Word had finally come from the Master himself! How had I missed it when earlier I'd sat shuffling Irving's correspondence like a cardsharp? How had I failed to recognise a hand so long cherished?

Of course, I'd written Whitman some months earlier, informing him of the impending tour and asking if finally we might meet. An *audience,* it would be, Caine, with the Poet of Poets, the Pope of Mickle Street.[14] Whitman had responded that he was not wholly well, and that I should write again nearer the desired date of our meeting; this I'd done the week prior. And here now was his response. I tore the envelope with my teeth and shook the note free.

"FRIEND ABRAHAM," began his note, the block letters of the salutation fast ceding to a scrawl: "My dear young man.—Your letters

---

13. Walt Whitman, of course.

14. Whitman was then resident on Mickle Street, Camden, New Jersey, a ferry's ride from Philadelphia and so a half-day distant from New York City.

have long been most welcome to me—welcome to me as a Man and then as an Author—I don't know which most. You have done well to write me so unconventionally, so fresh, so manly, and so affectionately all these years.—And now you are in Need."

Had I written as much, or had the Master inferred it? I cannot recall; but doubtless I had hoped that Whitman would somehow save me. I wonder now if he hasn't, for how I hold to his words! I will *re-build my life* upon them, Caine. Let it be *a new Stoker* you see when next we meet, when next you're able to cut for me a slice of your London leisure, busy though you must be. The words to which I refer? Of course you will wonder, and so:

Whitman's handwriting was familiar to me from his many replies to the letters I'd written him whilst at Trinity,[15] but now I found age in its forward slope, frailty in the slashed-at *T*'s and dotless *I*'s. I'd heard it said that Whitman was not well. I'd even heard his death rumoured on more than one occasion. And so I'd neither pressed for my audience with a second appeal nor held out much hope of having one granted. That said, reading Whitman's denial of my request was a blow, a blow indeed:

"My physique is entirely shatter'd—doubtless permanently—from paralysis, age and sundry ailments—And so it is, FRIEND ABRAHAM"—Whitman has always enjoyed teasing my name out so—"I cannot tell you to come at once to Camden. It seems that we two friends shall part this plane never having said Hello, but neither will we have to bear a last Good-bye. Death is a breath upon my neck now.—So it is that I return your younger letters under separate cover. Let it be you and not the coming crawlers o'er my estate who decide their Fate." And indeed I found said packet amidst the massed letters.

"I see the pain in your pen," concluded Whitman. "And to assuage it I can only offer this—that each man must somehow sign God's name to the letter of his life. Do so yourself, FRIEND. Good-bye."

Here then were my last words from Whitman. Worse: They told of

---

15. Trinity College, Dublin.

his imminent death.[16] Need I confess that tears fell anew, Caine? Here was news *most* unwelcome. My heart shattered as the whisky bottle had. And amidst the most jagged shards were a few Wildean ones, I confess it; for Wilde lately went to Mickle Street for an hour of claret and converse! It is a tale I've too often heard him tell. Oh, but *pish, pish,* to hell with Wilde. Better to read again the Master's admonition:-

"Each man must sign God's name to the letter of his life. Do so yourself."

However will I, Caine, when my *own* name pales so, and my life seems absent of all purpose?

Alas. Alack & Alas.

Oh, but glad I am that Whitman took it upon himself to settle my letters. A reader with neither sympathy nor understanding might see in them a means of embarrassing me, or worse. More about said letters anon; but first let me tell the present tale to its end:

The surgeon's knock gave me a start. The man entered when I bade him do so, only to stand there, stupefied, staring at the bloodied sill, wall, sheets, &c. Soon he fell to shivering from both the sights and the chill. Luckily, the staffs of such hotels as the Brunswick are well schooled in discretion. Their guests pay a premium for its provision. Still, in the course of the extempore surgery, I sought to explain myself with sketchy references to whisky—now the room reeked of it—and stuck windows, &c. The medico listened with professional sympathy and made no further mention of the blood. Indeed, having sewn my skin, he offered to arrange for a second suite, one in which I could stay the night whilst the present room was ranged, set right. Soon I'd signed myself into these rooms as "Walter Camden," bringing with me naught but the passel of letters returned by Whitman and a draught which the surgeon said would help in the summoning of sleep. I thanked the man, stating, quite plainly, that "Mr. Irving need not be bothered with . . . *all this.*" And though

---

16. Rather premature, as it would turn out: though Whitman was indeed unwell, he would not die for another four years. If he and Stoker corresponded further—as seems likely—we have no record of it.

the surgeon refused recompense, his nod told me I'd secured his silence.

Thusly did I settle into that second suite saying *To hell with Henry Irving, too,* and about to re-read my old letters. You'll not wonder, Caine, that I called up a bottle of the Brunswick's best to ease the twin pains of surgery and squirm-inducing self-assessment; for I wrote the first of the letters sixteen years ago, when, aged twenty-four, I was certain, *certain* I'd found in the Master's work words with which to anchor my soul.

"I am," I'd written to Whitman, "a man of less than half your age, reared a conservative in a conservative country, and who has heard your name cried down by the great mass of people who mention it." And so it was at Trinity then: one read Whitman *in private.* I went on:[17]

"I am writing to you because you are different from other men. You are a true man, and I would like to be one myself, and so I would be towards you as a brother and as a pupil to his master. . . . You have shaken off the shackles, and your wings are free. I have the shackles on my shoulders still—but I have no wings." Mercifully, I grew somewhat more prosaic and presented The Facts which then seemed to me pertinent, though why I presumed Whitman would be interested in my biography I've no idea. The presumptions of youth, I suppose.

"After an invalid childhood,[18] I have grown well and am, at present, six feet two inches high and twelve stone weight naked, and used to be forty-one or forty-two inches around the chest. I am ugly[19] but strong and determined and have a large bump over my eyebrows.[20] I

---

17. The ellipses that follow are Stoker's, not mine. He must have deemed the deletions too "squirm-inducing" for inclusion in his letter to Hall Caine.

18. True. Though the diagnosis is unknown, Stoker did not walk before the age of seven. Bedridden, he read, setting aside his books only when his father pushed his bed nearer the window so he could watch his siblings at play upon the strand.

19. He was not.

20. Allowed.

have a heavy jaw and a big mouth and thick lips—sensitive nostrils—
a snub nose and straight hair." Oh, Caine, the shame of having
described myself so! "Sensitive nostrils"? Good God! It's a wonder
Whitman ever wrote in reply.

"I am an Athletic Champion with a dozen cups on my mantel. I
have also been President of the College Philosophical Society as well
as an art and theatrical critic of a daily paper. . . . As to my personality,
mine is a secretive nature.[21] I am equal in temper and cool in
disposition and have a large amount of self-control. . . . I have a large
number of acquaintances and five or six friends—all of which latter
body care much for me. Now I have told you everything I know about
myself, " and I suppose I had. Would that I had signed myself *Abraham
Stoker* and set my pen down; but no:

"It was with no small effort that I began to write and I feel
reluctant to stop." Reluctant, indeed. "I hope you will not laugh at me
for writing this to you, but how sweet a thing it is for a strong and
healthy man with a woman's eyes and a child's wishes to feel that he
can speak to a man who can be if *he* wishes father, and brother, and
wife to his soul?" Oh, my.

There I lay upon my second bed in the Brunswick, mortified at
having re-met my younger self. Such a meeting is one to which most
men of middle age would not gladly go, agreed? (Yes, yes: I know *you*
would agree, Caine.)

As the storm came on without, a second rose within. My "need."
What was the need Whitman had referenced? And how would I have
shaped it into words if Fate had found me at the Master's knee?

"The wife and child"—he would surely have inquired—". . . how
are they?" And what might I have said? The truth?

True it would have been to say, to admit, that it is Henry Irving
rather than Florence Stoker to whom I am *truly* wed. I have long been
his close associate and most intimate friend. Surely I know him as

---

21. And so it was, much to the bane of later biographers, myself included.

well as it is given any man to know another. Indeed, Henry and I are so much together we are each able to read the other's thoughts. Surely you have seen, Caine, the same capacity in a husband and wife who have lived together long years and who are accustoming to working together *at life*, and at understanding each other? Yet it is not with Florence that I share such a bond. It is with Henry. And so it has been since first we met, nay since first I saw him upon the stage and we set off together on a path of sympathy which somehow has eventuated to . . . to *this*.

The place was the Theatre Royal, Dublin. The St. James's Company was on tour, and the piece chosen for the fateful night found Irving in the role of Captain Absolute.[22] To this very day, Caine, I can close my eyes and see Irving upon that stage, so different was his performance, nay his very *presence* from anything I—or anyone else, for that matter—had ever seen. Yet days passed and no mention was made of the performance in the papers. Of praise there was none, none at all.

You'll recall, Caine, that some years prior I had gone round to LeFanu offering to watch the city's stages for the *Mail*, though first my studies and later my work with the Civil Service precluded this becoming more than a sometime hobby.[23] And so it was that when next Henry Irving played Dublin, he found his Hamlet roundly and soundly praised.

The very day my review appeared in the *Mail*, word came round that Irving wished to see me. I was summoned to join his post-performance party at Corless's, where I partook of the famous hot

22. And so the play would have been Richard Brinsley Sheridan's *The Rivals*.

23. J. S. LeFanu: co-owner of Dublin's *Evening Mail*, yes, but more importantly the author of the early vampire novel *Carmilla*. It is likely Stoker had been introduced to LeFanu by the Wildes, whose neighbor he was in Dublin's Merrion Square.

Stoker is due some credit here. Prior to his unpaid employ at the *Evening Mail*, reviews of theatrical productions appeared at a day's remove from the performance, and so the traveling companies often found they'd left behind a hit. Stoker asked his bosses to extend his nightly deadline so that his reviews might appear in the next day's edition. Soon the practice spread, till now it is of course the norm.

lobster as well as other succulents from off that justly famed establishment's most excellent grill.[24]

It was not at dinner but afterwards that I learned that my host's heart was something towards me, as mine was towards him. He had learned that I could appreciate high effort: I could *receive* what he could *create*. This would become the basis of a relationship as profound, as close, as lasting as can be between two men. Revisiting that hour of deep emotion, each for the other, threatens to unman me now as I write, Caine; for yes, I can only wonder: How has it devolved to this untenable situation, this nameless Need I meant to confess to Whitman?

Alas, it was at the post-prandial party in his rooms at the Shelbourne that Henry Irving changed the course of my life; for he announced that he would recite *for me* Thomas Hood's poem "The Dream of Eugene Aram."

The effect of this on my person was prodigious. I sat spellbound. Outwardly I was as of stone; naught was quick in me but receptivity and imagination. All thoughts of self-existence ceased. And after the recital I sat reduced to hysterics; though here I hasten to add, Caine, not in my own vindication but rather to further attest to Irving's power—though you know it well yourself—that I was no green youth gadding about with back-stagers, looking to yield to the least emotional force. I was, as men go, strong, strong in many ways. I was then in my thirtieth year, and had been, for nearly ten of those years, a salaried clerk in the service of the Crown. Indeed, in addition to my journalism and the short, serial stories I engaged upon when able—trifles, trifles all—I was then completing that drowsy tome upon which my renown as Author seems destined to rest, rather as a crow upon carrion. I refer of course to my dry-as-dust *The Duties of Clerks of Petty Sessions.*[25]

---

24. It would seem Stoker put down his pen only to take up a fork, yet his contemporaries never go beyond "burly" in describing him. And if Stoker's habit of remarking upon meals is given to Jonathan Harker in *Dracula*, Harker's wife, Mina, is made to share her creator's fascination with trains: ". . . I am the train fiend. . . . I always make a study of the time-tables." *Dracula*, chapter 25.

25. Drier than dust, in fact.

The Petty Sessions court service had been established in 1827 to deal with minor offences—sheep theft and such like, country crimes typically settled amongst the Irish by the taking up of cups

Though my tears on the night in question were a surprise to all present, less surprising would have been the news, some months later, that I'd thrown aside the Civil Service to cast my lot with Irving; for I'd accepted his offer of the Lyceum's management, telegraphing my YES! to H.I., c/o The Plough & Harrow in Edgbaston.

As the Lyceum, the *new* Lyceum, was to open with *Hamlet* on 30 December, I met a touring Irving on 9 December in Birmingham, having in the meantime altered my whole life: I had married; for Florence—whose father I'd had to assuage re: the present security and later pension I was abandoning—had agreed to speed by one whole year an event already arranged. Of course, Henry was mightily surprised—and I daresay none too happy—to find I'd arrived in Birmingham with a wife in tow! And so it was, Caine, that I came to swear my allegiance twice in the span of one week. Doubly-wedded. Doubly-bound. And destined for I knew not what.

All these years later, and Florence is far away, in *every* way; but oh, how Henry hovers! Yes, it is Henry to whom I am truly wed, Henry to whom I am truly bound. And he is killing me, Caine! He is bleeding me dry! Oft-times I fear I can neither leave him nor live. And if I were desperate last week at the Brunswick, I am only slightly less so now due to Whitman's admonition. To the Master I'd written asking—much as the ancients had asked the oracle at Delphos—*How am I to live? How am I to survive?* Not in so many words, no; but still Whitman had read my Need between the lines and replied.

"Every man must sign God's name to the letter of his life."

Yes: I shall hold to his words. Upon them I will rebuild myself, my *self*. For what is the opposite choice?

Friend Caine, my heart and hand have had enough, and I must compose myself before our arrival at the Academy, which the conductor's call tells me is imminent. I must now don the mask of goodly Uncle Bram and see to the performance, the players'

---

and cudgels, in that order. Stoker's codification of the travelling clerks' duties remained in use for more than a century, and to it the rural Irish owe many an uncracked skull.

problems, &c. Need I write that already I long for curtain-fall? But I long, too, to keep your company upon these stained pages, and so I shall return to this letter as fast as Fate allows. Be sure of it.

Till then, I am, S.

BRAM STOKER'S JOURNAL

20 March, 2 a.m.—No sleep now. And so: this diary I've too long ignored.

We arrived back here at the Brunswick not an hour past. En route, and despite the soothing shimmy of the special, we all of us were wound too tightly to sleep, indeed were rather wild after making such a success amongst the cadets. Even H.I. came from his car to watch the lesser lights play at charades, and I fancied I saw a smile upon his lips as E.T. gently mocked his Mathias.[26] Of course, he had not a word for me; but still I am forgiven. I see it. I know it. And I am thankful, for his genius holds sway with me as to-night I fell anew.

Henry Irving was genius at West Point, and four if not five hundred cadets were witness to it alongside myself. What a wonderful audience they were! There they sat upon their benches in the mess-room, looking like a solid mass of steel: uniforms of blue and gray, with buttons of brass; and their bright young faces clean-shaven, and their flashing eyes—all this and more lent force to the metaphor: a solid mass of steel, indeed.

And the attention, the understanding of the audience could not, *cannot* be surpassed. Many of the cadets had never seen a play—so I heard it said, and often—yet not a line of *The Merch.*[27] went amiss. There was not a single point of the plot that did not pass for its full value. They attended to the trial scene—wherein E.T. as Portia is seduction itself &

26. The lead role in *The Bells,* which was a cornerstone of Irving's early success and thereafter a staple of the Lyceum's Company's repertory.

27. Shakespeare's *The Merchant of Venice.*

H.I. as Shylock wields my kukri so disturbingly well (and how the sight of the knife chills me now!)—as if they were present at a court-martial. Such rapt attention inspires an actor, and never more so than this night. So, too, did the applause inspire us all as it rose at the end of each act.

Of course, the in-loading earlier in the day had been a trial of another sort entirely. Already we were light, as regards costumery and stage-craft, word having come down from the Academy that no stage *proper* would be available to us. So it was that Irving declared that we'd mount the play as in Shakespeare's day. To this end, notices were set upon an easel beside the stage: *Venice: A Public Place; Belmont: Portia's House; Shylock's House by a Bridge; &c.* The costumes worn would be simple. And we encountered but one problem re: props; which of course a still-angry Henry insinuated was somehow *my* fault. Problem was, the lights available to us in a soldiers' mess-hall were insufficient to distinguish the lead trunk from the silver one in Act V, Scene III. "And so Portia's suitors"— this Henry railed at me from the makeshift stage, silencing the assembled Company—"will have but one trunk of gold and *two* of silver to choose amongst! Where is the sense in that, Mr. Stoker?"

"The sense, Mr. Irving," I countered from afar, "is in the text. A child could follow the *sense* of the scene if only it were played *as written.*" This last angered him, as I'd known it would; for all present caught my allusion to Henry's penchant for playing the Bard *not* as written but rather as it pleases him.[28] Our little row ended when H.I. stalked off the stage, calling for both his dresser and his dog and ready to curse me roundly to whichever showed first.

But in the end all went well. *Better* than well. At play's end there was that wondrous pause—as ever there is—and then, as if acting upon a single impulse, every one of the cadets rose and, with a thunderous

---

28. Stoker is backed here by no less a source than George Bernard Shaw, Irish critic, playwright, and Nobel Laureate, who was never a fan of Henry Irving's and blasted him time and again for what he deemed the actor's "Bardicide," going so far as to say:

  "Henry Irving was an illiterate mutilator of every piece of fine dramatic literature he laid his hands on. Like all old actors, he slipped in the most puzzling way from complete illiteracy to the scraps of shrewdness and wisdom he had picked up from Shakespeare and the plays he had acted."

cheer, threw his cap up. For an instant the room was blackened as if by bats. And oh, the cheering!

There was a significance to this cap-tossing that we understood only later, when it was explained to us, *sotto voce,* by an underling of the Secretary himself:

According to the American Articles of War which govern the Military Academy, a cadet's tossing his cap—*except* at the express order of his commanding officer—is an act of insubordination punishable by expulsion. To-night, however, those fine fellows were forgiven for finding this to be the means best suited to the expression of their feelings; and, strange to say, not one of their superior officers, least of all the Secretary himself, seemed to notice so dire a breach of discipline.

Splendid, splendid it was, and every eye was brimful as Irving took to the forestage to make the speech requisite to such an occasion, the last line of which I well recall and here record:-

"I cannot restrain a little patriotic pride just now," said he in his most measured, most mesmeric tones, "and I will confess it. I believe the joy-bells are ringing in London to-night as, for the first time, it would appear the British have captured West Point."

Whereupon there rose a great *Hurrah!*

Splendid indeed.

All were in a transport of delight. For my own part—and I have been in the theatre each time Henry Irving and Ellen Terry have played *The Merchant*—I never, *never* knew it to go so well as to-night. Genius indeed.

Of course, it fell to me to recall the company to earth—to such thankless tasks I have grown accustomed; for I had informed Mr. Macallister of the New York, Ontario & Western Line that the all Lyceum cast, crew & accoutrements would be aboard the special by midnight. By my watch we rolled at one minute past.

Now the clock creeps unto 3. Where is sleep? I want a walk, but this cold seems contagious of death, and I am wary of wandering the streets again. And so here I sit, wearied yet wide awake. Reading up this page, I am reminded of my love of the Guv'nor, of his genius; but then here lies my blood-let, bandaged hand, testifying to . . . what, precisely?

Is it too late to take up my letter to Caine? *Q.:* How much can I confess? To Caine? To myself? Alas, this much at least:

Forty-odd years of a life lived, and what have I to show for it but another man's achievements? If Henry be King, I am naught but his Shadow Prince, topped with an ever-tightening crown. Naught but a shadow. It is true. Without him I shan't even be cast.

Sleep. Where is sleep? I summon it with whisky. Far better now to dream than to think.

LETTER, BRAM STOKER TO HALL CAINE (CONTINUED)

21 March 1888

Dear Caine,

I resume this letter two days on, swearing to finish it now that we are returned from West Point *a great success.* At present, Henry has convened the designers onstage, for he asks, nay insists on their further refining the lights for *Faust;* and so it is that I am able to steal some minutes backstage—all but secreted amidst the fly ropes and curtain folds!—to finish this bloodless letter to a friend.[29]

Thankfully, the Star is dark to-night, as to-morrow we shift from *The Merchant* to *Faust,* with which we'll close before steaming home. And—all praise!—I find myself forgiven, and once again in the Guv'nor's good graces; for, in Henry Irving's world, forgiveness is comprised of two factors: the passing of both Time and Tests.

It has been ten days since *I failed him.* Time enough, it would seem; and earlier to-day I passed the latest—and hopefully the last—of his Tests. Of which more anon; but first:

How was it that I fell into disfavour? I was a half-day *disappeared,* as

---

29. Stoker would finish the letter, of course, but its thirty-six pages would require posting in two envelopes (extant), each addressed to "T.H.H.C., Greeba Castle, Isle of Man," and each bearing the admonition *Confidential,* twice underscored.

And "bloodless" is a reference to Stoker's having begun the continuation on unstained stationery.

Henry puts it; for I did not "return" to the Brunswick till mid-morning of the next day, Monday, leaving the premises by a lesser exit only to re-enter by the main. From my newly-ranged room, I sent word to Irving's suite that I was returned and well, and wished to explain my absence in person. Irving replied that he was glad of the news but could not see me at present. Neither could he refrain from scribbling at the end of his quite curt reply the prior night's take; which, though scanty, showed his discipline favourably as compared to mine: the proverbial show had gone on. In truth, the larger part of Irving's pique may be owing to his suspicions as to where I had disappeared to; which suspicions were not allayed when I told him, finally, of a maiden aunt resident on Staten Island to whom the favor of a visit is owed by any Stoker passing within these precincts. In the course of said visit, I had incurred the injury to my hand. So I said. So I lied.

Henry was having none of it, of course; but there the matter lies. Let him suspect, let him stew. He cannot claim the All of Me. Were I to tell him the truth—the truth of my weakness and my worries, the truth of what I'd done to myself—he would only add it to his armory. Henry can be cruel like that, though of course now he says, oh so simply, that I was missed, that I was worried over once the storm came on and I could not be found.

And indeed the storm did come on. Little did I suspect that Sunday morn that snow would soon fall to the height of my hip and that winds would drive it into drifts towering to twenty feet. Still, people tramp about with squares of carpet tied to their shoes, and fires yet burn in the tunnels cut through the drifts so as to do the melting work of a cloud-occluded sun. Quite a calamity it has been. Newspapers name more of the dead every day. Most of them are found frozen.[30] Yes, Caine: I was lucky indeed, having set out from the Brunswick in the state of upset already described.

So yes, I suppose I *had* disappeared, as far as Henry knew: an

---

30. History attributes more than four hundred deaths to the Blizzard of 1888, one hundred in New York City alone.

occurrence unique in the long years of our acquaintance. He has *never* not known where to seek out his Stoker. But lest you sympathise with a worried Henry Irving, let me add that he was worried for himself as well: the Guv'nor is unfit to govern.

Left to manage the Lyceum Company, *his* company, on his own— and on a day, no less, when all was *in extremis* owing to the storm— Henry Irving reverted to that discipline that has stood him in good stead for so long: He insisted that the Lyceum would play the Star that Sunday eve though all the other theatres had shuttered against the still-strengthening storm. He intimidated every member of the Lyceum Company, back- and forestage, into reaching the Star that night for an eight o/c curtain. All did. All save yours truly. And a triumphant Irving threw open the doors a mere twenty-five minutes late, cursing me all the while, to be sure; for, ever and always, at the Lyceum or elsewhere, it is *I* who open the theatre doors.

Of course, I have had it from E.T. that the audience was scant and the orchestra more so: a few hardy types comprised the former, a harp & two violins the latter. Still, the show *had* gone on. Doubtless my absence played a part in Irving's deciding to play: He would and could make do without me. As I suppose he did. Now he is armed all the more: He doesn't *need* me. Yet still, in the Time since, I have been subjected to his Tests; and the details of the latter would be too menial to mention if I were not certain they'd amuse you.

To-day's first Test: I was to find a horse for *Faust* less "healthful seeming" than the one I hired Wednesday week. ("Swaybacked, Stoker! More mangy!" came Henry's command.)

And Test the second: I was to secure a bunch of roses for E.T. (as Margaret) to have at her side onstage—if a particular play does not allow for flowers, H.I. brings a bouquet to E.T. in her dressing room ½ hr. prior to performance, this w/out fail—though prop flowers would surely suffice for the play itself, let alone to-night's dress rehearsal. Regardless, Henry wanted roses. And these, mind, I was to find in a city yet to thaw.

The roses I did find, albeit at famine prices: $5 a bloom!

Extortionary! And damned I am if I didn't tell the florist so! As for the poor horse, well . . .

Taking a tip from one of the local carpenters in our employ, I hied to a marketplace none too distant from Madison Square. There, tethered to carts of commerce, I found a selection of beasts of burden hardly worthy of the word "horse." I was quite saddened by the sight, in fact; but still I paid a devilish drayman $25 for his helpmate. But as I led the pitiable nag back to the Star by its reins— I dared not mount her, lest my girth be the reason she finally give up the ghost!—I found that I was being followed. In short order I was accosted by one, then two persons, who strewed at my feet, like so much manure, accusations of my having abused a beast that had been mine but for a quarter-hour! Their cries drew a crowd. Hisses were heard.

My protestations were in vain, and I escaped a dire fate—a constable came, and "jail" was not the worst of the words bandied about—only when someone in the ever-constricting crowd heard me say, nay *holler* the name Henry Irving. (No sense in hoarding a currency like fame, Caine, as no doubt you know.) As this fellow had seen our *Faust* when last we played it in New York, he asseverated, *much* to my relief, that the play did indeed call for a horse that already had its forelegs in the grave.

Thusly did I escape the scene; but as for the ol' bone bag—who'd have done quite well in the role, I must say, and would have lived out her last days in luxury—she was requisitioned from me by the constable. Indeed, I was made to trade the reins for a citation, and the accompanying fine was twice what I'd paid for the pitiable creature! Such that the tally of the day's tasks was $25 for five red roses and $75 more for a near-dead horse I had lost. Brilliant, that.

Of course, it all made for a fine story once I'd returned to the Star, spun some Irish round the reality, and recounted it to the assembled cast and crew. Even H.I. had a laugh. "Oh well, Stoker," said he, happy to hear of my late humiliation. "At least you've come back to us and are accounted for." He even clapped me upon the shoulder as he exited upstage right, calling out to Harker that he had better touch up the prop horse in our possession, as "our real one has lately gone to glue." So it is I know that Henry has forgiven me; and just when I'd come to hope he'd let me go.

Alas, must, *must* close & post this letter, as the longer it lingers the less inclined I am to sign/seal & send it, showing myself as low as I've lately been. (I am better now by a bit—blessed be Walt Whitman—so worry not!) But if I cannot confess such things to you, Caine, then to whom can I—

Damn him! Here comes Henry calling my name. And so now I close for true.

Sto.

TELEGRAM, BRAM STOKER TO FLORENCE STOKER

23 March 1888.—The countdown begins! 33 *Faust*s remain. Homeward 1st May, due at Liverpool 8th. S.S. *Germanic.* Do not bother to come. Will train home with Henry.

BRAM STOKER'S JOURNAL

3 May [1888]—aboard S.S. *Germanic* to Liverpool, whence London; seas rude.

2 days seaborne, with 6 more to go. Have been too long gone, but many worries arise re: finances, the Lyceum, *the new life*, No. 17 [31] &c.; but I hold to the belief that changes for the better are aborning. They *must* be.

As ever I do, I have been sleeping well at sea—a blessing, this, and

---

31. The Stokers were then resident at No. 17 St. Leonard's Terrace, Chelsea. Census returns indicate a household of five, including one Mary A. Dunhunter, cook, and Ada B. Howard, parlor maid. It would seem appearances were being kept up, and we may safely assume that Florence Stoker knew little of the financial shoals onto which her husband had drifted.

doubtless attributable to the fact that Irving & Co. are, perforce, at present, *still*. There is much talk, but not much *to do*. Save for poor Harker, of course, who has his orders for Henry's newly-decreed *Macb.*, such that he sketches non-stop, joking all the while that he might as well surrender his London rooms and move in to the scenarists' shop upon our return, for there he'll surely be from debarkation through to *Macb.*'s debut. (*Q.:* Is Henry's hope of going-up by year's end realistic? *Mem.:* Check that no else is planning to mount a *Macb.* w/in a half-year of ours.)

It is our great & good fortune to find ourselves sailing in the company of Cowboys, for Captain, nay *Colonel* Cody[32] takes his Wild West spectacle to London's West End. So it is that the hold of the *Germanic,* were she to go down in this red weather, would loose upon the sea floor such a collection of props & costumes & animals, &c.—theirs & ours combined—as to stun Neptune himself.

Of course, the Cowboys fancy themselves the more fortunate for having *our* company: they lined the gangway as we came aboard, welcoming us with war whoops, &c. The actors having been thusly flattered, it has been no great trick to get them to entertain; and so, after dinner, when normally the sexes would split—he to his port & cigars, she to her tea—we of the S.S. *Germanic* retire to the parlour ensemble, and there the hours fall away fast as we charade, recite, sing, joke, and otherwise amuse ourselves. It is a joy, truly, and—to the extent that I partake—a distraction *most* welcome to me at present. Indeed, I shall now set this pen in its stand and dress for dinner; for I am lead-bellied, and these heaving seas cannot deter me from such feasts as last night's:

Oysters on the half shell to start, along with olives and salted almonds, whence we progressed through a soup of squash (w/ an excess of garlic), fish (genus: unknown), entrée (unremarkable), and a most excellent remove of Mallard Ducks w/ Currant Jelly. (*Mem.:* Get jelly recipe for Florence, or rather Mary.) The parade of desserts had at its

32. Wm. Frederick Cody, AKA Buffalo Bill, b. 1846, d. 1917.

fore a Plum Pudding w/ Brandy and Hard Sauce *(exquisite!)* but ended with a savoury that suited *not at all:* Herring Roe on Toast. Salt on Pasteboard, more like. Yet we all attend the dinner bell impatiently—for the fare, yes, but also for all that follows—and there it is now: I hear it above the storm sounds.

Later. Returned from dinner. Indeed, the sea has come to a boil, and many amongst us are unwell. Those of the Wild West would no doubt fancy a return to the plains at present, and the Lyceum lot would opt to play the rag-taggiest, most rat-ridden of theatres as long as its boards were still. Only the meanest brute could fail to sympathise with the women aboard, some of whom refuse absolutely to return to their cabins. Having piled their pillows and rugs, they camp upon the parlour floor. "Safety there may be in numbers, ladies," cautions our Captain, "but that old saw makes no mention of seasickness, I'm afraid"; but still the green-complected ladies refuse to decamp. Of course, Ellen is not amongst the sickly. She is quite well, in fact, but as she has already roiled the sorority somewhat—by being, simply, herself: the New Woman whom they both envy and deride[33]—she *acts* unwell whilst yet nursing the worst of the lot. That said, she could not refrain, at table, from telling me of a Cowboy's wife—to call her a Cow Mistress seems unkind—who lately confided to E.T., with tears in her eyes, that "sea-sick is worse'n two acres of toothache."

2 a.m.—I take to these pages a third time to-night, if only to confess that I am as unsteady as the sea; for E.T. and I have just been some hours in Henry's company. Henry, who can talk of nothing nowadays but our distant *Macbeth*.

Indeed, he said he was in a quandary re: the staging of the weird sisters' scenes—ought there to be music when Macbeth first meets the witches upon the heath? &c.—and he was hopeful of hashing these things out with us. And so, all but bursting with bonhomie and opining

---

33. New Woman: a term much in use in the day, and not always flatteringly. *Dracula*'s Mina Harker is meant to be such a one.

that hot toddies were *surely* in order on such a sea night as this, Henry asked if we three mightn't repair to his cabin and order some up. Ellen and I were loath to leave the larger group, but Henry's "asks" are, of course, commands, and he is not to be denied: when either inspiration or insomnia strikes, Henry Irving seeks and *shall have* company. So it was we three sat together some while. The balance of talk tallied, as ever, to Henry's favor, and I left his cabin with a list of things *Stoker will see to.* Still I hear him, expounding, pontificating, *playing.*

It was hours ago that I began to long, *long* for solitude and the clarity that sometimes comes when I set pen to paper, as here. Yet there is no clarity now, none at all. Just whisky and words I dare not write—a sea of words on which my heart tosses as surely as does this ship.

Can it be that I've come to hate him? There, it is written.

LETTER, BRAM STOKER TO HALL CAINE

4 May 1888

Dearest Caine,

I have just now received your letter dated 15 April and addressed to me c/o the Star, for the fools there "forgot" to give it to me upon its arrival. Glad I'll be, friend, to return to the *controlled* surrounds of St. Leonard's & the Lyceum—even though it is Flo. who controls the former and Henry the latter!

Briefly, as regards your letter, you owe me no apology for its brevity. To have met my epistle with one of equal length would have availed no-one—neither you, who would have been taken too long from your truer work, on which the world waits; nor I, who, were I to receive thirty-odd pages from *your* pen would be even more mortified at having written as many with mine. What's more: No such obligations exist between those who sympathise. That is a lesson I have learned from Lady Wilde, who insists that friends should speak or write *as they will,* letting candour show their mutual concern.

Of course, I second your motion that we see each other soon. Assuming I survive this crossing—a safe assumption, sayeth the Captain, as the worst of the weather lies behind us—and land at Liverpool the 8th instant, to espy your person upon the quay will please me *no end*. In that eventuality, I shall happily over-night in the city. If, as I suspect, you cannot come, St. Leonard's or your city rooms in Victoria Street shall suit at your convenience, and I shall content myself with posting these pages from Liverpool in lieu of a proper embrace.[34]

Now let that be an end to "business."

Your suggestion that I seek to leaven my mood and sort my thoughts by writing a memoir of another, happier time is one I have considered at some length; and I believe I shall start forthwith. "Writing maketh an exact man," to quote Bacon, and *exactitude* is what I am wanting now, exactitude of heart and head. Purpose, in a word.

Yes indeed, I find I am eager to begin the project even though I have never been much of a diarist. I shall hold as my goal the posting of both this letter and an achieved *aide-mémoire* upon our arrival in Liverpool, assuming you cannot come to take *personal* possession of said pages and see proof of their prescriptive effect. (Hope dies hard as concerns any encounter with Hall Caine!) But before I begin, let me address, albeit cursorily, a few points raised in your letter:

Firstly, as regards the American friend you reference—and about whom, Caine, I must say, you are uncommonly reticent[35]—by all means send him round to the Lyceum at any time. He is a doctor, you say? And knows London well? Be assured, Caine, that I shall meet him as a friend, as of course any friend of T.H.H.C. is, perforce, a friend of mine.[36]

Secondly, as you are kind enough to enquire about my cut, I am

---

34. According to Vivien Allen's *Hall Caine: Portrait of a Victorian Romancer* (1997; Sheffield Academy Press), Caine always kept rooms of his own in London and seems to have secreted himself away in the city when not at Greeba Castle.

35. Reticent indeed.

36. Words Stoker will come to rue.

pleased to inform you that it has closed and starts to scar; which scar, I fear, shall be worthy of Miss Shelley's monster.[37] Alas, it shall serve as a reminder, a sort of *memento mori,* warning me of what might have been. Blessedly, I have stepped back from that abyss. I am well, or leastways better; and mine will be a new life, henceforth. And so:

What better way to begin anew than to return to those days when you and I both were newcomers to London, steeds—ha!—reigned to the chariots of our chosen gods? And so the calendar recalls me to mid-August of 1881, for it was then I learned from Lady Wilde that Rossetti—whom we all knew to be Great yet still presumed sane—had taken on a new secretary: You.

Aide-mémoire

What follows is undertaken upon the command of a friend—Thomas Henry Hall Caine; and to him it is addressed.[38]

In late 1878, my wife, Florence, and I re-located to London from Dublin, letting, for £100, six unfurnished rooms in Southampton Street, very near the Lyceum Theatre; at which latter place I was bound by salary to Henry Irving. As finances seemed to allow it—salaried at £22/week, I bethought myself a veritable Midas amongst men—I brought into my own employ both a cook and a lady's maid, meaning to spare my young wife the wider world just outside our door. However, it was not long before we, at my wife's ~~insistence~~ suggestion, resituated ourselves.[39]

---

37. Reference here, of course, is to Mary Shelley's *Frankenstein.*

38. "Command" seems an interesting choice of words here. Is Stoker less willing than he lets on to undertake the memoir? He earlier writes that Caine simply *suggested* he do it. But does a suggestion become a command when one friend is steeling himself to ask the other for a sizeable loan, as Stoker was?

39. Here the reader might spare a thought for the otherwise contemptible Florence Balcombe Stoker.

Though she was twenty-one at the time—eleven years younger than Stoker—Florence might as well have been ten, so coddled had she been all her life in Dublin, where she'd only ever had to be beautiful. (The author George du Maurier referred to her as one of the three most beautiful women he had ever seen.) Florence, who'd never left home unchaperoned, now found herself in the streets of Covent Garden, amidst its tenements and lowly taverns, and amongst people—"peddlers, pick-pockets, porters, and prostitutes"—new to her and none too pleasing. One can hardly fault Florence for suggesting, or rather insisting, on the move to Chelsea.

A lease was taken at No. 27 Cheyne Walk, Chelsea, an area abounding in antiquities and the traces of great men. I, however, knew the neighborhood thanks to a great woman: the estimable "Speranza," Lady Jane Wilde. She, along with her husband, Sir William Wilde, had been a second set of parents to me whilst I was living in Dublin yet longing for a London life; and glad I was, indeed, the day I had word from Lady Wilde that she, in consequence of Sir William's decease, would be joining her sons, Oscar and Willie, in London.[40] Specifically, she had recently arranged rooms for herself and Willie at 146 Oakley Street, very near Cheyne Walk, thereby doubling, nay trebling the appeal to me of No. 27 and leading me to lease it.

I had been somewhat out of touch with the Wildes of late, and was most eager to remedy that upon receipt of Lady Wilde's announcement, implying, as it did, that there'd been no lasting rupture in her regard for me.[41]

And so it was that by 1881 I was resident in Chelsea with both an old friend returned to me, in Lady Wilde, and a new one about to be made, in you, Caine.[42]

Though Lady Jane and Willie would decamp to Grosvenor Square by year's end, she revived her salon—her Saturday at-homes—whilst living on Oakley Street. This she did seeking only companions and like-minded converse, and those Londoners who cut her did so cruelly.[43] Of course, others cut her these days, but for different reasons entirely, on

---

40. "Consequence," indeed. In fact, and in Victorian parlance, Sir William Wilde had left his wife "horribly involved." Indebted, in other words. Ruined, in to-day's terms.

41. By "rupture," Stoker would seem to reference an odd but little-known fact of literary history: Florence Balcombe had broken off a long-standing engagement to Oscar Wilde in order to marry Bram Stoker.

42. Nota bene: no mention here of fatherhood. Irving Noel Thornley Stoker was born on 13 December 1879.

43. Perhaps so, but Lady Jane Wilde, AKA Speranza of the Nation, had hardly set herself up for a warm welcome in London.
    From 1846—and spurred by the Famine—she had been publishing some of the most violently nationalistic poetry ever to come out of Ireland. That alone would hardly have put her in contention for London's new Socialite of the Season, but the lady further lessened her odds of social success by the application of a fashion sense which the kind referred to as "personal," the unkind "inappropriate" or worse.

which topics I shall say only this: Unlike her sons, Lady Wilde has ever been the very soul of discretion, a fact perhaps best illustrated by a story I alone can tell, a story that will bring you nearer the heart of Speranza than you have yet come, Caine, which is as I would have it; for, as I have earlier sworn that your friends, *all,* shall be mine, let the obverse be true, too: Take my friend for yours. And so:

It may be said that I was orphaned rather late in life. My parents took to the Continent in 1872, when I was twenty-six. With them went my two younger sisters. We five brothers stayed behind. Abraham, my father, had, over the course of fifty-odd years in the Civil Service, faithfully served four monarchs—the Georges III and IV, William IV, and Victoria— retiring with the gift of a gold pocket watch and a pension that fast proved insufficient. And though we had never been Castle society,[44] we boys had had our educations seen to and were on our way, as it were, by the time my parents and sisters left Ireland, not as expatriates but rather as refugees needful of stretching a pension in Switzerland, where room and suitable board could be had for five francs/per day.

By this time I had left Trinity College, Dublin, and joined the Civil Service myself. My sanity in the face of that sameness put forth by the Service was preserved by going to the theatre five nights out of ten. Thusly did I come to crave Art, to need it as the end cap to a day of drudgery. And though I had heard rumours, it was not until I accepted the invitation of a classmate—Willie Wilde—and accompanied him home at Christmas, that I learned that though some wonderful people *made* art, even more wondrous were those who lived it.

The Wildes were then resident in a large, darkly opulent and deeply draped manse of Georgian origin at No. 1 Merrion Square. It was a corner house with balconies beyond number and a staff of six. It was, at once, both mere miles and a world away from the cold Clontarf home of my childhood.

No. 1 featured a lofty entrance hall with a wide central stair—a *car-peted* stair, mind: I had never seen such opulence before. And I had time

---

44. The true Protestant bourgeoisie, in other words.

enough to take it in that day, for Willie, who'd headed off I knew not where, had told me to wait there. Off the foyer was a room, a library whose walls showed shelves bowed by the burden of leather-bound books, hundreds, nay thousands of books. Its floor was covered in carpets that told of faraway countries, and everywhere, *everywhere,* there was bric-a-brac to boggle the mind. The mantels, too, seemed to sag beneath the weight of astrolabes, candlesticks, ceramics, shells, &c. There were the requisite clocks as well, though the lot of them were unwound and stared out stupidly from beneath their bells of glass. Tiny tables were laden and ever at the tipping point; one would brush by them to one's woe—over they would go, and down would come, with a crash, this or that collection of this or that collectible *thing.* Flowers, dried, dying, and fresh. Fossils. Waxed fruit. Such a surfeit of *things*! No flat surface was spared, not even the huge desk sitting center-all: books lay there in disarray amidst inkwells of horn and heartwood and even bone—Sir William Wilde set his preferred pen, which he rarely let rest, into the eye socket of a small and seemingly mammalian skull, its tip sunk in a pot of ink that had been placed where once there'd been a tongue—and there were sheaves of paper showing scribble all the way round, scribble which appeared, from where I stood, as disordered as ants at a picnic, but was, doubtless, the work of one of the Wildes' overly fine minds.

Yes, if Willie had told me to wait in the foyer, there I would wait. And wait I did, cursing my friend all the while. Then suddenly there came from upstairs the clap of a closing door. This was followed hard by a brace of ladies' maids fluttering downstairs as if to escape a spray of shot. They were nothing if not birds roused from the reeds by the report I'd heard. They attempted to bow to me as they descended, heads down, daring not to break stride. When the one nearly tumbled ass over teakettle, as we Irish are wont to say, the other fell to laughing. *Exeunt giggling,* as it were, save that these maids were pursued not by a bear but by Lady Jane Wilde.[45]

---

45. Reference here is to one of Shakespeare's few and more famous stage directions, from *The Winter's Tale:* "Exit, pursued by a bear."

There she stood at the top of the stairs, staring down and seeming to teeter. Never before had I seen such a . . . a *mass* of womanhood.

"And you are . . . ?" From her tone I knew that the true answer was also the wrong one, but still I said:-

"Abraham, ma'am, or rather just Bram. Bram Stoker."

"I see," said she. "Well, Mr. Just Bram Stoker, I suppose you are aware that you are *not* the Swedish Ambassador. In that, the maid who announced you was much mistaken."

"I am aware of that, ma'am, yes. . . . I've come with Willie, who—"

Lady Wilde met the utterance of her elder son's name with the snap of a silver fan. "Say no more," said she, whereupon she began her slow descent. Slow not for show, mind, but because it took some care to set into motion *all that she was.* Into play came sundry laws of physics and Society both, and I saw why it was she was displeased to waste the effort of her entrance on me, the Ambassador of Naught.

I stood staring. It was rather like watching a ship putting out to sea.

The lady clung, then, to the better side of sixty. Only in late years has Lady Wilde consented to the crawl of the calendar, though she long ago succeeded in confusing it.[46] Such was the impression Speranza made upon me that evening that these long years later I cannot recall the Swedish Ambassador at all—though he did indeed arrive to dine at No. 1 that night—yet I recall our hostess in all her many particulars; so:

She wore a gown of crimson silk, its volume as indebted to the lady herself as to the several crinolines she wore beneath it. Here and there, atop the silk, there'd been sewn dew-like patches of Limerick lace, and round what had once been a waist there was wrapped a golden scarf of Oriental origin. Her face was full-fleshed, and of an uncommon length, and her hands I must describe similarly. She appeared rather more handsome than pretty: her face was plastered with white powder, and her black eyes smouldered like coals above an avian nose; dark, too, was her plaited and piled hair, which she had seen fit to top with a

---

46. As various biographies I have consulted in the preparation of the *Dossier* put Lady Wilde's birth date in either 1821, 1826, or 1829, let us agree to take the mean and say she was a quarter-century older than Stoker.

crown of gilded laurel. Supernumerary to this last, most classical touch, her broad bosom bore a collection of brooches, making her seem a sort of mobile mausoleum.

When finally Lady Wilde berthed at the bottom of the banister, she put forth her other, fanless hand. In it she held a handkerchief reeking, not redolent but *reeking,* of rose-essence. I held my breath, took her hand, and came up from my kiss saying, "You will forgive me, madam, I am sure; for I would *very* much like to be the Swedish Ambassador. Alas, fate is sometimes unkind."

At this the lady let go a slow smile. "Well said, Mr. Bram Stoker. Dare I deem my entrance not wasted after all?" Whereupon she whispered, "A fearful bother, it all is sometimes. I was *very* much enjoying a reworking of *Prometheus Vinctus* up in my boudoir, and would have preferred to—"

"Aeschylus, then?"

At this she dipped her topmost chin and batted her lashes. "In*deed,*" said she.

My knowledge of Greek tragedy having won her to my side, Lady Wilde laid her hand on mine and asked that I lead her into the parlour. Finding that room yet free of the expected company, the hostess bade me sit beside her. This I did, delighting as she deigned to apprise me of the three rules requisite to success at her table. In this she showed me a most uncommon courtesy, for the larger lot of her guests were left to fend for themselves and, failing, as often they did, waited a long while for their second invitation to dine *chez* Wilde. The rules, then, were these:

1. Epigrams are much preferable to argument, ever and always;
2. Paradox is the essence of wit; and,
3. Insignificant people should avoid anecdotes.

"Are you, Mr. Stoker, insignificant?"

"Only as compared to present company, ma'am."

"Oh, yes," said she appraisingly, "Willie has done well to-night. Typically it is As-car who delivers me social treats such as yourself." Her younger son has always been *As-car* to his mother.

Later, the bell having rung, Lady Wilde invited me, not Willie—Oscar was "elsewhere" that evening, as often he is nowadays as well—to escort her "*à table*." This I did clumsily, catching myself up in her skirts and causing her to list towards starboard. Righting herself, she said, as if to excuse us both, "One atones for being occasionally somewhat over-dressed by being always and absolutely over-educated." [47]

Lady Wilde sat me at her right. The Swedish Ambassador was at her left. When he failed to stimulate Speranza in her native tongue—which he spoke *bouncingly*—she resorted to his. [48] Left, as it were, in the dust of Swedish discourse, I turned my attention to the table's far end, and there I found the second life-friend I would make that night: Sir William Wilde; who, though we were eight at table, with the Ambassadress at his right, sat reading a book between courses.

I liked him of an instant. And though our close acquaintance would be cut short by his death, I have never yet, in all the years since, met a wiser man. I shall, however, allow that his reputation as the least likely of libertines was *not* unearned; for he was indeed rather slovenly of habit, rather simian of aspect.

It was some ten years prior to my meeting the Wildes—1864, then—that Dr. William Wilde both segued to Sir William and saw his new title sullied by his being made party to a most unfortunate, well nigh ruinous, court case. At question were charges of heinous conduct brought against him by a former patient, one Miss Mary Travers. As that case is yet widely spoken of—and the particulars are surely known to you, Caine—I shan't offer details here. [49]

---

47. This very line later appeared in Oscar's *The Picture of Dorian Gray*. If Stoker has his dates right—and it seems he does—Lady Wilde's words predate her son's novel by some sixteen years and give credence to Stoker's earlier claim that Wilde's work was, in large part, "larcenous." But can one be liable if the line is stolen from one's own mother?

48. Lady Wilde was, amongst other things, a polyglot, fluent in ten languages. She had learned Swedish preparatory to Sir William's being awarded the Order of the North Star by King Karl XV in 1862.

49. As the modern reader may be less well versed than Hall Caine in the infamous court proceedings of the nineteenth century, I offer here the first verse of a smoking-room ballad both men would have known:
"An eminent oculist lives in the Square.
His skill is unrivaled, his talent is rare,

Though acquitted of all charges in the Travers affair, it was yet a much-reduced Sir William whom I met that first night at No. 1. Infamy and the habit of over-work had taken their toll on him. Indeed, he seemed reduced in every way; for, after dinner, when our party repaired to a secondary parlour, I saw that Sir William, in addition to being much older than his wife, was much shorter, nay altogether *smaller* as well.

And when Sir William approached me where I stood at Speranza's side, it was only to look up into his wife's face in search of the sign—yea or nay—telling him whether she deemed me worthy of his time. Evidently, an answer was given in the affirmative, for soon I was invited into Sir William's *sanctum sanctorum,* that library-cum-study off the foyer, where, behind closed doors, we proceeded unto cigars and the discovery of a shared interest: Egypt.

Sir William had toured that Land of Mysteries for the first time in 1838. It was he, in fact, who, having seen Cleopatra's Needle lying as it had for centuries beside Pompey's Pillar, began the campaign to bring the monolith to its present placement on the Thames Embankment.[50] That night, as we sat in Sir William's library surrounded by more volumes than I had ever seen in private possession, no few of their spines showing the name Wilde—his as Author, hers as Authoress—my host told me the story of his having discovered a mummy in shallow sands near Saqqara.[51]

I sat listening, raptly, for the gifts of the storyteller run amongst the Wildes. And a lie it would be were I to say that the hairs upon the backs of my hands did not rise up when, at story's end, and after a most effective pause, Sir William nodded towards a sarcophagus lying upon an iron stand in the library's far corner.

And if you will listen I'll certainly try
To tell how he opened Miss Travers's eye."

50. Odd that Stoker should place this as primary amongst Sir William Wilde's many accomplishments, which included pioneering eye/ear surgery, radicalization of the treatment of the deaf, advancements in the fields of anthropology, folklore, and, yes, Egyptology.

51. It falls to me to inform the reader of the *Dossier* that Stoker would appropriate the Saqqara story some years later, using it to frame his 1903 novel *The Jewel of the Seven Stars,* itself now mummified. Among Stoker's considerable oeuvre, *Dracula* alone is immortal. Ironic, that.

"It isn't," said I. "It cannot be!"

"It is," said a smiling Sir William; ". . . and it can."

I was up and at it in a trice. "But however did you . . . ?"

"It was no matter at all, really." Sir William caught up to me and now busied himself with the re-stacking of books which had been stacked, discreetly, upon this centuries-old sarcophagus, making it seem but a roughly hewn, gaudily painted table. "The laws of export are rather more lax than they ought to be, and coin accomplishes the rest. I had only to pay taxes comparable to those that would have been levied were I importing a comparable weight of salted fish."

"Indeed?"

"Very." Sir William went on to assure me that he'd spared the mummy a worse fate at the hands of smugglers less well intentioned than himself. "I suppose I *could* have left him in Cairo, true. But I have promised young Budge that I shall bequeath it to him, or rather to the British Museum . . . in the end."[52]

Before lifting the lid of the sarcophagus, Sir William scurried about the library locking its doors and turning low its lights. "It would not do to let the servants know," he explained. "Doubtless they'd league up to demand more wages, what with there being another member of the household to attend."

As a child confined by illness to my bed, I developed the habit of dreaming whilst awake. I conjured caves near Clontarf full of whisky oared in by smugglers. I conjured pirates aplenty. Then, too, began my fascination with secret languages, with ciphers. It was this last that led me to the legended hieroglyphs of Egypt, whence I travelled in many a waking dream. But never, never had I dared imagine the moment now come—here, at hand, was an actual mummy!

At hand indeed. The mummy had been partially unwrapped, and as I aided Sir William in raising the lid of the sarcophagus, the first thing I

52. Budge, here, is E. A. Wallis Budge (later Sir), then an Egyptologist of growing repute in the employ of the British Museum and later its Head of Antiquities. It is to Budge's translation of *The Book of the Dead* that we still turn to-day, more than one hundred years after its initial publication.

saw within was a golden, glinting finger stall capping the third digit, the flesh of which was black and desiccate and put me in mind of a child's licorice stick. "Young Budge and I began the unwrapping some months back," whispered Sir William, as if the mummy were a child asleep in its crib, "but, our friend here being rather bitumous and brittle—a bad job by the embalmers, I should say, done on the cheap—we thought it wise to desist. We made it no further than the hand, the bones of which—"

"Bones?" I asked. Somehow I'd not considered there'd be bones.

"Yes, of course," said Sir William. "The bones *pop!* when touched, rather like glass tubing. It gave me quite a start when first I heard the sound."

His *pop!* had startled me such that I had fallen back from the sarcophagus, leaving Sir William to struggle with the weight of the lid. "I say, Stoker, if you wouldn't mind . . ."

I re-took my share of the weight at once, with apologies. "It's just that—"

"Yes, yes, I know. Rare it is to meet a mummy, *wondrous* rare. . . . Touch it."

"No, no," said I, sniffing the spiced air of the Ages as it rose. "I'd not care to bother . . . him or . . . her?"

"A him, assuredly," said Sir William. "We found a mummified frog upon his privates, representing rebirth, yes, but seeming also a nod to Osiris, who—"

"Who, when he was dismembered by his brother, Set, had his penis thrown into the Nile. To be devoured by frogs."

"Well done, Stoker. Well done indeed. Yes, our friend here is a male of the Late Period, or so says Budge. Six hundred B.C. or thereabouts. . . . Go ahead, then."

Indeed, I had begun to reach my hand toward the mummy's, but just as I touched my fingertip to his, there came a sharp rap at the library door, and:-

"Darling? Open up, darling." And once she'd pushed wider the door Sir William had unlocked, Speranza swept in, chiding her husband; so:-

"Horrid, *horrid* of you, sir, to hog the most handsome and least Swedish of our guests." Sidling up beside me, Lady Wilde laced her arm through mine. "Why, oh, why, husband," said she with a sigh, "could you not have been accorded honors by a country more accustomed to converse? France, for example, would have suited. Or Italy. The Italians seem an amenable, amiable lot."

"I shall look into it, my dear," said Sir William with a wink. The oculist's standard line.

The Wildes then let go of the game, for Lady Wilde had fast taken the lay of the library. With a nod towards the opened sarcophagus, she said, in tones only slightly less sardonic, "So, Mr. Stoker, I see that my husband has introduced you to the eldest of our three sons. He is not the most amusing, mind you, but he is certainly the best behaved."

"He has, ma'am, yes. *Most* extraordinary."

"On successive visits," said Speranza, grandly, "you will note, Mr. Stoker, that the doors of our home are barred to the *merely* ordinary."

As indeed they were. True it was, too, that there would be many more visits succeeding that first. I dined with the Wildes often in those years, the last of Sir William's life, and at their table I saw shine the leading lights of Dublin life. Often I would go round to No. 1 from the rooms I shared in nearby Harcourt Street with my brother, Thornley,[53] and I would enter unannounced; for, as we hovered over his mummy in the half-light, Sir William had said that I should consider his library as my own. "On one condition."

"Sir?" Of course I'd have agreed to any number of conditions, as already I'd espied the first volumes I'd borrow: Sir William's own *Superstitions* and his Lady's *Collected Poems.*[54]

---

53. Thornley Stoker had, at the time of which Stoker writes, recently been appointed to the post of visiting surgeon at "Dean Swift's Hospital for the Insane," or St. Patrick's Hospital, Dublin, a position similar to that held by *Dracula's* Dr. Seward.

54. Reference here is to Sir William Wilde's *Irish Popular Superstitions* (1852), in which Stoker would have read of the *dearg-due,* or "red bloodsuckers" of ancient Ireland, as well as the *Tuatha De Danan,* or "deathless ones." Of equal interest, of course, would have been Lady Wilde's work, poems as well as stories replete with references to the supernatural.

"What do you carry upon your person," asked Sir William, "that is of most value to you?"

"Why, this, I suppose," said I, proffering the pocket watch that had been given to my father upon his retirement. It had passed to me upon my father's recent decease, and it served me as rather more than a time-piece: it was an object lesson in How Not to Live; that said, I loved my father very much and would have been loath to part with his watch, which now I held up by its fob chain, as a mesmerist might have done.

"Upon the desk, just there," said Sir William over his shoulder, for he was halfway up a ladder and trying to reach down a hollowed-out volume of Herodotus, "there is a box of smallish proportions. Do you see it?" I did. It was of hammered gold, and filigreed. "The key to that box I keep in this book. If, sir, I find your watch within that box, I shall know that one or more of my books has left this room with you, and that it or they are in your good care. I seek no other assurance, nor stipulate any other conditions." Whereupon Lady Wilde, standing solemnly by all the while, cleared her throat, rather pointedly.

"Oh yes, yes," continued Sir William, taking the cue. "And if, Mr. Stoker, you enter this room to find me at my work, bent over a book or a blank page, pen at the ready, I beg of you, please, do not speak until spoken to. My train of thought rides lightly upon its rails these days, I'm afraid, and I suffer derailments not well, not well at all."

"Not a word," said Speranza, forefinger raised to her lips. And with a tilt of her head towards the mummy, she added, "And hush-hush, too, about you-know-who."

"Not a word," said I, thereby sealing an oath that both granted me access to the city's finest private library and occasioned my never knowing the correct time, for my watch was ever in that box. It is not over-statement to say I read, or at least considered, every volume in Sir William Wilde's possession. (Not so his wife's: Speranza's library was upstairs and off-limits to all and everyone, including her much-indulged sons.) And it was some while later, as I sat in Sir William's chair one day at noontide, considering which of his volumes would return with me to

Harcourt Street, that I saw for the first time—and here, Caine, I come to the point I mean to make—. . . I saw The Woman in Black.[55]

Having signed out from my desk at the Castle,[56] and having traded my half-hour luncheon for a trip to the Wilde library, I'd gone round to No. 1 at noon. I was eager, I recall, for a bit more Euripides and some Shakespeare. I'd not supposed I'd see Speranza, for she rarely dressed or descended before mid-afternoon, loathing daylight as she does. Already a pall had fallen over No. 1, for Sir William had been some weeks in bed, and we had had, of late, an unfavourable prognosis. His end was near.

I entered to find the servants standing about teary-eyed. Oscar was at home, and Willie—whom Oscar said had been away "on alcoholiday"—was due presently. It was as I stood in the foyer talking to Oscar—and asking quite innocently about Florence, to whom he'd introduced me some weeks previously—that I, or rather *we*, heard the hall door open; for surely Oscar and the servants, despite all evidence to the contrary, saw and heard as I did and were aware of the woman, dressed all in black and closely veiled, who had come into No. 1 wordlessly and now, unmolested, stole through the foyer and up the stairs. Yet no-one looked at her. Extraordinary! Was this an apparition? Could no-one *see* the woman but me? How else to explain the abject *non*-occasion of her coming?

I watched the woman's progress with slackened jaw, and as my thoughts turned from Oscar and the servants to the constabulary—here was an intruder, surely!—I wheeled around only to find myself alone in the foyer. Oscar and the servants had scattered. So, too, had The Woman in Black disappeared into the upper reaches of No. 1. What was I to do? My options were few, for I would *never* have dared ascend those stairs uninvited or unaccompanied; and further, I was due back at the Castle

---

55. Stoker indulges here in something of an inside joke. *The Woman in White* was an absurdly popular novel amongst the Victorians, and one to which Stoker turned often, borrowing its structure for both *Dracula* and this its precursor, the *Dossier*.

56. Dublin Castle; where Stoker worked in his position as Clerk, Second Class, in the Civil Service. Clerks could only absent themselves from the Castle with the permission of the Senior Clerk, and were accountable for all their time as measured in half-hour increments. Later, upon his appointment as Inspector, Petty Sessions, Stoker's situation would be less restrictive, but only slightly more stimulating.

in—I guessed—a quarter-hour, no more. So it was that, tucking Euripides and the Bard underarm, I took my leave; but when I returned two
days hence, again at noonday, again I saw the black-clad visitor. In she
came, and upstairs she went, wordlessly, whilst I stared.

My puzzlement was slow in ceding to suspicion, for still I was green
in the ways of the world. Indeed, my suspicions would not be confirmed
until Oscar and I, some years later, met to mingle our weeps in a common cup and put the business of Florence behind us. Only then did we
speak of The Woman in Black. Doubtless it was I who brought her up.
And my relief at learning the truth was greatly tempered by learning,
too, what Lady Wilde's love had cost her.

The Woman in Black was, of course, Sir William's last and preferred
mistress. And every morning of his slow decline unto death, she had
come to No. 1, ever in black, always veiled, to sit at her lover's side.
Oscar held that his mother was, nay *is,* incapable of so vulgar a sentiment as jealousy; but I rather suppose she paid a dear price those dark
days. Not one woman in a thousand would have tolerated the presence
of a rival at her husband's deathbed, but Speranza did, and bade her sons
and servants do the same, in silence; for she must have known that Sir
William loved the woman, and she could not begrudge him the happiness her presence afforded him.

Still, she, Speranza, was Sir William's lady, and he was her knight. I
believe she did right. And I believe, too, in their love, such as it was; for
I myself have learned that there is but one vantage point from which to
judge a marriage: from the inside looking out.

Would that Oscar had learned from his mother's lesson in discretion;
for, devoid of it himself, I fear he sets himself up for a fall.

Aide-mémoire (continued)

As said, it was indeed Lady Wilde who told me that you, Caine, had
come to London as Rossetti's new "man."

The month was August, the year 1881; and the occasion of this news
was Lady Wilde's resumption of her Saturday-afternoon at-homes—or

conversazioni, as she calls them—that had been so popular in Dublin. Of course, her London salon was slow in attaining a like popularity.[57]

I arrived to find Lady Wilde's rooms crowded to less-than-critical mass. The bell being broken, I knocked upon the door at No. 146 Oakley Street. An Irish Betty answered in time, squinting, and taking it upon herself to apologise for the dimness within. "Shure, it's her Ladyship that likes to turn daylight into candlelight. Follow me, if you're able," said she, whereupon I proceeded to the salon proper through low-ceilinged, dark-paneled passageways. Several persons sat upon the stairs. Others milled about. As I stood in the shadows, I heard my name called, and called again, and followed the sound, shouldering my way to where Lady Wilde sat.[58]

"Mr. Bram Stoker," came the standard greeting.

"Lady Wilde," said I, bowing precipitously.

"Tell us," said she, making free with the royal we, "how does Mrs. Stoker fare these days?"

"She is well, and sends her regrets."

"Her regrets are well received, as ever they are."[59]

I nodded. "And you, milady, are looking *quite* well." Indeed, she was resplendent in a gown of purple silk set off by a matching headdress and golden earrings that depended to the level of her many brooches. The air around her was redolent of roses, as ever it is. Bangles could be heard upon her wrist as she withdrew her hand from my kiss.

"I *am* well, sir," said she, "quite." And, beckoning me closer, she spoke on:-

57. Stoker is too kind here. Speranza, newly impoverished and unhappy at having had to leave Ireland, was a long while establishing herself in London. She only did so at the time in which—not *of* which—Stoker writes, that is to say 1888; and her ascension was due entirely to Oscar's increasing renown. In 1888, he accepted the editorship of a popular magazine, *Woman's World,* and published his *Happy Prince and Other Tales.*

58. Another visitor diaried: "Went with mother to see Lady Wilde to-day. There she sat all alone in her glory in such wee rooms that mother and I later wondered how she had gotten into them—she seemed rather like a ship in a bottle."

59. Stoker would seem to allude to a lingering chill in family relations; and indeed, though Lady Wilde appears to have fast forgiven Stoker, still she begrudged Florence for having cast her As-car aside.

"Would that one could say the same of poor Miss Potter, there. Do, Bram, make yourself useful: Go tell the poor dear that to dress in tints of decomposed asparagus and cucumber flatters her face *not at all*. And she oughtn't to speak so much. With such a face, she ought to be still, still and very grave." She smiled, slyly. "Oh, but I am serious! If she doesn't remove herself at once I shall be forced to rearrange my candles. See how she *steals* the light that belongs, by rights, to the baronet beside her?"

Speranza referred to votive candles set in alabaster vases ringed round with red fringe. Their light was pink, and wholly insufficient. This, it was whispered, was owing to the lady's finding herself in reduced circumstances: as she could afford but one servant, and that the aforementioned bumbling Betty, she found it both easier and more economical to keep her rooms dark rather than clean. Of course, I was accustomed to meeting Speranza in shadow, and told those who spoke ill of her surrounds that Lady Wilde had long shunned natural light.[60]

Lamenting still the appearance of Miss Potter, Speranza said:-

"If only As-car were here, he'd somehow tell her—"

"Oscar is not here?" I asked. In truth, I was relieved to hear he was elsewhere.

"He is not. My As-car is absent, which *so* disappoints; but I read in *Punch* that he is making quite a stir on his American tour." Whereupon she feigned shock to say, "Do you know, Bram, that there are those who come to my Saturdays only in the hopes of finding As-car here? I find I have become *his* mother, when formerly he was *my* son; but that is, of course, very much how it should be, and how I would have it."[61]

---

60. Some of Lady Wilde's contemporaries, Shaw and Yeats among them, went so far as to suggest that Speranza's disdain of light was symptomatic of a sort of gigantism.

61. Speranza demurs here, as she was arguably still the most famous—or infamous—of the Wildes.

Indeed, Oscar would write of his first American tour—on which he did make quite a "stir"—that he was happy to find himself known as Speranza's son; for his mother was well remembered as both poet and patriot by those who had emigrated at the time of the Famine. Even as late as 1891, when the Dublin magazine *Lady of the House* held a poll to name the "greatest living Irishwoman," Speranza took 78 percent of the vote.

Speranza then clutched at my arm. "Oh, Bram, I am in a bit of a quandary: I do *so* wish As-car would write more, even though that would leave him less time to speak, which he does so wondrously well! But you *will* speak to him on the point, will you not, Bram? As an older brother ought to? Our Willie is of no use in the matter."

What was I to say to Oscar Wilde? It mattered not: he was, then as now, as impervious to persuasion as to public opinion. And so it may be said that I lied to the lady in replying:-

"I will speak to him, of course." And then, seeking to set the conversation upon a different tack, I asked:-

"Have you heard the rumours about Rossetti? . . . He is at number sixteen, you know, just a few steps from our number twenty-seven."

"Rumours?" Speranza drew herself up at the prospect.

I nodded. "Our Noel is sometimes woken by Rossetti's peacocks parading in the common yard. They are in fine voice, I assure you. An outrage, really—that menagerie he keeps, and the neighbours are very much set against him at present, owing naturally, to the rumours."

"Of . . . ? Oh, *do* tell, Mr. Stoker. Rumours of what?"

"Of the elephant, of course."

Speranza fell back, her hand upon her heart. In truth, her hand hovered some inches from said organ, separated from it by an ample bosom and that bib-like bit of brocade onto which her brooches were pinned. "Speak on, Mr. Stoker. What*ever* can Rossetti be planning with a pachyderm?"

"It is said . . ."And here I paused, much to the lady's anticipatory pleasure. "It is said that he means to keep one in the yard and train it to wash the windows of Tudor House."

"*Santo Cielo!* You cannot—"

"Oh, but indeed I *can* be serious, and am."

"An elephant? Here in the heart of Chelsea? Too rich, too rich by far!" Whereupon sympathy overtook her, or nearly so. "Oh, the poor man— poor only in spirit, mind, for they say he is rich as Croesus. Surely he has gone mad. . . . You know, I have it from a most unimpeachable source that

Rossetti cried like a child at the loss of his wombat. But an *elephant?* The mind reels![62]

"Help me up," said Speranza, proffering her hand. "As gossip goes, I am very much indebted to that Countess in the corner, just there, and Rossetti's elephant ought to square my account nicely." And so she set off—audibly so: the jangle of jewelry, the swish of silks—saying:-

"Do look in on Tuesday next, Mr. Stoker. We'll take a late tea. There's a matter I mean to discuss with you, a matter of books. . . . Quite sad, really. I shan't sully my Saturday in speaking of it now.[63]

"But as regards Rossetti, I hear he has a new man—Crane or Banes or some such. No, no, it's Caine. A Liverpudlian, they say, though Thursday last he appeared rather more like a Lilliputian; for as I coached past, I saw him dragging a trunk of but medium size up the stoop of Tudor House and succeeding none too easily. You will learn more, Mr. Stoker, and tell me all on Tuesday. . . . An elephant, you say? My word!" And, like a sawed tree, she timbered toward the unsuspecting Countess.

Caine. . . . I had heard the name before.

Ah, yes: *Liverpool,* hadn't Speranza said? Didn't Irving, as opening nights drew nigh, always direct me to ensure that a certain Caine be asked to come from Liverpool on behalf of its *Town Crier?* Indeed he did. And wasn't it that same Caine who, when little more than a lad, had reviewed Irving's *Hamlet* in terms so pleasing to the actor that he'd had Caine brought round to his rooms to meet him?[64] It was, indeed. And now this Caine had finally come to London, and was resident with Rossetti in a house a half-block from my own. Most interesting, this.[65]

---

62. Rossetti did indeed keep a wombat—which he was wont to nurse on his lap, upside down, whilst tickling its tummy—and which he much mourned. The Pachyderm Plan? It grows more plausible the deeper one delves into Rossetti's biography.

63. It is likely the lady refers here to having to convert her library to cash, as she had had to do with Sir William's library—Stoker's library—before departing Dublin.

64. Much as Irving had done with Stoker, some years later. Caine's acquaintance with Irving actually predated Stoker's: the year of "the lad's" review was 1874, when Caine was but twenty-one.

65. Had Stoker sensed a rival upon the scene? If so, one sympathizes. Hall Caine was a man who,

Rossetti had taken up tenancy in Tudor House in 1862, inconsolable after the loss of his beloved Lizzie.[66] He leased the whole of the house, sub-leasing three of its many suites. On opposite sides of the first floor were the poets Geo. Meredith and Algernon Swinburne, the former mild in manner but the latter inclined to drink and, when drunk, further inclined to grease the banisters of Tudor House and take to them naked. A more sobering influence was provided by Rossetti's brother, Michael.[67]

In time, Tudor House was emptied of all tenants save one: Rossetti wanted no company; but solitude soon devolved to seclusion, then delusion, whence he worsened unto addiction and, finally, insanity. As proof of the latter state, one need only reference Rossetti's treatment of his Lizzie, long years after her decease.[68]

In the two decades prior to Caine's coming, there had passed through Tudor House a procession of help. Coincidentally, when Caine first wrote to the erstwhile poet in 1881, soliciting a sonnet for a planned anthology, Rossetti had just hounded from his employ the latest of his secretaries. With Caine still in Liverpool yet longing to live the literary life in London, Rossetti sought his help with a commission in the former city, one that had grown complicated. This Caine saw to, successfully.[69] As recompense he was invited to sup at Tudor House, where a grateful

---

though six years Stoker's junior, had already met and impressed Henry Irving with skills much like Stoker's own. It bears remembering that Stoker, in August of 1881, was yet very much enamored of Henry Irving, and happy in the great man's employ.

66. Wife, not wombat.

67. Rossetti's brother, Michael, was Walt Whitman's English publisher. A sister, Christina, was herself a poetess of repute.

68. Stoker leaves me to explain.
   Rossetti, in a gesture that has since endeared him to Romantics yet horrified his contemporaries, had his wife exhumed years after her burial. In the passion of her passing, he had buried with her many of his unpublished poems. These he wished to recover. Lest any readers doubt the impression this had upon Stoker, they are referred to *Dracula*, chapter 16, wherein Lucy Westenra, thought to be dead but decidedly not, is dug up and done in none too nicely by her fiancée, Arthur Holmwood.

69. After months of negotiation, Caine succeeding in seeing Rossetti's *Dante's Dream of Beatrice* installed in Liverpool's Walker Art Gallery, where it remains to this day. By "successfully," Stoker no doubt refers to the 1,500 guineas Caine got Rossetti for the painting, a sum comparable to £75,000 to-day.

Rossetti—who'd turned from poetry to painting in the hope of greater profit—conferred upon Caine rights absolute to Swinburne's former suite. The offer was accepted with alacrity.

(Is the foregoing fair enough, friend? I have distanced you here for ease of recollection; but you will of course correct these pages *at will*.)

It was not long after Speranza's news that I met Hall Caine for the first time. To effect this took nothing more than a word to Henry Irving, who, quite happy to hear that young Caine had come to London, deputed me to invite him to the backstage dining room. Caine and I fast found ourselves the sharers of innumerable sympathies, interests, and much else besides, and we began to pass our (too few!) hours of leisure in each other's company, whether fireside at my No. 27 or in Caine's suite down the street at No. 16, Cheyne Walk, Chelsea.[70]

I had been to No. 16 a half dozen times before finally meeting Rossetti. Typically, Caine and I had sat in the parlour, our talk attuned to the rhythm of Rossetti's pacing in the studio above, and Rossetti had come to seem only slightly more real than the house's infamous haunts.[71] And when finally Rossetti did show himself, the presumed presence of such spectres was *not* dispelled: He seemed a ghost himself!

Here was a man old beyond his years, of medium height and inclined to corpulence, with a face more round than ovoid. His longish

70. Among the "innumerable sympathies" Stoker refers to, we may safely number the following:

Their shared state of artistic servitude and/or indenture; their love of the theatre; their literary ambitions; their nocturnal lifestyle; and the sexless marriages each would make. These marriages we may less safely attribute to what modern biographers refer to as the writers' homosexuality, presumed latent in Stoker's case but active in Caine's. That said, we moderns must tread lightly through the world of the Victorian homo-social, reminding ourselves that the word "homosexual" would not even enter into usage until 1892.

71. One such was a woman wont to appear upon the stairs; a second kept to the scullery, while a third "lived" in a disused bedroom overlooking the Thames. This was a topic on which Rossetti was silent. Once, when Caine offered to sleep in the affected bedroom, and so dispel the myth of its guest, Rossetti forbade him to do so. When pressed to explain himself, Rossetti would say only that he had seen and heard the dead.

Compare this to the welcome given to Jonathan Harker by his host at Castle Dracula: "You may go anywhere you wish in the castle, except where the doors are locked, where of course you will not wish to go. There is a reason all things are as they are, and did you see with my eyes and know with my knowledge, you would perhaps better understand." *Dracula*, chapter 2.

Compare, too, Rossetti's three ghosts with Dracula's daughters.

hair had thinned and was a shade less gray than his beard. And he was pale, eerily pale, with wide eyes that were black at their centers and ringed round, kohl-like, from want of sleep.

Indeed, Rossetti, fearful of his dreams, disdained sleep. He would paint as long as the light allowed. The idle hours of deepest night were a torture to him. He would roam the shadowed halls of Tudor House— always in those knee-length sack coats of his own design, paint-stained and buttoned tightly at the chin—along with its sorority of sprites, laying himself down at dawn with the last of his strength. I wondered if Rossetti's delusion—and deluded he surely was—was owing more to his sleeplessness or to the means by which he battled it: namely, the chloral to which he'd long ago grown accustomed and to which he now was addicted.[72]

Caine had learned of the chloral shortly after coming to live at Tudor House. Rossetti himself confided in Caine that he regularly took sixty grains at nightfall, following that in four hours' time with sixty more, and so on: enough chloral, in short, to send ten men to their dreams. Rossetti's doctor assuaged Caine somewhat, saying his patient was not taking all the chloral he thought. The doctor, in collusion with the dispensing chemist, had arranged for the dilution of the doses. And happy the doctor was, surely, to now consign the phials to Caine, to hand him the key to the traveller's cabinet in which they were kept, first directing Caine to give Rossetti one phial per day *and no more,* no matter how he pled.

Of course, Rossetti was ever after Caine for the key to the cabinet, for more chloral. And when Caine himself indulged in sleep—and an indulgence it must have come to seem—Rossetti would rifle through the house in search of the key, and, if fortune led him to find it, he would feast like a glutton come upon grub. Caine would wake to find his idol quite literally fallen. There Rossetti would be, bottles in hand,

---

72. "No man knows till he has suffered from the night how sweet and how dear to his heart and eye the morning can be." *Dracula*, chapter 4.

    As regards chloral: it is a clear, colorless, and slick liquid rendered from the action of chlorine on ethanol. When mixed with water, it becomes chloral hydrate, a powerful soporific, the strength of which was not appreciated by the Victorian-era doctors who prescribed it so freely.

upon the floor of his studio, or the cold stone of the scullery, or once, most ignominiously, in the mud of the common yard amidst his peacocks.

If having to care for an addict slowed Caine's literary ascendance, still he progressed. Readying his long-planned anthology, Caine was most pleased to find that no poet of renown ignored a request from Rossetti himself; and the older man was happy to write such requests, at once soliciting sonnets on Caine's behalf and introducing him to literary London.

In time, Rossetti grew accustomed to my presence and suffered it well. Indeed, we three sometimes sat through the small hours of the night playing at poker or descanting, each in his turn, upon our chosen topics. Thusly was I present at No. 16 the night that the bill of Rossetti's addiction came suddenly due.

In the weeks prior, Rossetti's craving for chloral had grown. He verily stalked the halls of Tudor House searching for the key. When finally, and rightly, he supposed the sleeping Caine had it upon his person, he stole into the younger man's suite. Caine woke with Rossetti's cold hands upon him and started, terrified. Rossetti, debased, fell back from the bed, bowing his apology, the tears upon his face moon-silvered.

On the night in question, Rossetti was more restless than usual. Caine, reading aloud from Tennyson, kept one eye trained on his charge as Rossetti paced, ever more slowly, till finally he fell upon the studio sofa—crumpled, really, nearly missing its cushions—and announced, with a sigh, the loss of all feeling on his left side.

As Caine descended to summon a doctor, I carried Rossetti down to his bed.[73] Rossetti, with his eyes shut, seemed a corpse; or worse, a revenant in repose. Life was yet quick within him, but I saw few signs of it. Indeed, Rossetti never rose from that bed in which I laid him down, and in it he dwindled undo death, achieving it—*Requiescat in pace*—on Easter Sunday, 9 April 1882.

73. A wise allocation of duties, it would same, Stoker standing 6'2" to Caine's 5'3".

LETTER, BRAM STOKER TO HALL CAINE[74]

8 May 1888

Dear Caine,

Enclosed please find my brief memoir. I thank you, friend, for
suggesting that I write it. It did indeed distract me from to-day, from
things *as they stand*. Still, you shall see that not all my memories are
fond ones. Alas, I find I cannot outstrip sadness, Caine, try though I
may. And I am wary, most wary of this return home.

We draw ever nearer Liverpool, & London, & the resumption of
Routine. What it will be like, I cannot guess, but I hold tightly to
Whitman's admonition. I *shall* write a new life, a new letter that may
someday merit a godly signature. Oh, but it shan't be easy:

H.I. paces like a lion in its cage. Once he is loosed upon
London . . . Alas, I fear that much of his busy-ness will fall to me, as
ever it does. Have I told you he is determined to mount his *Macbeth*
by year's end? *It shall be*, says he; but first we have our *Merchant* to
re-mount for those who have missed us.

Must now tidy my trunks but wanted this prefatory note ready for
posting along with my memoir; for I suspect I shall not see you upon
the slip in Liverpool. I understand your disinclination to show
yourself on the mainland—owing, of course, to those most tenacious
tax-men you reference—but still I say *Come!* Come you must, Caine,
for we've much to discuss.

And I say again: Have your American friend come round to the
Lyceum at his convenience.

Suddenly it seems I am in a mortal hurry! Land has lately hove
into view, and the Co., to a one, revert to their needful selves, verily

---

74. On stationery of the White Star Line.

drumming upon my door. And so I close, Caine, thanking you for the respite I found in the enclosed pages, the writing of which has reminded me how truly I am

Yours,
Stoker

TELEGRAM, BRAM STOKER TO FLORENCE STOKER

8 May 1888.—Landed in L'pool. 2 pm finds me at your door. Pls. see that Noel nap accordingly.

Bram.

The Second Epoch

THE NIGHT

LETTER, BRAM STOKER TO HALL CAINE

14 May 1888, Monday

Dearest Caine,

It is more than a month now that I am returned to the resumption of routine, *all* routine, and I find myself with a question to pose:

Am I wrong to wish my wife illiterate?

Lest you think I jest, I forthwith list those volumes, acquired in my absence and arrayed before me now as I write upon my slope at the dining-room table, in which Florence finds countless things with which to worry both herself and me; viz:[1]

Ward & Lock's Home Book: A Domestic Cyclopaedia. A Young Wife's Perplexities, the title of which promises much more than it provides. And of course there is *The Lady's Every-Day Book*, subtitled *A Practical Guide to the Elegant Arts and Daily Difficulties of Domestic Life*. Daily difficulties, indeed. And of course there is the venerable Mrs. Beeton's *Book of Household Management*.

Too, there are no few volumes on the general topic of Domestic Economy, though the pages of these are yet uncut. Were they cut, still my wife's piled library would be testament enough to the fact

---

1. Short of videlicet; from the Latin and meaning "that is to say, or namely."

that she has not read widely on the topic of Economy, Domestic or Otherwise.

I needn't tell you, my most generous friend, that at present I find myself somewhat over-extended. Florence does not know of this, nor of your loan; this is how I would have it.[2] In truth, she *cannot* be told, by which I mean that to share our situation with her would be as futile as casting seed upon stone. The truth of it would not take root. She cannot comprehend, cannot *allow* for realities other than her own. She is child-like in that regard, and inclined to fault reality for its failure to accede to her dreams.

And on the subject of children, I have before me now Florence's *Advice to Mothers on the Management of Their Off-Spring.* This, too, she cannot have read, unless it counsels coldness. Oh, Caine, am I too cruel? I fear I am. Of course, I would write such words as these to no-one but you; yet still, in re-reading these pages, I find I must resist *the crumpling urge.* And indeed, if once I loved Florence for being child-like, how can I now chide her for the same quality? How can I fault her ignorance of the Ways of the World when it is I who hide those ways from her? Can I at once gild her cage and complain that she does not fly from its opened door? I cannot. Oh, Tommy, doubtless your judgement is more sound than mine; and so I say, B-U-R-N T-H-I-S L-E-T-T-E-R! if you feel it the right and proper course, *do.*[3]

That said, it is true that I came back from the tour to find my son further distanced from his mother—and thus, by association, myself—owing to an excess of discipline. Not of the corporeal sort,

2. Again, Caine's success bears mentioning. His fourth novel would sell in excess of a quarter-million copies its first year in print. Such numbers would try the friendship of any two authors, surely; but further complicating the friendship was the fact that Stoker had had to borrow from Caine £600, a quite considerable sum. Caine, it seems, gave the money gladly. That said, Caine would soon find himself deeply indebted to Stoker in his turn, owing not to money matters but rather to a certain favour asked of his friend.

3. Stoker either copied all his correspondence before sending it—which seems very Stoker-like in its surety, yet unlikely, given how busy he was—or asked that his letters be returned to him once he had determined to compile the *Dossier.* Also, smudges throughout the *Dossier* may indicate Stoker's occasional use of manifold-paper, a precursor to carbon paper. In any case, we can be glad that Caine disregarded Stoker's directive in this case.

of course; rather I refer to *rules*, more rules than a boy his age could ever abide.

Noel's French, of course, continues unto fluency, but when I dared to suggest that our Mlle Dupont be sent back to Dieppe with letters of praise and a *merci beaucoup* for services rendered to our son, Florence cried, cried mightily. And, wily as women sometimes are, she fast alluded to my recent absence—no means atypical, it must be admitted—and her dart found its target; for even when we do not tour, still my London duties find me asleep when my son is awake, and vice versa. The odd afternoon when I am able to strip to shirtsleeves, lie upon the carpet, and invite the child to climb upon my mountainous self—Florence complaining all the while of the rising dust thus occasioned—can hardly be called fathering. And each time I leave for the theatre, it is to Noel's cries of "Stay, Papa, won't you please?" It both maddens and saddens me, Caine, to stand so justly accused.

Alas, domestic life has come to seem naught but a circle of anger and apology, a circle set to turning, day in and day out, by the silence of all that is left unsaid. It verily leeches the life-blood from me, and often, Caine, I have envied you both your Greeba, high on its hill, and your bachelor rooms in town—to which, as you have written, you hope soon to come. Glad I am to hear the news, too, as there is *much* between us that would be better said than read. Come at your earliest convenience, won't you, please?

Meanwhile, tell me: How fare your Mary & Ralph? Are you happy at the head of your household now that your confession has come—I trust I may call it that, Caine, without offending—and all was set aright in Edinburgh? Can it be that those secret Scottish vows were spoken two years ago?[4] *Santo Cielo!* as Speranza would say.

Apropos of Lady Wilde, I know she'd *very* much like to find you at one of her *conversazioni.* Might you be here Saturday week? If so,

---

4. Stoker digs at Caine here with this allusion to "secret Scottish vows," as the *Dossier* will make clear.

perhaps we three may proceed to Lady Wilde's ensemble—I refer, of course, to your American friend, who has written me of his arrival and of rooms taken in Batty Street, and enclosed, too, an advert for his patented Pimple Banisher. I must say, Caine, my interest in the doctor is piqued. Quite unique, he seems. I hope he comes round to the Lyceum rather soon.

Later. I broke off from this letter before its close, Caine, and wisely so: I find now that a spot of tea has much improved my mood. And though my marriage bed has long been cold, I cannot let my heart assume a like chill as regards my wife. To do so would be caddish, unkind. So I shall do my best to keep our shared cage at No. 17 shining with gilt; and as for guilt of the other sort, arising from the lie, I shall somehow let go of it. Oh, but, Caine, a cage this house, *this life* does sometimes seem!

In closing I shall confide that I had hoped the much-insisted-upon move to this house from Cheyne Walk would renew things, would better them; but it seems that was rather too much to ask of four walls and a roof. This house holds what the other held, and if my wife was right in referring to our former home as haunted, she knew not that the haunt was her medal-hung husband and not the drowned man who died upon her dining table.[5]

Stoker

5. This cryptic paragraph sent me down into the shallow pit of Stoker biography, where I quarried the following:

Stoker, when yet resident at No. 27 Cheyne Walk, ferried to and from the Lyceum upon the Thames. On 14 September 1882, as the *Twilight* approached its dockage at the end of Oakley Street, Stoker saw an elderly man leap overboard. Reaching down, Stoker succeeded in taking hold of the man's coat; but the would-be suicide resisted rescue. Nonetheless, Stoker stripped down and jumped into the river. Drawn from the Thames, the nearly drowned man was taken to the Stoker home. There he succeeded in his goal, dying upon the dining table.

Some contemporary press accounts criticized Stoker for his actions, saying that a family man was wrong to risk life and limb, as indeed he had. On the lighter side, the *Entr'Acte* opined that "Mr. Irving is fortunate in having for his manager a muscular Christian like Mr. Bram Stoker. Should the popular tragedian ever get out of his depth, he knows that his faithful Bram is ready to take the necessary header and be to the rescue." In the main, Stoker was lauded as a hero, receiving the above-referenced bronze medal from the Royal Humane Society.

As for Florence, who'd stood by as the suicide expired atop her Morris-style mahogany dining set, built to accommodate between ten and twelve *living* guests, she immediately launched a relocation campaign. Finally the Stokers did relocate, moving around several Chelsea corners to No. 17 St. Leonard's Terrace, where they are resident as Stoker writes in mid-May of 1888.

JOURNAL OF BRAM STOKER

16 May, Wed. [1888].—Theatre yesterday, 10 a.m. to 3 p.m. & 7 p.m. to 4 a.m.

Hired: Lydia—Lavinia? Lucia?—no, *Lydia*, Mrs. Lydia Quibbel; the widowed auntie of I Forget Who, sent round by same to see H.I. about employment.

"Stoker!" came the call, the same that chills every member of the Company.

I found the Guv'nor standing backstage, near the B. Street entrance.[6] "Whatever is the matter, Henry?"

"Why, nothing, nothing at all." Something was the matter, of course, and it took no great prescience to see that it had to do with the old woman standing at Henry's side. "Stoker," says he, "may I present Mrs. . . ." But as he misremembered the name, the lady herself offered it:-

"Quibbel, sir. Mrs. Lydia Quibbel. 'Ow d'y'do, sir?"

Henry resumed: "She is the mother—"

"The aunt, sir."

"Yes, yes, the aunt of I.F.W. You know the man well, Stoker, do you not?" This last accompanied by the sly arching of a brow.

"I do. I do indeed," said I, joining Henry in the lie. "A fine fellow, *most* fine."

"Yes, yes. Now, Stoker, the nephew has sent Mrs. . . . Rather, this fine lady standing before us has come round to see if we mightn't have some work for wages," which words Mrs. Quibbel took as her cue to soliloquise upon her recent sorrows. It was some while later that Henry, having attained, imperceptibly, the Burleigh Street door, indeed having opened it to the street, interrupted the lady; so:-

"Yes, yes, terribly sad, terribly. My sympathies are infinite, madam."

---

6. The Burleigh Street entrance to the Lyceum Theatre was reserved for the exclusive use of Henry Irving, Ellen Terry, and Stoker.

Whereupon his brow reshaped itself, betokening *Thought*. This could mean but one thing: I was soon to be assigned a task. And sure enough:-

"Stoker," he asked, "haven't we those many cats that want looking after?"

"We have, Henry, yes; but, as you'll recall, the two women you had me hire last month are doing the looking-after at present."

"Two tenders, you say?"

"Yes: *two*."

Whereupon Henry, one booted foot having achieved the street beyond, said, "Well, there you have it, then. Let this good woman look after the two women looking after the cats. See to it, Stoker." And the stage door slammed shut, leaving me in the dimness to shake the hand of the Lyceum Theatre's new Tender of the Tenders of the Cats, whose salary, whose pounds & pence, I suppose I am *to conjure*, loaves-and-fishes like.

Later. 3 p.m.—Tired to-day. The B.C. did not disband till nearly 4 a.m. last eve.[7]

Tea just ordered up to the office. Shall write till it arrives in the hopes of staving off sleep – could curl up in the safe at my side and sleep my life away; but alas.

Caine's American doctor came by yesterday. Quite the oddity, but I think he might prove amusing. Certainly, Henry enjoyed studying him last evening for tics and habits of character, &c. Indeed, Henry and Dr. Tumblety kept on chatting long after the last of the guests were gone. E.T., however, seemed to loathe the man on sight, *very* unlike her. (*Mem.:* We were eight at table: me, Henry, Ellen, our scenarists Harker & Hawes Craven, Dr. T., Sarah Bernhardt, and Damala. Menu: Lamb cutlets,

---

7. B.C. is the Beefsteak Club, AKA the Sublime Society of Beefsteaks: the backstage room where Irving and his invited guests dined in Gothic splendour. To the gridiron—original to 1735 and a survivor of two fires on the site—which was suspended from the ceiling, Stoker added a modern range intended to vary the fare from the rumpsteaks of old. Armour lined the panelled walls on which were hung portraits of Irving's artistic forebears—David Garrick, Edmund Kean, William Charles Macready—and of course Whistler's full-length portrait of Irving himself as Philip II, the last accorded pride of place.

mushrooms in butter, lentil pudding, claret, & of course Bernhardt's beloved Champagne.)[8]

Both Sarah and Dr. Tumblety were expected in the course of the week; that they both arrived on Tuesday was most fortuitous. Or so it initially seemed.

I had just met w/ Harker at the Guv'nor's direction. I was to reiterate to him—unnecessarily, of course, as Harker is proving himself first-rate as both artist and employee—Henry's initial thoughts re: the backdrops of *Mach.* Too, I was to suggest to the Scot that he make himself available for the research trip Henry hopes to take to E'burgh. And so he will, happily. (*Mem.:* When? Who else?) As such business was quickly seen to, I was surprised to hear the office door creak back upon its hinges a short while later to disclose Harker, seeming rather more stunned than otherwise.

"Harker," said I, looking up from my ledger. "What is it?"

"Down in the painting room"—thusly does he refer to the sub-stage space in which he and Craven work their magic—"...there is a man come to see you, sir."

"A man, you say? Come to see *me?*" Harker does not yet know me well enough to have heard my cynicism.

"Yes, sir. A man." And—it being plain he wished to speak on—I waited. Nothing.

"Harker," said I, "you are new to our little family here, and *most* welcome indeed; but let it fall to me to inform you that, innumerable times in the course of the day, any given day, men, women and ... *what-not* arrive on these premises needful of seeing me, or so they all say. Twice as many beings come seeking the Guv'nor, though of course it

---

8. According to Stoker's own *Personal Reminiscences of Henry Irving* (1906): "Sarah Bernhardt spent pleasant hours at the Lyceum—pleasant to all concerned.... Several times when she arrived in London from Paris she would hurry straight from the station to the theatre and see all that was possible of the play. It was a delight and a pride to both Irving and Miss Terry when she came; and whenever she could do so she would stop to supper. The Beefsteak Room was always ready, and a telephone message to Gunter's would insure the provision of supper. Those nights were delightful. Sometimes some of her comrades would come with her. Marius, Garnier, Darmont or Damala. The last time the latter—to whom she was then married—came he looked like a dead man. I sat next him at supper, and the idea that he was dead was strong on me. I think he had taken some mighty dose of opium, for he moved and spoke like a man in a dream. His eyes, staring out of his white waxen face, seemed hardly the eyes of the living."

is I who must meet them as well. . . . So, my good man, fear not to inform me that a man has come to see me. But may I ask, Mr. Harker: Has this *particular* man a name?"

"I did not ask it, sir."

"I see," said I, for it is fun to tease the handsome Harker. When rattled, he rouges and his Scottish *r*'s roll like rocks in a rail-box. "You'd be further in my favour if you had asked his name; . . . but tell me: Where is this nameless man at present?"

"Where I left him, sir; or so I suppose." And there stood the humble Harker, still wanting to say more; the which I elicited with:-

"Now, Mr. Harker, if you have—"

"Mr. Stoker, sir," said he, his courage summoned, "you may see scores of folks at your door in a week's worth o' days but I doubt you see many the match of this chap."

"Come now, sir," said I. "Speak plainly"; whereupon Harker came further into the XO[9] and with paint-stained fingers passed me the card he'd been asked to present, upon which was writ:

Dr. Francis Tumblety, &c.

"Ah, the American. He is not unexpected." I stood, returned the ledger and notes on last night's take to the safe—along with this very book—and quit the office, hopeful of handing over to a friend of a friend but one half-hour of my day, as I'd little more than that to spare. And down I went into the theatre's depths, accompanied by Harker.

En route I discovered exactly how it is Mr. Joseph Harker has come to us. "So then," I said, "you hail from Edinburgh proper. You'll be a right tour guide for us when we go."

"I do, sir," said Harker. "And I will, sir."

"You must call me Stoker, Harker. And you must *not* call me Uncle Brammy behind my back, as the others do. Understood?" In fact, the nickname does not bother me in the least: I simply find it fun to have at young Mr. Harker.

9. Executive office.

"Yes, sir," said he. "Stoker it shall be, sir."

"Ah, yes, well," said I with a sigh, "that's a start, I suppose."

Harker's story surprised me not at all. It seems that long ago his father—Harker the elder—then somehow affiliated with Edinburgh's Royal Theatre, extended a kindness of some sort to a young Henry Irving. Henry had despatched the debt with the late hiring of Harker the younger, who is, blessedly, *talented*. His case is quite unlike that of Mrs. Quibbel; who, I fear—even if she proves suited to serve as an extra, puffing out a party scene in *Much Ado* or coming on as a commoner at the start of *J.C.*—shall sup on the Lyceum teat till the end of her days.[10]

. . . Tea has come, and gone. Naught refreshes like a sandwich made of early cucumbers. I resume:

I found the scene shop uncommonly quiet. Typically, there are children at play amidst the scattered, half-achieved bits of stagecraft.[11] Yesterday there were no children. In a corner, two carpenters finished repairs to the beams of Portia's Belmont, which bore the brunt of the sea's having heaved the *Germanic* so. This gladdened me: the Guv'nor is unbearable when made to "make do" with scenery &/or props that are in any way imperfect; and so I was eager to inform him that the newly perfected beams of the castle would be upright, onstage, that very evening, as indeed they were; but first:-

---

10. *Julius Caesar*, of course; with particular reference to Act I, Scene I: "Enter FLAVIUS, MARULLUS, and certain Commoners."

11. This reference to children at the Lyceum may refer to Gordon Craig, Ellen Terry's son from an earlier, failed marriage, who, in adulthood, would become a noted theatrical designer and theoretician. (Ellen Terry seems to have borne Theatre as a dominate gene: her great-nephew would be John Gielgud.)

It may also refer to Noel Stoker, said by his father, in his *Reminiscences*, to be "adept in the application of gold leaf."

However, it is safe to assume that Stoker does *not* refer to Henry Irving's two young sons, who, though both would become actors, hadn't much of a backstage life at the Lyceum. As legend has it, Florence Irving once met her husband in the wings with, "Do you plan, Henry, on embarrassing me like this nightly?" After which Henry Irving moved into rooms of his own, never speaking to his wife again. She, however, was always present in his box on opening nights, glowering down on the stage and ready with some subacid comment. This was the woman, who, after all, had trained her boys to refer to their father as "The Antique," and Ellen Terry as "The Wench."

"Wherever is he?" I asked this of Harker; for, though the workshop was reasonably well lit, I saw no stranger within it.

"There, sir," said Harker. In his tone I heard regret, regret that he'd not pronounced further upon the stranger in the course of our coming downstairs. But now he'd no need to: Following Harker's finger toward a far corner of the room, I saw step from the shadows a most remarkable man.

"Thank you, Mr. Harker," said I, words at which the scenarist happily took his leave of me, of the shop . . . of the American.

Surely, Tumblety ought to have crossed the room toward me. Propriety dictated he do so. I, of course, would have played my part, so that we, meeting for the first time, would do so in a spirit of . . . neutrality, as it were. But there the man stood. Worse: Though merely standing, he seemed somehow *to preen*. Harker rose higher in my estimation: He'd been right: I'd rarely seen the like of this Dr. Tumblety.

Sensing keenly my duty to Caine, I crossed the room to meet the man where he stood; but my progress was arrested when there came from behind him a snarling, bone-toned, knee-high hound. A miniature, or Italian, greyhound. Beribboned in black at the neck. I was as thankful that I'd worn my horn-hard boots—I'd have punted the pet to Timbuktu—as I was to hear its master call the hound back, with apologies. Said Tumblety, then:-

"Your Mr. Harker seems a well-made man"—how very odd an opening gambit—"and quite capable as a craftsman. Is that so, Mr. Stoker?"

"It is, sir; though it might well be argued that he is more artist than craftsman."

"I meant no offence," said Dr. Tumblety.

"Then—on Mr. Harker's behalf—I take none." Whereupon, whilst holding still to Dr. T.'s proffered hand—too warm, too moist, too recently come from its glove—I asked, "Are you a connoisseur of stagecraft, sir?" This, though, was not my foremost question. It was a far greater wonderment that the American—and with a dog, no less!—had made his way down to Harker's den unannounced.

Said Tumblety in American tones, now inflected, now flat, "A connoisseur? I am afraid not, Mr. Stoker. I do, however, very much admire such dissemblers as yourself, able to . . . to suborn reality with your talents."

"Ah, there I fear you misspeak, sir: I am not to be included in talk of the talented."

"Not at all," said Dr. T., dismissively. "Our Thomas tells me otherwise. He has long spoken highly of you."

Thomas? Surely he meant to refer to Caine; but if so, he used the more formal name our friend has long disdained. Thusly was I led to ask:-

"How long have you known . . . our Thomas?"

By now our rapprochement had been effected: I'd gone the greater distance, hand outstretched, but Tumblety had come a step or two from the shadows to take my hand in his; and in the course of his doing so, I'd heard the clack and spin of . . . spurs, large spurs which now I saw were affixed to the heels of his boots. I've never seen the like, leastways not in London. Then again, of Dr. Tumblety, in his entirety, I've never seen the like anywhere.

Before me stood a man of middling height, perhaps a head shorter than myself, who seemed my senior by ten years or so.[12] He was well complected, healthful, hale—handsome, even. His eyes of jet were deep-set beneath black brows. His moustache was of the blacking-brush sort, full and perhaps overly tended, tapering to its well-waxed ends. Such a moustache would seem rather excessive were it not for the rest of Dr. T.'s . . . excess. Indeed, Tumblety looked as though he'd already had the run of our costume shop, save that the Lyceum stores cannot lay claim to such an ensemble as he wore yesterday, and which made him seem equal parts sportsman, soldier, and harlequin.

His suit was sewn of a woolly plaid in which puce and sundry greens vied for supremacy, though the combating colors seemed now to be

12. Tumblety is, in fact, thirteen years senior to Stoker in 1888: 55 to Stoker's 42.

signatories to a most tenuous truce, each making the best of a worsted situation.[13] This suit the doctor had seen fit to top with a hat both peaked and plumed and somewhat militaristic, though I'd have been hard put to guess what regiment it might have represented. The hat was balanced— if "balance" be the word—by boots of shining black leather that rose nearly to the knee. To these were attached the aforementioned spurs which had scraped the shop floor when finally Tumblety had moved to meet me.

His handshake was unpleasant, rather off-putting. These were not the hands of a man accustomed to main labor, clearly. Gloves, it would seem, yes, have long been the doctor's custom; but these he'd removed to show long fingers the nails of which bore—like his boots—too high a sheen. When it seemed the doctor had held to my hand quite long enough, I withdrew it. At this, something flashed up from deep in his dark eyes: now he held my gaze as surely as he'd held my hand. For a moment it seemed he had hold of my will as well. (*Q.:* Might the doctor dabble in mesmerism? Must ask this of Caine.)

Wondering, *whoever is this Tumblety?* I began to question the man, but only as a new acquaintance would. "Have you been in London long, sir?" I realised the gaffe at once: Hadn't the man already written me of his recent arrival?

"Days, merely," said he. "I am brought here on business."

"I see," said I. Caine mentioned only that the doctor dealt in patent medicines, Tumblety's Pimple Banisher being his prime decoction. Cuff links of hammered gold and inset stones bespoke success in the endeavour. On we spoke, our topics quite typical, till finally I, yet discomfited by the doctor's dark gaze, asked if he cared to tour the theatre. He did care; and very much so, it seemed.

We set off; but time and again, as his hounds—two, there were: a second had come from the shadows, and Tumblety had allied the two dogs by a common lead such that they strode side by side—as his hounds

13. The pun is of particular interest, as from it we may conclude that Stoker is yet somewhat amused by Tumblety.

and their master followed me through the labyrinth of the Lyceum, from the scene shop to and through its below-, back-, and forestage areas, I had the feeling they'd all three been in the theatre's bowels before. I can offer no proof of this, and indeed the doctor said, twice, perhaps three times, that he had not explored the theatre at all before happening upon Harker at his work.[14]

Unhappily, our party happened upon Henry backstage. I made the mistake of mentioning our mutual friend, Caine, whereupon H.I. invited Dr. T. not only to last night's *Merchant*—a common enough courtesy— but also to the supper in Bernhardt's honour which was to follow. I'd rather he hadn't, as I had now to phone Gunter's to alter arrangements. Too, I found myself more and more disinclined towards Tumblety's company. Odd, but there it is, writ. Still, I smiled through the Guv'nor's invitation, and even smiled through its ending with the inevitable, "Stoker will see to it."

(*Mem.:* Prompter has just come to inform me that last eve. the second-act curtain came down at 8.42, two minutes off pace. Odd of Henry not to have noticed. Must speed our strutting Bassanio from Act I, Scene I: "In Belmont is a lady richly left," &c. *See to it.*)

Tumblety sat last night in the Guv'nor's box, his hounds quite literally at heel, and was all compliments after the performance. At supper I sat him btw. E.T. and Damala, and for this Ellen shan't soon forgive me. She, so typically *at ease*, was tense and teased her napkin all night long. At first I thought this might be owing to the presence of Miss Bernhardt; but no, it was Tumblety. Miss B. seemed to disdain him as well, sending few words his way. Tumblety seemed neither to notice nor mind. For my part, I sat marvelling at the dead-seeming Damala. Poor man. Opium, is it? Or has he simply faded from the Divine Sarah's leeching away all his light? Regardless, his paleness, nay his *opacity*, is much to be remarked upon, and as now I have remarked upon it, why not close?

---

14. Stoker later amended this comment in the margins of his journal: "Neither Jimmy A. at the stage door nor Mrs. Foley in the lobby logged the mid-afternoon arrival of the American. *Most* strange."

Will cable or write Caine—*must;* but first will see, *must see,* to this Bassanio business before H.I. hears of it.

LETTER, BRAM STOKER TO HALL CAINE[15]

Thursday, 17 May 1888

Caine, my recondite friend,

This to acknowledge your recent short note—too short, unless my cable asking *What of this Tumblety?* has been misdelivered.

You needn't thank me for meeting your American friend, as any friend of T.H.H.C. . . . &c., but *do,* Caine, convey what it is you know of the man. *Most* unique, he is.

As Tumblety has now seen our *Merchant* twice and seems much to fancy our little Lyceum, I ask that you answer those questions one cannot ask a new acquaintance. Never would you compromise me, Caine—the notion is patently preposterous; but if I am to vouchsafe your Dr. Tumblety's return to London capital-S Society, I feel I must needs know more about the man. And in haste, if you please, for he has heard of Lady Wilde's Saturday at-homes and very much wishes to accompany me to Park Street,[16] two days hence. Share *something* of the who/what/where/when & why of the fellow so that I might more ably answer Speranza's many questions. Of course, far better it would be if you could shake the tax-men from your tail and come to town yourself, in lieu of a letter. But, barring that—and I do sense that solution is, at present, barred—send some history of the man.

Apologising for my insistence in the matter of the American, I remain,

Yours, tried & true,

Stoker

15. On letterhead of the Lyceum Theatre.

16. Lady Wilde had removed to 116 Park Street, near Grosvenor Square, some years prior.

P.S. *Macbeth* comes on swimmingly. Henry is much bent upon the lot of us heading to Edinburgh *to research*. If you can join us, send dates that suit, I shall plan accordingly. Much fun it would be to return there, for haven't we many fond & mutual memories of the place, Henry and myself and you and, of course, your young Mary?[17]

MEMORANDUM TO THE DOSSIER [18]

After the April 1882 death of Dante Gabriel Rossetti, Thomas Henry Hall Caine moved from Tudor House, taking rooms at No. 18 Clement's Inn; these he shared with one Eric Robertson, who was then, as now, unknown to me. Caine had already contracted for his *Recollections of Rossetti*, and his sonnet anthology was upon the presses. In addition, it had been agreed that he would remain resident in London to report on goings-on for the Liverpool *Mercury*, writing both its "Literary and Theatre Notes" and contributing to its annals of crime. Indeed, Caine was often in the courts by day and in the East End by night; and thusly did he acquire much knowledge re: the seamy underside of London life.

Caine also took charge of the *Mercury*'s obituaries. Previously, it was with great difficulty that newspapers covered the death, especially the

---

17. The arrival of Tumblety and the consequent withdrawal of Hall Caine seem to have emboldened if not angered Stoker; and here he muscles his absent friend somewhat with an allusion to the tenderest of topics: his wife, Mary, and his marriage, which topic he takes up in the *Dossier*'s next entry.

18. Typed, undated, unsigned.

Here, for the first time, Stoker breaks form. It seems he returned to the *Dossier* at a later date, adding this memorandum as a sort of *explication de texte*. He would not have done this lightly, for in both the *Dossier* and later in *Dracula*, Stoker stands committed to the narrative device first tried by Wilkie Collins in *The Woman in White*; compare:

This, from Collins's 1860 preface: "An experiment is attempted in this novel, which has not (so far as I know) been hitherto tried in fiction. The story of the book is told throughout by the characters of the book. They are all placed in different positions along the chain of events; and they all take the chain up in turn, and carry it on to the end," with this, as adapted by Stoker and printed prefatory to *Dracula*:

"How these papers have been placed in sequence will be made manifest in the reading of them. All needless matters have been eliminated, so that a history almost at variance with the possibilities of latter-day belief may stand forth as simple fact. There is throughout no statement of past things wherein memory may err, for all the records chosen are exactly contemporary, given from the standpoints and within the range of knowledge of those who made them."

Stoker's reason for inserting the memorandum here soon becomes clear.

sudden death, of persons of note; Caine contributed to the revision of this process by writing obituaries of the well-known whilst yet they were alive, filing these for instant use upon the subject's decease. Thus, many of London's luminaries vied for Caine's attention, wishing to meet him in public houses or private rooms and, over pints or port, eulogise themselves; for, to contribute to one's one obituary—"Caine's columns," as they came to be called—was *to have arrived*. So it was that even death came to serve an aspirant Hall Caine.

At this time, Caine and I saw each other increasingly less. We were no longer neighbours, true; but also, Caine grew somehow . . . secretive. For the longest while, I would not know why. I wondered if I had proved faulty as a friend. Now, however, I know his reasons; and, as said knowledge is necessary to the sense of this *Dossier*, I impart it here with Caine's permission, so:

Having no servants, Hall Caine and the aforementioned Mr. Robertson had their meals sent up from a coffee shop in Clare Market. A common enough occurrence, this, amongst unmarried men of the city. Common enough, too, would have been the familiarity, perhaps even the flirtation,[19] which soon developed between Messrs. Caine and Roberston and the girls who regularly brought up their meals, one of whom was thirteen-year-old Mary Chandler.

Though I am told by Caine that his behaviour towards Miss Chandler was beyond reproach, still trouble came; and, as often trouble does, it took the form of a male relation. The girl's step-father—wishing to rid himself of Mary, who was, to him, naught but another mouth to feed—accused Caine of gross improprieties. Words such as "ruin" and "blackmail" were heard, or leastways implied. As the "Maiden Tribute" campaign had recently appeared in the *Pall Mall Gazette*, much was then being made of the illicit trade in young girls. Caine could not risk being tarred by such a brush. This his accuser knew, and so the man pushed beyond the pecuniary: soon, *most* improbably, Mr. Robertson had moved from the rooms at Clement's Inn to make way for Mary Chandler. Caine

---

19. A loaded word for the Victorians: a "flirt" was a woman halfway down the road to ruin.

now had responsibility for the child; his options, it seemed, were two: adoption or marriage. As the former seemed too public a plan and the latter too private,[20] Caine came up with a third option:

He committed Mary to school at Sevenoaks, some distance from the city, thereby buying himself time, time in which to decide: *What to do?* For better or worse, if not yet in sickness and in health, Mary was his; for Caine knew all too well what would happen to her if she were left to fend for herself on the London streets.

Though Caine was ... *admiring* of Mary, it soon became clear the girl was smitten with him. Another man might have felt more: Mary, when finally I met her, fully one year into her tenure at Sevenoaks, showed herself a beauty. Her skin was pale unto opalescence, her eyes were blue and her hair honey-toned. She was doll-like, tiny enough to suit the diminutive Caine. In time, Mary was reinstalled at Clement's Inn, and those few who found her there were both told she was seventeen and sworn to secrecy. I was such a one.

To me, later, an in-his-cups Caine said that Mary had much benefited from her schooling at Sevenoaks, where the primary topic of study was wifehood; but Caine made no mention of marriage, not to me and not to Mary. Indeed, he kept young Mary hidden whilst further establishing himself in literary London. Then a thing equally improbable and inevitable occurred: on 15 August 1884, Ralph Caine came wailing into the world.

To hide a false wife was one thing, to hide a false family quite another. *What to do?*

Caine and company decamped from Clement's Inn. Wife and child were installed out in the Worsley Road, Hampstead, whilst Caine took rooms at Lincoln's Inn, where he, to all appearances, went about his bachelor ways. Meanwhile, Mary, still two years shy of her stated seventeen, raised Ralph whilst recording in her scrapbooks—which yet she maintains—every step of her "husband's" ascendance. Caine came to the house when he could, and indeed doted upon Ralph. Mary, for her

---

20. Not to mention illegal.

part, wanted marriage and, in protest against Caine's putting her off, kept her hair long and her skirts short.[21]

In 1884, Mary and Ralph were removed to Bexley Heath, to Aberleigh Lodge in Red House Lane, whilst Caine kept to the city proper. Now that I knew his secret—if not all its particulars—our friendship was resumed. That same year, Caine's first novel, *Shadow of a Crime*, was published. Caine, having found his authorial feet, as it were, felt himself steady enough to inform the Liverpool Caines of the London ones; yet still he would not marry Mary. As she was now sixteen, it would have been legal to do so; but no. Meanwhile, book followed book, and Caine became a known name.

Finally, in September of 1886, having wearied of both the secret and of Mary's insistence upon marriage, Caine came upon a solution. In truth, the idea was mine, or should I say Shaw's? For I had recently read a most bilious article by George Bernard Shaw, the topic of which escapes me, wherein he scorned the marriage laws of Scotland, which required naught but that bride and groom declare themselves before witnesses. As we of the Lyceum Company were then readying to play in Edinburgh, I suggested to Caine that he, Mary, and Ralph come along. He agreed. So, too, did Mary, quite. No-one else was *in the know* save Irving. And so it was that on the third day of September, betwixt matinee and evening performances—and with Henry needfully disguised, half made up as *The Bells'* Mathias—we five found ourselves comprising a wedding party: myself and Henry Irving, along with Caine, Mary, and a toddling Ralph. By that declaration sufficient to the Scots, Thomas Henry Hall Caine, thirty-three years of age, married Mary Chandler, twenty-three. (The bride was, in point of fact, and *finally*, seventeen.) Serving as witnesses were one Angus Campbell, Coachman, and John McNaughton, Hotel Waiter. (Irving, wearing Mathias's cape, was perfectly suited to play Campbell the Coachman. I

---

21. The opposite, then, of "suitable" behavior: new mothers were supposed to pile their hair high and lower their hems.

served as the Waiter.) And by the time our curtain rose that night, the Caines had begun their descent down the length of the kingdom towards Torquay. There they all three celebrated a honeymoon of sorts, returning to London some days hence, their union legal at last, their secret shed.

Rather, that *particular* secret had been shed. Caine, of course, had others. Only lately have I learned that one such is named Tumblety.

JOURNAL OF BRAM STOKER

20 May, a Sunday; irises rising, but I am not in heart to describe beauty.—Flo. & Noel off to Grim's Dyke.[22]

A note came round from Speranza on Friday last, begging my company at yesterday's *conversazione,* which I had hoped to miss; but as it was signed *La Madre Dolorosa,* I sent back surety of my attendance. Said, too, that I would come in the company of one Dr. T., as the man had *much* impressed upon me his hope of meeting O.[23]

As for Caine's coming to join us, he did not. There has been no word from Caine in quite some time. Hence, I know little more of his Dr. T. than I can glean for myself, and when on occasion I have dropped the stone of his name into common Society—having partaken little of Same, busy as I've been—it has quickly sunk, rippling not at all the waters of truth or rumour. *He* remains a mystery, too much so. This discomfits me. *He* discomfits me. And lest I hear from Caine soon, I shall

22. Country home of W. S. Gilbert, of Gilbert & Sullivan fame, a Beefsteak regular and "particular" friend of Florence Stoker.

At Grim's Dyke, Gilbert maintained a zoo that must have amused young Noel. Gilbert pleasured in his colony of lemurs and monkeys, the founders of which he'd brought back from Madagascar. Two Persian cats and six mongrel dogs had places set for them at the Gilberts' supper table. And if this seems an unlikely sphere for Florence Stoker, it must be remembered that she happily went wherever she would be admired; and W. S. Gilbert seems to have admired her much, so much so that there was talk and allusive cartoons appeared in *Punch,* none of which seems to have concerned Stoker himself.

23. Oscar Wilde, of course.

consider my debt to the Manxman paid, and this Tumblety of his shall take no more of my time.

In truth, he has taken too much of it already. Were it not for his obvious means and the rooms he has let in town—in Batty Street, of all places—I would think he were resident at the Lyceum. He comes & goes as he pleases; moreover, and despite my admonitions that they pay greater attention to their tasks, one of which is logging *all* Lyceum visitors, both Jimmy A. and Mrs. Foley miss the American whenever he comes. It is as though he has found an unknown door. *Most* strange, this. I have informed the doctor of our logging habits—saying our insurers insist upon them, when in truth it is Henry who so insists—and asked that he comply. Further, I have put my own hound onto Tumblety and his two: the ubiquitous Mrs. Quibbel has, in short order, proved herself rather . . . resourceful, and has twice reported to me of finding Dr. T. both in the costume shop and the loge. What he was doing in the former I have no idea. In the latter, he passed the two hours prior to curtain in feeding his hounds by hand. My own hands are now somewhat bound in the matter of the American, however, as H.I. is much taken with him and his strange manners, such that when next Irving plays Richard III or Prince Hal or Prospero, he will no doubt incorporate into said roles of crook-back, crown prince, and conjurer certain of the American's characteristics.

H.I. has even gone so unaccountably far as to tell Tumblety that whilst he remains resident in London, he may dine at the Beefsteak Club *at will*. Such terms of invitation are rarely heard from Henry Irving. Indeed, Liszt was the last.[24] . . . A mesmerist, indeed, is this Dr. T., for it would seem he has the iron-hearted Henry Irving in his hold.

I see I have given some pages over to Dr. Tumblety himself when I'd intended to use this quiet to write of yesterday's visit to Speranza's

---

24. The composer Franz Liszt had sat in Irving's box for the 99th performance of *Faust* and was feted afterwards in the Beefsteak Club. In Stoker's *Reminiscences* of Irving, he offers this interesting, Draculian description of the aged Liszt: ". . . fine face—leonine—several large pimples—prominent chin of old man—long white hair down on shoulders—all call him 'Master'—must have had great strength in youth."

salon in his company, where a most interesting and tempting invitation was extended to me; so:

Tumblety came round to the house at half four, as arranged. Florence was in a froth and drove poor Ada to distraction, this despite my having told the maid, having *insisted,* that neither tea nor refreshments of any kind be served. This, quoth the wife, was most uncouth and even unkind of me. "I'll not be *shamed* so," said she. And so it was I acceded to refreshments of the lightest sort. Florence, of course, over-spoke me in secret and told Ada to prepare a proper tea. This a teary-eyed Ada served some minutes after Tumblety had been shown into the parlour by our Mary, herself done up in a new dress-apron so lace-laden at the collar and cuffs, so befurbelowed about the neck as to make her seem a species of serving Iguana. There I sat in silent contemplation of *the cost of it all* whilst Florence hosted the American on her own.

He can be quite charming, this Tumblety; though I have noticed, too, that when he does not *strive* to charm, he falls far short of doing so, and people—women in particular—take against him, as has E.T. Not so Florence, however. As the American was *all* charm yesterday afternoon, my wife sat in receipt of same till the clocks slowed to a crawl. I very much wanted to hasten to Lady Wilde's and ascertain the cause of her dolour; too, I was eager to confer Tumblety unto the company of others. But I had first to suffer an interminable tea; in the course of which I had to suffer as well, the sight of Mary drawing from a low cupboard, under Florence's watchful eye, pieces of a Wedgwood service acquired in my absence. How these foreign tours cost me!

Tumblety revealed little of himself to my wife as I listened. Cagily, he responded to her every question with a compliment. Then Noel came down from on high in the company of Mlle Dupont. Quite the proper young gentleman, he is, albeit a bit Continental in his habits. Oddly, I found that I was loath to leave wife & child alone in the parlour with Tumblety when Florence suggested that I fetch from the diningroom mantel our preferred picture of Caine. I asked Mary to retrieve it, and when she handed the gilded frame to Florence, who in turn handed it to Tumblety, something seemed awry; for Tumblety said, or rather lamented, how long it had been since he'd last seen our mutual friend. Is he not welcome at Greeba Castle? Oughtn't Caine to come to London to greet a friend of such long standing? I might have answers to these and other *Q*.s if only Caine would write, or call, or come. As he has not written, and will not call—refusing, still, to install a phone line at the castle—and is disinclined to show himself in London owing to these Tax Wars he wages, I am left to guess as to the state of his relations with Tumblety, past and present.

At long last, Florence freed us; and only as we set out towards Lady Wilde's did I remark what it was the man wore. Were we headed anywhere but Lady Wilde's, I'd have blanched; but, blessedly, the lady is not to be outdone, even by one as . . . as sartorially splendiferous, may I say, as Tumblety. Speranza would meet Tumblety in his furred cuffs and Ephesian shako[25] with equanimity, if not admiration. Meanwhile, there I'd stand at his side—for as short a while as possible—in my funereal suit of blue serge, thankful that at least he had unscrewed his spurs and boarded his hounds at Batty Street.

Indeed, there sat Speranza dressed in an entirely departed style: a dress of sizeable black and white checks set off with accents of black tulle and silk and accessorised with tiny bunches of bundled wheat, such that she appeared more harvested than dressed. "Mr. Stoker, Mr. Stoker," came her call, and towards it I proceeded with Tumblety in tow.

"Lady Wilde," said I, "allow me to present Mr., or rather Dr., Francis Tumblety. He is a good and long-standing friend of Mr. Hall Caine, who sends his regrets and very much wishes he'd been able to join us to-day."

"I imagine Mr. Hall Caine," said Speranza, grandly, "is quite busy at present at his Grubby—"

"Greeba," said I. "*Greeba* Castle."

"—busy at his castle," said she, sniffily, "burying all his newfound coin." Turning to Tumblety, she asked, "But mustn't we, sir, find joy in our friend's good fortune?"

---

25. Evidently the military hat, peaked and plumed, earlier described.

"We must indeed, madam. It is only proper, and propriety is an English trait I've long admired." With this riposte—had he not heard the humour in Speranza's words?—Tumblety kissed our hostess's hand. I have seen him touch the hind-quarters of his hounds with less disdain. This, Speranza sensed, of course; and so it was she said:-

"You are welcome here, Mr. Dr. Rubbertree; however—"

"Tumblety, madam. The name is Tumblety."

She tapped at her ear. "My apologies, sir. . . . I meant only to say that propriety is a word best applied to tradesmen, I find. Here we've no interest in the *merely* proper."

"Duly noted, madam. . . . May I ask, is your son present to-day?"

"He *is* here . . . ," said she, squinting into the dark, "somewhere; but I fear that if you wish to speak to As-car—or rather listen to him—you shall have to make your way through his many admirers. I have had word· that a covey of your countrymen, your *concitoyens,* came here directly from their ship's mooring at Chelsea Bridge in search of my son and—"

And never before have I seen someone turn on his heel and head off whilst yet Speranza spoke, but this Tumblety did. "Well . . . " huffed Speranza.

I apologised, adding that I could not account for the man. Leaning nearer, I confided, "Caine sends no word at all, none, yet asks that I indulge this friend of his."

"How very curious of Caine."

"Indeed," said I, and the silence which ensued ended with:-

"But surely, Bram"—and she beckoned me nearer with a beringed finger—"you know you need *never* apologise to me, not from this day to my last. Your kindnesses to both myself and my late husband are well remembered."

I nodded. I bowed, just so. And then I did the lady the favour of returning to her preferred topic: "Oscar, you say, is present to-day?"

"He is, yes; which explains, I suppose, this uncommon crush. Since his American successes, As-car is followed hither and thither, with *Punch* reporting such pith as, 'Mr. Oscar Wilde has cut his hair,' et cetera. It is preposterous!"

"And, milady, you love it."

"Yes, you devil, I do. . . . But cannot the boy spare a moment for his widowed mother? He is forever in the company of that Mrs. Langtry[26]— *there*, there she is"; whereupon Speranza nodded toward a clutch of *salonistes,* none of whom I could discern in the uncertain light. "Why the woman would wear mauve I've *no* idea. One would think she'd try to live down her history rather than flaunt it. . . . What will it be next? Pink ribbons? Disgraceful, it is!"

I smiled my assent: disgraceful indeed; though I'd neither notice nor care if the Prince himself took to sporting pink ribbons.

"And if my As-car isn't arm in arm with Miss Langtry, or amongst those . . . those sporting fellows he finds I know not where, then he's fending off a swarm of social-women hopeful of being mentioned in his *Woman's World:* 'Mrs. Black looked very well in green, and Mrs. Green looked very well in black,' et cetera. I tell you, Bram, it's too much, *terribly* too much."

And so here I had the cause of Speranza's dolour: Oscar's growing renown—upon which she has *planned,* & over which she has sometimes *schemed*—is depriving her of his company. She is jealous of the world. So be it. I'd feared worse, for Speranza is not well: She has suffered much from her reduction in circumstances and takes every chance to condemn her many *"creditori."*[27]

Relieved to learn that Lady Wilde was otherwise well—and with Tumblety having set off on the scent of Oscar—I determined to take my leave then and there; but Speranza teased me into staying with:-

26. Lillie Langtry was the mistress of the Prince of Wales.

27. Lady Wilde was dependent on the rents from family properties in Ireland, though these were collected, at best, inconstantly. Otherwise, her sons helped her as they could. How could they not, when such appeals as this factored in the family's correspondence:

"If I am to be left in mere pauperism," she once wrote to Oscar, "I see nothing for it but to take Prussic acid and get rid of the whole business at once—for I will *not* undertake the struggle for daily bread, which I see is my probable future fate. So dies Speranza. Goodbye. . . . Now I must go and do my tasks in the house. *La Madre Povera*" (Quoted in *Mother of Oscar,* by Joy Melville: 1994; John Murray Publishers).

In fact, Lady Wilde did undertake just such a struggle for her daily bread, writing pseudonymously, for Oscar's *Woman's World,* those same types of society articles Stoker says she so disdained.

"Do be sure, Mr. Stoker, to say hello to my Irish poet, wherever he is. He says he knows you. A Trinity connection, if memory serves. . . . Ah, there he is, leaning against the mantel." She nodded towards a tall young man at room's end, a man too young to have been a schoolmate of mine. "He has a fine, fine forehead: We shall hear from him in the literary world, of that I'm certain. Oh, but *do* tell him to un-slouch himself. His bones are his, after all, and he must bear the burden of them." She called me nearer to say:-

"His name is Yeats, and he's been nose to nose with Oscar's Constance for fully an hour. You will tell me, won't you, Bram, their topic of discourse? I do not mean to pry, mind, it's just that I rather worry about our Constance."[28]

Yeats, had she said? *Ah, yes,* thought I in the long minutes it took me to cross the room, here must be the son of John Butler Yeats, who'd been some few years ahead of me at Trinity. We'd long been out of touch, but as I neared the conversing couple, I recognised the young man I'd met nearly ten years ago, when, early in my tenure with Irving, the older Yeats had brought his son to the Lyceum, writing first to say that the boy—Billiam, I believe he called him—was most fond of Shakespeare. I'd arranged a box, if I recall rightly, and arranged, too, that father and son should meet Miss Terry afterwards. Yeats the younger, then but thirteen or so, had proved impervious to the lady's many charms; but here he was now, grown quite tall and, yes, slouching, though far be it from me to admonish him for that.

"Sir," said I, proffering a hand, "I know your father. Never did Trinity see his like—some men paint, others speechify, but few do both as well as him. Likewise do I know your lovely interlocutor here; though you talk to her so intently, I am loath to interrupt. Do say you forgive me, both of you."

28. William Butler Yeats, then twenty-three, would win the Nobel Prize for Literature in 1923. As for Constance Wilde, she had married Oscar in 1884 and already borne two children by this time— Cyril and Vyvyan; but she had only just begun to bear, too, the lengthening line of Oscar's "sporting fellows."

I was of course forgiven, and further salutations were seen to. Still, the weight of the words I'd interrupted could be felt, verily felt—rather as the arthritic are said to feel rain yet to fall. I had indeed interrupted speech of some import. And so I decided: I would bid them good-bye and be on my way. It was just as well; for, as I'd not seen Tumblety in some while, I could now blamelessly take my leave of him. However, as I spoke those remarks prefatory to departure, Constance, dear, sweet Constance Wilde, cut me off; so:-

"Do stay, Bram. Indeed"—and here she and Yeats shared a look—"we have been wondering how long Lady Wilde would wait before sending you our way, as I earlier asked her to."

Whatever did she mean? Were the women complicit in a plot of sorts? Sly Speranza. Cunning Constance.

It was Yeats who answered the question. "A word with you, Mr. Stoker, was the day's objective for both Mrs. Wilde and myself. In achieving this we enlisted, yes, Lady Wilde." He peered out from behind circular spectacles that cast him in an owl's role. A forelock of blackest hair fell over that brow on which Speranza sees greatness writ. For my part, I saw but the father reflected in the son, and as the sight made me feel old, quite, I may have countered too curtly with:-

"Whatever do you mean, sir? It is my habit to speak plainly, even on Saturdays. Pray make it yours."

"Bram," said Constance, soothingly, "we wish a word with you. In private."

How deucedly odd, all this. "Privacy," said I, "is not the salient trait of Speranza's salons, as you know, and—" But before I knew it, Constance had taken my arm and was leading me from the room, Billiam coming behind.

We three had passed through the hallway where Wilde, halfway up the stairs, was holding forth on All & Everything. He looked much as I'd seen him last, and much as he does in the myriad photographs which weight the walls of his mother's home. I did not see Tumblety amongst those standing in rapt attendance. And as I had not seen the American, I was pleased to think he had not seen me.

Stepping into the scullery—of all places—we surprised the Betty taking a long pull upon her flask. The scent of sloe berries lingered longer than she. "Really," said I to my captors, for so they seemed, "I cannot imagine what—"

"There will be a meeting, Bram, two weeks hence, on the first of June. A meeting of . . . of a new society which we feel will be of interest to you. Brief: You are most, *most* suited for membership." This from Constance, whom I'd never known to speak so directly. Who, I wondered, was the "we" she referenced? For whom did she speak?

" 'Membership,' you say? In what kind of society? Pray tell."

"A secret society." This from Yeats, finally; whereupon he and Constance simply stood there, staring at me. There ensued a silence *most* awkward.

"Well, sir," said I in my turn, "if this 'society' be so secret as to preclude you and Mrs. Wilde from explaining yourselves further, I'm afraid I must decline your invitation. We have been quite busy at the Lyceum of late, and now Mr. Irving has announced his intention to mount *Macbeth* before—"

With rather too much cheek, I thought, Yeats interrupted me:-

"Mr. Stoker, excuse me, please; but Lady Wilde has told me of the long hours you spent in Sir William's study, both with and without the man, listening to his tales of Egypt and studying on your own. I have spoken to Budge, too, and he—"

"Is this society concerned then with travel to the East?"

"No," said Constance, "not travel, and not the East in general. Rather it is Egypt in particular that interests us; and, more particular still"—here she lowered her voice to a whisper—"the secrets and truths of ancient Egypt."

"Truths, you say?"

"Indeed," said Yeats, his handsome face quite stonily set, his bright eyes holding fast to mine. "Have you, sir, heard of the Order of the Golden Dawn?"

"I have not," said I, words which seemed to touch a nerve in Constance, for she then said, rather apologetically:-

"Oh, Bram, I fear we were wrong to broach the subject with you to-day, and here of all places—tucked in a scullery with a *conversazione* going on beyond!"

In fact, it seemed I could hear the salon disbanding. As I longed to take my own leave, and as the stink of soiled pots and pans piled in the sinks was somewhat mephitic, I said with some acerbity, "Yet introduce it you have, Constance. Why not continue on, then?"

She took both my hands in hers, as if we were about to waltz. As for young Yeats, he surrendered to a sudden interest in the scuffed tip of his shoe. Finally, in confidential tones, Constance set in; so:-

"Bram, for some while now, whenever I've seen you, I've seen . . . something. Dare I call it . . . disquiet? Oh, Bram, forgive me. I would never presume so, except I know that same disquiet." She stood so near me now that her head was back at an awkward angle, and as she looked up into my eyes, I saw tears welling in her own. "We are searchers, Bram, both of us. No: *all* of us." I assumed she referenced other members of the aforesaid Order. "Together we are stronger than if we each stand alone, each search alone. And so we are inviting you to join our common search."

I knew not what to say. I was at once flummoxed and flattered: a secret society, and one wanting me for a member? What was it they were searching for, specifically? Amidst these and other questions I could not ask aloud, not then, I heard one answer, as it were: echoing in my head were Whitman's words. And if I am to sign God's name to the letter of my life, well, haven't I *to write* that letter first, to live the life, truly, and with intent? Yes. *Yes.* Perhaps a path toward that life was being presented to me in Speranza's scullery. Stranger things have happened, surely. And so I said to Constance, to young Yeats:-

"I shall consider your invitation. I shall consider it deeply." And so I shall.

We three having nodded, each to the other—which bespoke a sort of understanding, I suppose—Constance stepped toward the fore. She'd be the first to quit the scullery; but as she stepped into the kitchen proper, she started and nearly screamed as Tumblety suddenly appeared in front of her, naught betwixt him and her but his ridiculous hat, which now he held in hand. Constance recoiled. Yeats took her in: damning appearances, he nestled her into the crook of his arm, and—this being no occasion for introductions—together they repaired to Speranza's common rooms.

"Sir," said I to Tumblety, my ire up, "as you profess to admire English propriety, I feel myself at liberty to inform you that it is *not* considered proper, neither in England nor elsewhere, for a gentleman to eavesdrop so."

"Forgive me, Stoker." Too familiar, this, too familiar by far: He hasn't my permission to address me so. "I sought you out only to see if you were ready to leave."

I said nothing, and so Tumblety took my turn:-

"Shall we, then?" Regrettably, we then took our leave together.

Upon the street, Tumblety let it be known that Wilde had much amused him. I, in turn, let it be known that he could spare me the details. In my opinion, said I, Oscar has far to go to match his wit to his mother's and his worth to his father's. And at the earliest opportunity, I attempted to point the American towards Batty Street. "A roundabout route, that one," said he of my proposal, "wouldn't you say?"

"As you please," said I; whereupon Tumblety fell back into step beside me. He may have spoken more. I was silent, resolutely so, though inwardly I cursed Caine. When Tumblety decided to head off a few streets farther on, he did so with that horrid handshake of his and this, said—it seemed to me—with something of a sneer:-

"Well, then, Stoker . . . June first if not before." Whatever did *that* mean? But before I could ask him, Tumblety—with a tip of his foolish hat—took his leave. And I'd walked half a block more before I heard his words, truly heard them. Only then did I understand that he had indeed been party to the secrets of the scullery.

. . . I close, and duly, for the crunch of coach wheels upon the drive tells me wife & child are come back from Grim's Dyke.

LETTER, BRAM STOKER TO ELLEN TERRY

24 May '88

Dearest, Most Dutiful Daughter,[29]

Your Portia was resplendent last night, as ever she is. Henry sits at his desk across from mine here in the XO and asks that I add his accolades to this note, which now I do, appending X's and O's of a more intimate sort.

As per your request, lately made, re: your desired research into Lady Macb., I write to say that I hesitate, quite, to accompany you into the precincts of an insane asylum. That said, I realise, too, that a mere NO! from your ol' Ma shan't dissuade you; and so I wrote to my brother, Thornley, for advice.

A response come in to-day's post tells me that—owing to Thornley's intercession on his beloved brother's behalf!—we, you and I, shall be welcome at Stepney Latch on Wednesday week. Thornley writes, too, that we would be wise to visit in the forenoon, whilst the nocturnal inmates yet sleep and the matutinal ones are medicated. If the day and hour do not suit, let me know at once, as I am to write to one Dr. Stewart to apprise him of our details.

I hope you know what you are doing, my dear!

Your loving Ma, AKA,
Stoker

P.S.—Thornley advises that we go incognito, as we cannot assume that the insane are yet sane enough to leave the London press unread, and, were you to be recognised, *true* Pandemonium would ensue.

P.P.S.—Not *a word* of this to Henry, agreed?

29. Ellen Terry and Stoker referred to each other, oddly, as mother and daughter. An extant photo of Terry is inscribed to Stoker, "To my 'Ma'!—I am her dutiful child. Ellen Terry. Feb. '88."

JOURNAL OF BRAM STOKER

28 May—a spitting, sunless Monday.—Thornley's advice sought/ received: He opines that a New Woman such as E.T. won't be much the worse for having seen the inside of an asylum such as Stepney Latch. I shall of course accompany her, though Henry shall have my head if he hears of it! He would deem the scheme too dangerous, as well it may be. But I have long pitied Ellen Terry *the artiste* in one particular and one only:

Henry steadfastly refuses to work with her on the realisation of her roles. I have never had more from him on the subject than, "Best not to ask the hummingbird how she flies, lest—in considering the question— she fall"; but this bothers Ellen *no end.* And so it was that when she came to me confessing her dread fear of going-up at year's end as a half-achieved Lady Macb., and broaching the idea of researching the insane—itself insane!—I heard myself say that I'd see what I could do. *Stoker will see to it.*

And so I *have* seen to it: We are expected at Stepney Latch two days hence. There E.T. will observe the inmates in their surrounds and various states of delirium, hopeful of borrowing from the demonic and the docile alike. She shall go incognito, of course. Though I am known in certain circles, they are not circles of the Dantean sort, but Ellen's fame & face are equally recognisable in Hell as they are On High, surely. And so we are to meet to-morrow morn. in the Lyceum's costumery. There Ellen Terry will become someone else whilst I watch with envy.

Later.—Post-performance. To-night's Bassanio better: prompter tells me the two minutes are retrieved (and with H.I. none the wiser).

Un-tired. No desire to dine. The Guv. is off to the Garrick Club in unknown company (?). So I will walk till the markets open and the first cries of the costers come with the sun. Wh'chapel, will it be? *The Ten Bells?* No. Silence and solitude shall suffice this night till sleep sees me off, long hours hence.

(*Mem.:* Wire Constance to-morrow: Will attend 1 June. Send word of whereabouts, hour, &c.)

JOURNAL OF BRAM STOKER

29 May—Strangeness to-day. Strangeness, indeed.

As previously planned, and despite my late retirement last eve—walked miles to & thru Whitechapel—Ellen and I met to-day in the costume shop at 10 o/c sharp. Whilst partaking of breakfast—scones and lemon curd, consumed at the milliner's table amidst ribbons, feathers, &c.—we discovered, with scant surprise, that we were like-minded re: her Stepney Latch disguise.

We both thought it best she go dressed as a man. She has dissembled so onstage innumerable times. But then we thought better of the idea, for isn't it the mad*women* of Stepney Latch she means to move amongst? Indeed. And though an artificer as skilled as Ellen Terry might sit, be-suited, through a season of Parliament amidst unsuspecting M.P.'s, in breeches amongst the female Bedlamites of Stepney Latch she'd be found out, surely. And so it was we decided that a wig, much maquillage, and some widow's weeds would suffice as the bushel under which we'd hide her light. Far better a plan, this. Far safer. What's more, Dr. Stewart has given us but one directive: *Stir not the pot.*

We shopped discreetly for Ellen's disguise, lest the wardrobe mistress learn that the Lady of the Lyceum planned to meander amongst the mad. We allowed only that Miss Terry was to play against type in a production proposed, merely proposed, for a future season: a spinsterish ensemble was wanted. What had we in store? Alas, our costumer wasn't a full minute amongst the racks before she loosed a blue torrent the likes of which I'd not heard from a woman since . . . well, since last night's wanderings down the Whitechapel Road.

"Whatever is the matter, Mrs. Pinch?" Though this is not the lady's name, it is so common a practice of hers when fitting the players that it has stuck. Stuck like her pins, yes, and stuck like the dog-produced dirt now featured upon the worn heel of her side-spring boot.

"I ask you, Mr. Stoker, sir, 'aven't we rules about dogs 'avin the run of the theatre? Your sweet Drummie and the Guv'nor's Flossie excepted, ma'am, of course."

"Dogs?" I echoed, for I'd not yet seen nor smelt the substance in question. In truth, hearing of dogs astray in the Lyceum chilled me. "'Dogs,' do you say? Here?"

"Dogs I say indeed, Mr. Stoker, and yes: 'ere in the shop! What but a mutt would leave a like mess?" Mrs. Pinch hopped nearer where we sat to show the proof upon her boot, which proof was yet . . . fresh. "Really, Mr. Stoker, sir, dogs ain't appropriate to—"

"Dogs are *not* regular denizens of the Lyceum Theatre, Mrs. Pinch," said I, pronouncedly; "and I shall have further words with our gatekeepers, be assured of it."

"Thank you, sir," said she, dropping her bulk onto a chair and setting to work upon her boot with an old brush.

"Ellen," said I, "will you excuse me?"

"Surely," said she; but I could not tell if her thoughts, too, had hied toward Tumblety and his twin hounds. Before taking my leave, I cleaned up a second . . . coil of soil, may I say, and told Mrs. Pinch to take an inventory and report to me of any missing attire, *men's* attire.

To those at the Lyceum's doors, both of whom swore they'd been in their positions some two hours or more, I posed the now-familiar question: Had they seen the American on the premises that morning? They had not. Neither had Mrs. Quibbel. However, Mrs. Q. was able to inform me that the American had indeed accompanied Henry to the Garrick Club last night. Had Tumblety explored our costumery before going? No: the spoor was too new. Had he returned later, then, either alone or with Henry? If alone, has he a key of his own? His free in- and egress would seem to indicate so. Good God! Can Henry Irving have been so charmed, so hoodwinked, by the American as to have conferred upon him a key of his own? I shall not be surprised to earn an answer in the affirmative, for Tumblety's ... *influence,* dare I deem it, is downright mesmeric. Oh, but if the man has a key to any of our doors I shall insist, *insist* upon its immediate surrender.

Later. Henry not keen on my enquiry. Not keen at all. Words were had, yet here I sit wondering still: Does Tumblety have a key to these precincts? I must and will ask the man myself when next we meet, though happy I'll be if said occasion is a long time coming.

JOURNAL OF BRAM STOKER

30 May.—Night now after a day most drear; sleepless; and so I write.

Henry dined again last night at the Garrick with Tumblety. To spite me? To allay my suspicions?

I have not seen the American since Speranza's salon; but when I do see him, I will put my questions to him, and pointedly, too: Has he a key? And was it his dogs that dirtied the costume shop so? Surely it was. No other dogs could have done it, as the terriers are in fact no longer let to stray from the dressing areas, not since Ellen's Drummie came so perilously close to making her debut in *The Lady of Lyons.* What is more, I here record, Holmes-like, the indelicate fact that the tiny terriers do not produce spoors the size of those found in the shop.[30]

But whatever was Dr. Tumblety doing in the costumery? Thievery cannot be the motive; for why would he steal something he is free to borrow? Upon this point I learn little from Mrs. Pinch, who holds that the requested inventory is impossible, owing to her present work on *The Merch.,* her preliminary work on *Macb.,* &c. She'll discover what, if anything, has gone missing only when next she needs it, says she; and with that I must content myself.

Another question to put to the American: How long does he plan to

---

30. Reference here is of course to Sherlock Holmes, the character created by Arthur Conan Doyle (later Sir), another of Stoker's writer-friends more successful than he.

linger in London? I shall suffer him better when once again a sea separates us. *Many* questions remain for Caine, Caine, Caine! The Isle of Man might be the moon, so distant, so quiet is the newly-contemptible Caine.

...To Tumblety my pen too often returns. Did I not open these pages to tell of to-day's excursion to Stepney Latch? Indeed I did.

I went round to Ellen's house in a hansom. My *Bradshaw's* did not disappoint: We arrived at King's Cross in time to secure first-class passage upon the listed 9.14 a.m. train to Purfleet, where Dr. Stewart awaited our arrival.[31]

At the Purfleet station, I and one Mrs. Stevenson—E.T., of course, done up as a dowager searching out an asylum in which to stow a troublesome son—hired another hansom to take us to Stepney Latch. As its driver cast not a second glance at England's best-known actress, Ellen and I nodded, satisfied, and settled in for the ride, which was shortened by my promising to add a guinea to the fare if the driver delivered us at double-speed. The added haste, however, threatened to tip Mrs. Stevenson's gray wig from its north-south axis to one oriented east-west; but pins were soon applied to the task, and the coiffure came under control.

Soon enough we slowed before a place seeming perfectly suited to its purpose. A stony edifice spread its wings over untold acreage, this last delineated by a short wall fallen deeply into disrepair. Trees were innumerable upon the land. The place, the land seemed perpetually shadowed. A low and leaden sky improved the asylum's aspect not at all as we drove down its long drive. "Oh, my," mused Mrs. Stevenson as we passed beneath an iron arch on which was writ—or rather wrought—STEPNEY LATCH ASYLUM.

So long and noisy was our approach up the shell- and cinder-coated

31. *Bradshaw's Guide*, published between 1839 and 1961, provided railway timetables for all the routes in Britain. Stoker's well-thumbed *Guide* for the year 1888 is, in fact, part of the *Dossier*, and its perusal confirms a 9.14 train to Purfleet on the day in question.

Purfleet, fifteen miles east of London on the north bank of the Thames, is where Stoker will later situate Count Dracula's London estate and its adjacent asylum, run by a Dr. John Seward. (Compare to Dr. Thomas Stewart, already introduced to the *Dossier* and soon to reappear.)

drive that Dr. Stewart knew of our arrival before it had been accomplished. Out he came in the company of a nurse quite short, quite stout. There our hosts stood at the asylum doors. We'd hardly alighted from the cab, Mrs. Stevenson and I—only Dr. Stewart knew my companion's true identity—when our driver, fare and a guinea further in hand, rounded out and up the driveway in haste. Having first waved away the dust thusly stirred, Dr. Stewart and I applied our hands to the duties of introduction.

The nurse's name was Nurske, hard on the *e,* if you please; and so at first I thought Dr. Stewart had provided a pet name of sorts: Nursey. Oh, but here was no man's pet, and so I asked that he repeat the name. He did so, saying, to clear my confusion, "Yes, sir: Nurse Nurske it is." I then introduced my Mrs. Stevenson—mine, I say, for I'd named her: Stevenson's *J&H,* of which *all the world* still talks, sits beside my reading chair presently, so good, so *damn* good, I am cutting the pages at a snail's pace so as to savor the read.[32]

It was with actorly discipline that E.T. managed to stifle a smile upon being consigned to the care of Nurse Nurske; but there soon followed from my Mrs. S. a look that led me to ask Dr. Stewart for a word aside.

We walked two steps from the women. Behind me I heard E.T. speak platitudes appropriate to any occasion, even one as strange as this— words regarding the weather, the want of sun, &c.; all of which words Nurse Nurske met with a silence as stony as her place of employ. I had best be about my business then, and so:-

"Doctor," said I in low, clubbish tones—here were *words btw. Men*— "my brother Thornley insists that I convey to you his very best."

"I am indebted to your brother for favors conferred in Dublin, sir," said he, "and I shall remain indebted—happily so—for some while."

32. Author and novel in question are, of course, Robert Louis Stevenson's *Dr. Jekyll and Mr. Hyde,* published in 1886 and later played upon the Lyceum stage to great acclaim, not, however, with Henry Irving in the titular roles but rather Richard Mansfield. Stoker's presentation copy of the novel was part of the Sotheby's lot acquired by my relation. It is now in my possession, the final pages still uncut—interesting that Stoker found reason never to finish his friend's "*damn* good" novel about a man split in two.

"Well, sir," said I, "if that be the case, know that my brother is an inveterate forgiver of debts. I have had cause to discover this myself over the decades, again and again. . . . Now, as for myself and"—*clearing of throat*— "Mrs. Stevenson, I thank you for indulging what may seem to you a whim; but I assure you, sir, that if ever you have seen my companion upon the"—*whispering now*— "stage, you will understand that her art—"

"I have done so, Mr. Stoker, and often." His voice rose with excitement, and in so doing betrayed a slight accent, one betokening either an Irish birth or a green sojourn of some duration. "And though I am beholden to your brother—broth*ers*, may I say, for I am privileged to call George Stoker a friend as well[33]—your presence here to-day is owing, too, I must admit it, to the way in which Miss . . . or rather, Mrs. Stevenson moved me, deeply, when I saw her play in *Hamlet* beside Mr. Irving in Manchester. I could not pass up the opportunity to tell her so in person, even in surrounds as inauspicious as these; but rest assured, sir: I shall convey my compliments in whispers." Whereupon we four headed toward the asylum's oaken doors.

Ellen had recoiled from Nurse Nurske. Indeed, she now clung to me; and it was doubtless this that caused Dr. Stewart to say, assuagingly:-

"We have a wing, Mr. Stoker, Mrs. Stevenson, in which the sexes are integrated. And there we four shall be a *partie carrée* at all times; so fear not."

"Excellent," said I, commending the plan. This despite my disdain of the foreign phrase; for it put me in mind of Mlle Dupont, Noel, &c., such that I could only deem myself in dereliction of my duties as a father, being at Stepney Latch amongst the mad when I could have, nay *should* have, passed those hours at home. Alas.

"But be forewarned, sir," appended the warder, "that some of our

---

33. The youngest of the Stoker brothers, George was then in the early stages of a medical career that would be nearly the equal of Thornley's. He was a specialist in diseases of the throat, in which capacity he consulted often at the Lyceum; was a proponent of now-standard oxygen treatments for sores, burns, etc., based on methods he observed amongst the Zulus; and was the author of *With the Unspeakables; or Two Years Campaigning in European and Asiatic Turkey*, to which his writer-brother would later turn for its descriptions of Transylvania, a land Bram Stoker himself would never visit.

hardest cases are resident in the West Wing. We keep them in common as it's they who need the greater share of care, day and night." Hearing this, Ellen steeled herself; and I might have chided the doctor for frightening her so if I'd not decided in his favour mere minutes after having met him.

I quite liked him, yes. He was of Ireland, true; but also his face bespoke a solid character: a strong jaw frames his relative handsomeness, the latter marred only by his black hair being rather more recessed than his years would warrant. He is perhaps thirty, the doctor, no older; and it dawns on me now that Thornley likely taught the man in Dublin, or perhaps supervised his residency at Dean Swift's.

Only later, on the train back to London, would I wonder if perhaps Dr. Stewart doesn't indulge in some of the many medicaments he doles out daily. Sleep, to some men, is more a problem than a palliative; and the administrator of Stepney Latch showed marked symptoms of insomnia: a slightly tremulous handshake, and purpled disks beneath dark eyes. Little wonder it would be, too; for the doctor's private rooms must be within the asylum, the same we now entered to a chorus of howls and other auditory horrors the like of which would deprive the deaf of sleep.

Mrs. Stevenson kept close to my side, relieved that her role was one of few lines. She observed in silence, cupping to nose and mouth her violet-trimmed kerchief. "Oh, Ma," whispered she, mere minutes into our tour, "is it not terrible? I feel as though we've come to a human zoo."

"Some would say we have," I rejoined. "The stories I hear from Thornley would curl those horsey locks of yours, Mrs. Stevenson." Further referencing her wig, I added, with a leavening wink, "You'd best tug it forward a quarter-inch"; for, forgetting herself, she'd dislocated it, just so, with a scratching fingertip. My own scalp now prickled from the proximity of Dr. Stewart's patients, too. Indeed, the air at Stepney Latch seemed electro-static, as if madness were an emission of sorts.

I'd have been relieved if E.T. had turned to me then—in or out of character—and asked that we leave: I'd no need to see the insane myself, and still I doubted that she stood to learn a great deal from watching madwomen wailing at walls, &c. Moreover, the ever-tenuous peace at the Lyceum was dependent upon our timely return: H.I. could not be let to miss us, to wonder where we were. My *Bradshaw's* told me that the 2.20 train from Purfleet was the preferred one, returning us to London with time to spare. I'd see that we were on it. Meanwhile, our tour continued.

We passed through a common area in which a woman—white of hair, deficient of tooth—clawed at herself most indelicately. ("No place upon the stage for *that*," said I to Mrs. S.) Now another woman bowed deeply, as if we passed in a royal procession. A third asked if we'd brought the pastilles we'd promised her Sunday last and met our apologies with screams, screams that gave rise to others till the stones of the asylum verily rang. Quite disquieting, this; literally so. We walked away, ever faster; and this, mind, was not the ward we'd been warned of.

I pitied our hosts: To be insane in such a place was bad, terribly bad, but to be sane amongst the mad was surely worse. I could only hope Ellen might benefit from our having come. Myself? I would know no benefit but distraction. Amongst the mad, I gave no thought to those questions which have dogged me for days; such as: What have I committed to to-morrow with Constance and young Billiam? And what of Caine? Will I have to search him out in person? Or will this Tumblety take himself off, elsewhere? Tumblety, blasted Tumblety! Once again the man pilots my pen & drinks my ink; and I shall have reason to *re*write his name as I continue the tale of our visit to Stepney Latch; which now I do:

Having reached the end of a cold, long, and lightless corridor, albeit one blessedly less cacophonous than the common area, we came to a wide flight of stairs. These we ascended, as to do so seemed the proper course; but midway up the stairs, Nurse Nurske set to coughing. Either she was suffering a sudden-coming consumption or she meant to convey something to Dr. Stewart. The latter was the case, of course; but the doctor was distracted: ensorcelled by E.T.—as men so often are—he had taken this quieter time to lay his accolades at the actress's feet. This he did whisperingly whilst Nurse Nurske coughed herself hoarse. So it was that as we turned at the stair-top onto the wing marked *West*, we—all of us save Nurse Nurske, of course—were startled by the low-timbred and refined salutation that greeted us.

The words issued from a room three walls of which were covered in quilted sail-cloth or canvas. And there, before the fourth, iron-barred wall of the cell, stood the strait-jacketed speaker. "Good morning, Dr. Stewart."

Our host took a step back from the bars. The inmate, smiling now, offered a stiff nod toward Nurse Nurske while asking Dr. Stewart, "To what do we owe this call? It would appear social in nature, as I see Nurske hasn't her stick in hand.

"It has been so very long since you've brought me guests, Dr. Stewart, and though I thank you, truly I do, words of warning would not have gone amiss. I might have . . ."—here he strained to look back over his shoulder at his cell, and doing so showed where his restraints chafed: he bore a livid scar upon his neck, such as one might see on a victim of strangulation—"well, I might have tidied up a bit," concluded he, theatrically, sardonically; for there was nothing in his cell save some rudimentary plumbing and a rubberised pallet upon the floor.

"My apologies," said Dr. Stewart; whereupon he introduced the inmate to us as if the man were invisible, insensate, and not standing mere feet from us, albeit behind bars:-

"Mr. T. M. Penfold, fifty-odd years of age. Previously a cavalryman in Her Majesty's service. Sanguine temperament, great physical strength, morbidly excitable, and prone to periods of gloom—"

"I shouldn't doubt it," muttered Mrs. Stevenson.

Dr. Stewart resumed: "—and fixed, quite, upon self-mutilation, self-murder."

"Suicide," said I, staring at the inmate; and the moment I'd mouthed the word, I wished I hadn't. "But why . . . why the strait-jacket?"

"I am afraid that Penfold"—who was, of course, listening as intently as we—"would, if he were allowed the use of his arms, tear at his own flesh with his fingers. And further, there is the matter of his teeth. Too, the man has shown over the years a certain . . . *talent* for escape, let me say."

"Oh, my," mused E.T., clasping her kerchief to her mouth and nose, as if the words she'd just heard were themselves malodorous.

Much struck by the idea of a man—*this* man—bent on doing himself to death, were he able, I asked, "Do you mean, Doctor, that Mr. Penfold desires to ... to bleed himself to death? Or do we speak of carnivorous intent?" I'd adopted the doctor's habit of distancing the very *present* patient, only to be brought up short by Penfold himself:-

"May I respond to that, Dr. Stewart?" This, uttered in tones appropriate to any London parlour.

Dr. Stewart said nothing, and so Mr. Penfold spoke on:-

"What I wish, sir," said he to me, "is simply to die. Rather, I no longer wish to live. And, as no other means of suicide avails itself to me in this cushioned cell—neither utensil nor tool, not even a hardened corner on which to dash the brains from my head – the doctor speaks true: I would, yes, if able, tear and rend my flesh with fingers and teeth. Not with carnivorous intent, no, but rather to rid myself, my body, of its blood; for the blood, sir, is the life, and, as said, I have had done with life."

The blood is the life. Whence did those words come? Forthwith I was informed, by Penfold himself:-

"So it says in Deuteronomy 12:23, where the interdiction is, and I quote, 'Only be sure that thou eat not the blood: for the blood is the life.' But of course I do not wish to drink my own blood, Mr. Stoker. I would, however, see it spilled. I would watch with increasing relief, yes, if the red of life were to run from me."

So struck was I by the sentiment, so sanely expressed, that I was the last of our party to realise that Penfold had addressed me by name. It was Ellen's sudden, sharp intake of breath, her sudden taking hold of my hand, that alerted me. She may even have whispered what it was had happened. I cannot recall.

"Do we know each other, sir?" I prefer to think I spoke the words with equanimity; even so, this was naught compared to the cold smile of Penfold's reply.

"Perhaps," said Dr. Stewart, "we should leave Penfold now, as such talk as this is sure to upset—"

"To upset Miss Terry?" asked Penfold. We stood there thunder-struck. "Oh, I think not, Doctor. Miss Terry is very much . . . of the world."

"Sir," said I, stepping nearer the cell, "explain yourself." I'd have taken him by the lapels but for the bars between us—that and the fact that such jackets as the one he wore sport no lapels. The eyes into which I stared were hard and dark. I stood near enough to smell his soiled self. "And if you are the gentleman you wish to seem, you will address myself and not Miss Terry"; but Ellen had already drawn up beside me to ask:-

"However did you know?" I wonder: Was Ellen more abashed at being addressed so familiarly or by having her performance as Mrs. Stevenson deemed deficient? With actors one never knows: as Henry is wont to say, they never forget a hiss.

Penfold circled his cell. Never was an audience more rapt than we. Finally:-

"It was Mr. Stoker I recognised first, madam; but may I suggest you pay closer attention to your props when next you play . . . Mrs. Stevenson, was it? A lady of her supposed station does not carry another woman's kerchief, and yours, there, bears a rather broadly embroidered 'E.T.' in its crumpled corner." And so it did. "From the kerchief, I concluded—via a chain of deduction needful of but few links—that yes, before me stood the Lyceum's brawn and brain, Mr. Bram Stoker."

I did not appreciate being dismissed so. "I ask again, Mr. Penfold, and with lessening patience: Are we acquainted?"

"At present, it would seem so; but previously? No. Would that our common host might untie me, so that we could meet as men ought to: with a handshake."

"You trifle with me, Mr. Penfold," said I.

"If I do, sir, it is only to retain your company—company being a quite rare commodity here at Stepney Latch; and to pass the time, of course. . . . Of time, sir, I have entirely too much."

"Really, now," said Dr. Stewart, trying to turn our party back towards those stairs up which we'd lately come, "I must insist—"

Just then Penfold spoke on, and I daresay we all four hung upon his words.

"You do realise that we," said Penfold—meaning, presumably, his fellow inmates—"were once . . . *out there.*" He had been pacing, pontificating; but now he nodded, as best he could, towards his barred slit of window, adding, "And whilst *out there,* I once had the great good fortune to see you, Miss Terry, play alongside Mr. Irving. It was an occasion I shan't soon—"

"Lord alive!" This from Nurse Nurske, who, previously, in tallying the two-plus-two of our talk, had arrived at only three. Now here was four. "*Henry* Irving, does he mean? That would make you, missus, *Ellen Terry,* the Lady of the Lyceum."

"I am afraid it would, yes," said a chagrined E.T., stuffing the tell-tale kerchief into her purse. She'd have relieved herself of the wig, too, I'm sure, had it not been for the netting she wore beneath it. "I apologise for the charade, but . . ." and her words fell away unsaid. Meanwhile, Nurse Nurske sidled nearer the star. From the look upon her doughy face, in particular the twitching of her pug nose, one would have thought her hopeful of catching the scent of fame.

"Your Ophelia," resumed Penfold, "was sublime." Whereupon Dr. Stewart, forgetting himself, set to nodding like a spaniel being offered sausages.

"I thank you, sir," said Ellen, still feeling the fool.

"I very much envied the graceful death you conferred upon her."

"Such compliments are attributable to Shakespeare," she demurred, "more so than his players."

"Ah," said Penfold, "then I am right to disdain our Dr. Stewart for his refusal to free me; for surely he is the author of my fate, as Shakespeare was Ophelia's. Perhaps, were he possessed of an ounce, of a *scintilla* of art, he'd see at least the romance in freeing me, if not the reason; but alas . . ."

" 'Romance'?" quoted the indignant doctor. " 'Reason'? I submit only to science, Penfold, in protecting you from yourself."

"But I want no protection! How *dare* you condescend to me so?" And here came the bound patient, surging, as smoothly as his restraints allowed, to break upon the bars of his cell. *Crack!* went his jaw. His eyes fluttered, and it seemed he might faint onto the floor, but no . . . Here he was again, rather *too* lucid, blood spraying from his mouth as again he said, nay *seethed,* "How *dare* you?"

"Suicide," answered Nurse Nurske, "is a sin! You'd roast for it, you would."

"So, too, would you roast, if stupidity were a sin! No, I am wrong: Oily as you are, you'd not roast but *burn,* burn clean and quick." The nurse clenched her fists, and in wringing between them something unseen . . . well, it was evident she very much missed the aforementioned stick just then. Best not to know what might pass at Stepney Latch after our departure, after Mr. Penfold launched his appeal in earnest; so:-

"Mr. Stoker," said he, imploringly, "I no longer wish to live. Living pains me."

"Would not death?" I ventured.

"Dying, yes, perhaps; but not death. Death would be but . . . sweet oblivion, a surrender and a sinking away."

"We cannot be sure of that," said I in tones that would have won me no confidence in court.

"We cannot be sure," he agreed. "But suicide, Mr. Stoker, is a topic upon which you have thought often, is it not?" His reddened chin rested now on a cross-rail of the bars. The blood that bubbled on his lower lip as he spoke was discomfiting, yes, but his words were worse. I stared at the man, whose eyes were fired now, fired by knowledge of . . . of *me,* or so it seemed. However could he know of my blackest moods, of Manhattan, of what had happened there? He could not. He was not prescient. I'd only endowed him with a like sight, and for an instant only. He was, in point of fact, merely mad; though Mr. T. M. Penfold can appear quite sane, *quite;* as when he next said:-

"I was yet a free man, Mr. Stoker, and myself a resident of Chelsea some six years ago—it was six, was it not?—when you so famously interceded in that suicide attempt upon the Thames." Ah, at last: the explanation of how he'd known of me. Damnable *Punch*, damnable press.

"Mr. Penfold, I assure you—"

"Do you ever wonder, Mr. Stoker," he interrupted, "if you ought not to have interceded? If you ought to have let that man die?"

"The man who leapt from the *Twilight* into the Thames did die, Mr. Penfold, as surely you know if you—"

"Do not mistake my point, sir. You did not *let* him die. And so I pose the question a second time: Do you, Mr. Stoker, ever wonder if you ought to have let the man die?"

The answer is yes. And I *have* often asked myself that question in the years since. But of course I said nothing of all that.

"And be assured, sir: I followed the press upon the case *quite* closely, as my own life had lately devolved to something . . . something I wished to rid myself of."

Would he offer particulars? Ought I to ask for them? I hadn't long to ponder, as Dr. Stewart then spoke of his patient in tones rather more sympathetic than he'd earlier employed, though still he spoke not *to* but *of* Penfold, as if he were not present.

"Penfold," said he, "holds himself responsible for the deaths of his wife, two daughters, and an infant grandchild. Though the authorities deemed the deaths—by drowning: it was a boating excursion—accidental, still Penfold . . ." But Dr. Stewart desisted in his diagnosis, and indeed the look he then cast at Mr. Penfold was a pitying one. This was easily done; for there stood the man with tears in his eyes and blood on his lip, blood which must have tasted to him of the life he so disdained.

"It was after his first attempt at self-murder," resumed Dr. Stewart, in softened tones, "that his in-laws—and the law proper—remanded him to Stepney Latch; and here he remains."

"Yes," rejoined Penfold, glaring at his warder, "here I remain, *years* on."

"Penfold"—and again Dr. Stewart resumed his distancing discourse—"is of so fixed an intent he is dangerous. To himself, primarily, yes; but we must allow for the possibility of his murderous intent being directed toward others."

"Oh, make up your mind, Doctor! Is it me or society proper you're protecting?"

"Both," said Dr. Stewart.

This raised Penfold's ire once again. "Nothing, Doctor, *nothing* in my past life can possibly lead you to presuppose that I would be a danger to society if I were released. *Nothing,* I say. I have never hurt a fly."[34]

"I ask you," parried Dr. Stewart, "if, *if* I were to release you, would you set out immediately to harm yourself?"

"'Harm myself'? No, Doctor, I would not seek simply to harm myself. I would, however, seek egress from life by whatever means. Such is my right."

"God gave you life," interjected the nurse, "and only God—"

"God gives us two-legged brutes such as you to live amongst! By those lights, it would seem He plays rather loosely with the gift of life, and mightn't look too harshly upon its occasionally being refused, *with due reason.*"

"'Reason,'" quoted Dr. Stewart, addressing us. "He has *reasoned* thusly since his arrival at Stepney Latch, and so you see: My hands are tied."

"No, Doctor, only *my* hands are tied." Penfold spun round to show the long cuffs of his coat tied off behind him. "Free me, Dr. Stewart, and I shall gladly pardon you the pun. As for your persistence in keeping me penned up so . . ."

"I believe," said a worn Dr. Stewart, "we ought to proceed with our tour. This patient is overly excited."

" 'Excited'? *Excited,* you say?" Whereupon Mr. Penfold—and I came to begrudge Dr. Stewart his refusal to address his patient politely, to deprive him of the proper appellative—whereupon *Mr.* Penfold, I say,

---

34. Odd, this reference to flies.

Readers of *Dracula* will already have recognised in Penfold his novelised doppelgänger, Renfield, who is servile to the Count; and who, far from *not* hurting flies, ingests them and other lesser species in the hopes of subsuming their souls, via their blood, and thereby achieving immortality. The Penfold of the *Dossier* seeks the opposite, of course: suicide via exsanguination.

Such is the work of the fictioneer, I suppose: enfolding the real and the irreal.

began to run his forehead across the bars rather as—and here I must
beg pardon of a simile no better suited to the situation than the doctor's
accidental pun—rather as a lesser pianist would run the keys to finish
off a drinking song with a flourish. He did so down the length of the
barred wall, and back. The sounds of it—bone on bar—were as horrid
as the sight.

Dr. Stewart stood staring, stunned, whilst Nurse Nurske sprang into
action: from a hook beside the cell, she took down a heavy hood sewn
of canvas, its inside rubberised, and she entered the cell, brought the
inmate to the floor with moves vaguely Eastern in origin, and fastened
the hood over his broken and bleeding head. She took evident pleasure
in pulling its laces tight to the patient's skull. All the while, Penfold
cried to be let to die. Never have I heard words so plaintive. I confess
that my breath caught in my chest, and I might well have given myself
over to tears were it not for the needs of an already-crying E.T., the
which I tended as best I could, saying:-

"We will go, we will go . . ." and I continued to whisper cold comfort
into her ear, and ever louder, as now the ward rang with the imitative
cries of its inmates; meanwhile, Mr. Penfold's two warders—for Dr.
Stewart had sprung into action at his nurse's bidding—settled him upon
his mat. He quieted as doctor and nurse left the cell, but still his shoulders heaved as high as they could whilst he cried. I saw now how the
strait-jacket constrained his every motion: not only had he to move like
a diapered child, bow-legged and sway-backed, when upright, but bed-
ded down he could not even cry freely. The man's humiliations were,
nay *are*, manifold, and for his sake I hope he is indeed mad; but this I
have reason to doubt. Rather, he wants death. Simply so. And doubtless
Mr. Penfold saw a measure of sympathy in my eyes; for he then struggled onto his haunches and cried out:-

"Mr. Stoker, wait!"

"Yes, Mr. Penfold, what is it?" I went nearer the bars. I had to kneel
in order to hear the now-sane-seeming Penfold, for his words were
muffled by the hood, through the mouth-slash of which blood seeped,
just as tears moistened the crudely sewn eye-slits. "If, Mr. Stoker," said

he, "if you believe, as I do, that I have the right to end my own life; and if, Mr. Stoker, you were to convey that sentiment to whatever persons of power granted you access to this place to-day; I, Mr. Stoker, would remain indebted to you until the day my death be achieved. Do you understand me, sir?"

I stared at the man. I knew not what to say. I could not countermand Dr. Stewart, of course, but neither could I dismiss Mr. Penfold's plea: *Let me die.* I waited, and with silence did neither. "Good day, Mr. Penfold," said I, finally.

"Good day, Mr. Stoker," said he; and I am left to wonder what he heard in my non-words, in all I'd left unspoken. And what was it I'd meant to convey, exactly? I am left to wonder that myself. And to know, too, that for some while to come, Mr. T. M. Penfold shall people my dreams, both waking and otherwise.

"Miss Terry?" said he as we made to leave, Ellen and I both having grown eager for the world beyond the broken walls of Stepney Latch. "It has been my honour."

"Mr. Penfold," said she, turning back to Penfold. "I shall pray that if ever we meet again, it shall be under auspices pleasanter to yourself."

"You are kind, Miss Terry; but if I were inclined to pray, it would be that I never see your sweet face again, for the only auspices more pleasant to myself would preclude it. . . . Good day, Miss Terry."

"Good-bye, Mr. Penfold."

And hastily we took our leave of the asylum at Stepney Latch, having first to refuse Dr. Stewart's odd-seeming offer of tea.

The 2.20 from Purfleet brought us back to the Lyceum with Henry none the wiser. The ride was silent, save for:-

"Ma, did you see that . . . that *horrid* something in the eyes of poor Mr. Penfold as he spoke so accusingly to Dr. Stewart of his confinement? It unnerved me, quite."

"I am sorry, Ellen. Perhaps we oughtn't to have come."

"But did you see it, Bram? I believe it is that eye-fire, if you will, that marks the lunatic amongst us."

"I am sorry," I repeated. "I saw no such thing."

"Curious," said she, "*most* curious. I surely saw something in his eyes . . . something I hope to never see again. And perhaps you are right: perhaps we oughtn't to have come. It was folly on my part, Bram, for which I apologise. And if I learned anything at all, I fear I'll not know it for a long, long while." Whereupon silence was resumed, and we each retook to the landscape as it rolled through the frames of our respective windows.

Of course, I had seen the *something* Ellen had referenced. It sparked in the inmate's eyes. But what was it? I was less inclined than she to attribute it to lunacy. Menace, perhaps; the menace of the monomaniac, fixed upon his one idea, his one intent. Oh, but why admit as much to E.T. and scare her worse than already she was? For, had I spoken truly to my friend, I'd have had to say that yes, I saw the eye-fire—as she called it—at Stepney Latch, in the eyes of Mr. Penfold, just as I've lately seen it in the eyes of Francis Tumblety.

Who, if he shows at the Order's meeting on Friday, having inveigled an invitation from some principal fallen prey to his mesmeric ways, I shall cut most cleanly, most pointedly. Let Caine be damned and done for! Now I see I have indeed written past midnight into Thurs., 31 May; and so, one day more.

Pray let sleep fall fast as a final-act curtain. Pray let it be dreamless. And pray, pray may Friday's meeting hold meaning.

BRAM STOKER'S JOURNAL[35]

Sunday, 10 June, '88.—He was there.

A thing, something, I know not what . . . Brief: Something of lasting moment occurred Friday week—the 1st—such that now I feel that I write these pages for reasons other than my own. I must *record,* put down every detail *as it occurred,* yet by the use of cipher I will secrete these

---

35. This entry is enciphered and was entered into Stoker's journal more than one full week after his first experience of the Golden Dawn. In the interim, presumably, Stoker needed to re-familiarise himself with Bacon's cipher; but it is evident, too, that he researched the Order.

pages till passing time completes them. Yes, now more than ever, I am cognisant this is a Record I keep, though presently I have but a few fears and facts to commit to it.

I arrived at the appointed place at the appointed hour.[36] I was met upon the street corner by a boy who bade me follow him to a nearby door, numberless and red. He knocked upon same and fast disappeared, the coins thusly earned jangling in his pocket. The door opened, and there in the shadows stood C.W.,[37] who wordlessly ushered me down into an unadorned room whose high half-windows were at the level of the curb. She drew dark curtains. Naught but candles lit the scene now. It seemed not the time for pleasantries: neither families nor friends were asked after, and C., cryptically, said only:-

"Qui patitur vincit."[38]

To this I knew no reply. Thankfully, none seemed requisite. Rather, C. directed me to a corner of the room—it now seemed an antechamber of sorts—where there stood a tri-fold partition of carved mahogany upon which, despite the semi-dark, I could discern signs and sigils. C. herself repaired to the opposite corner and slipped behind a like partition. By the rustle of her silks, I knew she was changing. Finding a robe, a rope, and slippers—all white and approximate to my size—hanging before me, I followed her lead, removing my jacket yet wearing still my waistcoat beneath the belted cloak; but let me here state that were scepticism water, my kettle would have been fairly aboil by now. Had it not been for my fondness for Constance[39] and the fact that Billiam comes

36. The Hermetic Order of the Golden Dawn was a secret society, and Stoker—initially—respects this. Therefore, the precise location of the Order's Isis-Urania No. 3 temple is unknown, though some scholars situate it near the British Museum. It is my supposition that the Temple was not fixed at all, but rather moved and re-created as it suited its adepts.

As regards "the appointed hour," we may assume it was in the late afternoon or early evening, as Stoker's absence from a Friday night at the Lyceum would hardly have been tolerated by Henry Irving.

37. Constance Wilde, of course.

38. Latin for "He who suffers, conquers." This was likely the motto chosen by Constance Wilde upon her own initiation into the Order.

39. So much for secrecy.

of reputable stock, I might well have taken my leave of the Order then and there, before learning the least of its rites, rituals, and *raisons d'être*. And would that I had; for it is most decidedly *not* for me, this Order.[40]

Alas, I did not leave. And so, to continue:

Constance came from her corner dressed in a black tunic, a white cord wrapped thrice about her waist. Her slippers were red; they showed beneath the black bell of her robe like splashed blood as she approached me where I stood. She rose onto tiptoe to tilt my hood up over my head, kissing me first upon the cheek and whispering—quite incongruously, or so it seemed to me then—something about Sir William, pride, &c., whereupon she lowered my hood and, having donned her own, led me from the Pronaos[41] to the Temple proper.

There were twelve of us, total, in the Temple: ten adepts and two neophytes, of which I was one; but it was some while before I could count the costumed members of the Order, struck as I was by the Temple itself.

It—the Temple, or Hall of the Neophytes—was neither large nor architecturally grand. In fact, the structure itself was obscured by the extraordinary décor. The walls were impermanent: mere panels of painted canvas stretched taut over wooden frames, done much like the scenery of the Lyceum. There were seven such panels—each 8' or 10' high and 10' or 12' wide—set end to end, thus rendering the Temple heptagonal, tent-like. From these panels there swept upwards, towards the top of a golden pole standing center-all, as a support, great swathes of white silk. These, too, were painted, though "painted" does not suffice

---

40. As Stoker does not situate the Golden Dawn historically, here or elsewhere in the *Dossier,* I shall take this opportunity to do so.

The Hermetic Order of the Golden Dawn was founded in London in February of the year in question, 1888. The local Temple was inaugurated as Isis-Urania No. 3. Its original members were, variously, Qabalists, Rosicrucians, Freemasons, Theosophists, and other occultists. These adepts committed themselves to the evolution of, firstly, the self; and then, perforce and secondly, humanity in toto. This they sought to achieve via the *mysteria*—a series of secret, initiatory rites involving astrology, divination, alchemy, astral work, etc., progressing unto practical or applied magic, most particularly, and of greatest relevance to the *Dossier,* invocations for the summoning of spirit forms. And, to paraphrase Hamlet, "Therein would lie the rub."

41. So the antechamber is called.

as description. Here was high artistry, all of it betokening what little I'd learned of the Order's tenets, for:

All was Egyptian. As I stood in wonderment, staring at the walls whilst doubtless being stared at in turn by the adepts, I daresay my interest in the Order of the Golden Dawn grew. Constance had indeed referenced Egypt in drawing me towards the Order, but nothing she said had prepared me for what I now saw; however, all my hours in Sir William's library *had* prepared me to identify my sudden surrounds.

The seven silken panels that rose from the walls to comprise the ceiling illustrated the Am Duat, or *Book of What Is in the Underworld*. More specifically, upon the panels were painted the hieroglyphs and accompanying art that told of the King's nightly death—his journey through the Underworld with the sun god, Ra, in the Night Boat—and his rising, or reincarnating, the next day at dawn alongside the sun. There at the prow of the Night Boat stood Set, Protector of the kingly mummy depicted on the Temple ceiling with his spirit/soul in ascendance.[42]

As for the wall panels themselves, they were dense with depicted deities. Amongst these Hermes-Thoth was preeminent, as it is he—the Greco-Egyptian god of all mind-work—whom the founders of the Golden Dawn reverence, culling his *Hermetica* for the secrets of the ancients. Other deities I identified easily: jackal-headed Anubis, cat-headed Bastet, hawk-headed Horus, and bovine Hathor. Of course, Isis, Osiris, and Set were represented as well. Indeed, two whole panels were devoted to their story, which events soon to unfold upon these pages deem that I detail; so:

The reign of Osiris and Isis—brother and sister, husband and wife—

---

42. Stoker's use of "spirit/soul" here is telling, and begs some explication if one is to understand the "strangeness" earlier referred to.

The Egyptians were an almost absurdly spiritual people. As regards the Egyptian spirit/soul, they believed that the deceased were divisible thusly: into the *khat* (physical body), the *ka* (astral body), the *ba* (soul), the *khu* (spirit), the *sekhem* (life force), the *khaibit* (shadow), and the *ren* (name). Prayers, rites, rituals and sundry other gruesome processes—delve into the details of mummification, Ms. Durand, if you doubt me—were put to purpose to ensure that each aspect of the deceased was accorded a proper send-off, one enticing them to stay in the Afterlife and leave the living alone. A most tricky business, this, to judge from the *Dossier*.

is held to have been sublime, albeit short: it was brought to an end by the jealousy of their brother, Set. Assuming saurian shape, Set is legended to have slid into the Nile to tear his bathing brother, Osiris, to pieces. Isis, however, finding those body parts not fed to frogs and sundry other fauna, reconstituted and revivified Osiris long enough to conceive by him.

Suspecting that Set would seek to slaughter the rightful heir of Osiris, the pregnant Isis hid in the Nile Delta. There her son Horus was born. There, too, as feared, he was killed by Set. Isis, via rite and ritual, restored life to Horus as well; whereupon she rose in station to equal the great god Ra.

As for the heir himself, Horus would avenge his father and himself against the usurping Set. He appealed to a tribunal which decided in his favour: Horus was given the crown; Osiris—resurrected to have his heart weighed favourably against the Feather of Maat—was named Ruler of the Underworld and Judge of the Dead; and Set was banished to the desert, fated to evolve into the Evil One, the enemy of Egypt.

There stood Set on the Temple walls, devolved from Protector to be depicted as species-less, with an aardvark's snout, ass-like ears, &c. The portrayal was uncommonly horrid in aspect; the more so as . . . *things* progressed.

Though I was much distracted by the Temple décor, still I was conscious, quite, of a quickened heartbeat, of perspiring profusely. And still my thoughts churned. Was I a seeker like these others, and, if so, what was it I, nay *we,* sought amongst the secrets of ancient Egypt? The promise of a purposeful life? The path towards it? Or, *to sign God's name to the letters of our lives?* No answers came, of course; but the questions were brought into stark relief by what next I noticed:

A panel depicting that same Weighing of the Heart of the deceased, whereby a life's merit is assessed. What would be the merit of my life? What would be its worth? And if I wondered thus on Friday the 1st, I wonder all the more now.

The depiction was true to the 125th chapter of *The Book of the Dead,* wherein the scales of Anubis are described. Upon these the deceased has his heart weighed against Maat's truthful feather, Osiris standing by to despatch the deceased either to Paradise or its opposite. If the latter, he will first feed the worthless heart to the baboon-like Devourer seen slavering beneath the scales. This ritual—the Weighing of the Heart— was familiar to me from my studies; but oh, how *hard* it hit me then with Whitman's admonition foremost in my mind and the deities in array all around me and the adepts watching on as well. Indeed, it was to the adepts I then turned, yet aside from Constance—whom I knew only by the red of her shoes—I could but wonder who the others were.

Upon the temple floor, there'd been painted a compass rose, and so I can situate the adepts. On a dais to the east sat three hoodless men, Billiam being one. Their situation set them apart, but so, too, did their garb: they alone were hoodless, yes, but over their white robes they wore coloured cloaks, or mantles. Each had a headdress coloured in kind: a fold of cloth which rose up from the forehead to fall back over the head and onto the shoulders.[43] Upon their breasts, these three wore plates depicting the deities to whom, presumably, they were allied: left to right, I recognised Nephthys, Isis, and Thoth.[44] He on the left held a red sword; hĕ in the middle, a blue wand topped with the Maltese Cross; and on the right, Yeats had at his side a yellow, hexagram-topped wand, though he did not hold his implement as the others did, for evidently he'd been set the task of recording all that passed.[45] The two other men upon the dais I did not know. Both were senior to myself by some years, and both were bearded—greatly, brushily so—with the one in the middle wholly bald. Still I do not know who they are; for, since the day in question, Constance has twice refused me at Tite Street, and when fi-

43. A nemyss, this, like that famously sported by King Tutankhamen; however—and despite the Victorian craze for all things Egyptian—the reader is reminded that Tut's tomb would not be discovered for another thirty-four years, Howard Carter not disclosing it until 1922.

44. So the Temple Chiefs sat in accord with the known rules of the Order: left to right, they were the Imperator, the Praemonstratur, and the Cancellarius.

45. True; the Cancellarius served as secretary of the Order. That it was a young Wm. Butler Yeats serving as secretary is of extreme interest, and doubtless true. "The mystical life," Yeats would later write, "is the center of all that I do and all that I think and all that I write."

nally I forced my way before her, she would neither admit to having seen anything . . . *untoward* nor tell me through her tears the names of those whose testimony I might seek. And to interview the Yeats boy would avail me little, for Speranza—in whom I've yet to confide *all this*—says her Irish poet finds demons and divinities in the everyday.[46]

Seven other adepts, hooded all, sat strategically placed throughout the Temple. One was dressed as I was: Another neophyte? And a second wore white as well: the hoodless Hierophant who would lead the rites.[47] The others were clad in black and indistinguishable one from another save for the implements they held or the symbols they showed. Constance carried a censer now, and swung it round from her position on the south side of the temple.[48] Beside Constance—at the southwestern wall, near the panel painted with a red False Door like that common to Egyptian tombs and through which the spirits of the deceased are said to freely pass—there sat two adepts, identifiably male and female. He, showing the Eye of Horus upon his pectoral plate, was unknown to

---

46. One pities poor Stoker here and wants to help:

It seems likely that the bearded men in question were two of the Order's original members. The Imperator is likely to have been Dr. W. Wynn Westcott, with the bald Praemonstratur being Dr. W. R. Woodman, a retired physician and Freemason of whom little else is known. Westcott, however, whom history credits with founding the Order's Isis-Urania Temple No. 3, merits more of an introduction, but before offering one I must backtrack a bit:

The last quarter of the 19th c. was a time of renewed interest in all things occult, as ever it is when millenniums turn. (Witness our own Y2K tomfoolery.) The Victorians, however, were more prone than most peoples to this, as their days were defined by a Queen too dour for description and as science was fast debunking all that was left to them of spiritual, or even supernatural, explanations of the universe. Into this void—this Longing for the Larger—stepped many charlatans, spiritualists, so-called psychics and swindlers, none of greater interest here than the Russian-born Madame Helena Petrovna Blavatsky, founder—in New York City, in 1875—of the Theosophical Society.

Blavastsky claimed to be in contact with spirit teachers who were revealing to her long-hoarded secret doctrines, or esoterica. These guides—Serapis Bey, Polydurus, Isurenus, and John King by name—had chosen Blavatsky, said she, to carry on the work of Zoroaster and Solomon; that is, the Western, or Hermetic, tradition. This she was happy to do, for a while.

However, when, some years later, Blavastsky converted to Buddhism, shifting her allegiance to Eastern traditions—and guided now by Koot Hoomi, Morya, and Djwal Khul—she left her Western-leaning followers in the proverbial lurch. One such follower was Dr. Westcott, who went on to found the Golden Dawn along with Dr. Woodman and a third man, Samuel Liddell "MacGregor" Mathers, whom we may dismiss as a wacko, albeit a charismatic one; but more about Mathers to come, as it seems he served as Hierophant, or initiating priest, at Stoker's ill-fated induction into the Order.

47. The aforementioned MacGregor Mathers.

48. Constance Wilde was, then, the Dadouche, whose job it was to consecrate the Temple with fire. Or incense at least.

me.[49] She, however, I knew from the first of her many declamations: F.F., it was, holding high—for reasons still unknown to me—a red lamp.[50] The identities of the others I cannot venture to guess at.[51]

Oh, but I know too well, too well indeed, who the other white-robed neophyte was: kneeling beside me before a long table chockablock with I-knew-not-what, and separating us from the dais beyond, was Francis Tumblety. I knew him by his mien, by that haughtiness he cannot hide, and by those eyes of jet—veined with strangeness: the *eye-fire*—that shone darkly through his hood. He *had* come. How dared he? And who had he charmed to access the Order? Constance, whom he'd startled so when first she'd seen him outside Speranza's scullery? Doubtful. What about Billiam? I think not. The boy wants women in the Order, says Speranza, and only seconded me at her insistence. Who then? Regardless, the deed is done. *He was there.* And of said fact I was equally certain and displeased, the more so as the occasion—viz., the ritual into which we soon launched ourselves, quite fatefully, I fear—allowed for no discussion. I'd waited long days to confront the man, and now I could not, though I admit it: I did consider damning all the adepts and falling to fists with Tumblety.

Instead I knelt silently at the man's side. And before I knew it, our double-induction had begun. In this Tumblety took the lead, doing, dog-like, all the Hierophant bade him do. I was to follow in my turn.

49. Marginalia, in Stoker's hand, reads "Peck." Wm. Peck was the city astronomer for Edinburgh, and soon would found a Temple in that city—Amen-Ra No. 6. Later events described in the *Dossier* confirm that it was Peck present at the Isis-Urania No. 3 on 1 June 1888, serving as the Phylax.

50. Who "declaims"? Actors do. Thus, it seems Stoker here references Florence Farr, an actress second only to Ellen Terry on the London stage and so ideally suited to serve as Kerykissa, leading the rituals alongside the Hierophant. Stoker will soon confirm this, in fact.
It is likely Farr was drawn into the Order by Yeats, who was then vying for her attentions with George Bernard Shaw, a battle he'd soon surrender in order to commence his life-long pursuit of Maud Gonne; who, it should be said, may well have been an early member of the Order herself, though there is no indication she was present on the day in question.

51. There remain but three adepts: the Hiereus, the Hegemon, and the Stolistes. Only the Stolistes can be identified with any certainty. She is likely to have been Moina Mathers, née Mina Bergson; who, in addition, perhaps, to having lent her prenom to *Dracula*'s own Mina Harker, was the Geneva-born sister of the Nobel Prize–winning philosopher Henri Bergson and herself a graduate of the Slade School of Art in London. As the wife of MacGregor Mathers, and the earliest known initiate into the Isis-Urania No. 3, surely it was she who'd adorned the Temple so.

Meanwhile, I'd naught to do but kneel and watch. And watch I did, so that here I can record—in language plain and purposeful—all, *all*, as it passed. *Impossibly* passed.

The Hierophant—tall, lean, and rather handsome despite a scar running from the corner of his mouth high onto his left cheek[52]—came to where we two knelt. He spoke, but did so at such length that I cannot here commit his words to paper. I can say only that his speech circled the notions of Purification and Judgement, and those rites by which we would soon submit to same, undergoing the metaphoric weighing of our own hearts, i.e., Induction into the Order. Rather, it was all *meant* to be metaphor, transpiring upon the astral plane and imperceptible upon the physical. The neophyte need only submit to the ritual for the metaphoric work of the Weighing to be achieved; whereupon, I suppose . . . No. I cannot suppose anything at all, can only record what I was witness to when the astral and physical planes collided and metaphor was made manifest in a man, the American, Tumblety.

We—myself and Tumblety—had been told to kneel upon the *priedieux* by F.F., as Kerykissa. This we did. Before us was that table-cum-altar upon which was spread tools of sundry sort: a golden scales, shabti dolls, sistrums, &c.[53] The Hierophant expounded upon the symbolism of our surrounds and the tools. (He was, for the most part, accurate.) Upon the scales, Feathers of Truth would be laid on each of our accounts. Billiam stood by to record the foregone result. Happily, no Devourer of Hearts attended, ready to eat our vitals should either of us be deemed unworthy and despatched to Tartarus.[54]

---

52. A swashbuckling Mathers had been wounded in a fencing duel.

53. Shabti figurines were typically buried with the affluent dead to serve as an afterlife workforce; and sistrums are rattles used in summoning rituals.

   Here I must wonder what role E. A. Wallis Budge may have played in the Order. Surely, he'd have been sought as a member, as his contemporaries hinted. Was he an adept? If so, did he "borrow" artifacts from the British Museum for the use of the Order?

54. Tartarus (as Hell) is in fact a Platonic concept, one adopted by the Golden Dawn.

   Plato also believed in what he called a World Soul and the idea that an individual is capable of recovering knowledge from the divine, or Divine, if only he or she can recall something of what was surrendered upon reincarnating. The *Dossier* will posit whether the opposite be true: Can a deity reincarnate into a human host, taking on his or her knowledge, traits, etc.? This, of course, is commonly called possession.

It all came to seem rather silly, I must say. And as the marriage of so many myths and so much metaphor boggled my mind, I was relieved when the Hierophant turned to the ritual proper. A ritual, said he, of Purification: the Bornless Ritual.[55]

The Hierophant readied the Temple. The adepts knew their positions and assumed them in silence. The Stolistes progressed clockwise round the Temple, sprinkling water with her fingertips. Constance, as Dadouche, went deosil with her incense. The two bowed as they passed, whereupon the Kerykissa, standing west of the altar, cried out:

"Hekas Hekas Este Bebeloi"; and the purifiers with their water and incense sped round the Temple thrice more.

The Hierophant came nearer Tumblety and me. Turning to the cardinal points of the compass, in succession and beginning with the East, he opened a leather-bound text of some heft and read from its pages:-

"Holy art Thou, Lord of the Universe"; and turning to the south, "Holy art Thou Whom Nature hath not formed"; whence to the west with, "Holy art Thou, the Vast and the Mighty One"; and, finally, finding north, "Lord of the Light and of the Darkness." Turning again to the east, he made the Qabalistic Cross overhead and said:-

"Thee I invoke, the Bornless One," and the other adepts joined in, chorally, so:-

"Thee that didst create the Earth and the Heavens.

"Thee that didst create the Night and the Day.

"Thee that didst create the Darkness and the Light."

The others falling silent, the Hierophant went on:-

"Thou art Osorronophris, whom no man hath seen at any time. Thou art Iabas. Thou art Iapos."

The adepts rejoined the invocation, and with one voice proclaimed:-

"Thou hast distinguished between the Just and the Unjust.

---

55. Technically, *The Bornless Ritual for the Invocation of the Higher Genius.* Stoker's notes are so comprehensive here—in fact, the ellipses in this transcription are mine—we may conclude that he had the written ritual before him as he wrote.

"Thou didst make the Female and the Male.

"Thou didst produce the Seed and the Fruit.

"And thou didst form men to love one another and to hate one another."

Movement ensued, but as I know neither its point nor purpose, I do not detail it here. Humming, too, was heard; in this the adepts joined, serially, till the Temple verily thrummed. By now I was perspiring well past comfort. My knees and back ached. Tumblety, beside me, sat in a perfect, well nigh prayerful pose. If he, too, were uncomfortable, I saw no sign of it. However, I did notice the American's cologne: the scent of violets issued from him, and strongly so. Here was one more reason to dislike and disdain the man. I thought little more of it then.

Now the Hierophant dropped his voice to deified tones—showily so—and declaimed, "I am thy Prophet unto whom Thou didst commit the Mysteries, the ceremonies of the Magic of Light.... Hear me Thou.... Let me enter upon the Path of Darkness, and peradventure there shall I find the Light. I am the only being in an Abyss of Darkness; from an Abyss of Darkness came I forth ere my birth, from the silence of a Primal Sleep. And the Voice of Ages answered unto my Soul: 'I am He who formulates in Darkness the Light that shineth in Darkness, yet the Darkness comprehendeth it not.'"

Tumblety's broad, white-cloaked shoulders began to heave. Was he sniggering at this holy show? No. It seemed he had fallen to tears. I adjudged him a fool.

Meanwhile, the Hierophant and the Kerykissa busied themselves. What seemed but a dervish-like dance I can now identify as their tracing on the air the Spirit Pentagram of Actives and the Invoking Pentagram. Progressing round the Temple from the east, they thusly invoked the deities depicted on its walls; and though it seemed to me they merely flailed their arms about, they were in fact drawing those astral portals, as it were, through which the invoked deities could come. *Did* come.

This invocation took some time, and ended with all the adepts—save the three Chiefs upon the dais—joining in similarly; and so it was to the beating of their black sleeves that I attributed a sudden down-drop in temperature within the Temple. Or perhaps it was the up-draught from a cellar? Regardless, it was welcome until it set to swirling Tumblety's too-strong cologne. I turned my head from the scent, from its source, but I only dared turn so far, lest I offend the Hierophant. In truth, I did not fear offending him so much as I did not wish to draw his attention *to me*, for he focused now on Tumblety whilst yet addressing the Unseen.

"Hear me," said he, "hear me, and make all Spirits subject unto me, so that every Spirit of the Firmament and of the Ether, upon and under the Earth, on land and in water, of the Whirling Air and of the Rushing Fire, and every Spell and Scourge of God the Vast One may be obedient unto me"; whereupon he . . . In fact, I know not what he did.[56] But I liked *not at all* the words with which he ended, for their effect was such that Tumblety shuddered, visibly shuddered to hear:-

"I invoke Thee, the Terrible and Invisible God Who dwellest in the void place of the Spirit. . . . The Bornless One. Hear me and make all Spirits subject unto me." There were uttered more words of power, more names unknown to me. Acts were committed which I cannot accurately describe. Oh, but the cloying scent, the *stink* of violets seemed somehow to redouble as this was said in summation:-

"I now set free those Spirits that have come. Show yourselves."

Tumblety had fallen deeper in thrall to the Hierophant: from mere nodding to tears, and now whimpering. It was pathetic. I thought to leave. I could only hope that the Hierophant would busy himself with Tumblety whilst I sought the door; but I could not see the door by which I'd come. It might have sat behind any of the seven screens.

The Hierophant spoke now in a *basso profondo*, such that I assumed he'd ascended, if you will, from addresser to he—He?—whom formerly he had addressed. "Hear me now. This is the Lord of the Gods. This is the Lord of the Universe. This is He whom the Winds Fear. This is He who is Lord of all things, King, Ruler, and Helper."

---

56. We may excuse Stoker his confusion, as my copy of this same ritual states that at this juncture the Hierophant was to "make one complete circumambulation of the Temple deosil, to formulate the Angle of Kether in the Supernal Triangle of the Genius. Pass to the South, assume the astral god-form of Horus, and let the invocation proceed till Fire purges you of all blemish. Use Spirit Pentagram of Actives and Invoking Pentagram of Fire." Indeed.

"Who cometh down? *Who?*" This from the Kerykissa, addressing not the Hierophant but rather . . . Alas, she addressed her words to the Temple's walls, to its tent-like top. It is more precise, I suppose, to say she spoke to Those painted upon same. "Who?" she asked again; but I cannot aver that the Hierophant was answering her when next he said:-

"I am the Resurrection and the Life." Osiris, then? "He that believeth in me, though he be dead, yet shall he live. And whosoever liveth and believeth in Me, shall never die. I am the First and I am the Last. I am He that Liveth and was dead, and behold, I am alive forevermore, and hold the Keys of Hell and of Death." If not Osiris, then Isis, surely; for who else would speak so of reincarnation? "For I know that my Redeemer liveth and that He shall stand at the latter day upon the Earth. I am the Way, the Truth, and the Life. No man cometh unto the Father but by Me. I am the Purified." At which last all the adepts hailed the Hierophant, *huzzah, huzzah.*

It was then I saw the Phylax fall back from the False Door. As he did so, there came again that cold, violet-stinking current. This combined with the Hierophant's words to chill me to my core; for his voice fell lower as he said:-

"I have passed through the Gates of Darkness unto Light. I have fought upon and under the Earth, and come now to finish my Work, for who dareth banish me to the sands? To do this I shall pass unto the Invisible."

Odd, now, that I saw the adepts turning to one another; though I could not see their faces, of course, there was something . . . worrying in the swivelling of their hoods this way and that. As for the Hierophant himself, I saw, or rather thought I saw, his eyes back-roll to their whites and the scar upon his cheek redden and twist till . . . till it appeared like lips, lips threatening to split apart and speak. Horrid, this; and I attributed the vision to the hood I wore, to the sweat now running into my eyes, to . . . I knew not what.

The Heirophant was none too steady upon his slippered feet as he shuffled nearer the altar. I feared he'd fall upon it. Instead he gripped its edge, hard, and set to swaying the golden scales. Leaning over same—his head bowed, his back turned to us two neophytes—he continued to read. No: *not* read; for there the book lay atop the altar, closed. All present hung upon his every word as he continued extempore in a voice seeming not his own.

"I am He, the Bornless Spirit. I am He, the Truth. I am He, who hath wrought Hate and Evil in the world. I am He who casteth Lightning and Thunder. I am He whom the Showers of Righteousness shall not douse. I am He whose mouth ever flameth. I am He who hath come back from Condemnation. I am He who refuseth Exile. I am He who riseth from the sands Vengeful. I am He whose Heart was wrongly Weighed." Set? Could it be Set the Hierophant had sought to invoke? Surely not. To do so would render him a Satanist. Yet these were the words I heard—sure as I record them here—from the Hierophant, who now faltered in his speech as he turned round to show his handsome self gone horrid: skin of a milky white to match that of his back-rolled eyes, the long scar split wide and suppurating. When he spoke again, he did so nearer a trembling Tumblety.

"I am the Usurper. The Heart Girt with a Serpent is my Name. I am Set, risen for Revenge, risen to Right the Scales of Maat." Most extraordinary, this; and lest I doubted it, down from the dais came the three Chiefs. Billiam, I'd remarked, had stopped keeping his record. Now the Imperator and Praemonstratur came to the Hierophant, arriving only to catch him as he fell, crumpling to the Temple floor. He convulsed atop the compass rose. The adepts broke from their stations, but the Imperator stilled them with a risen hand; they returned whence they'd come, and watched in silence. As did I, knowing not what to do. My action, however, was soon decided for me.

I was leaning nearer the stricken Hierophant, desperate to determine if my eyes had deceived me yet again—for I'd have *sworn* his scar had now closed—when Tumblety came timbering toward me, falling off his *prie-dieu* onto mine, onto *me*, such that suddenly we two fell, entwined, onto the Temple floor. He shuddered, and the stench of him was sickeningly sweet as he lay atop me; but somehow it came not as a smell but rather a taste. I *knew* that it was the scent of violets, yet it came to me as a taste upon the tongue, a taste bearing no relation to the actual flower. I can only compare it to the bitterest of fruits.[57]

I was horribly disoriented, owing to the confusion of my senses, yes, but also my hood had twisted round in the fall and all was silken shadow now. I ripped the hood from off my head, and Tumblety's, too, just in time to see him return to consciousness: his eyes righted, and his jetty pupils focused on mine as he said my name, its two syllables eerily distinct, "Sto-ker." His head was nearly in my lap. Looking down, I saw that his left-side moustache was darkly wet; this I attributed to something having seeped from his nose or mouth, nothing more. "Sto-ker," said he again, this time with a palsied twitch of his lips that revealed opened flesh running from behind that same moustache onto his cheek. Here—*impossibly!*—was the Hierophant's scar.

To young Billiam, hovering overhead, I said "stroke"; for I had immediately sought a *saner* explanation of all I'd seen and had now arrived at one: Tumblety had suffered a Rossetti-like stroke. "He has suffered a stroke and . . . " And I left off speaking as Tumblety, of a sudden, rose, albeit as awkwardly as a newborn foal, to announce:-

"It is nothing, gentlemen. I am prone to minor seizures, is all." His eyes were steady. The scar, gone. And as he refitted his hood and adjusted his robe, he added, *most* astonishingly, "Let us resume." These last words seemed to echo through the Temple.

The Hierophant had come to consciousness some moments prior. He sipped now from the Stolistes' cup of consecrating water. The three Chiefs helped him to his feet. And as the shaken Hierophant came briefly out of character to offer an apology, to say that he was well and had merely over-worked of late, Tumblety interrupted to repeat:-

"Let us resume the ritual."

And this we did! I was stunned. I'd thought this strange session would

---

57. Here Stoker speaks for the first time of the relatively rare phenomenon known as synaesthesia, a condition in which persons perceive sensory stimuli via a sense other than the one being stimulated, i.e., seeing a sound, or tasting a shape. Of particular interest to readers of the *Dossier* is the fact that synaesthetic responses to stimuli are commonly attested to by two groups of people: creatives—artists, composers, writers, etc.—and those present at alleged instances of spirit possession.

surely be brought to a close now, that soon I'd walk from the Temple with the Golden Dawn in my past and Constance Wilde very much in my debt. But now, more than ever, I wondered if the American weren't a mesmerist of sorts; for he, a mere neophyte, had commanded the Temple Chiefs to resume the ritual—and they had obeyed him! Extraordinary, this. What hold might he have then over Henry Irving? Over Hall Caine? . . . Over *me*? For, evincing neither will nor wit, I found myself re-taking my own role!

I had suddenly gone gelid: I was all gooseflesh and cold sweat. The Temple itself was unaccountably cold, and now the silks overhead shivered on a sourceless breeze—no mere draught, this. Silhouetted atop the silks were slithering snake-shapes which I could not blink away, try though I did. It seemed I heard, too, the rasp of their scales upon the silks. I reasoned, *reasoned,* that this too must be shadow-work, that still my senses were confounded. . . . Alas, what can*not* we convince ourselves of? But is it not true that by disbelieving in Satan we confer unto him his very strength? And if ever we had the least faith in God, how then do we turn from His opposite when proof, *proof* of the Dark Prince is present, as surely it was on Friday the 1st?

Must stop this. Must simply testify here. *Record,* record all that came to pass.

The Chiefs re-took the dais. The Hierophant sat altar-side, and with what strength had returned to him shushed the adepts, some few of whom seemed on the verge of question or complaint. The resumption of the ritual fell to Flo Farr as Kerykissa, and she progressed with a wavering voice in which I heard the nerves of a first-night actress.

The Hierophant had ordained that a second Purifying Ritual be read, and this the Kerykissa did. Just whose influence led to the selection of the Invisibility Ritual, I do not know; but so it came to pass, most fatefully, I fear.

The adepts rearranged themselves slightly, but on balance it seemed to me the Temple was as it had been for the Bornless Ritual, the Stolistes and Dadouche circumambulating thrice to purify the site, &c. And when Constance with her censer passed the altar before which I knelt, she looked at me. In her eyes were wonderment and fear, and just when it seemed she might speak, the Hierophant hurried her back to her southerly place, beside the False Door. Having relegated the Kerykissa to her previous position as well—and rudely so: with a wave of his hand—the Hierophant then commenced the reading, or should I say recitation; for I could see that his downcast eyes did not move over the open book in his lap, and indeed they sometimes back-rolled as before. I had the impression, too, that he knew not what he said: here were utterances only, as from one whose consciousness has been altered. More, I could not reconcile the Hierophant's stricken self—verily, it seemed he might slip from his chair at any moment—with that voice, so strong, so sure, that fell first upon us neophytes before filling the Temple proper.

As for Tumblety, there he knelt, still so oddly redolent of violets. He, too, seemed over-strong for what he'd suffered, showing symptoms of neither stroke nor seizure, save for a flinching of his limbs that came coincident with certain words of the ritual. Indeed, it seemed to be Tumblety who knew the ritual as it was read; for, from the corner of my eye, I saw the movement of his hood where it hung before his mouth and by its billowing knew he spoke the text in time with the Hierophant. Oh, but then whose voice was it I heard, *heard* as though brambles were being drawn over all my body by an unseen hand.

"I adjure Thee by Thoth, Lord of Wisdom and Magic who is thy Lord and God. I adjure Thee by all the symbols and words of power; by the light of my Godhead in thy midst. I adjure Thee by Harpocrates, Lord of Silence and of Strength, the God of this mine Operation, that thou leave Thine abodes beneath the sands to concentrate about me, invisible, intangible, as a shroud of darkness, a formula of defence, that I may become invisible, so that seeing men see me not, nor understand the thing they behold.

"Lady of Darkness, who dwellest in the Night to which no man can approach, wherein is Mystery and Depth unthinkable and awful silence, I beseech Thee to clothe me about with thine ineffable mystery. I implore Thee to formulate about me a shroud of concealment. Aid me with your power, and place a veil between me and all things belonging to the outer and material world. Clothe me with a veil woven from silence and darkness, the same that surrounds the abodes of eternal rest."

I knew from looking at the Temple Chiefs that the Hierophant was neither reading nor performing the rite as prescribed. He made no motions at all, but sat hunched in his chair seeming half the man he'd earlier been. Yeats's pen was yet still, and now I saw him cast an eye towards the Temple's roof: Could he, too, see the snake-shapes writhing there, hear the rasp of their scales? Insects, too, there were now, hand-sized and scrabbling atop the snakes. I saw others of the adepts tilt their hoods upwards to watch, to worry that the silks would split and down onto us would rain the snakes and . . . scorpions. Yes, here were scorpions in the very heart of London! And I saw one, or thought I saw one, or would have *sworn* I saw one—its body white, its legs pale unto opalescence, its tail turgid and set to strike—disappear fast up the pant leg of the kneeling Tumblety; who, a moment later, stiffened before falling still, ecstatically so, such that I'd no doubt he'd been bitten and had pleasured in the bite.

No-one else had seemed to remark this, but off to the side I saw Constance glancing from the Temple's top to its False Door. Meanwhile, that incorporeal voice came ever stronger, though the priest and neophyte from whom, or *through* whom, it seemed to come were weakening, such that I readied to catch either if he fell, or leastways remove myself to safety before there came another tangle of limbs and senses. Meanwhile, I could do naught but listen as the voice now commanded:-

"Behold! He is in me and I in Him. I am the Alpha and the Omega, the first and last, and my life is a circle unto Infinity. I change, but death does not come nigh me. I rise now from the firmament of sands, my light that of Ra, my powers rendering impotent those of Osiris and Isis, of Horus the hawk." The voice began now to ululate, to vibrate, at once to use and to overwhelm the men's bodies through which it came, such that they, the Hierophant and Tumblety, shook, visibly shook, and choked even as they spoke what now I know to be the secondary names of Set:-

"For I am Apophis, I am Typhon, returned to the House of Maat to settle its scales."

How to describe that voice as it uttered the Setian names? The ululating—bizarre though it may be—is a sound of human dimensions; but the vibration accompanying the names could be felt, bodily. It moved the white silk of my sleeves. It stirred, too, the tent overhead, where the snake-shapes had taken on weight sufficient to sag the silks. And though I am a big man, little prone to fear, it was fear that stilled me then, and fear that caused my eyes to tear as that supernal voice spoke on:-

"Hear me, Lords of the Paths in the Portal of this, the Vault of the Adepti. Give unto me the blue-black egg of Harpocrates as a shroud of concealment that I may attain unto Knowledge and power for the ac-complishment of the Great Work and the execution of my will of Ge-nius. Let rise He who hath been unjustly banished to the Realm of Sands. Rise Aphophis! Rise Typhon! Rise Set, who will lay a host of hearts upon the scales of Anubis to show how false is the Feather of Maat! How false Horus the heir! How false Osiris and Isis, the Whore of the High World!"

Others of the adepts had begun to cry. Hoods were turning this way and that. Naught but our common concern anchored me to sanity: Were we not, all of us, seeing the Unseen?

The Imperator descended the dais and moved towards the Hiero-phant, who stayed him with one raised hand whilst with the other he took from off the altar an ancient sistrum—no replica, this—and rattled it, rattled it till it fell to pieces. He then applied both hands to scrawling on the air Spirit Pentagrams, both active and passive. At this the adepts cried out, such that all three Temple Chiefs called on the Hierophant to still his evil-summoning hands.[58] This he would not do, and so they turned from warning words to deeds. From the fracas that ensued, they all withdrew when the following happened concomitantly:

---

58. Evidently, Mathers was drawing the pentagrams with their two points upwards, not down, thereby paying homage to the world of matter and not spirit: evil, in a word.

I cried out; for I'd turned to Tumblety to see issuing from beneath his hood a thick, treacly liquid. It came copiously now, darkening his neck and collar. I thought bile had risen with his vomit to both blacken and thin it; but how could he heave up either effluent, still as he was? I might even have reached out to Tumblety then, save for:

Constance had cried out when I had; for the red-painted canvas of the False Door had split, loosing into the Temple a stench so sulphurous that others of the adepts retched. All the while the weighted silks above us writhed. So imminent did their splitting seem that Constance and others covered their heads. It was the Praemonstratur who called for order, order and obeisance; but still the ritual devolved to Chaos, to Pan-demonium proper. The adepts had either to flee the Temple or to fall, so horrid was the stench. My staying put may be attributed to my confused senses: variously I *saw* the smell in shades of red and *heard* the sight of the rent canvas as clashing cymbals. And so whilst the rest of the adepts fled the Temple, passing fast through the Pronaos to the street beyond and *away,* I stayed to witness the worst of it.

The Hierophant having fallen still, the Temple Chiefs—no-one remained save us five, and Tumblety—turned their attention to the American, who held his kneeling pose as if he were statuary. A steady thrumming could be heard coming from him. Had the voice of Set distilled to this? Still there issued from him that hellish effluent which now I knew to be the source of the violet stench, married to the dissipating sulphur come through the False Door. The silks overhead were blessedly still, unshadowed. Neither was the False Door animate, as earlier it had seemed. And so yes, to the American we all five turned, though somehow it fell to me to reach out and rip from off his head his hood and so disclose . . .

Oh, it was the very face of Hell, risen Hell!

His hair, all of it, whiskers as well, had reddened, appreciably so. His pate was slick with sweat. The skin over his cheekbones was stretched drum-tight. His eyes had back-rolled. And his jaw hung down, making of his mouth a horrid O open for the egress of the effluent and a distended tongue atop which . . . Oh, where are the words suited to such strangeness as this?

Atop Tumblety's tongue as well as his moustaches, his chin, his throat were—light-bright amidst the black spew—seven small scorpions: the seven of legend, given by Sequet to Isis to protect a young Horus from Set. But it was he who controlled them now, he who spoke their names through Tumblety; for the American, immobile but for his fluttering eyelids, incanted, again and again:-

"Tefen, Befen, Mestet, Mestetef, Petet, Thetet, Matet . . ."

It seemed the others heard the names as nonsense, if they heard them at all. Billiam, it was, who bent to touch Tumblety on the shoulder, as one would to rouse a sleeper. At this, Tumblety's black pupils rolled fast into place and the skin of his left cheek split. Blackness seeped. The stench was strong. And to the substance the scorpions scurried, as if to feed. And there knelt Francis Tumblety, stony still, unrecognisable save for his eye-fire, his white skin—slick with blackness, bright from seven white scorpions—and the heightened red of his hair.[59]

Yeats had fallen back from Tumblety, but now the Imperator made as if to wipe the stricken man's face. "Careful!" said I. "They sting."

My hood was now off, and with it had gone all pretence to secrecy; for the Imperator addressed me by name. "Whatever do you mean by 'sting,' Mr. Stoker? This man has sickened and wants only a good washing-up. Isn't that so, poor chap?" Whereupon he patted Tumblety on the shoulder, and he, Tumblety, turned to me. Would that I'd been able to turn away!

Instead I saw the seven scorpions disappear into Tumblety's

---

59. This from a friend working in antiquities at the Louvre, a woman both kind and incurious enough to answer my questions without posing any of her own:

Alternate spellings of Set, or Seth, were *Setesh* and *Sutekh*, the pronunciations of which may have been similar to that of the word for dessert, *tesherit*, itself similar to *tesher*, meaning "red"; consequently, Set, after his fall, became associated both with the desert and all things red, i.e., redheads, so uncommon amongst native Egyptians as to further associate him with foreigners and seal his status as the anti-God of the Egyptians, the Evil One.

Note, too, that Jonathan Harker's hair will turn suddenly white in the course of his pursuing the Count.

now-smiling mouth and the split of his cheek. I could hear their names being called: echoes, these seemed. Could the others hear nothing at all? Was I alone now in seeing the scorpions, in hearing a demon draw them away so? This I made to ask:-

"Can you not see—"

It was Tumblety who interrupted me, saying in his own silken tones, "Sto-ker." He smiled, he smirked as he said again the two syllables of my name: "Sto-ker"; and then he shushed me as one would a child.

"See, man," said the Imperator, having heard something else entirely, "he wants but a hand. . . . Surely you'll offer one, Mr. Stoker?"

I had no need, for a standing Tumblety clamped his hand to my arm. And I listened with incredulity as the Temple Chiefs offered him their apologies—*apologies!* Perhaps they'd proceeded too fast with too intricate a ritual . . . and wasn't the Temple over-hot to-day . . . and oughtn't the Order to disband for the day, &c.? *Hadn't they seen what I had?* Where was Constance? Where were the other adepts? Surely they would bear witness to all I'd seen. But no, they will not. Constance has taken sick to bed at Tite Street. Billiam over-boils with bull-shite, and I get no answer to the question: What did *you* see Friday last? Florence Farr denies she was present. Peck is returned to Edinburgh, whence I await his response to my two telegrams. It seems I alone amongst the adepts have not dived headfirst into the River of Lethe![60] Extraordinary, this. And I'd question myself, my sanity, if I did not fear the answer so. Instead I shall hold to *the facts,* strange though they be, and gather more as I may: which is to say *C-A-I-N-E.* I shall go to Caine. From him I will wring word of Tumblety. I will have the man's history from Caine *at all costs;* for I shan't get it from Tumblety himself. Of that much I soon became certain.

I had to quit the Temple, and quickly; but I saw I'd not be let to do so without Tumblety, for it was evident he'd earlier spoken of me to the Chiefs and doubtless used my name to lie his way into the Order, such

---

60. The River of Lethe, in Greek mythology, ran through Hades and conferred forgetfulness on those who bathed in it.

that now the sick American was seen as my responsibility. So be it. I would lead him from the Temple if it meant my own escape. And once out on the street, I would accost him. *Then* I'd have my answers, damn the man!

The Pronaos was empty of the adepts. They had all gone their separate ways, never, it seems, to speak of what they may have seen. The Chiefs, seeming somewhat dazed, donned their street dress and wordlessly took their leave. I saw a change in their aspect: forgetfulness yes, but however had it been conferred? Is there precedent amongst those present at . . . at a *possession,* for mustn't I deem it such, all that I witnessed within the Temple?

Questions. Too many questions. Must first procure answers from Caine.

And question the first shall be: What of the American now? For there has been no word of him for a week, and though I do not worry, I wonder. Oh, yes, I wonder; for:

We walked from the Temple in company, Tumblety and I. Neither of us spoke. We'd not taken five steps down the street—with Tumblety stumbling, seeming *most* unsteady—before I wheeled on the man. Or rather, made to; for something about him stilled me, and no questions, no accusations came. It seemed I had lost the power of speech. I simply stared at him—how long I cannot say—and just when I saw, or rather *understood,* that Tumblety was not breathing, that he stood before me corpse-still yet somehow animate, a creature akin to the dead un-dead of lore . . . alas, just then I heard a scream.

Turning, I saw by the late daylight that a hansom had tipped in the street. The scream had come—indeed, continued to come—from a female pedestrian fearful of the fallen, still-harnessed horse struggling mightily to extricate itself from beneath the weight of the cab. Its whinnying was horrid. A crowd gathered round passenger and driver, both lying akimbo upon the curb. Whistles could be heard summoning constables of the watch. From this I turned back to find . . . nothing.

Tumblety was gone. Disappeared.

It seemed doubtful he'd have ducked back into the Temple, and as

I did not see him down the length of street in either direction, I could only conclude that he had, yes, disappeared. However had he done so? I'd not been turned away from him so long, or had I? And just as I cursed the American aloud, I heard again his, "Sto-ker." Was he nearby still? Oh, but where? . . . *that I may go invisible, so that every spirit created, and every soul of man and beast, and everything of sight and sense, and every spell and scourge of God, may see me not nor understand.* Was he hidden, then, in the blue-black egg of Harpocrates, Lord of Silence? Absurd, this. I might have laughed at the notion had not my blood begun to run cold.

I walked away. I walked away whilst in my heart I ran, *ran*, such was my fear. I have never known its like.

And when I reached the corner, there came from behind me a sound, a report so shatteringly loud that I at once sought a wall against which to steady myself. Looking back, I saw a constable standing over the fallen, broke-legged horse, his pistol yet smoking, and I fancied—oh, but what is fancy now, in the face of such truths as I've seen?— . . . I fancied I saw the horse's blood flow from its nose to flood, verily flood, the street. There I stood, believing the blood-wave would come to break upon me. I watched for it, waited for it; till finally I went onto my knees at the curb to confirm its absence from the macadam with both my hands, holding them up to assure myself they were merely dirty and not blood-stained. Only then did I rise and truly run.

I ran not knowing where I went. I ran till the end of breath. Hours passed, hours for which I cannot fully account; and then finally I found myself on St. Leonard's Terrace, whence I proceeded home to No. 17. There I threw the useless bolt behind me.

Sto-ker. I heard it as I ascended the darkened stairs.

I slept from excess of soporific—no longer do I begrudge Rossetti the comforts of chloral—and, says Florence, would not be woken for eighteen hours, not even when Henry sent a boy round to see where I was. When finally I rose, it was to find my senses righted and my memories far, far too sharp. No dream, this.

In days since, I have not heard my name spoken so. In time I will. This I know.

Meanwhile—Henry Irving be damned—I set off to-morrow for the Isle of Man. There Thomas Henry Hall Caine will be made to answer for *all & everything*.

Now, sleep. I have sent word downstairs that I am to be woken in four hours, lest I miss the 8.12 to Liverpool, whence I will ferry to Caine in his castle. My questions are legion; pray shall my answers be legion, too, by luncheon to-morrow.

Pray, yes; for in the days since Friday the 1st, it seems I may have re-found my faith, both sides of belief's equation now being in balance: If before I doubted God, now it seems I know Him from having met His Opposite.

BRAM STOKER'S JOURNAL

Tuesday, 12 June [1888], returning to London from Liverpool.

Though still my stomach sways within owing to a rude crossing from Douglas[61] to L'pool over seventy-odd nautical miles of a distemperate Irish Sea, and though my penmanship at present testifies to the shimmy and shake of this railcar, still I write. I dare not delay. I must record my recent converse with Caine before time renders my memory inexact, retentive of substance but not our speech precisely as it passed.

Since those strangest of events which I shall here refer to only as Setian, I have been disinclined to leave home, not because I deem myself safer there than elsewhere but rather because, having seen what I have seen, I feel myself a stranger in the wider world and want none of it at present. Word was sent to H.I. at the Lyceum: I lied and said I was unwell—physically unwell—and from my slant atop the dining-room table I have seen to only the meanest of daily details. Let others undertake the rest. Although now that Henry has learned of my excursion to Caine—I know not how—I suppose I must return to the theatre and suffer his abuse when, in truth, having heard what I have heard from

---

61. Capital city and port of the Isle of Man.

Caine, I am sorely tempted to pack wife & child and set London at our backs, once and for all; for somewhere in the city lurks this Tumblety.

I went to Caine for two reasons, nay three, for the first must be this: He would not come to me! Reason two: Neither did he deign to write, such that I knew there to be a reason for his reticence and knew, too, that if only I could set him down fireside, as in days of old, if only I could unstopper his speech, I would have my answers. Reason three: None present at the above-mentioned Setian event will speak to me, and in the silence that has ensued, my sanity dissolves like toast in tea.

All last week, I wondered how much I could confide in Lady Wilde; for I would not worry her, nor could I appear to impugn Constance, of whom she grows ever more protective. Finally, I went to Speranza on Wednesday last; for she alone of all my acquaintances—all save Caine—has both a heart and brain capacious enough to . . . Brief: Believing in nothing, Speranza is capable of believing in anything. And as regards the super-natural, it was the pastime of both her and Sir William; and indeed, by her own work—both fiction and non- —she has contributed much to the topic.

Unfortunately, I found Speranza in the company of that bookman to whom she sells her beloveds in twos and threes so as to survive, and pity—which I dared not let show—prompted me to take my leave of Park Street in haste. Glad I am to have done so, too; for Caine has told me much, *much,* and I shall now return to Lady Wilde with . . . Well, though I haven't all the answers, not by a long stretch, the questions are clearer.

Oh, but poor, pitiable Caine. How his secrets took their toll, even as he spoke them. A terrible business, this. And it would seem that things have worsened in London, for the Guv'nor's telegram, lately delivered to Greeba Castle, summons me home *at speed.* But before I tell of my leaving the castle and Caine, I must first tell of my coming. I must *record* the particulars as they passed; and so:

I left out of Euston Station at 8.12 o/c, bound for Liverpool. I sent no word to Caine of my coming, but I had discovered from Mary—now at their Hawthorns house with Ralph—that Caine was indeed in residence at the castle. Alone, as best she knew. And so I set off to catch him unawares, to corner him as a dog does a cat; for he'd left me little choice.

Owing to delays no porter could explain, we were two hours late arriving in Liverpool. So, too, was the crossing to Douglas delayed: three hours more were added to the journey; such that I was *most* foul of mood when, finally, from aback the dray I'd hired portside, I saw the ivy-covered crenellations of Greeba Castle hove into view high above the Douglas-to-Peel road.

The drayman bore the brunt of my mood, which would shame me save for this: our progress would not have been slower if we'd had half a horse at the helm. Moreover, the Manxman insisted upon stopping midway. Slipping down from the dray, he said he'd a message to deliver to a certain publican, though I supposed he sought naught but a fast pint with which to slake his thirst. I sat steaming upon the dray, heated by both the afternoon sun and the islanders' stares. I was a *Stranger,* and so I took scant notice when two boys came barrelling out of the aforementioned pub and, having appraised me shyly, proceeded apace in the direction of the castle.

And so I ought not to have been surprised to soon find a steward of sorts standing at the lower gates of Greeba Castle, coldly enquiring into what business I had thereabouts. "My business, sir," said I, "is none of yours." With a few words more, carefully chosen, I suggested the steward step aside. He would not. He barred the way with his body, both fists locked onto the long bore of his rifle. I would have to wait under the watchful eye of the drayman whilst the steward carried my name up to the castle proper; where, of course, Caine converted it to apology and permission to pass. The drayman departed, the steward sneered, and I, satchel in hand, walked red-faced up to the castle.

"Friend," said I to Caine, who stood in his door dressed in a country suit of Knickerbocker tweed, "criminals have been known to escape Pentonville prison with greater ease." He looked worn, worried, and *un*surprised to see me. "Living under guard, are you? Has the reading public gone rabid?"

Caine responded to neither gibe in kind, as once he would have; instead he held to my hand overlong. Silence ensued, and in its course Caine seized my left hand with both of his. He shoved my cuff up and flipped my hand, searching out what he called my "Manhattan scar." From said inspection, I withdrew with a nod: *All is well* was conveyed, so, too, *Let that be the end of it.*

Looking down into Caine's face—as perforce I must if we stand but an arm's length apart—I found worry in his every feature. His brown eyes were wide, as ever they are, but brimful of tears as well. The bags beneath them bespoke sleeplessness, such that I, drawing conclusions I'd soon learn were false, observed:-

"I disturb you at your work." This he neither acknowledged nor denied. Indeed, he said nothing at all. "I'm afraid your reticence left me little choice but to come, Caine; for the situation in town has grown quite . . . complicated as regards your—"

"Quiet!" And looking about, this way and that, nervous as a fox at the heel of the hunt, he added, "No more now, not here . . . inside, *inside*"; and he all but pulled me into the castle proper.

Built but a half-century ago, Greeba Castle sits upon its hill like a cake iced with ivy, the same that hosts the "creepy-crawlies" that render the place repugnant to Mary Caine. That, and its distance from her beloved London. And so the castle seems Caine's alone. With his new-found riches, he renovates it, room by room, garden by garden. In so doing, he stakes a claim to Manxmanship, if you will, and keeps at bay, literally, those more tenacious members of the Her Majesty's tax inspectorate who insist that he is English—being Liverpool born—and, according to the laws of the mainland, falling ever deeper into arrears. It is a rich man's war Caine wages, and one from which I long ago recused myself, as both barrister and friend.

In the silence following upon Caine's strange salutation and his *insistence* that we enter the castle, I wondered how long it had been since I'd last heard his voice, for it is distinctive: quite deep, quite mellifluous for so diminutive a man. Indeed, were it not for his body, Caine's voice may well have carried him onto the stage. It was a dream he'd been loath to abandon, I know; and said dream was doubtless the reason he'd long worshipped Henry Irving. In a lesser man, such disappointment might've rendered down to envy; not so with Hall Caine.

Once we were in the foyer, Caine closed the door behind us and threw a battery of bolts. It was warm within the castle, airless and far too close. It was evident no window had been opened to the sea of late, as the weather surely warranted. The sounds of the locks yet reverberant, Caine took from his pocket a small, pearl-handled pistol and set it on a table beside the door. "Whatever is the matter, man?" I asked, wondering if Caine's glooms had finally gotten the better of him.

He came nearer, tilting high his red-bearded chin and locking his bleary eyes on mine. I was all sympathy: on the instant I forgave my friend for that silence of his that has vexed me so. "Speak, man," said I. "What is it?"

Caine sighed. "I might apologise to you, Bram, from this day to my last, might *die* with apology upon my tongue, and still I could never—"

"Good God, Caine, you're talking like a page torn from Scott."[62] The joke went well wide of its mark: Caine simply stared up at me. I saw it'd be best to let him speak, even if he'd devolve to tears in doing so.

Circling the dark-panelled foyer, Caine continued. "I am confident, Bram, that at times I am the densest-headed mortal the sky looks down on. Surely there has never before been anyone, *anyone* who could see as vividly as I sometimes can and yet be—eleven hours out of twelve—so blind and muddle-brained."

"I must think, Caine, that you rather overstate your case." In truth, I doubted he did: Hadn't he sent Tumblety to me? And, knowing I dissembled, Caine whispered:-

"Tumblety." He spoke so fast, and with such disdain, it seemed he might have spat the name.

"Tumblety, indeed," said I. "So he *is* at the crux of this, both here"— I nodded towards the pistol, lest my allusion to the battened-down castle be lost—"and in London?"

---

62. Sir Walter Scott, b. 1771, d. 1832; known as the "Midlothian melodramatist."

In response, Caine led my eye to the lintel above the broad door leading from the foyer; on it were words carved since last I'd visited, words from the Bard—*AYLI*, if I am not mistaken[63]—the which he recited:-

"'Here Shall Ye Find No Enemy But Winter and Rough Weather.'" He sighed till it seemed he'd exhale his very soul. "I fear," said he, finally, "that those words are no longer true, and that he of whom I'd reason to be wary might well— Oh, Bram, I've made *my* enemy yours. I fear it may be hard to forgive a friend that, though an eternity of apologies be said."

"Fear not, friend," I said, adding, rather as a sigh of my own, "... Tumblety." Caine reacted as if the name itself were an invocation and the man might suddenly appear. Alas, who was I to doubt he might?

"I *do* fear finding our enemy here, Bram; but I have taken precautions, I have taken pains." Such as, I supposed, the spying islanders and the armed steward; still, and rather brusquely, I bade my friend explain.

"I have read your letters, Bram, every one, and your telegrams, too. I know what has been going on in London."

"Why, then, didn't you answer? ... Deucedly rude of you, Caine, *deucedly*."

"I cannot excuse my actions," said he; "but perhaps I can explain them. I'd hoped, *hoped* Francis would bid a fast hello to Henry and yourself and then leave you be, but from your letters I learn that he is up to his tricks of old."

"'Tricks of old'? Whatever do you mean?"

He sighed. He circled the foyer, stopping only to peer out a window, this way and that, scanning the landscape. He slipped the pistol back into his pocket before continuing. "There are things, Bram, that want no words, things that ought not to be written, not even in those beloved ciphers of yours. One only utters such things under the worst duress."

"Secrets, I suppose you mean."

"Confessions," said Caine. "Or call them what you will. But as re-

---

63. Stoker is not mistaken: the quote comes from Shakespeare's *As You Like It*, Act II, Scene V.

gards Francis Tumblety, I can assure you, Bram, you know not the least of them."

"Nor, I fear, do you."

Caine's russet-colored eyebrows arched. Had I come with answers in addition to questions? "An unburdening, then? On both our parts?"

"Indeed," said I. "It is the reason I have come."

"And the reason I feared you would," said Caine; "for what I have to say—"

"Surely," said I, forestalling my friend, "such converse as this wants two comfortable chairs." I nodded towards the parlour beyond. "Shall we?"

"Yes, yes, of course," said Caine. "I forget myself. . . . I can ring for tea if you'd like."

"I'd *very* much like. The dirt of the city and the dust of the country have left me parched. . . . And for God's sake, Caine, throw a window open to the sea, would you? It is as stuffy as Victoria's boudoir in here." At last: a smile; but it faded fast as Caine refused, squarely, to air the castle. He would open no windows. To do so at present, said he, would be "unsafe." *Unsafe?* Alas, whatever Caine knew of Francis Tumblety, the tale I'd brought up from London would allay his fears *not at all.*

Tea having been brought and served, and with dinner having been ordered—baked whiting was all there was at hand, muttered an apologetic maid—Caine launched into his confession, which I hereby record with his permission; so:-

"Am I to bleed myself, Bram, for having been, as a boy, a bit . . . impressionable?" He leaned from his high-backed chair towards mine, towards me, whispering lest his words be heard by a servant at the door. Caine has, I fear, come into some upper-class pretensions of late, one such being the belief that servants have naught to do but go door to door, keyhole to keyhole, in an espial crouch; and so, as a precaution against same, he set a lathe-like instrument atop a small table near the parlour door. A few cranks of the instrument's arm and out came Caine's own voice. Astonishing, this.

"What on earth . . . ?" Though I had heard of Mr. Edison's phonograph, here was one in action.

Caine explained: He'd recently acquired the machine—and doubtless for a fair amount, too—so as to speak into it and thereby record, onto waxy cylinders, and by means yet mysterious to me, himself, reading his work aloud. This a secretary then transcribes. (*Mem.:* Investigate; surely there exists a whole devil's den of uses for such a contraption.)[64] There being more pressing matters at hand, I enquired no further into Tommy's new toy, yet to its scratching accompaniment we spoke, the *faux* voice of Caine obfuscating the real and so confounding any keyholers.

"'As a boy,' you say? How long have you known the man?"

"I first met him," said Caine, "in 1874. I was twenty-one; he, forty-one." Poor Caine raked his slender fingers through his ruddy beard and moustaches, mopped with a kerchief his receding brow—that he resembles Shakespeare is the highest compliment one can pay Thomas Henry Hall Caine—and fidgeted in his chair as if it were afire. His wide eyes avoided mine all the while. I hated to see him so; but alas, there were answers to be had.

"That *would* be the mathematics of it all," said I, "as you approach your thirty-fifth birthday, yes?" Caine nodded. Satisfied at having rightly pegged the American as fifty-ish, I continued, cruelly perhaps, "But at twenty-one, Caine, one can hardly consider oneself a boy."

"He was twice my age, Bram, and *made* of me a boy. I was . . . impressionable, yes."

"How so? What do you mean, 'impressionable'?"

"Really, Bram, I'll *not* be interrogated. And in my own parlour, no less!" Odd, such an outburst from Caine. My friend's fuse had shortened of late. I had best take care.

"Ah," said I, "I see it is my turn to apologise to a friend: I am sorry, Caine. I had supposed it might be easier for you if—"

"In due time," said he; "all in due time." Which adage Caine took to heart: there we sat some while in stifling silence, Caine studying the back of his hands, until:-

64. One of which would be *Dracula*'s Dr. Seward recording his diary onto a similar machine.

"I was yet living in Liverpool in '74, as you know, writing theatrical critiques for the *Town Crier*. . . . I'd not yet met Mary."

I nodded. "But you had made Henry's acquaintance, yes?"

"I had. Words of mine regarding his *Hamlet* had reached him, and he responded by requesting my presence when first he played the Prince at the Lyceum, as soon he would: All Hallows' Eve, as it happened: thirty-one October, '74."

Despite my trying to hold my tongue, to let Caine speak as he would, my impatience prompted me to say I knew that Caine had been present at the premier, knew, too, that afterwards he'd dined with Henry for the first time.

"But what you don't know is this: *He* accompanied me."

"Tumblety?" At which utterance, Caine closed his eyes and sighed his assent.

"You are quite correct," said I. "*That* I did not know." How odd of Henry not to have mentioned as much. Surely he remembers meeting the American in the company of Caine, albeit it fourteen years ago? Was this, then, the hook Tumblety had in Henry, the one by which he'd lately reeled in the somewhat gullible Guv'nor? Henry is an actor, after all: he can be had for a compliment; and I've heard Tumblety speak with a silvered tongue when it serves him.

"Yes," continued Caine, "Henry has known the man nearly as long as I—Francis having arrived in Liverpool that June, not four months prior to that Halloween *Hamlet*."

"From . . . ?" And as I was unnerved by references to the American by his Christian name, I appended, as if clarity had been sought, "Whence had Tumblety come?"

"From New York, I believe; but . . . *he*, Tumblety"—and so Caine acceded to my lead—"has always been a traveller. Or rather, I should say a runner."

"Had you mutual friends? Was it they who introduced you?" This, too, was cruel: an allusion to Caine's having beset me with Tumblety.

"No," said he, flatly. "We met via an advert."

The puzzlement upon my face must have been question enough, for Caine continued:-

"An advert, yes. In the newspaper."

"Surely not an advert for the infamous Pimple Banisher?" Despite his predilection for fancy dress—shared with Tumblety, it seemed—I would not call Hall Caine vain.

"Would that it had been," said he. "No, this was an advert offering . . .

"No, no: First let me backtrack and say, Bram, that, at twenty-one I was already unwell. Then, as now, my personal enjoyment of anything beyond the commonplace depended on the caprices of a torturing nervous temperament; however, I thought, then, that this might be righted. I thought . . ."

He fell silent, and maintained the state over-long.

"Caine? Continue, please."

"I thought," said he, finally, "that I'd done myself damage through . . . secret habits."

"Self-abuse, do you mean? . . . Friend Caine, be assured: The thought crosses the mind of many a young man." This I spoke over the lip of a teacup which might otherwise have hid a wry smile. Not so this day. "But whatever might a medical man have to say about that? And in a public advert, no less?"

"That consultations could be had in private. . . . That therapy of a sort was available."

"'Of a sort' indeed," said I, drawing a cross look from Caine. "And you sought out this . . . therapist?"

"Yes." Caine shifted in his seat as criminals do in the docks.

"Whose therapy consisted of . . . ?" But here I had returned to my barrister's ways. I determined to desist, to let Caine tell the tale as he would; viz., slowly, and with a shame that elicited my sympathy.

"Tumblety," said he, "had come from America with something of a reputation.[65] He was known there as the 'Indian Herb Doctor,' and in-

---

65. And several aliases, of which Hall Caine likely knew nothing.

deed much of what he prescribed did have a salutary effect. To that I can attest. So, too, did his company, at first; such that when—after my second consult—we repaired to his rooms and he told me he sought a travelling companion, the idea appealed, albeit briefly. As you know, I felt mired in Liverpool at the time. My life had stalled, yet I knew, *knew* I would prove a fine enough engine—ready to run the world, or London at least—if only I could find the fuel."

Alas, amongst literary friends one runs the risk of spoken metaphor; as when I now say it was I who took up the needle & thread of our converse to stitch in my turn, so:-

"'Briefly,' you say? What led to your disinterest in this post of . . . companion?"

As Caine sighed, and sighed again, I stood and stripped to my shirt-sleeves. "Ring for water, won't you, Caine? And some whisky to wet it?" This he was happy to do: it would afford him time whilst he waited for it, and fortitude once it was found. When each of us sat in possession of a tumbler poured two fingers high, we proceeded.

"What dissuaded me from the post of travelling companion, you ask. Well, it was his rooms; or rather, their contents."

"Which were . . . ?"

"Really, Bram, has Greeba been converted into a Court of Petty Sessions, then?"

"My apologies. Proceed."

"Thank you, I shall." Happily, he did so at an improved pace. "First I must say that Tumblety then—and perhaps now, perhaps still—cut quite a figure. He was a handsome man, despite his extremes of dress and deportment. When first I saw him in the streets of Liverpool, he sat astride a white horse, a pack of lashed hounds following behind."

"Damn those miniature hounds of his," said I.

"Then he has them still?"

"Two of the species, yes; and they have shat themselves silly in the Lyceum costumery."

"Henry must have *poured* it into his ear then, surely? The Archbishop would better suffer dirt being discovered in Canterbury Cathedral than Henry would in his Lyceum."

"And it was discovered, all right—by the boot-sole of a wardrobe mistress! But I didn't even tell Henry, for he is hoodwinked at present and has given Tumblety the run of the theatre *and* the Beefsteak Club as well. Indeed, if one dines there now, one dines with Tumblety. Until late days, at least. . . . I fear that Henry may even have given him a key of his own."

"'Fear'?" queried Caine. "I must ask, Bram: Do you speak casually, or carelessly, or do you truly *fear* that Tumblety has a key of his own?"

"I am inclined, Caine, to neither careless nor overly casual speech," said I somewhat huffily. "Yes: *I fear.*"

"I meant no insult. The matter is simply this: I fear the man myself, and with reason. Now it seems you've reasons of your own. I can only wonder at them."

"You wonder, Caine, because the scales of conversation yet weigh in your favour: your reasons first, if you will, with mine to follow."

Caine rose to change the waxen cylinder. I'd accustomed myself to the drone of this secondary Caine, but I was happy to hear the primary one say, as he retook his seat and reached for the whisky, "All right, then. Curiosity as to *your* reasons shall hasten me through mine."

"I shall not rue the advance in speed," said I, holding out my glass for two fingers more. In truth, I feared my turn. Caine's is a fine but sceptical mind, and though I knew he'd sat through séances and such when first he'd come to London, I'd no idea what he thought of all that nowadays. The tale I'd carried to the castle would tell me soon enough.

"All right, then," said a chagrined Caine once more. "Onward through the facts, and faster.

"The Francis of my early acquaintance was, as said, a handsome man, the possessor of a certain appeal. A charismatic."

"A quack, you mean. A charlatan."

"On the contrary," rejoined Caine. "I always found his diagnoses spot-on. Indeed, he ought to have kept to medicine proper and let lie those medicaments by which he prospered."

"He is wealthy, then?" I had supposed he was, but to have this con-firmed by Caine made me even more wary of the man. He had *resources:* unwelcome news, this.

"Quite," came the confirmation. "I once knew him to draw sixty thousand dollars on a Rochester bank—this in a single draught, mind. And I had it from the man himself that in his heyday his practices brought him three hundred dollars a day."

"'Practices'? In the plural?"

"Indeed. He partnered with others, travelling to oversee it all. Things first boomed for him in Boston, I believe.[66] In time, though, Tumblety's Pimple Banisher was well known in New York, Jersey City, Pittsburgh, and points as far west as San Francisco; north into Canada, too, as I recall."

"And by '74 he had come over in search of . . . English pimples, Eng-lish pence?"

"Pounds, more precisely," corrected Caine. "And a companion."

"But that was not to be you. You say you were dissuaded from his company."

"I was; but not fast enough, I fear. You see, Francis was what the French call *un beau-parleur.* Gifts, too, were given"; the acceptance of which—to judge by Caine's chin falling to rest on his chest—shamed him still. "Do you recall, Bram, those shepherd's plaid trousers I was so fond of when first I went to Rossetti?"

"Too well," said I.

"Well, I had them from Tumbelty, along with much else. We went about town together—dandified, the both of us; but yes, by the time a travelling companionship was spoken of, I'd decided against it, and squarely so."

"Owing, you say, to his rooms?"

"In a way, yes.

---

66. This after he'd been run out of St. John, New Brunswick, in 1860, upon the death of a patient, James Portmore; to whom, Tumblety testified, he'd given nothing but a "tincture of parsley tea." At the Portmore inquest, Tumblety was further accused of dealing abortifacients to prostitutes, notably one Philomene Dumas; to whom he'd sold, for twenty dollars, pills containing "cayenne peppers, aloes, oil of savine and cantharides." By the time Tumblety was acquitted of all charges, he'd already absented himself, slipping southwards into the States.

"He had established rooms in Liverpool some years prior, when first he'd come. He is wont to keep rooms here and there. But, again, it was not the rooms proper that put me off so much as their contents." A nervous Caine rose to draw the drapes against the dusk, leaving me to contemplate the coming catalogue: the contents of Tumblety's rooms. And though my imagination tends towards the morbid, nothing imagined could compare to the true contents as told me by Caine; for:-

"Wombs," said he, returned to his chair.

"Rooms, yes," said I. "You were about to tell me what it was in Tumblety's rooms that dissuaded you from keeping his company, or leastways travelling with him."

"I have told you," said Caine, "just now: *wombs*. Not rooms."

Whisky welled in my mouth. I swallowed it back to ask, "Whatever can you mean?"

And Caine explained. "Francis had told me he'd long ago turned from surgery. He was, he said, 'disinclined to cut.' He'd an abhorrence of blood and blades, both. Yet one night, whilst we sat sipping sherry in the company of two other men of his late acquaintance, one of our party proposed we step out in search of . . . females. Of the hiring type. At this, Francis railed. I thought he'd ask the man to leave. In fact, he did soon effect the man's departure, albeit indirectly, by . . ."

"Balderdash! Now I find I've advanced my tale too far. . . . You've got me speaking in pamphlets, Stoker, when it's novels I know!"

"This day does not allow for novelising, Tommy. Pamphlets it must be: precise and spoken apace, if you please."

"As you wish, Bram. As you wish.

". . . Let me first say this, then: I knew that Francis had put out word to the medical colleges that he sought wombs 'for study.' This aroused suspicion."

"As doubtlessly it would."

"And if enquiries were sent Stateside, the enquirers must have heard ill of Tumblety in return; for the rumours that arose may, I think, be dated to this time."

"Rumours?"

"Many," said Caine; "but I can either speed or stray, Bram. Which shall it be?"

"Speed," said I, "if you please."

"Denied by the colleges, Tumblety sought his 'samples' amongst the body-snatchers and death-dealers and lesser surgeries, and the result was a cupboard crowded with jars of sundry size and shape, in all of which swam the matrices, the uteri . . . the female organs of generation. And as this cupboard—more of a wardrobe, I suppose it was: broad and tall—stood quite conveniently beside the table at which we four had lately dined, Tumblety threw it open to his guests, having first asked the one—a randy sailor up from Limehouse—if he'd ever seen a woman's *diseased* . . .

"Oh, I know not what it was, but it was horrid, horrid! And, standing, he slammed down onto the table a jar in which there sloshed a yellowed—"

"Great God," I said. "Surely your supper party disbanded at that."

"You jest," accused Caine. "I hardly think—"

"I jest or I retch."

"May I continue?" And he did, explaining that Tumblety had once been affianced to, perhaps had even married, a woman whose dissolute ways he was late to discover. A prostitute, in point of fact.[67]

"I see," said I. "And the sailor types were . . . solace?" For one hadn't to squint to read between the lines of Caine's account. However, in phrasing the question so, I had impugned my friend, who answered in his own defence:-

"If you've been in Francis's company—"

"As indeed I have been."

"—then you know he can charm."

"I have seen him do so, yes. I have wondered if he mightn't be a mesmerist."

---

67. Who, it has often been supposed, may have given Tumblety a venereal disease of some sort. Whether or not this heartbreak of his preceded the above-mentioned accusations of Ms. Philomene Dumas is unknown, though the question thus raised is a valid one: Did Tumblety seek to avenge himself on Ms. Dumas or others in her line of work?

"He may be, for all I know. Years have passed since I saw him last, you understand. . . . Would that I could attribute my having kept his company beyond that evening to something as surreptitious as hypnosis."

"So, though you declined to accompany Tumblety on his travels, still you saw him?"

"I cannot explain," said Caine. Of course he meant he'd rather not be made to. "Suffice it to say I'd grown . . . fearful, yes. I was afraid to quit him cold. Amongst the rumours were some concerning another companion . . . a *prior* companion."[68]

"No need to explain, friend," said I. "No need." Thereafter we sat some while in silence, in sympathy. "Do, though, tell me what else you know of the man. Facts, if you please. Night falls fast, and I've much, *much* to tell when it is my turn."

"You've your satchel. Surely you'll stay the night? . . . Breakfast is fried bacon and brawn, served at eight, if that suits."

"It suits, yes, and nicely so. I thank you, Hommy-Beg."

"There's breakfast seen to, then; but what about dinner? Shall we dine now, and thereby speed ourselves toward cigars and port?"

"Capital," said I, "capital indeed." Whereupon bells brought the requisite help, and all was seen to. Within the half-hour, we were at table, bent over baked whiting and other such non-stuffs—spiceless, sauceless; for Caine says his stomach cannot abide the least culinary nuance. The table was long, but Caine had had our places set side by side: himself at the head, myself to his right. On the panelled walls hung portraited ancestry—someone's ancestry, though not Caine's—and the broad antlers of an elk. It was the latter that drew my eye, as if the truths yet to be told depended from its horns.

"Why," I asked, finally, "has Tumblety returned to London after all this time?"

---

68. Research leads me to posit that this was one Isaac Golladay.
     Tumblety befriended the much-younger Golladay—the nephew of two former congressmen from Kentucky—while living in Washington. The boy's father, however, formed a bad opinion of Tumblety, and when he sought to end the liaison, Isaac left Washington. Tumblety himself departed mere days later. Whether or not a reunion was effected is unknown. Known is this: Isaac Golladay was never heard from again.

"I haven't a clue," said Caine. "My best guess is that he has lately rendered some other city too hot to hold him. Scandals pursue the man. Or rather, he they. So it came to pass in '74, '75."

Before Caine returned to talk of the past, I had another question regarding the present. "You say you have not seen Tumblety since his return?"

"I have not," said he. "And I shall not. I told him so in terms quite emphatic."

"'*Told* him so'?"

"Very well: *wrote* him. You splice my words too fine. . . . Been reading Conan Doyle again, have you?"

"Wrote him, perhaps, in that same letter via which you foisted the fiend off on me?" Touché.

"He is hardly a *fiend*," said Caine, at which I could only clear my throat, tellingly. My turn would come. "I simply do not wish to see him again."

"And have armed both yourself and your steward to ensure that you do not."

"Our parting," said Caine after a pause, "was unpleasant. So, too, I fear, would our reunion be."

With arching brows, I begged for more, and had it, so:-

"All talk of Tumblety turned to rumour," said Caine, "and scandal ensued." As Caine offered no details, neither can I.[69] "I tell you: The man draws detractors like no-one I've known. Soon Liverpool had shrunk for him, owing, said he, to the machinations of certain medicos jealous of his money. And though he hot-footed it to London, he did not leave Liverpool without a fight—a fight in which, unhappily, he involved me."

Caine explained that Tumblety relished such tussles, the more so if they could be played out in the press. "Sales . . ." said Caine; "he was ever mindful of sales. And scandal drove sales, for Francis was very crafty at attributing all accusation, all calumny to professional jealousy."

---

69. Tumblety was, by now, well launched on a lifelong cycle of arrest and revenge. Charges against him would range from charlatanism to the peddling of pornography, from gross indecency to the corruption of youth, and, of course, murder most foul.

"I see," said I. "If others were jealous of his nostrums, then surely they worked. Up went sales."

"Precisely. And so no matter the enemy, Francis made it seem as if some cabal of medical men were behind it all." From London—to which Tumblety tried to lure Caine, and half succeeded: Caine was often with him in London, yet retained his Liverpool life—the older man convinced the younger to write in his defence. Their efforts progressed from passages in the newspapers to pamphlets. "Quite the pamphleteer, he was," said Caine; "but our joint effort was as naught compared to these." And from a portfolio which he'd earlier drawn from the locked drawer of his desk and carried to table, Caine now slid two specimens:

The first was entitled *The Kidnapping of Dr. Tumblety Upon Orders of the Secretary of War of the US,* and bore an imprimatur reading *St. Louis, 1866.* "A jest," said I, "surely."

"Not at all," said Caine, sliding toward me the second pamphlet: *Dr. Francis Tumblety—Sketch of the Life of the Gifted, Eccentric and World-Famed Physician.*

"My word," I marvelled, "the man is a megalomaniac." I forbore adding that *that* was the least of the problems he posed at present.

"The kidnapping pamphlet," said Caine, "is of an earlier date, and I have it from the subject himself. The second I secured on my own, as eventually it came to seem . . . prophylactic, if you will, to keep tabs upon Tumblety."

I sit now upon this London-bound train in possession of both pamphlets.[70] I have read them through with astonishment, as Caine had promised I would; more so the first, in which Tumblety exculpates himself from charges of involvement in no less an event than the assassination of Abraham Lincoln. Extraordinary, this.

It seems Tumblety—having abandoned New Brunswick and now Boston—had settled in the American capital. There he set about estab-

---

70. I am their possessor at present, as Stoker, deeming the pamphlets evidentiary, included them in the *Dossier.*

lishing himself.[71] Just what he did during the war the pamphlet does not say; but on 6 May 1865, Tumblety was arrested for complicity in the President's assassination some weeks prior. Evidently, a boy who'd once served John Wilkes Booth as a messenger had testified that one of Booth's companions was a known associate of the infamous Indian Herb Doctor. A case of mistaken identity, it seems.

Tumblety's adoption of the alias J. H. Blackburn—one among many—had led to his being confused with a Dr. Luke Pryor Blackburn. The latter was being vilified in the day's press as a Confederate, yes; but, worse still, he stood accused of having gone to Bermuda the year prior to secure fever-infected clothing which he then shipped to Northern cities and camps. One such place was said to be New Bern, North Carolina, where a subsequent yellow fever epidemic took the lives of two thousand civilians and soldiers. Whether the real Dr. Blackburn was guilty or innocent of such charges is not of import here.[72] For our present purposes, suffice it to say that it was the Blackburn confusion that led to Tumblety's arrest. And upon his release, Tumblety the Maligned made of himself a *cause célèbre*.

"My arrest," he writes in the pamphlet, "appears to have grown out of statements to the effect that the Dr. Blackburn who has figured so unenviably in the hellish yellow fever plot was no other person than myself. In reply to this absurd statement, I would most respectfully say to an ever-generous public that I do not even know this fiend in human form." A fiend in human form indeed.

71. Indeed. Contemporaries reported that posters advertising the Pimple Banisher adorned Washington's walls. A Colonel C. A. Dunham attested to having seen Tumblety in the capital some days after the Battle of Bull Run—21 July 1861—in a pose the Colonel described as "typical": dressed in a richly embroidered coat pinned to which were medals of unknown provenance, cavalry trousers showing a bright yellow stripe, riding boots, and his preferred spurs. Atop his head was a semi-military peaked cap. In such attire, said the Colonel, Tumblety was a frequent sight at the city's hotels as well as the War Department and Navy Yard, talking always of how he'd recently accepted but deferred an appointment as brigade surgeon.

72. As historians—not to mention the descendants of the real Dr. Blackburn—might take issue with Stoker's indifference, let me add that the doctor was acquitted of what he called "charges too preposterous for intelligent men to believe," and took up practice in Kentucky, where he fought a yellow fever outbreak in 1878 and was eventually elected governor.

"I do hope that the papers which so industriously circulated the reports connecting me with these damnable deeds, to the very great injury of my name and position, will do me the justice to publish the fact of my having been entirely exonerated by the authorities, who, after a diligent investigation, could obtain no evidence that would in the least tarnish my fair reputation," &c. Sales, it may be imagined, skyrocketed. And from this most profitable lesson—for which a prison stay may have seemed fair payment—Tumblety learned: thereafter he wooed scandal wherever he went, and often he won her.

Over the dregs of dinner, Caine told how the pamphlet he'd later penned had caused no such stir, for which he'd given thanks. "Already I wanted to rid myself of the man. London had its allure, yes, but at what price?" But Caine did not, or rather could not, rid himself of Tumblety, and the price to be paid—the *literal* price—is, I fear, yet to be determined; for:

As I left Greeba Castle some hours ago, after a night and morning most memorable, a chagrined Thomas Henry Hall Caine—honourable man—pressed upon me letters, very *personal* letters, written in the hand of Francis Tumblety and addressed to Caine himself. These I've now read, and . . . and good God! If, *if* the twin of this correspondence is yet in Tumblety's possession, well, then, the American has the means to ruin Caine, to blackmail him into bankruptcy, into oblivion. Into jail! For the first of these letters—dated 28 January 1875—begins in terms so intimate as to burn the ears of the world. Oh, Caine, dear Caine, I fear the fate that awaits you, friend. How, *how* will we avert it?

Alas. The first letter appears to follow upon a London rendezvous, for in it Tumblety references various . . . *pleasures* lately partaken of and writes, "As you have proved yourself most feminine, I feel under great obligation, and hope some time to be able to make suitable recompense." What to make of this?[73]

And Caine, *foolish* Caine, seems to have returned such letters *in kind*,

---

73. Here Stoker dissembles in deference to Caine. As a literary man—and one knowledgeable, surely, of his friend's predilections—he was more than capable of parsing the letter's quoted line.

yes; as Tumblety writes on another occasion, "It gives me infinite plea-sure to hear from you, as I should dearly love to see your sweet face and spend an entire night in your company. . . . I feel such melancholy when I read your amiable letter"—an "*amiable* letter": Whatever can Caine have been thinking?—"as it brings back the pleasing reminiscences of the past and only stimulates the affection I feel for you." Good God! Ruinous, such lines, *ruinous!*[74]

Another letter—one in which Tumblety plays the Persecuted One, and lists those Parliamentarians and other public men of repute who are sure to support him in his nameless cause—invites Caine to visit him again, as soon as possible; but he closes the letter by chiding Caine, telling him not to bring the printer's bill when next he comes, but rather *pay it himself.* The cheek! And in subsequent letters, Tumblety further turns his talk to loans:

"Dear boy, wire at once—forty. Wire, wire, wire!" Yet the older man is coy, too, cunning, closing the letter with: "Come here by the morning train. I must see you. Be a dear and bring the sum we spoke of." And he signs himself, "Yours affectionately, F.T."

More of the same follows, until an angry letter dated 4 August and posted, presumably, from somewhere other than London, as in it Tum-blety refers to having "moved on":

"Caine," it begins, "trifle with my patience no longer. Send me £2 to the above address no more no less a paltry amount than the £2 and this friendly correspondence shall go on, independent of these petty finan-cial matters upon which you insist. Fear not—no-one knows anything

---

74. It is perhaps difficult to convey to to-day's reader the danger then posed to Hall Caine by the supposed existence, or rather the potential resurfacing, of such letters; yet the *Dossier* itself hinges upon that very danger. It is this—exposure, in a word—that will keep Stoker and Co. from resorting to the authorities later on. Had they done so, Caine's world would have come crashing down.

Too, it bears mentioning that blackmail was a booming business amongst the Victorians. Let Oscar Wilde stand as illustration: some few years on—in 1895—similar letters sent to several of his "sporting fellows" would seal his fate, bringing on charges and a conviction under the Labouchere Amendment to the Criminal Law Act of 1885; which states (48&49 Vict. C.69, 11):

"Any male person who, in public or private, commits or is party to the commission of, or pro-cures or attempts to procure the commission by any male person of any act of gross indecency with another male person, shall be guilty of a misdemeanour, and being convicted thereof shall be liable at the discretion of the Court to be imprisoned for any term not exceeding two years, with or with-out hard labour."

about IT, and there is no fraud being committed upon you as I am not in the habit of telling people about my private affairs. You abuse me in suggesting I might ever speak of this, of US.

"I got your last letter forwarded to me here this morning and felt surprise at finding in it not the 2£ lately requested but excuses only. I am stopping here for 3 or 4 days and no more. Do not fail to send a postal order." Young Caine, threatened so, must have responded by posting the two pounds, for I have here a letter of slightly later date in which Tumblety recants somewhat, yet stops short of apology:

"You must have thought my last note imperative," he writes, "but the fact is I really required the money." (*Q:* Is Tumblety a man of means or not?)[75]

Said letter closes with, "I will do you a better favor than this before long." One can only hope that the favour alluded to was the burning of all letters similar to these in content or tone and addressed to Tumblety *in Caine's hand.* Oh, yes, ruinous such letters would be if they came to light now to shine upon the author of *The Deemster!* Caine's position is a parlous one indeed. Can such letters yet be in the blackmailing hands of Tumblety? If so, poor Caine may yet come to rue the day he first picked up a pen for *any* purpose, let alone to spill his heart toward the likes of a Francis Tumblety!

Later; nearer London.—I write again after a quarter-hour's respite, for with those infernal letters of Tumblety's in my left hand I could no longer steady my right. At present they sit smothering in my satchel, and there they shall remain. My heart is full from the trust little Tommy has shown me, and I shan't abuse it, *ever.* If eyes other than mine ever read those letters, we, all of us, will long ago have gone to dust. No: None alive shall ever see them. And that includes simple Mary Caine, who loves a man she hardly knows.

And this trust Caine has shown conferring the letters unto my care makes up somewhat, too, for the scepticism he showed last night when

---

75. He was. And so it seems either Tumblety sought to fleece Caine of what little money he then had, or something else—perhaps an alias he could not let fall—had separated Tumblety from his money for a short while. It cannot be known.

dinner was done and we repaired to his study, it being now my turn to talk.

I much preferred whisky to the proffered port, indeed had *need* of whisky if I were to find my words; and I sought to assuage myself further with a Havana cigar. There we sat, smoking in the study before a fire lately laid by an unseen servant; for the cold would come on with nightfall. And though it was stifling at present and would grow smoky as well, my repeated request for air was again refused. Caine's papers were piled all about, his books thrown helter-skelter. (*Mem.:* Caine's means of composition seems rather more *physical* than mine. Perhaps in heaving the odd volume I'd come upon a like success. If only.)

Over dessert, Caine had said he'd heard naught of Tumblety since he'd received a letter sent from San Francisco—in which Tumblety entreated Caine to come meet him in the American city of his, Caine's, choice—until a more recent letter arrived announcing his return to London. "Did the last mention money?" The night was late, my conversant a friend: Why not hasten to my point? (Already I'd caught the sulphurous scent of blackmail on the air.)

"No," said Caine, "but as I see where you are headed, let me say that the thought has already—and often—crossed my mind. But again, no: His last letter bore no allusion to . . . blackmail." Here was the first mention of a means of blackmail: extant letters. My supposition would be proved true on the morrow, all too true; such that now I know as well why a worried Caine sacrificed his Stoker to such a man: introducing us would have seemed a scanty price to pay in order to preserve the peace, to busy Tumblety in London and keep him at bay.

Caine fell quiet then. He occupied himself over-long with the lighting of his cigar. Now I wonder if he wasn't considering introducing the other letters, *all* the letters? If so, he desisted. As it was evident he felt he'd lowered himself in the telling of his tale, I sought to raise him up, saying he'd sunken *not at all* in my esteem, &c. Caine was having none of it. Already his mullygrubs had come, and I fear they shan't surrender him for many days more. (*Mem.:* Wire upon return to London: *Letters read. Friendship firm.*)

Indeed, Caine might well have retired then, save it was my time to talk, to tell what I knew of Tumblety. I set in. Five minutes later, Caine sat ramrod straight in his chair, his wide eyes afire, his jaw slack, and his cigar fast ceding to ash.

I'd decided not to mince my words. If madness be Caine's verdict, so be it.

. . . I have just sat some while in consideration of how men's minds close; how, as boys, we believe so much more than as men. Are *able* to believe so much more: bogeymen beneath our beds, pirates lying in wait in the coves of Clontarf, &c. As we age, our beliefs are drawn in, are pulled tight—by what: religion? the world, or our overly vaunted experience of it?—much as a miser pulls tight the strings of his purse; but the miser enriches himself, whilst we men are left bereft, believing in *single* things, *sure* things. And surely the goal of life oughtn't to be fewer beliefs at its ending than at its beginning, but more. A broadening is what's wanted; for one's ideas must be as broad as nature if they are to interpret nature. Alas, though a man's beliefs ought to broaden with age, the lot of most men's lives is a lessening, a narrowing over time. Not so Hommy-Beg, bless him, or surely he'd have shown me the door last night. No: Caine has proved himself the exception rather than the rule; and said proof was this:

He sat a long while in consideration of all I'd said—and I had said all, *all*—before pronouncing it "a scandal on common sense; and yet . . . and yet . . . There *are* mysteries which men can only guess at, which age by age they may solve only in part. Are we now on the verge of such a one?"

He stood to pace, a trait acquired from Rossetti, all the while fingering the pistol in his pocket. "Possession, you say? It rather sends one to one's wits' end, does it not? Though of course wit factors . . . well, it factors *not* a whit, for we enter now into another realm entirely. And we—men of *paid* imagination, after all—ought to be able to progress upon that path, no?" And then he said again and again, as if in time with his heartbeat, "Oh Bram, Oh Bram, Oh Bram . . . " till finally he waxed philosophical; so:-

"I have often wondered if life as we live it isn't merely the visible aspect of a far vaster, invisible conflict. Time and again, we find no reason that things have happened as they have. Strange, this. So how, then, can we refute that theory of the ancients—the same upon which the Greeks based their plays? Which is namely this: That invisible powers of good and evil—operative in regions above and beyond our control—wage war while working out our destiny.

"Mightn't some of these powers—whatever they are—be made manifest to man, even if accidentally so?" I said nothing, as capital-N Nothing was all I had left to say.

"Even our own forebears," continued Caine, "saw the devil's hand in everyday deeds. I daresay they attended Satan himself at every turn, whilst God, of course, was thought to be rather more ... shy. They cursed the one and praised the other daily, *thrice* daily in my grandmother's case. To her the world was full of spirits good and bad, ministers of God and His Enemy, such that she'd not have been surprised to see an angel spring from her teapot, or turn to find the Arch-fiend himself seated at her table.

"How is it they—be it the Greeks or my grandmother—had faith, whilst we, Bram, can barely muster belief?"

"Oh," said I, "I believe. Now more so than ever."

"I'd rather think you would, yes. . . . A demon, you say? Snakes and scorpions and such? Come as portents, signs?" He paced on in silence. The sea could be heard without, the fire within. Our whisky was gone, but I daresay no two men were ever more sober than we. "You, Bram, are a man free of all fiddle-faddle. This I know. This I have long known. So I believe all you say, if for no better reasons than that *you* say it; and, further, I cannot justify my disbelief. Too, if ever a man were to be asked to dance with the devil—or this particular devil, this risen god, this Enemy of Egypt, this—"

"Set," said I.

"Set" said he, "—well then, Francis Tumblety would be that man." Caine paused. He turned toward me. "Have you spoken of this to anyone else?"

"I have not, though I thought to talk to Lady Wilde, as she—"

"Yes, yes," said Caine, "you have always held her and her late husband in high regard."

"I have. Sir William would neither blanch nor blink at all this, but rather he'd seek to get to its bottom by . . . by whatever means. I shall do the same. And as Speranza shared, nay shares still, both Sir William's scepticism—which surely is wanted—and his erudition, I shall appeal to her. Only those who know much know there is more to learn, *much* more." [76]

"And Henry? Will you speak of this to Henry?"

"I will not: Tumblety has his ear at present, and Henry would think I mean only to malign the man."

"Malign indeed," mused Caine. "From the Latin *malignus,* meaning 'bad.' This *is* a bad business, Bram."

"So it is. So it is. But it may yet turn out well; for—" And I was spared having to lie further, as, concomitant with my last word, there'd come a *rap, rap, rap* at the castle door. Caine sprang from his seat, pulled out his pistol, and began waving it about wildly. "Calm yourself, man," said I, standing. "But who*ever* . . . ? And at this late hour?"

Caine was white, and wavering in his resolve. I feared he'd fire: at a shimmering window, at a maid come to see if we'd all we needed; and so I said:-

"I'll go." Turning at the study door, I meant to admonish Caine, to tell him to re-pack his pistol; but I said nothing. Better he have it ready to hand, for who knew what the night had brought to his door?

Of course, some few moments more and I knew: it was the steward, come to accompany the postman's boy. "A telegram," snarled the steward, "for Mr. Stoker." I drew forth a farthing for the boy, and thanked him. I shut the great door resoundingly upon the steward even as he went onto tiptoe to look over my shoulder, searching out Caine in vain;

76. Lady Wilde was a dear and trusted friend, true, but doubtless fresh in Stoker's mind was her recent publication, *Ancient Legends, Mystic Charms and Superstitions of Ireland, with Sketches of the Irish Past.* This she'd follow up in 1890 with *Ancient Cures, Charms and Usages of Ireland, Contributions to Irish Lore.* Though much of the research requisite to these volumes had been done by Sir William Wilde, it was Lady Wilde—herself no stranger to the strange—who brought them to fruition.

for the latter crouched now behind the study door, a discovery which startled me badly as I re-entered the room and disclosed him so.

"Good God, Caine," said I, "come from there and put that pistol up. You'd have shot the telegraph boy! And wouldn't *Punch* have had fun depicting *that* till your last day standing?"

"I fear *Punch* may yet have far more fun with me than that." It was a comment I could not have understood fully, not then; though now I do. "A telegram?" Caine held out a trembling hand: after all, this house was his.

When told the telegram was for me, my host was relieved. "Just as well. I want no news at present. You've provided quite enough to-night, Stoker, and my nerves are fraught." He fell heavily into his chair.

Returning to mine, I opened and read the telegram. "However did he know to find me here? Florence must have told him."

"Told who?"

"Henry, of course."

"Henry," said Caine, "could find you anywhere. A bloodhound, he is, so long as the blood be yours. But what does he say, Bram?"

I handed the telegram to Caine, who read it aloud:-

"'Come at once. Horrid incident.'"

There was panic in Caine's voice as he asked, "You'll not leave *now*?" And even if the hour had been earlier, and the packets still steaming toward Liverpool, I'd not have left till the morning, this morning, for I knew that my tale of Tumblety had taken from Tommy all hope of sleep and . . . alas, he'd not have fared well alone.

"No, no," I assured him, "impossible. The first boat of the morning will do. No doubt it's but some bit of theatre business badly seen to, or some impediment to the mounting of our *Macbeth*."

"Ah, yes," said Caine, "it's to be *Macbeth*. Finally."

"Yes, by year's end. Or so it is hoped—by Henry if not necessarily myself."

"Henry's talked of putting on the Scottish play for years. Why, we even spoke about it back when we all three were in Edinburgh, you'll recall."

I did recall, and said so. I recalled, too, the reason the Caines had accompanied us to the Scottish capital; but I left it to my friend to allude to same, as then he did:-

"Mary, by the way—"

"Of course," said I, interrupting, for a man ought to spare a friend such words as were coming. "Not a whisper." Though the revelation of the letters yet lay a half-day ahead, still I knew enough to swear I'd keep Caine's confidence as regarded Tumblety, as surely as he'd keep mine. After all, though Caine risks ruin, I run the risk of a bunk beside Penfold's in Stepney Latch!

"Perhaps," said I as we headed upstairs towards our suites, "perhaps we'll neither of us ever hear from the man again."

"One can but hope," said Caine. Whereupon he went into his room and threw several bolts behind him. I retired in my turn, thinking the resolution of this—*all* this, whatever it may be—will want rather more than hope.

In the morning, after the promised bacon and brawn, I took my leave of Caine, of Greeba Castle, wondering what further revelations lay in the letters I'd lately been handed with nary a word but a worried, *very* worried, look.

Mere minutes now to Euston, whence to Henry and his "horrid incident." Whatever it be, pray let it be *explicable*.

BRAM STOKER'S JOURNAL

Tuesday, 12 June '88, *later.*—Horrid indeed. And *his* hand is in this, surely.

Upon returning to Euston Station, I went straight to the Lyceum, arriving there to wonder why all the world was milling about. I hadn't time to set down my satchel before I was beset, first by Jimmy at the stage door; secondly by the two tenders of cats who sat huddled round she who tended them in turn, Mrs. Quibbel, whose tears precluded her customary salute; and thirdly by Henry, who, I'd been told manifold times in my progress toward the XO, attended me there. En route I learned naught but that the incident, whatever it had been, had occurred in the Beefsteak Club the night prior; yet I could not connect that fact with Mrs. Quibbel's fresh tears: Whatever had she to do with events as they passed in the Guv'nor's private dining room?

Henry explained, but this Record needn't show his surliness in doing so. Suffice it to say that, in the opinion of Henry Irving, I have no right to absent myself more than one half-hour from his summoning call. Tommyrot! But so he holds. Alas, said he:

Mrs. Quibbel had come to her post earlier than usual yesterday, Monday instant, 11 June—11 a.m. o/c, said she; by which hour I would have been well launched toward Liverpool. "Or so she has sworn," said Henry, seated at his side of our double-desk.

"Have you cause to doubt her?" I asked, taking my own seat, my back to the opened door. "And whatever do you mean 'sworn'?" Had Henry interrogated Mrs. Q. himself? The answer was slow to come, for Henry Irving often acts rather than tells his tales, and tiresomely so.

"The lady," said he, thus casting a slight aspersion upon Mrs. Quibbel, who, though she has proved herself both amiable and utile, is certainly no lady, ". . . the lady has sworn that she arrived before luncheon and let herself into the Beefsteak Club. To ready it, says she; to tidy it if need be." Had Henry dined there the night prior, Sunday? If so, with whom? Could Tumblety so dissemble himself as to pass—and pass as what: *un*possessed?—in common company? I did not know, of course, for I'd absented myself at curtain-fall Sunday last, eager for these pages, sleep, and that early-morning train that carried me to Caine. "Tell me, Stoker," said Henry, "have you enlarged the woman's responsibilities so that now she is charged with tidying my dining room?" *His* dining room. Indeed.

"With all due respect, Henry, I doubt Mrs. Quibbel's job description goes to the heart of the matter."

"Heart of the matter indeed," said he with a sniff, assuming now the aspect of Shylock in the *Merchant*'s trial scene, for Henry has little *self* on which to rely in realities such as these. "This Mrs. . . ."

"Mrs. Quibbel," said I. "Quibbel."

"She let herself into the Beefsteak—by means mysterious, might I add—no doubt with purse or pockets suitably empty and ready to be stuffed, and—"

"Have you reason, Henry, to impugn the woman so?" I doubted he did, for hadn't I just passed her, still on the property? He'd have surrendered her to the authorities, happily, or kicked her to the curb himself if she'd been caught pilfering his pantry. So I would have to be Portia to his Shylock; but oh, let this play end, thought I, wondering still what the "horrid incident" was. I yet hoped it would turn out to be trivial, but with Henry I would not know till all the facts were told, or rather played.

"Well," said he, "whatever her reasons . . ."

"I have discovered Mrs. Quibbel to be *most* conscientious at her tasks," said I, failing to add that one of her tasks, of late, had been keeping watch for Tumblety.

"Be that as it may," said Henry, "yesterday eve, whilst alone in the Lyceum Theatre"—as if I might wonder what theatre he referenced—"she entered my private precincts to find . . ."

"Yes?"

"That the grill was yet warm . . ."

"As sometimes it is, Henry, hours after the last of the guests—*your* guests—have left."

"Aha," said he, raising high a crooked finger, "but I had no guests Sunday night. Had you been here, of course, you'd well know it." He slammed his hand down atop the desk as he added, "Someone else had laid the fire in question."

Having long been sympathetic towards the lesser members of our Lyceum family who have to make do, post-performance, with cold meats, &c., whilst the aroma of roasting beeves wafts through the theatre, I said, "Perhaps, Henry, someone thought to play the Guv'nor for once. A simple change of locks shall preclude its ever happening again, and . . ." And, thought I, render inutile Tumblety's key, if indeed he has one. *That* was something Stoker would see to at once, if only Henry would give the order; but no:-

"You mistake my point," said he.

"You've yet to arrive at it," said I.

Henry stood to his full height. He seemed now to be playing equal parts mad Mathias and Hal rallying the troops,[77] and I shan't here discount the effect: it was disquieting. Indeed, my words had been rash, perhaps, and I might well have apologised had not Henry then hastened to his point, which was this:

Mrs. Quibbel, entering into the Beefsteak Club, had found its pendant grill still warm, nay hot, and upon it, laid crosswise, were the charred remains of what she at first took to be hares. They were not. They were hounds. Tumblety's hounds, eviscerated and laid there to roast.

"Good God," said I, sitting back heavily in my chair.

"The poor beasts were burnt beyond recognition," said Henry.

"Burnt whilst alive?"

"Not at all. They'd been split and cleaned, albeit clumsily, and the innards lay . . . lay splayed across the table—*my* table, yes."

"The innards?" I asked.

"The innards," said Henry.

"All save the hearts, of course," whereupon I started and wheeled round, for these last words had come from behind me. In the doorway of the XO stood a man in every way middling—middling of height, of weight, of appearance—middling in every way save for the reputation I attached to his name as Henry then spoke it:-

"Stoker, have you met Inspector Frederick Abberline, Scotland Yard? He is not unknown here on first nights."

Had I? In my confusion I could not recall, but leave it to Henry Irving to tap the top of Scotland Yard. "Sir," said I, standing.

---

77. The former the haunted hero of *The Bells*; the latter Prince Hal, or Henry V, from Shakespeare's eponymous play.

"Mr. Stoker," said he, meeting my salutation with a nod. "Horrid, this."

"Horrid indeed," said I. The *hearts*, had he said?

"It is early days yet, of course," said Inspector Abberline, "but all answers are tending in the same direction." He stepped into the office, towards me. We shook hands. His was warm; mine, I fear, had gone quite cold. And there we stood, as he said, "Tell me, sir: What do you know of this man, this American"—he read the name off a pad as small as his palm—"this Tumblety?"

The Third Epoch

THE NIGHT
WITHIN
THE NIGHT

BRAM STOKER'S JOURNAL

Wednesday, 13 June.—Who is this Abberline?

Middling, yes—half a head shorter than myself, with brown eyes and browner hair: bald atop, but with bushy moustache and side-whiskers; a whispery sort, seeming more a clerk than a constable; let alone an inspector 1st class; fifties coming on fast, I should think[1]— . . . middling, I say, in every way save one: his repute. Indeed, I did recognise Inspector Abberline from the occasional opening night, when he'd have been accorded two seats, perhaps even in the Guv'nor's box, and I had only to ask around town—discreetly so—to find out more:

It appears that Abberline has lately been transferred to Scotland Yard from CID,[2] H Division, after 14 yrs. service in & about the slums of Spitalfields, &c., 25 yrs. service in toto. Knows all the strata of London life, from the working women of Whitechapel up to Henry Irving. (*Mem.:* Ask Caine if he knows Abberline from his slumming and court-crawling on behalf of the *Town Crier.*)[3]

Now that Abberline has been spared Spitalfields and accedes to the Yard, I suppose we may be seeing more of him at the Lyceum.

1. Frederick George Abberline was actually forty-five in 1888.

2. CID: Criminal Investigative Division.

3. "Slumming": a term used by the Victorians to denote, with irony, one's placing oneself amongst one's inferiors in a place beneath one's station, usually in the pursuit of illicit pleasures.

Doubtless his present work will earn him seats to spare. Oh, but *damn* Henry for bringing the Yard into this! Things grow complicated now, re: Tumblety.

What did I know of the man? Abberline wondered and wanted to know.

"Not a great deal, Inspector," said I. We were walking now, side by side, down and through the theatre towards the Beefsteak Club. Henry, of course, led the way.

I had not had to feign my surprise at hearing the news of the hounds back in the XO, but I had insisted, at once, on being shown the site; in so doing I succeeded in buying myself some time, for I'd been caught unawares. What would I say? What *could* I say? Certainly not the truth. Not even *most* of the truth. Indeed, the *least* of it would soon lead to Caine, and I cannot, *will not,* compromise him so. No. I would have to lie: white lies, lies of *o*mission rather than *c*ommission.

"Not a great deal, Inspector," said I in response to the second iteration of the question. "I have met the man on occasion, and usually in the company of Henry here," whereupon the Guv'nor wheeled round, showing a brow furrowed by the business at hand: Who'd dared defile his dining room?

"With Mr. Irving, you say?" Abberline scratched something onto his pad with a stub of pencil drawn down from amidst his side-whiskers. Henry was heard to harrumph. We all three resumed walking.

"Yes," said I. "He—Tumblety—has sometimes dined with us here at the Lyceum since . . . " I paused. Was I already offering more than was requisite? But Abberline caught me out:-

"Since . . . ?" said he.

"Since his arrival in London." And lest I seem too recalcitrant, I added, "Sometime in early June, that would have been."

"I see," said the Inspector, making note of same. "An old friend, then?"

Here I saw an opportunity to hold back the name of Hall Caine whilst calling out Henry on the topic of Tumblety. "Henry," said I, "am I wrong to recall the American's presence at your first Lyceum *Hamlet?*" This, of course, I'd lately learned from Caine.

"You are not," said Henry, the words thrown back over his shoulder.

"So, then, Mr. Irving," asked Abberline, "he *is* a friend of long standing?"

"Hardly that," said Henry, "hardly that." And, turning back to us both, he added, "I meet many men, Inspector, few of whom become friends." Abberline nodded in seeming sympathy, and Henry spoke on. "What's more: We cannot conclude that the doctor played a part in this barbarism simply because the hounds are presumed to be—"

"Who else can lay claim to two tiny hounds?" This I asked, purposely over-speaking Henry, for I know he roils at having his lines trod upon and I hoped his ire would prove of interest to Abberline; but Henry spoke on as if I'd not said a word:-

"—simply because we presume the hounds are his, or rather *were* his—poor creatures—and he has not come round in a week or so." Hadn't he? I left it to Abberline to ask the obvious question, the answer to which was:-

"No, Inspector, I have not heard from Francis"—and so: infernal Francis Tumblety had wangled his way onto a first-name basis with Henry Irving—"since last we supped at the Garrick. I am afraid I shall have to resort to my social calendar if you require a more precise date." But nothing more was said upon the point, for we three had arrived at the Beefsteak Club even as Henry spoke.

There was that aroma of flame-charred flesh, save this time it had arisen from neither beeves nor fowl but rather . . . hound. I fairly retched. And my stomach was settled not at all at seeing two maids-of-all-work, hired from I knew not where, scrubbing a deep stain from the table's end: Henry's end. Doubtless he'd soon charge me with replacing the table. *See to it, Stoker.* A third maid tasked herself with the grill itself, though this, too, would have to go.

Though the canine victims of the crime—the *horrid incident*—had been removed, still it was unsettling to consider the scene, the deeds lately done. "Pardon me, Inspector: Did you say that the hounds were dressed elsewhere than here?"

"I did *not* say, Mr. Stoker. . . . But yes, we may suppose they were."

"As surely there'd be more blood hereabouts had the perpetrator done his surgery on site?" Abberline said nothing. His silence was meant to discourage further speculation on my part: doubtless the men of Scotland Yard encounter many a would-be Holmes these days and curse Conan Doyle for it. The Inspector did, however, meet my eye at the word "surgery," which I'd chosen with care: though I could not tell the truth about Dr. Tumblety—whatever *that* may be—neither would I exonerate him. Surely this was his handiwork, and practised upon his own pets no less! And so let hounds of a higher order have at him, let Scotland Yard set off on his scent and pursue him till they . . .

Oh, but what might the man say if found? Who might he incriminate? Me, the secret ritualist? Or worse: Caine the catamite? Oh, damn Henry Irving indeed, and damn this Abberline as well! What to do? *What to do?*

(*Mem.:* Must copy out these pages and post them to Caine *at once.* Tell him he is likely to be summoned to London. Too, send word round to Speranza: *Must meet.*)

Inspector Abberline pursued me on the point of my acquaintance with Tumblety. I said only that, at his request, I'd introduced him into Lady Jane Wilde's salon on a Saturday late last month. On the instant, I damned myself for having said Speranza's name: Would Abberline go to her next? Happily, he did not take the name down. Wilde, though, is a name unlikely to slip the mind of any Londoner at present. I worried, too, that he'd draw from me more names: Yeats, Constance. Blessedly, he did not, but he surprised me when he asked instead:-

"Did you not, Mr. Stoker"—and here he glanced down at his pad— "suggest to the wardrobe mistress that perhaps the doctor had stolen items from the costume shop?"

Thank you plenty, Mrs. Pinch. "'Stolen'? Not at all. Having found proof, proof of the dirty, doggish sort . . ."

"Understood," said Abberline.

"Having found seeming proof that Dr. Tumblety and his hounds had been present in the costumery, I simply asked its mistress if anything had been borrowed. 'Stolen' is a newspaper word, Inspector, and one of the mistress's choosing, not mine." And with a dismissive, dissembling laugh I had at Henry, via the Inspector, saying:-

"I hardly think, sir, that our good Guv'nor here would gift a thief with a Lyceum key of his own and—"

Abberline interrupted to ask Henry the question I'd long wanted answered: Had Tumblety a key?

"No indeed," huffed Henry in response. "He was welcome here, and will be welcome again when he returns, as I'm sure he will be able to explain all . . . all *this;* but a key of his own? Nonsense." He glared at me. I had best prepare for punishment, for listed tasks of the punitive type. Stoker shall be *seeing to this* & *seeing to that* for some while, I'm afraid. So be it. I'd long wondered and worried re: Tumblety's means of in- and egress; but now that I had my answer, it gave rise to another question:

However had Tumblety come and gone so freely *without* a key? The man moves as mist! Surely he'd no need of the Invisibility Ritual read over him by the adepts! I jest, jest as best I can at present; but what if that ritual found its effect and Tumblety now has such stealth, such mysterious means of movement as . . . as the blue-black egg of Harpocrates? Crazed, *crazed* I am to even consider such! But alas, I have seen what I have seen, and I shall *not* doubt myself; for that way madness lies.

More questions were asked of us in the Beefsteak Club. I divulged little, and Henry even less; for the Guv'nor is keen on accusing Mrs. Quibbel of complicity in the crime, if not the crime itself. "Follow her and you'll have your answer," said he to Abberline, who seemed rather less sure. Yet when Henry insisted that I fire the woman, it was Abberline who intervened, saying it'd be wiser to keep the suspect close at hand some while. To this, Henry unhappily acceded. And finally, with promises of cooperation &c., I bade the Inspector adieu and let Henry escort him to the stage door. By the time Henry returned to the XO— as no doubt he did, having rehearsed the earful he'd offer me—I had taken my leave of the Lyceum and was headed home.

I have avoided Henry thus far to-day; and I shall continue to do so till a quarter-hour before curtain, by which time he'll be Shylock and I shall be spared both his wrath and his wonder, for I am undeserving of the former and cannot answer the latter with what few truths I possess.

BRAM STOKER'S JOURNAL

Thursday, 14 June, post-performance.—I entered Speranza's boudoir earlier to-day with an excess of apology.

"Please, Mr. Stoker," said she, "desist! How can such apology be called for? Have you been adding to my family's infamy? I rather hope you have! Say all the bad you can about us, Bram, lest the world not take us Wildes seriously." I had no interest in Speranza's wit this day, and showed her so by my absent smile. Now she knew I had come to her with reason, indeed had *insisted* on seeing her, though the hour was—by her lights—*un*reasonable.

"Oh, but *do* speak, Bram. Speak bold and true to your Speranza before you burst!" And she patted the bed beside her, where I was to sit.

I had gone round to Park Street at noon and again at one, twice leaving word with her Betty that I came re: *something of great import;* and so, when finally Speranza rose—half past 2, this was—she assented to receive me, still abed but already at work, dressed in what she refers to as her "literary attire": a stayless dress of white lawn with a bonnet to match; for, she asked, how can her mind be free to answer to divine inspiration if her body is not? "Although . . . ," said Speranza, stoppering an ink bottle and setting her lap desk aside, "far be it from me to invoke the divine these days. The Muses, I'm afraid, have thrown me over in favour of my son. And this daily, undignified, and merely mechanical employment of pen and ink is killing the last vestiges of the divine within me." And lest I mistake her meaning—that she wrote now for money and nothing more, nothing *noble*—she added, with a sigh, "My creditors are carnivores, Mr. Stoker."

"I am sorry to hear it," said I; and as Speranza had never before spoken to me of her penury, which is greatly worse than mine, I ventured to suggest that as Oscar was doing well—or at least better—so, too, must she be. She replied only by saying that her second son was "a good boy" before turning the converse back towards myself. "How it vexes me to see you so, Mr. Stoker!" For there I sat, chin to chest. "What is it, *what?*"

Walking the streets of Grosvenor Square whilst waiting for Speranza to rise, I'd wondered how best to broach my impossible subject. Perhaps it would be best to broach it via its very impossibility; and so it was that I blurted out, finally:-

"I have seen the impossible, Speranza."

She moaned. "Oh, my, this *is* serious. But I fear, Bram, you've been too long amongst the English—pray summon your Irishness and get about the business of *telling* me something. Do so poetically, if it pleases you, but *tell* me something. Facts, please. And fast!"

I said again that I had seen the impossible; whereby Speranza saw that I was at a total loss and said, with a sigh and a wry smile:-

"No, dear, *not* the Impossible. The Impossible is in Paris at present." She fluffed her pillows and settled back onto them, saying, "But if you *have* seen As-car Fingal O'Flahertie Wills Wilde, I am at least relieved to hear he has returned to London—what he does amongst the French I've *no* idea, but 'tis not for a mother to wonder—as Constance has been *quite* unwell of late, and the solitary life on Tite Street suits her not at all. The boys bedevil her, and she speaks to me of unfounded fears.... I worry for her, Bram, truly I do."

"I have not seen Oscar," said I; "but tell me: What troubles Constance so? Not her health, I hope." I knew full well what was troubling her; for it troubles me, too.

"Not her *physical* health, no." And Speranza—not known for her subtlety—tapped at her temple, twice, with an ink-stained forefinger. I said no more of Constance, save that Speranza should give her my regards when next the two met.

"That, I fear, may be some while from now.... But alas, Mr. Stoker, out with it now: Speak!"

"Yes, yes," said I, breathing deeply. "What ... what do you know of possession?"

Speranza paused not a moment before saying, "I am Irish. I know only of *dis*possession."

"Speranza, please. This is quite serious, and difficult for me."

"Well, then, Mr. Stoker, though it be difficult for me, I shall stow my *bons mots*." She reached for a scrap of paper and withdrew her pen from its pot. "Do, though, let me write that last one down." This she did, adding, "As-car will thank me for it."

She sat up straight now. She laced her long fingers and settled her hands in her lap. She stared at me, her eyes wide. She was, in a word, *serious*. I might have cried then, for I feared losing a friend. What if Speranza deemed me insane? Oh, but blessed lady, blessed friend, she did not. Instead:-

"'Possession,' you say? Of the Popish sort?"

"More or less. Spirit possession, we may say. Demonic possession."

"My word. . . . I see by your furrowed brow and bagged eyes that this is no idle enquiry, no research for a fiction."

"No. There's the British Library for that. What I need is wisdom, and so I came in search of a Wilde."

"Well done, Mr. Stoker. Well done. . . . Now, I suppose there are particulars?"

"Oh, yes," said I, "many."

A half-hour passed, in the course of which I told Speranza *all & everything*. I left out Constance's involvement in same, of course: a family matter, that. When I finished with talk of Tumblety's charred and heartless canines, Speranza, who'd sat up in the course of my confession, fell back amidst her pillows, muttering, "I liked that man not at all, *not at all*." And for a long while, she said nothing more, her eyes alternately wandering, finding no focus—I wondered if she heard voices, or leastways sought them—and then boring into my own as if to search for madness there. Evidently she found none; for she proceeded to pronounce:-

"Firstly, we speak of this to no-one, not yet. Stoker, Caine, and Speranza: We three shall keep our own counsel."

"Agreed," said I; for silence suits me fine at present.

"Secondly, return to me to-morrow at three. I've a friend in Rome sitting deeply in my debt. I shall wire him to-night and have him hasten his reply."

"A priest?" .

"Formerly, yes, and possessed of a fine mind. I shall tell him it is a question of *my* research, and he will advise accordingly, send useful books, et cetera. . . . To-morrow by three, I shall know more. And I shall summon my Irish poet as well."

"Yeats? . . . To have from *him* substantiation of my claims?"

"Yes," said Speranza, "as I'm sure you'd have me do. The boy-man bears all the signs of genius, but I shall test him, test the tethers tying him to a world larger than this. Let him prove himself, finally: magus or fraud."

She was right: Yeats's testimony—if she could cull it from his claptrap—would be of benefit to both Speranza and myself, and maybe Constance, too.

"And we ought to learn more of this Order," said Speranza. "When I put forth your name for membership, Bram, I'd no idea they dabbled so deeply in the spirit realm. I apologise if . . ." And I'd never before heard Lady Wilde leave a sentence unsaid to its end; but perhaps she was simply distracted, scrawling out a few lines to both Yeats and her Roman. These I would wire to poet and priest myself when later I wended my slow way home, listening in the streets for *Sto-ker, Sto-ker*.

As I stood to take my leave of Speranza, she surprised me by asking why it was I sought such answers. What was it I meant to do with—or rather *to*—this American? Save him? Exorcise him? "I should think," said she, summarily, "that you and Mr. Caine would be happy enough to never see him again. Mr. Caine, especially so."

"We would indeed," said I; "but that, I'm afraid, is unlikely to even-tuate." What *was* it we meant to do? I thought a long moment before saying I had no idea, no idea at all—I hadn't, and still don't!—before adding that whatever we did, we'd have to do it alone: no authorities. Caine stands to lose too much.

I thanked Speranza. If earlier I'd feared what she would say, now I wondered how I'd ever doubted the woman.

"You are welcome," said she, beckoning me nearer, lower. I bent, and she enveloped my face in her hands. She bussed my cheek. And, holding to my beard as a baby might, tugging at it, hard, she smiled as she said, "*Bienvenue* to the invisible world, Bram, that spins in the shadow of ours. . . . Sir William believed in you. He swore you'd see the shadows one day."

And as I descended towards her front door, blinking back tears, already Speranza was calling down behind me for her Betty, calling for certain of her books to be brought to her in bed, *"pronto!"*

LETTER, BRAM STOKER TO HALL CAINE

Saturday, 16 June '88

Dearest Caine,

Events of the week want recounting, surely, but I have had to wait till now, for which I apologise. It is, however, as well that I waited; for I have more, *much* more to report at present—2.35 a.m.—as I have just returned home from a long walk with Henry through your haunts of old, Whitechapel & its surrounds. And I use the word "haunts" advisedly; for there, to-night, I saw . . . No. I'll get to that, to him him *him*, in due course.

For now let me simply say where things stand, or seem to. *Real* things. For I fear that imagination runs riot with me now. Oh, forgive me, friend. I am not well at present, and if ever I was adept at the narrative art . . . alas; but art plays no part in such news as I have to impart.

First, as regards Lady Wilde:

Blessedly, *I am believed.* Broad is her mind, broader still her spirit. Moreover: She has had confirmation from an Irish poet who was present at the Setian event. Rather, as she wrote in her note:

"My Poet declines to come to me at present; and so I wrote him again, chidingly. I have here his reply, which is tripartite. Says he, 1.

Something passed, yes; 2. He knows not what, precisely; and, 3. He asks that I never speak to him on the subject again. Rather more forthcoming was the Roman. Come round at once for more. *Speranza.*" Of course I went at once.

The referenced Roman is a priestly friend of Lady Wilde's. She has had word from him re: possession; of which more anon, but first . . . Oh, Caine, I am fractured! Let these pages reflect the disorder of late days.

Forgive me, friend, for failing to wire you re: the *horrid incident* that attended me upon my return. I waited to do so in the hope of having more facts; but still facts are few, and these are they:

Someone—doubtless it was *he*—roasted his two hounds on the suspended grill of the Beefsteak Club, having first removed from them their hearts. Horrid, indeed! Worse: Henry has brought down upon us the watchful eye of an Inspector from the Yard, one F. G. Abberline, whose watch was once Wh'chapel &c. If you know anything of the man, wire it at once. Fear not, Caine: I have kept your name from Abberline, if not Speranza. Again, fear not: She is a woman well versed in the ways of the world and spares her scorn for simpletons. Artistes are to her antinomian; and as no laws apply to them, none may be broken.

Oh, how I wish you were here, Caine! I fear that these out-moded means of communication may prove inadequate as the days draw on. Install a telephone machine, won't you, please? And set a packed bag by your door, for it is likely you shall soon be summoned to London— let us hope it is by me and not Inspector Abberline!—and doubtless the notice will be short. And when you are summoned, Caine, come! You must. Lady Wilde and I shall want you here to complete our trinity. For *he* will show again. Indeed, he already has, this very night.

Oh, but first, as regards the Roman:

He posed to Speranza this question: Did she enquire as to perfect or *im*perfect possession? I shall assume your ignorance re: the difference—as the Roman assumed Speranza's, and she mine—and explain, so:

In instances of imperfect possession, the possessed fall prey
to . . . to the invader, let me say, yet still they remain themselves. The
possessed body is shared, and so it is that struggle ensues and an
exorcist may intervene, shifting the balance towards the possessed. In
perfect possession—much the rarer, says the Roman—the possessed
surrenders himself. He is willing, as it were. He is complicit. (And if
ever a man courted the chthonic, the Infernal, surely Francis
Tumblety is he!) And as the perfectly possessed surrenders his will,
no struggle ensues, and without the struggle, exorcism is
inefficacious—that is, *NOTHING CAN BE DONE.*[4]

If this be the case with Tumblety, he is become the truest of
evils.

Caine, Caine, Caine, whatever shall we do? *Something,* surely; for
we cannot hope to have heard the last of the man, nor of the demon
within him. But alas, man and demon are one if he be perfectly
possessed! So it is *this* we must ascertain. Conceive of it, Caine, if you
can: We must find the fiend and determine whether he be imperfectly
or perfectly possessed. If the former, the Church may hold out some
exorcising hope—ritual may yet undo what ritual hath wrought. If
the latter, and if Tumblety be perfectly possessed, then Evil is
amongst us and . . .

And the Roman writes that murder is the sole means of dealing
with such a man. Destroy the man and the demon must, perforce,
depart.

Murder, yes! But before you think me mad, Caine, let me say again
that Tumblety has already come! Or was it I who went to him, *drawn*
to do so? Regardless, I know now his haunt.

Prefatory to the tale, I must perforce report that Henry and I have
had a rapprochement of sorts, owing in large part to the horror of the
hounds. He cannot deny that this, coupled with Tumblety's
disappearance, casts the American in a new and decidedly less
favourable light. Slowly he accedes to the common opinion of the

4. Here Stoker's underscoring has torn the page.

man whilst yet refusing to admit he may have misjudged him. For my part, I have said only that it is hoped—by me, by you, by all but Inspector Abberline—that we have seen the last of Dr. Tumblety. To further assuage Henry and also to keep Abberline from darkening the Lyceum door, I have had to fire an innocent woman: Mrs. Lydia Quibbel, by name; but as the particulars bear upon this Record not at all, I spare you that tale of tears and say again that yes, Henry and I have had a rapprochement of sorts, and so it was that after to-night's performance I joined him in his walk, as often I used to. Bedeviled by our cocky Bassanio, Henry's ire was up; and so the walk would be both brisk and long, as indeed it was:

We went all the way to Whitechapel.

Henry is often keen to be seen by other slummers—once, whilst in his company, we happened upon the Prince of Wales—but not so this night; for still he seethed. And having left the Lyceum in haste, still he wore Shylock's black cloak, the same which shows Antonio's spittle so well.[5] As he'd hardly un-made his face, his pallour drew such stares that I suggested he pull the cape's collar high. This he did, but of course the cape and collar were of no avail when, at Henry's insistence, we went into The Ten Bells for a tin, repairing to his preferred table in the corner to watch, or rather "to study the lesser of our species at their work." Happily, Henry was not recognised.

As now the clock rounds onto 3.00 a.m., it was perhaps two hours ago—mere minutes it seems!—when we re-took to the streets. It was Henry's wish to walk some more through the warren of Whitechapel. I, however, yet entertained some hope of sleep. I told Henry this, but he would not hear me. In such moods as he was in to-night, he wants company at all costs: it might be me, or it might be Jack the Monkey who so amuses the masses now at the Regent's Park Zoo.

Compromising—rare enough an act with Henry Irving—we

---

5. Act I, Scene III, *The Merchant of Venice*, where the play tells us Antonio has often spat upon Shylock the Jew. How the Lyceum played this, I don't know, though Stoker here states that spittle—or its facsimile—came into play nightly. Odd, then, that Henry Irving would wear the same stained cape offstage.

agreed to take a final pint at the nearest public house, whereupon we'd part, I to head home, Henry to do what he willed.

Soon we'd alighted at The Red Lion on Batty Street, east of Berner Street and just off the Commercial Road. Here Henry was recognised, and so his mood improved. We might have drunk all night had the both of us been so inclined. Instead only he was; I nursed my ale whilst I stared out the window, whilst I listened, and listened, and listened some more to Lyceum business. Then I saw Tumblety.

In fact, it was Henry who saw him first. "Stoker," said he under his breath, "do I know that man?"

"What man? Where?"

"Right there. Staring in from the street."

Tumblety had nearly pressed himself against the plate glass, but with the lamplight behind him being . . . ; or perhaps it was the shadows that . . . ; alas, I did not see him at first. But there he was. Staring. Staring, indeed. Now my blood ran cold. Here was Tumblety, returned; but worse: Henry did not know him!

"Why, Henry," said I, "that is he! That is—"

"Who, Stoker? Do I know the man? Does he . . . matter? Ought we to wave him in?"

. . . that I may go invisible, so that every spirit created, and every soul of man and beast, and everything of sight and sense, and every spell and scourge of God, may see me not nor understand. Extraordinary, this.

"No!" said I. "You . . . you do not know him. No need to wave him in, Henry, no need at all." Still Tumblety stood staring, staring at me though it was Henry who said, into a hand cupped to receive a false cough:-

"See how he stares at me, Stoker. I like it not a bit."

"Nor I," was all I said in response. Oh, but how could Henry see yet *not* see Tumblety? Had the Invisibility Ritual conferred upon him . . . *powers of confusion,* if not invisibility proper? Henry *saw him not nor understood.* Yet I saw him. I understood. And I heard him as well:-

Sto-ker, Sto-ker, came his call.

If Henry spoke, I heard him not, for my every sense was tuned to

Tumblety, standing there, behind the waved glass. His body beneath
its concealing cloak seemed somehow to writhe, to gyrate, such that
he appeared humpbacked. Simply, his body seemed not wholly his
own. I wonder, Caine: Would *you* have known him? Or did the ritual
confer some means of sight upon me and me alone as I knelt beside
him, as Set ascended? It is a question, Caine, that I fear you will have
occasion to answer, for it would seem our choice is to be this: haunt or
be haunted, hunt or be hunted.

As I stared, as we—Tumblety and I—stared at each other, he
incanted my name, *Sto-ker, Sto-ker,* though his lips were immobile till
finally his face broke into a smile the likes of which . . . Alas, though I
wanted desperately to look away, I could not, and so it was I saw the
proof of his possession:

The skin of his face went taut as drum skin. Gone were wrinkles
and all signs of wear, of age. And as he smiled wider, the skin of his
left cheek split from the moustache up, just as it had in the Temple,
and the same black, treacly substance seeped forth. The sudden
back-rolling of his eyes to their whites seemed to be for show, for
they rolled back fast to show the eye-fire. *Sto-ker. Sto-ker.* Amidst this
strangeness, I heard Henry ask, "Why doesn't he move on, then,
Stoker? Are you sure I do not know the man, that I am not slighting
someone of import?"

I could not answer. I *wanted* to answer, for to dissemble seemed the
wisest course; but my voice was stopped in my throat. I could do
nothing save sit and stare. And Henry was witness to none of it!
Neither the hellish show happening on Batty Street nor the further
proof of *strangeness* that came when I found upon the back of my hand
a scorpion, two inches long and white as light. As I flinched from it, as
I sought to flick it away, Henry chided me. "Whatever is the matter,
man? You're behaving as odd as our fellow out there on the street."
Now here was a second scorpion clinging to my palm till I succeeded
in shaking it off. Things worsened as I went down onto a knee to
search the filthy floor for the scorpions. They were, of course,
nowhere to be seen. And neither was Tumblety still in the street when

finally Henry pulled me to my feet, asking, "What the devil's gotten into you, Stoker?" What the devil indeed.

"Where . . . ? Where . . . ?"

"The man has moved on, and finally. It takes all types to make a world, Stoker, does it not? . . . Have another? I rather think you should." Already Henry was motioning towards the barman: two fingers raised in a circling gesture.

"Whisky," I whispered. "Whisky, please." And as Henry moved off to see to our drinks, well . . . something there was that drew me to the door of The Red Lion and out onto Batty Street. Once out in the street, I saw no sign of Tumblety, and neither could I hear his intoning my name; but he'd been there! The air was redolent of violets. And on the sidewalk where he'd stood, there was blood. I bent and took it onto my fingertip. Blood, yes, and fresh. Was it his, or had he held a bleeding thing beneath his cloak?

Henry came out to where I stood and asked if I were well. I said I was. "Come now," said he, taking my elbow. "A whisky will do you good."

To this I assented, but as Henry led me back into The Red Lion, I saw something shimmering in the street, taking the lamplight just so. Stretched to a foot in length, furred—I knew on the instant what it was. I sent Henry into the pub, saying that perhaps I was not well after all and implying—hands fast to belly, back hunched—that I might in fact need to spill the contents of my stomach into the street.

Henry half watched with worry through the window, trying to afford me the privacy such sickness begs of a friend. Of course, I was not sick in the street, but rather I bent to the thing seen, spread wide the wings of my coat to conceal what I was doing when I drew my kerchief from my pocket and . . . and prodded the newly cut cat onto its stomach to see that yes, it had lately been slit and eviscerated. I'd no need to prod further to know it lay there absent its heart.

Stok-er, Sto-ker. The call came again, this time dissolving into laughter.

Back in The Red Lion, I downed the waiting whisky and ordered another. I bade adieu to Henry as best I could, hired the first passing hansom, and offered its driver double to deliver me home at speed. Now here I sit, about to sign this letter to you, Caine. In it I have detailed the strangeness of recent days, of recent hours. I shall now fold it, slip it into its envelope, seal and send it to you, retaining sense enough to say, SAVE THIS; for I am ever more certain that we write a Record that ought to be retained, let to stand as our testament—last or not—to the Evil we witness.

S.

LETTER, BRAM STOKER TO HALL CAINE[6]

I am in receipt of your recent letter. Indeed, days have passed since its receipt, days in which I have been at pains to reply, for each time I sit down to do so, I find that my pen stalls and the same question echoes back to me: How, Caine, can you impugn me so?

Can you possibly think that I have not questioned my own sanity of late? You imply that I have not, and further presume to do so for me. This seems hardly the act of a friend, let alone a co-conspirator. Need I remind you of certain letters likely in the *possession* of a certain ~~friend~~ fiend of yours?[7] Need I remind you that prior to your introducing me to Tumblety I was merely unhappy, whilst now I know no words for what I am. You, however, seemingly do: *insane*. Alas, if ever my sanity does leave me, Caine, it was you who showed it the road.

Do you recall a day late in '86 when we were in Edinburgh together? So, too, was Henry there. And we three, on the eve of your wedding vows, on the eve of your extricating yourself from a situation all but untenable—by a plan which was both perfect and mine, might

---

6. This letter is both undated and without salutation, though I think it safe to assume that Stoker sent it sometime after his letter of 14 June 1888, as clearly he takes issue here with Caine's reply to that letter.

7. Uncommonly "cute" of Stoker, this punning.

I add— . . . we three friends, I say, repaired to a tavern in the very shadow of that shadowed city's castle, high atop the Royal Mile, and there drank ourselves down to a state of raw honesty during which you, Caine, confessed to having once peered into a perfectly fine mirror only to find *nothing at all.* Insanity? Did I spill so damning a diagnosis on the table between us? I did not. I would never. Why, then, do you do so now? Why cannot you extend to me the courtesy Speranza has shown? It is *faith in a friend.* It is the same courtesy I extended to you in Edinburgh when you confessed to your very *self* having once disappeared.

In closing I shall say only this: Quit your castle and come to London, and let us see if it is not your name we begin to hear whispered in the streets. Till then, till you stand in this city at my side to see what I see, to hear what I hear, you may call me insane; know, however, that until such time I call you coward.

Yours, formerly,

Ab. Stoker

BRAM STOKER'S JOURNAL

Sunday, 1 July.—It is one month since the Setian event, and two weeks since I wrote so coldly to Caine. (No response.) Two weeks more and the Lyceum shutters, the season ends.

Lately I have been away from the pages, this Record, as blessedly Tumblety has neither shown himself nor spoken my name. (*Q.* If I hear him, is he near?) The watching, the listening, weakens me, though the waiting is worst of all; for he *will* come again: his incanting my name seemed to promise as much. And so I watch the shadows, and fear the silence lest it bear my whispered name as spoken by Tumblety, by Set, by the spawn of that dark marriage I witnessed one month ago.

But I *must* forbear, and will. Two more weeks of *The Merch.* shall see us to season's end, whereupon Henry will *away* to the Mediterranean. So too shall Flo. & Noel go to Dublin for highest summer. And I shall be home alone. Unless of course I leave as well. Shall I leave? Can I stay? Shall I write again to Caine (*Q.:* An apology?) and ask him to come?

Questions, naught but questions; and whilst awaiting answers I busy myself. As I am useful, so, too, shall I remain sane.

Night now, deepest night; but I fear the onset of sleep, I fear my dreams, And waking, I wonder if still I sleep, if still I dream this darkling dream. Worse: When finally I realise I am awake—quick with life, wanted or not—my thoughts hie to poor Penfold. Why? *Why?*

BRAM STOKER'S JOURNAL

14 July, Saturday, 2 a.m.[8]—It is done, another season survived. The Lyceum shall lie dormant a short while, too short a while, I fear; for already all Henry's talk turns to *Macb.,* viz. how goes it w/ Harker's sets? & when are we all to head to E'burgh? & what of beetles' wings to adorn Lady Macb.'s dress? &c. I have promised to wire him at sundry ports of call along the Riviera, for he sails to-morrow from Southampton with Lord & Lady Garner with plans to put in shortly at Nice.

F. & N. safely in Dublin these two days. Speranza stays in town. And news of news: Caine wires that he will come! Soon. He swears it.[9]

Maids away as well. House too quiet. Shall I walk in search of sleep?

Later, nearly 5 a.m.[10]—Fool! Who but a fool would so tempt his greatest fear? For I went to Whitechapel.

There I saw an old friend.[11] As she lives not far from Batty Street, I

---

8. Early morning, then: Sunday 15 July.

9. Whether Stoker wrote his planned apology or one came from Hall Caine, I cannot say: the *Dossier* neither contains nor makes mention of either. Suffice it to say that by mid-July of 1888 the men were once again allies and friends.

10. The journal shows three successive versions of the 5 a.m. entry, each slightly more legible than the last but all three identical in content. These are not drafts; rather, they appear to be the rote work by which Stoker tried to steady his hand and heart.

11. One wonders who. A working woman of Whitechapel?

Daniel Farson, Stoker's grandnephew, held in his 1975 Stoker biography that Stoker sought sexual solace outside his marriage, going so far as to attribute Stoker's slow death—and the weirdness asked if she knew a man fitting Tumblety's description. She looked at me queerly and said she did not; but here the blame is mine, for I struggled to describe the man. Was his hair the black it had been when first I'd seen him, or was it reddened still from the effects of Set? Would his oddly tautened skin make him seem much younger than he was? Would the split skin of his cheek have scarred? And what of that crook-backed stance that made his body seem not his alone? Alas, I fear I made a hash of it all, describing many men in one. So I said no more, only bade her beware.

"Of . . . ?" she asked, whereupon I took my silent leave.

I lingered over-long in Batty Street when I ought to have hurried home. Indeed, I ought never to have gone! Whatever was I up to, walking those fetid, fogged streets, watching, waiting for *it*. And of course it came: *Stoker, Stoker,* faster at first before devolving to the heartbeat of *Sto-ker, Sto-ker,* with a laugh of sorts underlying it all.

Meanwhile, I walked, very nearly *ran,* this way and that; but then . . . nothing. My name came no more, and the laughter lessened to silence, silence broken only by the bells of St. Botolph's, the hooves of horses, the din of those within the pubs, heedless of a demon come amongst them.

Was I searching him out? What might I have done had I turned a corner to see Tumblety step from the fog? Would I have known him? Is he himself at times? If so, can he be spoken to, reasoned with? Can he speak and reason in his turn? Or is he always subject to Set? Far better if he appear the freak he has become; but I fear this is not so, for is not the devil the Great Dissembler? Alas, more questions; and all I know for certain is that while I wandered Whitechapel, the fiend hurried himself here, to my home, such that now this gruesome game is well & truly joined; for:

Upon my stoop, he left a horrid tableau: a calico cat with a mouse in its claws.

---

of his later work—to tertiary syphilis and its symptoms. However, I am inclined to side with the majority of biographers who attribute Stoker's death to the aftereffects of stroke.

Something there was that drove me to scoop up the corpses and hurry into the house. I cannot say if he called to me, *Sto-ker, Sto-ker,* but something there was, of that I am certain. I knew it at the nape of my neck. Was he near? Is he near still? Near and unseen?

Here I sit, listening, waiting. And writing writing *writing* by lantern light. At break of day, I shall scrub the blood from the stoop. And I shall take up a spade and bury these bloodied things in the back yard. Meanwhile, I find I cannot move, will not move, have not moved save to do what finally *I had to do:* finger the split cavities of the creatures—cat & mouse—to confirm what already I knew: They are as heartless as the Batty Street cat, as heartless as he who does these deeds.

BRAM STOKER'S JOURNAL

Wednesday, 18 July, *sun rising.*—Only resolution and habit allow me to make this entry. In truth, only resolution and habit allow me to live. I am so miserable, so low-spirited, so sick of the world and all in it—including life itself—that I would not care if I heard this moment the flapping of the wings of the angel of death.

Resolved: To the Brit. Museum to-day at the earliest hour. Search out Budge and bring to bear upon him the name of Sir William Wilde. None better than Budge to speak to the question of Set, the Scales of Anubis, the Devourer of Hearts, &c. (*Mem.:* Must remember to dissemble, dissemble as the devil does; an *academic* matter, this.)

Speranza reads on re: possession, but little has availed her of late. Still, her Park Street salon—*conversazioni* adjourned at present—is the port in which we weather this strangest of storms; oh, but are we worthy vessels on such a sea of wonders? Metaphor. Have I no weapons but words? Meanwhile, I doubt and I fear and I suffer thoughts I dare not confess to my own soul. Oh, pray may God keep me, if only for the sake of those dear to me!

Resolved: To Euston Station to-day to meet the 1.46 train. Caine comes grudgingly but comes *to-day!*, I having cajoled and cowed him onto the 10.14 a.m. from Liverpool. He wires in advance that he will stay in his own rooms: Albert Mansions, 114 Victoria Street, nr. W'minster Abbey. Mightn't I set them in readiness, the Author asks, as he has let them fall into disuse of late? My wire in reply: *Stoker will see to it;* but sarcasm is lost on Caine. Humour has never been his long suit, and wealth worsens him. Still, I shall see to it, after I find Budge. May even stay w/ Caine if his rooms prove serviceable, as doubtless they will. Oh, but what then of the cemetery No. 17 has lately become, myself its secretive sexton? He has haunted this house! Damn the man, *damn him* though it be redundant!

Resolved: To Park Street to-day w/ Caine. There we three shall finally be one: the Children of Light, says Speranza, indivisible against the Dark. We are to make a plan. Or perhaps we shall all three wake to sanity in strait-waistcoats and take the place of Penfold!

Resolved: To Budge "on business," whence to Albert Mansions, whence to Euston Station, resolute all the while.

BRAM STOKER'S JOURNAL

20 July, Friday, *late.*—Good God, how many other lairs might the fiend have found?

No. Stop. As there was a certain method, a *resolve,* to my late enquiries, so, too, shall I put them down here in sequence; and so:

I was at the British Museum on Wednesday last when it opened. Budge was not to be found—he digs at present; somewhere distant—but from an underling of his in the Office of Antiquities, I borrowed books relevant to the Creation Myths of the Egyptians—Osiris, Isis, and, of course, Set. Budge I will find another time.[12]

Breathe. I breathe, seeking to slow my heartbeat & steady my hand.

It is night as I write. The Night Within the Night. And if latter days

---

12. It seems that no Child of Light succeeded in involving E. A. Wallis Budge in the Tumblety business, as his name soon disappears from the *Dossier.*

have taught me to despair of sleep, *this* recollection, this Record of Wednesday last, *18 July 1888*, will surely render to-night white as well.

It is at present Caine's turn to keep watch, and this he does from the parlour beside the dining room in which I write. Silence surrounds us; a silence that no doubt will cede to the call, *Sto-ker, Sto-ker*, . . . oh, but *when* will it come? This waiting may well be the worst of it!

In truth, Caine suffers more than I, though he hears not the call. Poor Caine: I so fear for his nerves—nerves that might lead to a too-twitchy trigger finger—that I have temporarily deprived him of his pistol. He sits, just there, in the darkened parlour, sunk down beside the sill, spying over it to the yard and street beyond, waiting, waiting and no longer wondering if I am sane; for now Caine, too, has been converted: He believes; for now he, too, has seen. . . .

No. Must, must, *must* write of events *as they passed;* and so:

Caine arrived Wed. a.m., the 18th inst. His train was on time. Mere minutes in one another's company and all was forgiven. Apologies were passed, this way and that. Caine laughed to have called me crazed. I laughed to have called him coward. As Caine was shy to see Speranza, it was well that I'd already brought Budge's books to Park Street and left them with the Betty. Further, and at my friend's request, I wrote to delay our luncheon. Soon enough we Children of Light shall convene in Speranza's salon for a *conversazione* of another type entirely. And then Caine will see that Speranza, though she is free with petty judgements, will not presume anything at all re: the affairs of his past, Tumblety, &c. Moreover: Surely we have progressed past the petty unto the profound, and must turn all our talk toward *a plan,* a plan to stop Tumblety on our own whilst keeping clear of the Yard. ("No authorities," I reassure Caine; though now I wonder if he won't come to ruin anyway, such is his present state.)

We—Caine and I—took a pint for strength near Euston Station. The sky was cloudless and high, and the sun scoured the streets of all shadows. And though the day itself did not conduce towards fear, still Caine and I, as if by common instinct, went to a deep and dark corner of the chosen pub, sitting far from the street-side windows. Our beers we lifted in a wordless toast, to friendship, to forgiveness, and to a fast resolution of this fiendishness. Food was ordered. Caine commented upon my absence of appetite, and I realised he was right: I have not eaten much of late, but my burliness bears it well. Were I to try to set something upon my stomach, I fear I would find the food passed back—this, no doubt, is owing to all I've seen of late, all I see still; and to this horrid show of things *seen* must now be added the odour of Tumblety's having come again.

Stay. I speed, and ought not to. Breathe, breathe, *breathe*.

Luncheon ended, and by hansom we hied to Victoria Street, to Albert Mansions, to Hall Caine's London rooms; to which I'd never been and had not gone earlier, their airing-out having come to seem quite secondary.

Caine had forgotten his key, but the landlady—cheered to find the famed Author returned to his rooms after a long absence—happily handed him another; whereupon we two climbed to Caine's chambers. Arrived upon the second-storey landing, I paused to compliment Caine on this arrangement: rooms, *private* rooms of his own in which to write. My envy—of which I said naught, naught at all; for had we not tacitly toasted to friendship a half-hour earlier?—was short-lived indeed; for as we stood upon the landing, Caine fumbling with his key, I caught that scent, the violet scent that tells of Tumblety's violation by Set. And there was a second scent besides: a ferric tang, redolent of rust and newly-turned earth. That also was a scent I'd caught too often of late: blood.

I took the key from Caine and bade him stand aside. I opened the door. I entered. It was dark within the suite and horribly close, and whilst I walked with care to draw the drapes and throw high the sash, I felt my shoes alternately stick and slip upon the bare wood floor. And at first, having discovered the drawn drapes to be of crimson hue, I, turning, assumed that the round table sitting center-all was covered in a similar fabric; but wouldn't a tablecloth drape the table and hang evenly from its edge? No tablecloth, this.

By the circle of coagulant shimmering on the hardwood floor beneath it, I knew the redness atop the table to be blood, blood that had run to both cover the table's surface and drip from its side to fall upon the floor. The sudden intake of air from Caine confirmed it; for he had followed me into the blood-redolent rooms to see what already I have described.

Fear the first: *Was the fiend still here?*

Caine drew from his pocket his pearl-handled pistol. With a wavering hand, he pointed it this way and that, finally training it so long upon my still-shadowed self that I, in short order, took it from him, set him down, locked the door against any comers—i.e., a too-solicitous landlady coming to see if Caine had all he needed—and only then, having lit a lamp against the last of the shadows, only then did I set about searching the suite for Tumblety.

As I'd supposed, he was not there; oh, but he had been of late, for he had made a secret shambles of the Albert Mansions.

I lit candles not for illumination but against the stench, and by their flickering light I returned to see Caine no longer sitting but standing now, and shivering as if from cold.

"What is it, Tommy?"

"Leave. Can . . . can we not just leave, Bram? Please?"

"Do you suppose—" I began.

And indeed Caine *had* supposed something, for like a child's overwound toy he sprang now toward the door. With fingers both fumbling and fast, he'd undone two of the door's three locks before I could calm him. "Now, now," said I, setting my hands heavily upon his low shoulders, "think well, Caine: Do you suppose Mary may have . . . ?"

"Have *what?* Come here to bathe in blood? Opened a surgery on the side? . . . And what's more, Bram: Mary knows nothing of these rooms."

"You, Caine," I ventured, ". . . are *you* certain there can be no other explanation for— perhaps—"

"Oh, Bram," interrupted Caine, "two plus two is very often four, don't you find?" He returned to working the last of the locks and said again, or rather pled, "Can we not just leave, *please?*"

"Leave this scene for the landlady to discover?"

"The police, then. Let us leave it all to the police!"

"To whom we will report what, exactly? That your city rooms—rooms, might I add, kept private from your wife—have lately been the scene of inexplicable slaughter, or bloodletting at best, then tip our hats and say 'G'day'? Or should we simply hand them Tumblety's letters and save the man the bother of arranging your ruin? . . . No, Caine, we cannot just leave. Neither can we summon the police. We must—"

"Surely you don't mean to suggest that *we*—"

I interrupted, meaning only to say that the rooms were ours to scour and range, like it or no; but now I heard myself speaking rather more summarily, as it seemed Caine hadn't heard, truly *heard,* what I'd said. "Have we not agreed, Caine, that circumstances"—by which I tacitly referred to a secret society whose membership comprised the leading lights of London life, as well as certain indiscreet and potentially ruinous letters to which a witless Caine had signed his name, *and* the visions I have seen, *and* the sounds I have heard, *and* the animals putrefying at present in my own back yard, &c.—". . . have we not agreed that circumstances as they stand preclude our confiding in the police?"

Caine let my logic lie. Said he, "Very well. But all that blood! My own runs cold at the sight of it, the *stench* of it. Oh Bram, oh Bram . . ." I worried that Caine might faint, but greater was my wonder at how Tumblety had accessed his suite.

The Tumblety I saw in Batty Street, his person twisted and his face drum-tight, is unlikely to have sidled past the concierge without raising her suspicions. And so I can only conclude that he *is* able to dissemble and does not always show the influence of Set. He can pass as *un*possessed. He can win people to his ways. If this be true, the danger he poses is redoubled. And what mightn't he accomplish now, with his magic, with his blue-black invisibility, with his money and the meanest of motives, all the while in league with the Adversary, Set? How many hearts mightn't they harvest?

When finally I took my first step towards the far side of the room, my soles sucked harder at the hardwood floor; for the blood had congealed. Which meant, did it not, that when first I'd stepped in it, nearer the table, it had been fresher? Had Tumblety only lately absented the suite, the shambles? Had he left us this fresh ... evidence, knowing we were coming? If so, he was watching. He was near. I said none of this to Caine, of course.

The table. Six feet round and hewn of solid mahogany. Its top was slick with blood, blood which dripped onto a carpet showing a blue design through the ruddier shades of stain. Nearer now, I could discern bits of viscera in the blood, and the wood of the tabletop had been nicked by knives. These observations I made aloud to Caine, but my poor Watson had all he could do to keep hold of consciousness, though it was he who then asked, "What the devil?" while pointing to a black bag that sat beneath the table.

What the devil? indeed.

"Thornley," I said, squatting to better see the bag.

Through the kerchief clasped to his mouth—against the blood only, for I doubted he caught that heady perfume of possession—Caine queried, "Your brother, Thornley? ... What are you saying, Bram?"

"Thornley has just such a bag. It is—if I am not mistaken—a doctor's kit, a sort of travelling surgery."

I nudged the bag into the light with the tip of my boot. I then bent, prised wide its opening, and proceeded to draw from it knives of every type.[13] The knives—from cleavers to the finer blades used for filleting—bore blood both dried and fresh. And there were shears and small saws utile to the disseverance of bones: post-mortem appliances.

"Whatever does he do with all these ... tools?" In truth, I cannot recall, and so cannot here record, which of us spoke that question, but I can say that neither of us responded; for the answer was borne on the blood, as it were. And it was then, as I stood contemplating same, that I heard him:

Sto-ker, Sto-ker ...

"Caine!" said I, startling my companion, who kept his kerchief

13. Lest he accuse Stoker of destroying valuable evidence, to-day's reader is reminded that finger-printing played no part in the detection of crimes in England prior to 1901—a development, by the way, owing much to the advocacy of Sir Francis Galton, a half-cousin of Charles Darwin.

clasped to his mouth with one hand whilst holding the other over his heart, as if to guard against its extraction. "Caine, can you hear that?"

"Hear what?"

"Listen," I said, for still the name, *my* name came. Nearer? Louder? "Oh, can you not *hear* that, Caine?"

He swore he could not. I dared not explain what it was *I* heard, lest Caine panic. But neither would we wait to see if my name, so spoken, betokened the coming, nay *the return,* of Tumblety to the Albert Mansions.

"Let us go," I said. *"Now."*

Caine, though eager to do as directed, to finally take his leave, to relinquish his rooms for once and for ever, questioned me. *Why now? What do you hear? You say you smell something?* &c.; but these and further questions I forestalled by saying:-

"Go! Tell the landlady you will return in a few days' time. Meanwhile, she mustn't disturb your rooms *at all*—speak clearly on this point, Caine. But do tell her to alert you at once—by messenger sent to St. Leonard's Terrace—if anyone else comes to these rooms, day or night."

"Should I ask her who, if anyone, has already been here?"

"We know who has been here, Caine; we know it all too well. And I've reason to believe that your landlady has not seen him." *. . . that they may neither see me nor understand.*

"But oughtn't she be made to account for all the keys, Bram? Surely Tumblety has somehow secured a key, for how else might he have . . . ?"

"The fact of his having been here is already that, *a fact;* and I fear that the few answers we may have from the landlady are not worth the risk of rendering her suspicious. Remember, Caine: We must safeguard this site. It is yours, after all." Lest he miss my meaning, I added, "These are the private rooms of Thomas Henry Hall Caine." And "Scandal" was the first of the words alluded to. "Ruin" the second.

"What's more," said I, "it seems Tumblety hasn't need of keys to come and go as he pleases." To Caine's raised brows, I replied, "I cannot explain, not now; but suffice it to say that, keyless, he nonetheless has had the run of the Lyceum. And may still." This notion heartened me not at all; for the shuttered Lyceum would seem a suitable lair, now that we'd discovered and deprived him of the one at Albert Mansions. No-one would look for him there, not now, leastways not Inspector Abberline. This he must know; for he is clever: well he knew that word of his return to London would keep Caine at his castle, thereby freeing his bachelor's suite for Tumblety's use. But had he learned of the rooms by natural or super-natural means, and if the latter . . . ? I was wondering thus when I heard him again:-

Sto-ker, Sto-ker.

"What is it, Bram?"

"Come," said I, "let us lock the door and leave." This we did. I had with me Tumblety's black bag: his tools of butchery. I had no idea what I would do with them, but as I knew what *he* would do with them, I bethought myself to deprive him of his blades and thus render his red work more difficult.

We were in a hansom, fully halfway home, when I realised that Caine was speaking to me. I had been so intent on hearing, or blessedly *not* hearing my name so intoned, that I had not heard Caine speak. I apologised.

"I was simply saying that I shall abandon that suite at once and take rooms elsewhere in—"

"You shall do nothing of the sort," said I.

"Begging your pardon, Bram, but if I mean to—"

"Those rooms must remain in your name some while longer, I'm afraid." I stared at Caine, waiting for him to take in my meaning.

"I suppose they are not, at present, ready to be re-let."

"Indeed not."

"And I suppose, too, that we ought to play our cards close to the vest till this infernal business be at an end—no sudden changes, I mean to say. . . . But what of the suite, Bram? If we cannot turn it over to the police, neither can we leave it as it is. And *I* will not, cannot return there—"

"No, no," said I, "not us; but someone must right the place before eyes other than ours see it and suspicions regarding its present state fall on you, as doubtless they would do."

"Yes, yes, of course. What's wanted is a charwoman type, a maid-of-all-work who—"

"No maid can suppose *that* is what's meant by 'all-work.' . . . What's wanted, what's needed, is a woman at once discreet and desperate."

"But who, Bram, *who?* The clean-up must commence at once. You scare me with your talk of my being seen as complicit in, in . . ."

"Fear not," said I. "I know just the woman." And I did. Rather, I do. "But tell me, Caine: Have you cash at hand?"

"I do indeed. And as concerns this matter, Bram, you may consider the store limitless."

"Fine," said I. "To-morrow we shall hire our woman."

To-morrow did, of course, eventuate into yesterday, *Thurs., 19 July;* and so I can record that we went with Caine's cash to search out and secure the services of Mrs. Lydia Quibbel, the Lyceum's recently let-go Tender of the Tenders of Cats. But first:

We returned to St. Leonard's Terrace from the Albert Mansions. I was grateful—and grateful I remain—that Florence & Noel have gone to stay some weeks with Thornley in Dublin. There they shall be safe, surely; but what's more: No words could have convinced anyone who knows him that Caine was well. He is *not* well, and I wonder if he won't do himself to death with his worrying. Indeed, sedation came to seem in order as Caine peppered our Wednesday-night converse with such questions as, "What if someone *had* gone into those rooms in my absence and seen . . . ?" and such exclamatory comments as, "Bram, what fools we were! We ought to have looked for the letters!"

Said I, with assuagement, upon the latter point, "It is doubtful, don't you think, that Tumblety would stash the letters in the rooms of the very man who'd most like to see them destroyed? And let me remind you further, Caine: We have had *no* indication from Tumblety that he means to blackmail you." Though true, this was a statement neither of us believed. "And as his . . . his *work* in that suite was recently done, the risk you have run of discovery has been minimal." I did not add that the risk had increased of late, for nothing piques the interest of a landlady more than the admonishment that she keep clear of a locked door; and before Caine could arrive at the same conclusion, I suggested:-

"Brandy?"

"Oh, yes, please," said Caine, and we sat a long while with the bottle between us, sipping, then swilling, and finally progressing unto whisky as I told Caine all I knew of the Osirian myths, of Set, some of it gleaned from my own readings and some of it lately learned from Speranza. And all the while, Tumblety may have been . . . Alas, it never dawned on me that Tumblety, having had *his* den disturbed, would seek to disturb ours in turn; and I cannot account for having forgotten those carnal calling cards he had left of late, yet I did. Doubtless I *wanted* to. And I'd even opened the parlour window, so that Tumblety may well have been there in the bordering bushes, listening as I held forth to Caine on all things Setian; for *he was there* sometime prior to dawn. Of this we'd soon have proof.

As I myself have had resort to laudanum of late, I knew I had enough in store to offer some to Caine later that evening. He accepted with alacrity, whereupon we both rose to retire to our rooms, carafes in hand.[14]

Amazingly, I slept a short while. More amazingly, when I woke, my first thought was not of Mr. Penfold but rather of the open parlour window: Florence would have had my head for having left it so, for having exposed the furnishings to the dirt and dust of a London night, a London dawn. Indeed, it was dawn when I woke, the habit having been established of late: best I find any carcasses left lying about before they be espied by the neighbours, the early-coming carters of coal, or the blue-smocked butchers' boys working the Terrace. Only then did I realise I'd left the window open to more than dirt: I'd left it open to a demon.

Down the stairs I flew in naught but my nightshirt.

Shutting the open window, I progressed sill to sill: nothing, no death

---

14. Laudanum: a hydro-alcoholic solution containing either 1% morphine or 10% opium. Its being widely available and commonly used to calm the nerves, bedside carafes of the stuff were common then.

left for my discovery. So it was that with hopes of a bloodless Thursday I went into the scullery to do the minimum of what the maids usually do. (*Mem.:* Send word to Ada and Mary that they are free to stay away *as long as they like,* with pay. Speak to Caine on the latter point.) Already I'd put off those costers who come to the door daily, telling them that as both the missus and the maids were away, 'twas Bachelor's Ways for me till further notice, &c., and just as I thought, *No need to listen for the door,* I realised I had not checked the front stoop. It was then the day went luckless; for:

Spread diagonally and stretched to its full length, there lay the flayed carcass of a large dog. Naught but the head had been left intact: the rest was skinless and raw, *horrid.* Its cavity had been opened towards the door, towards where I stood barefoot on the threshold. One step more and I'd have slid in its viscera, ranged in a red-show upon the stoop. So large was the canine, the carcass—here was a hound many sizes larger than the two he'd tried to dispose of at the Beefsteak Club— . . . so large was the carcass and so *artful* its arrangement, I could see clearly where the heart had lately lain. As I stared at that absence, there came from the cavity, crawling forth over the entrails, first one, then a second scorpion, white as the still-dawning light. And just as the scent of violets rose to my nose, I heard behind me that sudden intake of breath that presages a scream.

I turned round to find Caine standing there in his nightclothes. Fortunately, he was able to forestall the scream; and indeed here was Caine converted to a Man of Action: He backed into the house horrified but returned quickly with that sheet Mary uses to cover the couch when the coal is delivered. (*Mem.:* Replace this before F.'s return).

We buried the hound in its now-bloody shroud in a hole that took us nearly an hour to dig. In the course of doing same—as stealthily as daylight allowed—I spoke of the scorpions and the violets only to discover that indeed Caine had neither seen the former nor smelt the latter. I heartened somewhat at being believed, but nothing more was said on the subject. I refilled the hole and concealed it as best I could with squares of cut sod whilst Caine set to upon the stoop with bucket & brush.

We were to meet up over the scullery sink, there to cleanse ourselves of our respective filth—soil in my case, blood in his; but the look
upon Caine's face when he came to join me made me fear he'd been
found at his work. The truth was worse: He had discovered something
half-stuffed in the letterbox. A scroll of sorts. He'd not dared to read it.
Wordlessly, with red and trembling fingers, he handed it over to me.

The paper was parchment-like. The words were written in what
surely was blood.[15] And as I unfurled the scroll to its full length and
weighted it down upon the chopping block, my eye fell to its signatures,
plural; for there were two.

The first, I knew, was Francis Tumblety's. To this, Caine attested as
well; although, said he, "It shows a feebleness new to me."

"Not feebleness, I fear, but rather its opposite: a strength he cannot
yet control." A super-natural strength attributable to his possessor.

"Whatever is that?" Caine pointed to pictures sitting left of Tumblety's signature. These were more steadily written, or rather drawn,
and I knew of an instant what they were; for I'd found the same strand
in a book borrowed from Budge. I explained to Caine that here was Set's
hieroglyphic signature:

"Good God!" exclaimed Caine.

"No," said I, "... not a *good* god at all."

Caine, standing at my side, struggled to read aloud the note's scribbled, stilted English, which I here transcribe as accurately as I am able,
underlining those words written in the hand of Francis Tumblety so as
to distinguish them from that secondary, stronger-seeming hand that
showed the influence of Set:

15. On the original—contained in the *Dossier*—someone, presumably Stoker, has traced over the
blood letters in ink.

"My heart, my mother; my heart, my mother! My heart, my being! May naught oppose me at Judgement and may there be no opposition to me Returning now to the Presence of the Chiefs who caused my Name to reek, and may there be no second condemnation of Set by He Who Keepeth the Balance! Heed me, Thou in Whom dwelleth my *ka* and *khaibit*! [16]

"I heed You, mighty Set. I heed He who strengthens my limbs. May You come forth through me. May You use me. May You Rise and be Redeemed!

"And may thou hearken to and heed the coming Judgement so that thou may spread word of He Who Hath Been Wronged. Thou will sayeth that the heart of Set hath been weighed anew and that His Heart-soul hath borne testimony on His behalf and that He hath been Redeemed upon the Great Balance. Thou will sayeth that there hath not been found Wickedness in Him and that He hath not committed any Evil act and that He hath not set His mouth in motion with Words of Evil. This they say Set did whilst He walked the earth. And so the Scales of Truth fell against Him!

"You were adjudged wrong, mighty Set.

"Heed well the Weighing in the Balance of the harvested hearts of Set!

"I will pay heed. I will harvest the hearts.

"Onto the Balance shall go the worthless hearts to show as false the Feather of Maat and to show the Truth of Set! Set shall be Rightly Judged against these hearts and Set shall Rise and be the Beloved Lord of the Two Lands. He shall sit amongst the Favored Ones.

"So shall it come to pass, mighty Set.

"How great Set shall be when He Rises!

"Great the mighty Set! Rise the mighty Set!

"Let no man bear testimony against Set in the presence of the Keeper of the Balance! He who speaketh against Set shall have his heart devoured by Am-mit and have his Heart-soul bound in fetters in the

---

16. *Kha* (astral body) and *khaibit* (shadow); see *The Second Epoch*, note 42.

Boat of Millions for all Time, for Set is Time and Set is greater than all gods. So Set decrees.

"I am Am-mit. I harvest and devour hearts at Your bidding. I shall rip the hinderers even if their hearts be worthy. I shall rip them as You command it.

"So commandeth Set."

Only as I let the scroll fall back onto the scullery table did I realise I'd taken it up. Caine and I watched as it curled unto itself like . . . like a scorpion's tail. Indeed, we stood there some while before Caine quoted from the scroll, so:-

"'I shall rip the hinderers. . . .' Am I right in reading that as a threat, Bram? To us: the hinderers?"

Caine wanted me to say he was wrong. This I could not do.

"And if we are worthy, who then might the worthless be? . . . I don't suppose he means literary critics."

"No," said I, heartened by the humour—as rare as it was ill-timed—for it assured me of Caine's sanity and set my fears of his nervous collapse at a remove, albeit a *slight* remove. "We cannot know who the worthless may be, not yet; but I recall to you the fact that I saw Tumblety in Batty Street, and have heard him elsewhere in Whitechapel . . . and is not Whitechapel chockablock with those the world deems worthless?"

"Oh, my," said Caine; who then swallowed hard before saying, summarily, "This work he sets about is not done. This scroll is prophecy. Prophecy and threat. Prophesying that some poor 'worthless' sot is soon to fall victim to Tumblety's mistaking metaphor for . . . for murder! And threatening we hinderers besides!" With a gesture towards the yard's freshest grave and a look down at his unwashed hands, Caine concluded, "This dog was slain to warn us."

"Secondarily so, I would suppose," said I. "Primarily, I fear, it was but further practice for Tumblety as Am-mit, the harvester, the Devourer of Hearts. After all, the poor hound's heart was ripped from it. . . . Mouse to cat to hound to—"

"*Homo sapiens?* Good God, Bram! A progression through the species, do you mean to say?" Whereupon no further words were wanted, and so we set to scrubbing at the sink, each of us silent and staring as the dirt and blood swirled darkly down the drain.

I needn't record that we weren't much in the mood to breakfast yesterday after . . . *all that*; but neither did we wish to stay in a house so lately violated. Thus it was that we dressed fast and betook ourselves some blocks away to The Hare and Harp, where we perused the morning papers, rather desultorily, it must be said, as already we'd had news enough from the shadow world; but then, finally, our tea having gone cold, our toast having hardened, we both of us struck upon the same plan—this business about the blood and an amenable maid—and thereby brightened a bit.

I drew from a pocket paper & pencil and began a letter addressed to Mrs. Lydia Quibbel, lately the Lyceum's Tender of the Tenders of Cats; meanwhile, I confessed to Caine my guilt at having had to let the lady go:-

"I was quite vexed at having to sack her," said I, truthfully. "I rather liked the woman, and what's more: She'd proved herself most useful to me at the Lyceum, watching for Tumblety as a hare watches for hawks: a service I secured, mind, with withdrawals from the Lyceum's petty cash."

"Well," said Caine, "if a bit more of my cash puts her back in your employ, I shall consider it money well spent, well spent indeed."

I had earlier secured from a cat tender Mrs. Quibbel's approximate address: King George's Street, Great Walworth; and in a note addressed to that place, I put forth the following particulars of our proposal while offering to pay in direct proportion to "the unpleasantness of it all":

1. She would go to 114 Victoria Street, the Albert Mansions.
2. She would do so at night, alone, taking care not to be seen.
3. She would climb to the rooms whose bell bore the mark *HHC* and use the enclosed key.

And, 4. She would brace herself for what she'd see—". . . an accident involving a most unfortunate patient of a surgeon-friend of mine . . ."—

and set about ranging the rooms, scrubbing the blood, &c. Again, proper recompense was promised.

I closed, stating that she would need to see to this soon. Of course, I made it clear she could decline and simply return the key by the next post; but should she accept the charge, she had only to send a trusted boy round to St. Leonard's Terrace, No. 17, with said key and word of the job being done, whereupon I'd hand over her reward.

We left The Hare and Harp to post our note; and, events being what they were, or rather are—which is to say: *urgent*—I determined that Speranza could sleep-in some other day, some soon-coming day when we were no longer beset by an ages-old demon and his Devourer of Hearts. Likewise, Caine could steel himself to her company *now*, if you please. And so: Towards Grosvenor Square we went. It was scarcely 2 p.m. when we arrived, so early by the standards of 116 Park Street that still the Betty slept; but both maid and mistress woke to my insistent pounding.

"Messieurs Stoker and Caine," said Speranza, settling herself amidst pillows as puffy as her eyes, "I trust you have good reason for barging into my boudoir in the middle of the . . . day."

"Yes, Speranza," said I, "we have *very* good reasons for coming round at the very private hour of"—I drew forth my watch to read it, showily—"quarter-past two."

Speranza gasped. "It is even worse than I thought! I shall simply have to avenge myself by someday sending a knocking someone round to *your* homes in the middle of *your* night."

"Send a sharpshooter, Speranza," said I, "if it's our sleep you mean to target."

"Indeed. You both look ghastly. Sit yourselves somewhere, gentlemen, before you fall, but do *not* draw those shades! . . . I simply deplore daylight. It is too vulgar, too vulgar by far."

Speranza knew I respected her, and therefore her habits, such as they were: I'd never have disturbed her sleep without very good reason indeed, nor brought a relative stranger into her private rooms, as now I had. For his part, Caine's *dis*-ease was evident: he sat like a truant dragged before the headmistress whilst Speranza, with a nod of her still-bonneted head, said, as salutation:-

"Mr. Hall Caine, sir. . . . News of your great success precedes you here, such that I must say I am happy we are not yet friends, for when my friends succeed, it saddens me. Indeed, something within me dies. I cannot help it. The success of strangers, however, heartens me, and so it is I am able to say to you, sir, in the French fashion: *Félicitations!*"

Caine was flummoxed. "Why, . . . why, thank you, Lady Wilde."

"And though we may not *yet* be friends, Mr. Caine—'tis but a matter of minutes, I suppose—still, you have seen me, now, in this relative state of undress; and, what's more, our Mr. Stoker has us hunting demons *ensemble;* so I really must insist that you call me Speranza."

"Thank you . . . Speranza."

Soon the bleary-eyed Betty had brought a terrible tea. The pudding looked as though it had been dug up from the garden: it had a fungal aspect to it and sat untouched for the length of our stay. And Speranza had neither thanked nor dismissed her maid before the latter slammed the bedroom door and descended, stomping like a Prussian on patrol. Unfortunately, this show prompted Caine to ask:-

"Speranza? Indelicate, this; . . . but can your maid be trusted?"

"*Certainly* not," said the lady, feigning offence. "Who, Mr. Caine, wants a trustworthy maid? Where is the fun in that?"

I said to a confused Caine that he could surrender his fears of Speranza's maid meddling in our affairs. This Speranza seconded, saying, "'Tis true, Mr. Caine. My maid's deafness is surpassed only by her disinterest.

"But you, sir; let us speak about you and your most *enviable* position."

Caine began to demur, but Speranza corrected him. "No, no, I refer neither to your *inky* triumphs nor the monies thusly derived—money is a topic best left to merchants, sir, not *artistes* such as we are; rather my envy stems from Mr. Stoker's telling me you are on the verge of involvement in *un vrai scandale!*"

Whilst Caine blanched, I, trying to leaven things, laughingly said, "And Lady Wilde knows whereof she speaks!"

"Indeed I do," said Speranza. "We Wildes were the stars of many a scandal back in our Dublin days. And though scandals are not always pleasant to endure, Mr. Caine, they are *won-der-ful* to survive."

"I shall be happy to take your word for it," said Caine, coldly, "as I hope neither to endure nor survive any scandals featuring myself. I trust you take my meaning, Lady Wilde?"

Indeed she had; and by the slowness with which she removed her bonnet and tidied her coiffure, Speranza conveyed to Caine that he had spoken out of turn. "Do you suppose I mean to threaten you, Mr. Caine? Or is it that you keep your humour locked in your castle's keep? . . . Your mien, sir, is suddenly that of a cat in a corner."

This was not good, not good at all. "Now, now," said I, "it has been agreed amongst all parties present that our secrets, *all* our secrets, shall be held in trust. Perhaps it would be best if such vows were made aloud, now that we are in company? Caine?"

"Assuredly. And I would ask that discretion be used as regards the *in*discretions of my youth. Further, I hold that we would be unwise to solicit the belief of anyone save those present—here, now—of things *un*believable. What can come of it but the Queen's offer of room and board in Bedlam?"

"Indeed. Speranza?"

"Mr. Caine, forgive me. I did not mean to make light of your situation, which is a most regrettable one. This I understand. It is simply that I hold to a long-standing preference for being spoken *of,* period, no matter the words applied. You may one day understand, sir, if ever the world ceases to utter *your* name." Caine nodded to the lady, who added kindly, "Though surely the world will continue to speak the name of Caine for quite some time to come."

"So, too, Wilde," rejoined he. "Your Oscar's genius is spoken of in the streets."

Poor Caine. I can only wonder as to the scribbled state of his first draughts; for this, too, had come out all *wrong,* and again it fell to me to intercede:-

"Friends," said I, "we've much to discuss, and a plan to formulate. Shall we, then?"

And so we did; though our discussion was more akin to reportage, each of us speaking in turn. Caine confided in Speranza re: his history with Tumblety. This I thought rather brave of him, and so, too, did she. Speranza then spoke—and simply as well—of what she'd learned of possession from her Roman friend, which already we knew, then added to the topic what little she'd learned from Budge's books. For my part, I apprised Speranza of late events. And by the time Caine and I testified together re: what we'd found in the Albert Mansions and afterwards at No. 17 . . . well, suffice it to say the tenor of our talk had changed.

"Are you in danger, Bram?" asked Speranza as she sat bolt upright in bed, spilling her tea only to blot it, absently, with sundry pages of manuscript. "Tell me true."

"I may be," said I.

"Then so, too, are you, Mr. Caine; and I refer to more than just those delicate letters of yours coming to light."

"But you, Speranza, have nothing to fear. The fiend can know nothing of your involvement."

"Your talk, my dear Mr. Stoker, is hollow, and I rather fear you patronise me with it. We cannot presume to know what this Tumblety knows. We cannot even presume what he *is,* or has lately become. And these calls you hear, these carcasses you find on your property, the sudden ease with which the man appears and disappears, well . . . No. Do not suppose for a moment, Bram, that our adversary does not know all, *all* who stand against him." Speranza was right, of course, and I shuddered to think of having put her in harm's way.

"Oh, Speranza, forgive me. I did not know—"

"I understand, Bram: You did not know the man when you brought him here. However, you, Mr. Caine, did; and that is a matter with which you alone must reckon."

"What ... what can I do *now*?" This from Caine; who, seemingly in-spired, then added, "We could all three head to Greeba! We'd be safe in the castle."

"Thank you, Mr. Caine," said Speranza. "And though typically I ac-cept all invitations to castles upon principle, I am not sure we can be assured of our safety anywhere at present. Moreover, if we were to hide, we'd be hiding only ourselves."

"Why, yes, of course," said Caine. "Who else *would* we hide?"

I picked up Speranza's point. "If we were to secrete ourselves away, Caine, what then would become of the unsuspecting? Of 'the worthless'?"

"Good God Almighty," said Caine, falling back heavily in his chair, "what have I loosed on London? ... You were right, Bram: I *am* a coward."

"Nonsense, Mr. Caine, if you were a coward, you would not be here now. It may even be argued that you are the bravest amongst us, as it is you who stand to lose something more than ... life; for those who hold that the reputation of a dead man never changes are, I fear, quite wrong."

"I ... I ... " began Caine, but he finished with a most plaintive moan.

"Self-recrimination," said Speranza, "is like a rocking chair, Mr. Caine: it is something to do, yes, but it will get you nowhere. What's wanted here is a plan."

"Indeed," said I. And so it was that we set about formulating one. By dawn of this day—Friday—we were able to refer to it as fixed. Unfor-tunately, after all our talk, talk this way and that, said plan is comprised of little more than:

Watch and wait.

And that is what we do at present, as Friday cedes to Saturday. Caine keeps watch at the window, and we all three wait, we two here, Speranza behind her bolted door. Though I worry about Speranza, it is Caine who needs taking care of. Indeed, as we sat trying to sup some hours ago, my bell was rung and poor Caine nearly slipped his skin. But it was only

Mrs. Quibbel's hired boy come round to deliver word of her success. This he did by holding out Caine's key and saying the one, well-rehearsed line the lady had charged him with:-

"Mrs. Q.," said he, backing from my door even as he spoke, "swears that if you forget her, she'll forget you."

I nodded my understanding, and before I could draw forth a coin the boy was off and running towards the river.

So yes, we watch and we wait. And I write, *have written*, rather; for now I close to take up position in the darkened parlour, at the watcher's post.

BRAM STOKER'S JOURNAL

Saturday, 21 July.—Neither of us saw him, though one of us watched the yard *all night long*. (*Q.:* Does he—Tumblety, if not Set—want us to pursue him?) This vigil is killing Caine. He does not know how long he can stay in the city. If I call him coward now, he will be crushed. So, too, would I be if he called me crazed. But so we are, both of us: cowardly and crazed! Who would not be, amidst such strangeness as this?

Meanwhile, we watch. Meanwhile, we wait. Pray may we never have occasion to say we waited too long.

BRAM STOKER'S JOURNAL

Wed., 25 July.—Caine still here, though his bag sits packed at his bed's end.

TELEGRAM, BRAM STOKER TO LADY JANE WILDE

Th., 26 July 1888.—Receive us to-day at 3.00. New plan needed— Plan of Action.

Bram

BRAM STOKER'S JOURNAL

Fri., 27 July.—Having risen at dawn—the effect of the laudanum lessens, and, unlike Caine, I dare not up my dosage—I cased the property for carcasses; finding none, now I sit to write my way into another day. I must be exact, must seek the sanity orderliness can confer; and so, in summary:

Ada & Mary stay contentedly away, Caine paying their wages.

Henry still at sea. Have wired him: *All is well & correspondence quiet; Harker proceeding apace,* &c.

Florence & Noel in Dublin, where they shall *safely* stay some while longer.

Have sent a tentative invite to Thornley: We may need to speak, as & where it suits him—London? Dublin?

. . . Have breakfasted now: a bit of eggs & hash. Pray may it stay on my stomach and settle me sufficiently to recount yesterday's conference w/ Speranza; so:

We walked to the Wilde house in silence so I could listen: no calls came; and Caine heard my report with due relief. (*Q.:* Is this silence a good or bad sign? We cannot know.) Rounding onto Park Street, we encountered Oscar on the sidewalk before No. 116. Or nearly did. I espied him stepping down onto the sidewalk and heading in the direction opposite to ours. As he was yet within hailing distance, I sped my step, raised my hand, and readied to call out to him, only to be arrested by Caine.

"*Hsst!*" It was that or a comparable sound that came from my companion. "Is that not Wilde? I'd know him anywhere—that body of his seems built of boiled potatoes."

Rather unkind, this, but so be it. Said I, "I'd have thought it was the green velvet suit and top-curls that betrayed him."

"Curly hair to match the curly teeth," sneered Caine. "And that suit of his is absurd!" This from a man in his Knickerbocker tweeds of an orange hue.

"What reason have you, Caine, to cut the man so?"

"I've no interest in keeping the company of a metropolitan sodomite the likes of Oscar Wilde," huffed he.

Indeed? Well, this was too much. And so I said—in my best barrister's voice, meant to allude to the Laws of the Land—"Might I remind the honourable Mr. Thomas Henry Hall Caine that he himself was once a 'metropolitan sodomite'?"

Caine coiled; but he soon thought better of it, un-balled his small fist, and said, simply, "Stoker! How dare you?"

"No, Caine," said I, "how dare *you* malign a man you know not at all, and he the son of my, nay *our,* devoted friend?"

"Well . . ." stammered a contrite Caine, "one hears rumours red enough to rouge the ears, that's all."

"And with the release of certain letters, friend, similar rumours regarding *you* will quickly turn to truths."

"That's quite enough, Bram, *quite* enough." And so it was, for we'd each made our respective points: mine being that Caine had spoken cruelly, his being that Wilde scared him; for whether Caine knows it or not, that is the truth: Wilde simply scares him.

By now we'd lost our chance of encountering Wilde in the wild, as it were; for he'd disappeared down the street, walking briskly and seeming to recite from pages he held in his hand: a play script, no doubt; for Speranza tells me Oscar fancies he'll try his hand at theatre now, and asks would I be so kind as to read the results?[17]

If Caine was chagrined by his show of contempt for Wilde, the feeling must have deepened as we entered Speranza's salon to find her all but illuminate from the filial visit. "Did you not see As-car? If you missed him, it was by minutes, merely; for he—"

I interrupted, cursing our ill luck at having missed the man.

"Oh, well," said she, settling back into her seat, "perhaps another

---

17. Wilde would not only try theatre, he would revolutionize it. By the time of his later fall—his conviction, in 1895, on charges of gross indecency—he would be supreme in the London theatre, *An Ideal Husband* and *The Importance of Being Earnest* running concurrently. Whether Stoker read any of Wilde's plays prior to their performance is unknown, but none were ever produced at the Lyceum Theatre.

time. Though of course poor As-car is *mortally* busy, doing this, that, and the other thing, here, there, and elsewhere. To you, Mr. Caine, As-car asks that I convey his *especial* regards, and so now I do."

"Thank you, Speranza," said Caine. "You may return them in kind."

"I shall. I shall indeed," said she with a smile, happily tapping the book nearly lost in her lap amidst flounces and furbelows and folds of fabric, fabric whereon polka dots battled broad and blindingly bright stripes. (*Q.:* Am I in league with *damselfish?* These friends of mine are not ones for hiding lights under bushels.) As I approached Speranza for a kiss, I saw that the book was a text of Russian grammar. I saw, too, that several pound notes protruded from its pages: the point of Oscar's visit had been pecuniary, at least in part. Speranza, shyly tucking the bills deeper, showed me the book's spine and explained, "I used to covet news of the world when waking; but now—what with the two worlds being rather confused, thanks in no small part to you gentlemen—I prefer to start my days with a difficult declension. Nothing, I find, cleanses the mind like the predicate nominative case of certain Slavic verbs."

"So I've always held," said Caine; but as ours was hardly a social call, Speranza let the slight lie, and soon we were about our stated business.

"This new plan of yours, gentlemen—this Plan of Action, as you put it— . . . well, let me just say this: Our watching, our waiting has proved both ruinous to our nerves and dangerous to London at large, or least-ways its population of domestic pets. So I, too, have struck upon a plan, and I shan't be surprised to find we are like-minded in the matter."

"Possession," said I.

"Indeed," said she. "We return, perforce, to this notion of possession; or, more to the point: imperfect as opposed to perfect possession."

Speranza took it upon herself to explain, to clarify our common thought. This she did as Caine and I settled into our seats, our too-tiny seats set amidst the dimness, the pinkness of her salon. Said she, with concision:-

"We must choose one of two roads: the high or the low, if you'll pardon my simplicity. The high road is the Church road—high not by my assessment, mind—and the low road splits unto the many paths of paganism. If we find ourselves upon the Church road, we may yet have recourse to the rite of exorcism: I have a priest standing at the ready. If, however, Tumblety leads us onto the low road, well . . . I fear we may find the way uncharted; but we will deal with *that* in the eventuality. For now"—and here she paused to look from me to Caine and back again—". . . for now there is but one question that wants an answer. Without it, we cannot choose our road. Without it, we can only continue to watch and wait. And in doing that, we know not the risk we run."

I agreed, and said so in the simplest terms. Caine was slower to come around: "The question, then," said he, "if I understand it rightly, is whether Tumblety be imperfectly or perfectly possessed?"

"That has been and remains the question, Mr. Caine, yes," said Speranza.

"All right then," said Caine; "but however are we to ascertain . . ." It was then that certain practical aspects of the problem hit home with him. "Oh, no. Oh, no."

"How else, Caine?"

"I am afraid Mr. Stoker is right. I am afraid the fiend must be found." And snatching up a square of cloth that covered the chair beside her, Speranza disclosed tools utile for whichever road we find ourselves on: crucifixes for the high, pistols for the low.

I had to help a quivering Caine to his feet, and, doing so, I said, "Look at it this way: At least the waiting is over"; for it is decided: To-night we go to Whitechapel.

BRAM STOKER'S JOURNAL[18]

Sunday now, a.m., 29 July '88.—The sun in its daily course shines on no house more miserable than this; for he has returned. *To this house.* A white rat found to-day at dawn upon the dining table.

---

18. Stoker's marginalia: "Exp. [expurgated?] version of same copied-out/sent by Sunday's post to Park St."

The rat's body was intact. He had not harvested the heart. No need; for it was not death so much as a message he meant to deliver: If we no longer wait, neither does he. If we now hunt, so too does he.

I told a waking Caine that I discovered this latest upon the front sill, and *that* news hit him hard enough. If he knew that finally his worst fear has been realised—that the fiend has entered here in defiance of our locks, and with our watch lately abandoned, and whilst we slept— well . . . I fear he would flee. As it is, Caine now sits across from me at this freshly-scrubbed table, scribbling I know not what, whilst I record; so:

We left Lady Wilde's on Friday, fearful but determined. In our pockets were our pistols and crucifixes. It was hoped we'd soon know down which road we were to go in pursuit of Francis Tumblety; for we had agreed that we would go to Whitechapel at nightfall to search out the Adversary. This we did, stopping first at the Lyceum to 1. ensure that it was yet secure; 2. disguise ourselves; and 3. stall, if the truth be told.

The Lyceum is a city unto itself, and we stood no better chance of exploring all its warrens and darkened ways than we would those of Whitechapel; that said, a more-than-cursory look about the theatre told me it was yet secure. This seemed suddenly sensible: Tumblety has already fouled the Lyceum as lair by leaving his half-burnt hounds to be discovered there; to return to it would be against his savage habits, surely. Too, he may already have fifty such lairs in London.[19]

From the XO, we proceeded to the costumery, Caine, in particular, being bent on going into Whitechapel incognito. As his notion of incognito was a satiny vest into which was sewn a label reading *Page/Party Scene/R&J* and pasha-esque pants puffed at the thigh, I said, dryly, "It isn't dress-up we're about here, Tommy. You look like a boy Hindi in the Raj's employ. . . . Allow me, please."

A half-hour later, I had Caine dressed in a black, three-quarter-length cape which I set over his shoulders myself, lest he see its label reading *Jessica/Merch. o' Ven.* "There, now," said I, "that suits, and literally so."

19. As will Count Dracula in his turn.

Caine acceded, yet soon snorted his derision as I chose for myself a dun-colored cloak and broad-brimmed hat, a smaller version of which I set atop Caine. Then, in Henry's dressing room, and using Henry's paints—an offence for which the Guv'nor would send me to the gallows—I rendered Caine's pale skin rather more . . . ruddy. Too, we borrowed Henry's half-glasses, for if anyone were to recognise Caine, it would be by his wide eyes.

Finally, we set off afoot; and we had nearly achieved the Minories when Caine suggested I tuck away my watch-chain, it being "a sure indicator" there was a watch of worth resident at its end. Said he, condescendingly, "Tempting one to do ill-deeds sees that ill-deeds are done."

"What penny poet sold you that?"

"I am quite capable of penning such *poésie* myself."

"True, true," said I, slyly, "not to mention prose no less . . . *musicale*. I *have* read your latest, after all." In truth, I was grateful for Caine's censure, the watch in question being my late father's; but still I looked at my companion askance: I could not reconcile his having come to Whitechapel with his increased sense of . . . *ease;* for his step was well nigh jaunty, now we were in the East. When I queried him on the point, Caine replied with what seemed a confession of sorts:-

"Stoker," said he, stopping, turning, staring up at me, "each man has his West End and his Whitechapel—it's just that mine have long been rather more than metaphorical."

"I see," said I, supposing I did: Caine referred to his days reporting on the lowest crimes of us Londoners, in which role he'd had occasion to trawl these selfsame streets. If he meant something more, his meaning was lost to me. Truer to say I soon grew distracted, and had neither the time nor tendency to delve deeper; for, in the course of our bantering we'd taken a few corners too fast and now found ourselves standing before swinging slabs of meat pendant from iron hooks the size of my hand.

Here was Aldgate Meat Market, the blood-stink of which—a smell grown too familiar of late—ought to have alerted us to the site; yet it hadn't. So it was we were at once surprised, revolted, and stilled to inaction. There we stood, our senses making the most unwelcome connections between the hanging carcasses, the carts piled high with hides, and all we'd lately seen and smelt of death. It was Caine who finally broke the silence, and with a quote no less, one that came to him easefully:-

"'Ancient, let your colours fly; but have a great care of the butchers' hooks at Whitechapel; they have been the death of many a fair ancient.'"

I knew the source to be Beaumont & Fletcher's *Knight of the Burning Pestle,* for Henry, by his own admission, had been an abomination in the same play as a much younger man—he'd heard hisses rise from the pit in Glasgow, and still he holds that serpentine opinion against *all* Glaswegians—and when later he took over the Lyceum, he banned those two fellows of Shakespeare's from his stage. Needless to say, the words were all too apt on this occasion, such that I rejoined, "Well, I might name one *un*fair ancient whose death, whose *second* death I very much hope to speed, by hook or by crook."

"Here, here," said a seconding Caine.

Soon we'd set the butchery of Aldgate at our backs. What we found, however, might well be deemed worse.

Whitechapel. That labyrinth of licentiousness. A warren, indeed, wherein there lives the worst of what man devolves to when deprived of ... *everything,* even light; for the wider streets and slimed alleyways of Whitechapel are lit—if "lit" be the word—by gas lanterns standing at long intervals, and the citizenry's cry of "More light for lower London!" yet goes unheeded. I wonder: What would become of the West End were it deprived of its electric light? Would vice invade to a similar extent? Would it, too, slip into such Cimmerian shadow as to make Milton blush?[20] Indeed, it is as though the underworld has risen up as Whitechapel. And so what better place for Set to seek out? What better place for his Devourer of Hearts to hunt the "worthless"?

... I fear for Caine. I have just risen to escape those last words writ

---

20. The reference is to John Milton and his epic poem *Paradise Lost,* which added the adjective "Cimmerian" to Webster's dictionary, c. 1580: "very dark or gloomy; 'under ebon shades ... in dark *Cimmerian* desert ever dwell.'"

and to somehow gather sufficient strength to proceed; and, looking over Caine's shoulder at the sheets on which he has been writing—with a pen seeming somewhat palsied—I found his penmanship much the poorer: his nerves work upon it. I must watch him for further signs of nervous dissolution. It may yet fall to me to send Caine from London for his own sake, even if it means I must go this alone.

To resume: The everyman's map of Whitechapel goes beyond those bounds established by the parish authorities of St. Mary's to include Aldgate, Spitalfields, and much of Mile End besides. It features such poetically named places as Fashion Street and Flower & Dean Street, Breezer's Hill and Angel Alley, but little poetry is to be seen upon those streets. Indeed, the area's dimness may be a blessing, for it conspires with the common fog to render down to shadow such sights as ought never to be seen, the very same we've seen these two nights past; for yes, we went to Whitechapel Friday night and—having found no sign of Tumblety—returned the next night as well. As Saturday was the more eventful excursion—understatement, this, of the severest sort—to it I speed.

Saturday is pay-day amongst the poor, and one finds them, that night, fast succumbing to those wily half-sisters, Liquor and Sin. They throng the public houses, speaking in ever louder keys as the night progresses, seemingly intent on drowning both their sorrows and the voices of their boon companions. In the pubs, they progress unto . . . *fleshier* thoughts, the which I begrudge no man; but out on the streets of Whitechapel this too often means the hiring of an unfortunate, likely to be drunk herself, and a loveless coupling—a bestial rutting, really— done in some dark alley or on a stair landing or behind a lockless door. And when the sun rises on Sunday, the working poor find their penury redoubled, for they have spent those monies marked for meat, for John- ny's new boots, for sundries, &c. It is a cycle readily seen on their faces when one walks amongst them, and the sight saddened me on Saturday night as it never has before.

Alas, in time we betook ourselves to Batty Street, where I'd last seen the fiend. It seemed as logical a place to loiter as any other. An hour of propositions and pity passed slowly and with no sign of Tumblety. We agreed that a pint in The Red Lion would be our reward for having waited, for having watched. A second pint followed fast upon the first, and by its lights we let down our guard: we removed our hats; and so it was that as I sat on the stool beside a beer-emboldened Caine, trying to convince him to hand over his *two* pistols to me for safekeeping, I heard my name spoken:-

"Mr. Stoker?" I nearly spun myself off the stool. "Why, surely it is. And Mr. Hall Caine as well, unless I'm very much mistaken."

"Indeed, it is the Messieurs Stoker and Caine," said my too-accommodating friend, heedless of the danger in our having been discovered. "And to whom . . . ?"

"This," said I with a kick to Caine's stool, "is Inspector Abberline of Scotland Yard." Caine looked at me. *Yes,* said I with a half-smile. *Not good. Not good at all.*

Hands were shaken, platitudes passed; but it was not long before the Inspector went to work:-

"Is not the Lyceum closed at present, Mr. Stoker? And does not Mr. Irving summer in the South of France, even as we speak?"

"It is," said I, ". . . and so he does." Though people, meeting me, always ask after Henry before following up with a second question regarding myself, still it sometimes rankles; and so, from habit, and a bit snidely, I added, "But surely that information falls far from your purview, Inspector?"

He managed a slow smile before stepping back to look us up and down, appraisingly; whereupon—with a twist to the waxen tip of his right-side moustache—he wondered aloud, "Gentleman, why are you—"

"Oh, *this?*" It was my turn to appraise our dress. "This is nothing."

"'Nothing'?" quoted the Inspector. "Well, if you do not, at present, play upon the Lyceum stage in some lesser role, one can only conclude that you are in . . . *disguise* of some sort."

"'Disguise,' do you say?" I was graceless in my attempted denial of the word: I laughed far too loudly, verily roared with laughter; and I must have struck the publican as a sort of chained bear, freshly baited, for he fast appeared to ask Abberline if all were well. It was whilst the Yard-man appeased the publican that Caine came up with a plan.

Said Caine, confidentially, when Abberline returned his attention to us, "Right you are, Inspector: Indeed we *are* in disguise." On the streets, my work upon Hall Caine had seemed sufficient; but beneath the Lion's naphtha lights, he—with his rouged skin, half-glasses, and slim-cut cloak—looked rather too much like a lowly wizard, or Alexandria's first lady librarian. "You see, Inspector, well . . . it was all my doing. Stoker here is just a game sort, up for anything. Isn't that right, Stoker?"

I'd already dived to the bottom of my beer, whence I now offered up an agreeing grunt. And, holding to that same position, I listened as Caine put the Inspector off by saying that, owing to "the worldwide success" of his latest novel, and certain unscrupulous pressmen intent on bandying about the name and likeness of Hall Caine, &c., &c.; . . . and further, by touching upon such points as pride, fame, and money—viz., *success:* the one topic sure to shut off another man's converse as though it were a spigot—Caine finally succeeded in sending Abberline back to his corner table. There—to judge by the company he kept: three soiled boys in caps, informers all, surely—he resumed the role of St. Whitechapel, Savior of the Slums.

"Come," said I to Caine, "let's go. That was rather too close for comfort." As we left, salutes were shared. I liked Abberline's not at all: he ran the brim of his bowler hat with a forefinger, too knowingly for my tastes. And once we had left the Lion, I asked aloud, "What's he doing here? I have it from reliable sources that he's been elevated out of these precincts to the Yard." In response, Caine muttered another adage of sorts—"Once Whitechapel is in the blood . . . ," or something similar—but still I complimented him on his fast thinking, whereupon he walked Batty Street a foot taller than before.

By now the hour was late, we were feeling the mingled effects of both fear and two tall beers, and we'd seen no sign of Tumblety. "Whatever were we thinking?" By my mumbled question, I'd only meant to marvel that we'd ever hoped to find our needle in the Whitechapel haystack; but Caine proffered a response, summarising our Plan of Action as if I'd forgotten it.

"Oh, Tommy," said I, stifling a smile so as not to condescend; and just then . . .

"What is it Bram? Are you unwell?"

Suddenly I was. For I had heard my name; and not, this time, in the insinuating tones of Inspector Abberline.

"Is he calling you?" asked Caine.

I nodded.

"Is it . . . is it sufficient to draw a bead on him, Bram?" Logical this, but the call isn't that species of sound. Rather, it comes from nowhere and everywhere at once.

Sto-ker, Sto-ker. He was calling me, yes, but did he mean to draw me, or distract me, or scare me back West, out of Whitechapel?

By then we'd regained the Commercial Road, where the din threatened to drown out my name if he spoke it again. Did he speak it again? Was he speaking it still? But it was more than the din that undid me, for once again my five senses were as confused as they'd been in the Temple at the ascent of Set.

I remember stumbling into an alley, wanting to quiet the world and quiet him as well; for though we'd found Tumbelty, or rather he'd found us . . . alas, *what now?*

A frantic Caine was asking me questions, and though I could see his mouth moving, his words were nonsensical, and I could not respond. And the tighter he held to my arm, bracing me, bracing himself, the more I felt—no *smelt* . . . orange blossoms? In Whitechapel! Madness, this! When Caine let go my arm—he says I wrenched it away—the scent disappeared, but so, too, did I fall back against a brick wall, where a protruding stake—blessedly too blunt to do damage—brought a second scent, this one bitter as burnt coffee. All the while, the chatter of sewing machines rose from a low window as waves of white light.

Sto-ker, Sto-ker. No nearer, no louder, but it was the only sound that still was sound, pure sound, and insistent.

Railcars rattling somewhere in the offing were as ice touched to my fingertips. An organ-grinder's music came tartly to my tongue. Yes, here again was that sensory confusion, and owing to it *all the world* was drawn into doubt, such that now I know what it is to lose one's mind. Yes: On the streets of Whitechapel on Saturday last, I feared for my sanity even as it seemed I was losing it.

I stumbled deeper down the alley, coming to lean on a lamppost. A small crowd had gathered round its shed light to watch an old man put his trained white rat through its paces. I suppose I was taken for a slumming drunkard, and so ignored.

Caine, poor Caine, tried to penetrate my sensorium; but in speaking to me, in touching me, he only worsened my state. I saw the fear on his face but could not allay it. He was fearful for me, yes; but he further supposed my confusion was attributable to our enemy's close approach, and so he scanned the crowd and outlying shadows for Tumblety. Meanwhile, I could only cling to the lamppost, could only watch the man and his rat. Was that Italian the man spoke? I did not know, could only hear his words as the green of new leaves. Still, I stared at his show as if entranced.

With naught but a square of white rag, the rat upon its plank was made to mimic, successively, an old woman, a monk, and a shrouded corpse. *Sto-ker, Sto-ker.* The show drew laughter and cheers; but when the man took off his cap and went round with it, his audience married the dark and disappeared. *Sto-ker, Sto-ker.* So, too, did we abandon the man, for I abandoned consciousness as well: I fainted into the sluicing filth of the alley, coming-to only as a stranger far stronger than Caine aided him in settling me into a hansom. *Sto-ker, Sto-ker.*

The last I can recall is Caine's shouting up to the driver my far western address, for the words as he spoke them were salty, redolent of the sea. Then I slipped away a second time, waking halfway home to learn from Caine what had occurred. Now my senses were re-ordered: so said a pinch to my palm and the aromas of the London night.

Returned here to No. 17, Caine—poor, pitiable Caine—had all he could do to help me down from the hansom, into the house, and up to bed, where, last night, I slept like I have not slept since those long-ago

Trinity days devoted wholly to sport; and just as I used to wake still weary from those contests, so, too, did I wake this morning to find my senses stiffened from hard use. I sat some while on the edge of my bed, gathering strength. Still it was dark. I thought of Mr. Penfold, as is my habit of late: a sort of prayer, it seems. And when I lit a lamp, I heartened to see its flame leap up—neither taste nor hear but rather *see* the flames, as one ought to. Then I listened for and heard, *heard* the first of Chelsea's birds. And as I descended in my nightshirt, I heard only the echo of last night's *Sto-ker, Sto-ker.*

Caine yet slept his laudanum sleep, dreamt his induced dreams. His habits of late led me to believe he'd sleep for some while. So it was I hoped to open these pages, to record our Whitechapel night before I'd have to assuage a woken Caine. But having drawn back the draperies to let into the dining room the rising light, I turned back to find beside my writing slant—there on the table, where I'd just set my morning tea— that same white rat in its white shroud, save now it no longer played a corpse but had become one.

Rather had been *made* one. As I lifted its tiny shroud to find the rat intact—the heart unharvested—a breeze blew into the room from behind me, bearing that violet scent I've come to abhor. Could Caine have left the window open? No. Here was a man who kept his hilltop castle closed tight as a casket. So it was I knew how Tumblety had come in the night. Had come into my home to leave word, as it were: *I, too, am watching. I, too, can hunt if I choose.* Now I knew both the how and the why of his coming, and the knowledge chilled me.

I sat at the table, my hands yet too tremulous to take up my tea, when Caine came hurrying downstairs, earlier than expected and calling my name in concerned tones. He cheered to hear that I'd woken with my senses intact, but his relief was short-lived; for I told him then of the rat, which I'd already conferred to the dustbin outside the kitchen door.

"Where . . . where was it found?"

"On the front sill," I lied. Caine cannot know that Tumblety entered here last night, entered and might have easily ascended the stairs and gone to Caine as he slept. To do what? Harvest that same heart he once tried to win? No. Caine cannot know that this house is no longer invio-late. (*Q.:* How then can Florence & Noel return to it? The maids? How, then, can Caine and I stay?) Lest Caine press for details, I changed tack and asked him to recall all he could of the stranger who'd helped him load me into the hansom last night.

"Why, he was . . . a gentleman, I should say. Perhaps midway between us two in height, and rather more stocky than not."

"How old a gentleman?"

"He was easily fifty, . . . yet quite strong of limb. He verily handed you up into the cab himself. So: perhaps younger than fifty. Forty? Thirty, even?"

"Hair color?"

Caine thought a long moment. "I cannot recall."

"Moustaches?"

"Why, yes, certainly. . . . Or is it mutton-chops I'm remembering?"

"What about an accent? Did he speak?"

"He spoke to offer his assistance, and he spoke again to bid us God-speed as we headed home. An accent, you ask? Why, I'm embarrassed to say I cannot recall."

"Nothing more? If not of the man proper, then of the incident itself?"

"Well," said Caine, "there was Abberline, of course."

"Inspector Abberline? What of him?"

"I would swear, Bram, *swear* I saw Abberline standing on the Com-mercial Road as we headed off." Had he then trailed us from The Red Lion? If so, why?

"What was Abberline *doing,* Caine?" I tried to master myself by sip-ping my tea, but cup and saucer yet clanked in my hands.

"Watching I suppose. . . . Oh, Bram, I don't like that man at all. There I was, worried sick, with you teetering on the edge of consciousness, and what does he do from across the road? Runs his finger round his hat, just as he had when we took our leave of the Lion. Did he offer help? Not at all. Can you fathom it, Bram? A public servant, such as Abberline, not offering to assist a—"

I cut him off to ask, "What *more,* Caine? Anything more?"

"Why, yes; but . . . but the particulars of the night are all so con-fused!" Caine sat now, heavily. With his elbows on the dining table, he set his broad forehead into his hands and hid his face from me. "Bram," he began, "I . . . I . . ."

"Do not be bothered, Hommy-Beg. You were simply . . . confused, yes; as any man would have been under the circumstances." . . . *that they may see me not nor understand.* And I said nothing more, least of all what it was I suspected: That Tumblety had been in that alley beside us, that it was he—the dissembling fiend!—who'd offered his help, he who'd handed me up into the hansom, and he'd who'd set the rat on my dining table as proof of same.

As for Inspector Abberline: Why *wouldn't* he have followed two slummers in disguise, the one famous and the other not unknown, and both of them allied to the Lyceum, lately the site of the still-unsolved "horrid incident"? Or perhaps he is in the sometime employ of the press, members of which would pay handsomely to hear what Hall Caine was up to in Whitechapel Saturday last.

No: I said none of this to Caine. Instead I invited him to take his tea and toast, though there both sit yet, untouched. As there Caine sits, still, scribbling. Perhaps he keeps a Record of his own, though I think it more likely he simply surrenders himself to his writing habit much as another man might lie down in an opium den to lose himself similarly.

As for my own Record, this Record, I close now by committing to it this question: What if the Enemy leaves me my heart but takes from me my mind? What then?

BRAM STOKER'S JOURNAL

Thurs., 2 August '88.—As I must do something or go mad, I write this diary.

The Plan, once again, is Watch & Wait. This we have done these five days since Saturday last without *effect:* no more dead things deposited here, no calling of my name, &c., but neither have we learned how the demon dominates Tumblety: perfectly or imperfectly. TO LEARN would mean TO RETURN to Wh'chapel, but Caine cannot do it, I will not risk it, and Speranza agrees. So: We Watch & Wait, damning this Plan of Inaction and going about our lives as best we can.

Caine studies my *Bradshaw's*, longing to leave. Yet still he stays, and we while away the days reading the tale of maddened *Macb.* whilst at night we seek sleep via sundry drugs. Speranza sleeps all day and at night tasks herself with translating a terror-tale from the German.

The maids stay away w/ pay; but what of Flo. & Noel, due to return mid-month? Ought they to remain in Dublin? Ought I to take Thornley into my confidence re: all & everything? Much, *too much* to mull whilst again we watch, again we wait.

TELEGRAM, BRAM STOKER TO LADY JANE WILDE

8 August 1888.—Waiting over. Receive us at 2 to-day. God help us in this.

B.S.

CUTTING FROM THE *MORNING ADVERTISER*, 8 AUGUST 1888

BRUTAL MURDER OF A WOMAN.

At about ten minutes to five o'clock yesterday morning John Reeves, who lives at 37, George-yard-buildings, Whitechapel, was coming downstairs to go to work when he discovered the body of a woman lying in a pool of blood on the first-floor landing. Reeves called in Constable Barrett, 26 H, who was on the beat in the vicinity of George-yard, and Dr. Keeling, of Brick-lane, was communicated with and promptly arrived. He immediately made an examination of the woman, and pronounced life extinct, giving it as his opinion that she had been brutally murdered, there being multiple knife-wounds on her breast, stomach, and abdomen. The body, which was that of a woman apparently about 5ft. 3in. in height, complexion and hair dark, wore a dark green skirt, a brown petticoat, a long black jacket, and a black-bonnet. The woman is unknown to any of the occupants of the tenements on the landing on which the deceased was found, and no disturbance of any kind was heard during the night. The body was removed to the Whitechapel mortuary, and Inspector Elliston, of the Commercial-street police-station, placed the case in the hands of Inspector Reid, of the Criminal Investigation Department.

The superintendent of the buildings, Mr. Francis Hewitt, has made the following statement:- "When I was called this morning, shortly before five o'clock, I saw the poor woman lying on the stone staircase, with blood flowing from a great wound over her heart. There were many other stab wounds of a frightful character on her. Up till half-past three this morning some of the occupants here passed up the staircase, and therefore the murder must have taken place after that, for the deceased was not there then. It is my belief that the poor creature crept up the staircase, that she was accompanied by a man, that a quarrel took place, and that he then stabbed her. Although the deceased is not known by name, her face is familiar. She is undoubtedly an abandoned female."

BRAM STOKER'S JOURNAL

Thurs., 9 Aug. '88.—C. & I to Speranza's yesterday at 2 p.m. to consult.

Said she, "Yes, but what of the heart? This article mentions"—and here Speranza had recourse to the *Advertiser* article, which I'd brought and which now she read again—"'blood flowing from a great wound over her heart.' The poor woman! Dreadful, *dreadful.* But still: What of the heart? Was it harvested, as you are wont to say? If not, perhaps the murder is . . . merely that: a murder."

"I know no more than you, Speranza. Details are yet scarce."

"Details . . . ," adjoined Caine, "yes: it is details we need, and *that* detail in particular." He'd not said much prior to this, nor would he after. He is unwell, and though we all fear that the blood of the woman murdered in George Yard may be upon our hands—God help us—Caine fears this, *feels* this, deepest of all.

Said Speranza, "What about this Inspector you reference? Can you ascertain more from him?"

"No indeed," said I. "In point of fact, I'll not be surprised if he comes to me seeking details."

"Whatever do you mean?" This from Caine.

"Need I remind you that we are allied in the Inspector's mind to a series of events ranging from grilled hounds to bad disguises to my taking *literal* leave of my senses and fainting in Whitechapel, verily at the Inspector's feet?" In enumerating the reasons we wouldn't be seeking the favor of information from Inspector Abberline, my voice had risen, prompting Speranza to say:-

"Calm yourself, Bram. Neither you nor Mr. Hall Caine can be suspects in the Inspector's mind."

"To the murder? No, no; impossible. Yet the man must have questions he'd like answered. I have no doubt, no doubt at all, that Henry's return—which is imminent, I hasten to say—shall bring Inspector Abberline round to the Lyceum once again. But . . ."

"Speak, Bram," urged Speranza. "But what?"

"I know another man in the Yard. Perhaps he . . ."

"Try it," said Speranza. "Try it, Bram, but by all means: Be careful! There are a few very simple questions which, if asked, must make perjurers of us all."

(*Mem.:* Simpson? Swenson? No: *Swanson.* Well met at the time of the Thames suicide. Came to the Lyceum later as my invitee.)

"Oh, please *do* be careful," said a querulous Caine. "It seems every time we poke about somewhere, we find something!"

"That, Mr. Caine, is the point of poking about," said Speranza.

"I know it is," said he, "but still . . . all this *detection*. Must we, really?"

Yes, we must; but neither Speranza nor I bothered answering Caine, whose chin had quivered even as he'd asked the question. (*Q.:* Mightn't it finally be time to send poor, petrified Caine back to his castle? His commitment is to *in*action only.) Alas, our conference ended as we all three agreed I will write to Inspector Douglas Swanson, Scotland Yard, in discreet search of details.[21]

CLIPPING FROM *THE TIMES*, FRIDAY, 10 AUGUST 1888 [22]

Yesterday afternoon an inquiry was opened at the Working Lads' Institute, Whitechapel-road, regarding the death of the woman who was found Tuesday last with 39 stabs on her body at George-yard-buildings, Whitechapel. Detective-Inspector Reid, H Division, watched the case on behalf of the Criminal Investigation Division.

John S. Reeves of 37, George-yard-buildings, a waterside labourer, said that on Tuesday morning he left home at ¼ to 5 am to seek for work. When he reached the first-floor landing he found the deceased lying on her back in a pool of blood. The deceased's clothes were disarranged, as though she had had a struggle with someone. Witness saw no footmarks on the staircase, nor did he find a knife or other weapon. As he was frightened, witness did not examine deceased but at once gave information to the police. He did not know the deceased, thus described: Age 37, length 5ft 3, complexion and hair dark; dress: green skirt, brown petticoat,

---

21. It is to be hoped that Stoker did his homework before contacting Inspector Donald—not Douglas—Swanson; but whether or not Swanson was Stoker's source within Scotland Yard, it soon becomes evident he had one. In this instance, however, the details sought seem to have been found in the popular press, i.e. *The Times* (see next entry in the *Dossier*).

22. Pasted into Stoker's journal.

long black jacket, brown stockings, side-spring boots, black bonnet, all old.

Police-constable Thomas Barrett, 226H, said that the last witness called his attention to the body of the deceased as he walked
his beat. PC Barrett sent for a doctor, who pronounced life
extinct.

Dr. T. R. Killeen of 68, Brick-lane, said that he was called to the
deceased, and found her dead. She had 39 stabs on the body.
She had been dead some three hours. Her age was about 36, and
the body was very well nourished. Witness has since made a post-
mortem examination of the body. The left lung was penetrated
in five places, and the right lung penetrated in two places. *The
heart, which was rather fatty, was penetrated in one place, and that would
be sufficient to cause death.*[23] The liver was healthy, but was penetrated in five places, the spleen was penetrated in two places, and
the stomach, which was perfectly healthy, was penetrated in six
places. The wounds generally might have been inflicted with a
knife or a dagger, as one went through the chest-bone. Witness
is of the opinion that all the wounds were caused during life.

The CORONER said he was in hopes that the body would be
identified, but three women had already identified it under three
different names. He therefore proposes to leave the question
open until the next occasion. The case will be left in the hands
of Detective-Inspector Reid, who will endeavour to discover the
perpetrator of this dreadful murder, one of the most dreadful
imaginable. The CORONER records that the assassin must have
been a perfect savage to inflict such a number of wounds on a
defenceless woman in such a way.

---

23. Underlined in—presumably—Stoker's own hand.

The CORONER afterwards addressed the Jury, who returned a verdict of Willful Murder against some person or persons Unknown.

TELEGRAM, BRAM STOKER TO LADY JANE WILDE

10 August 1888.—Organ intact, but was its removal sought; hence, the butchery?

B.S.

LETTER, BRAM STOKER TO HALL CAINE

14 August 1888

Dearest Caine,

I trust that you and yours are safely ensconced at Greeba, and that your return trip to the Isle was easily seen to and speedily accomplished. You do the right thing, friend, and as you sit there in safety beside your wife and child, know that I shall keep you apprised of developments here—of which *there are none.*

It seems the M. was simply that, as Speranza suggested. Horrid though the details be, there was no harvesting of the H. Neither have any gifts been brought to me here at No. 17. And so again I watch and wait, adjudging you, Caine, neither less a man nor a friend for your inability to do either *one moment longer.* I understand. Your leaving was for the best, for yourself as well as your family. I, too, shall have to make a new plan soon, for Florence and Noel are due back from Dublin. And Henry is to arrive in short order. Doubtless he'll be a devil of another type entirely. Already he writes to ask after plans for the *Macb.* trip to Edinburgh. Won't you join us in Auld Reekie? Henry would be thrilled, and my sentiments on the subject warrant no words.

Highest regards from Lady Wilde, who joins me in wishing that we will see you in London only as friendship requires, *and no sooner.*

Yours, simply,
Sto.

P.S. I remind you again, Caine, of those provisions discussed re: F. & N. and the unlikely event, *the wholly unlikely event,* of my sudden decease.

BRAM STOKER'S JOURNAL

Fri., 17 Aug.—I hate having to lie to Caine; but I am hopeful that if ever he discovers my lack of candour, he will forgive me for it.

If I were to write that I have heard my name called these last days, either Caine would have to upbraid himself for not returning to London, or, worse, he would return, and I'd have his nerves to contend with in addition to my own. No: He cannot know. Neither can Speranza know *all & everything,* leastways not that I have re-taken to the streets of Whitechapel. The worry of it would ruin her, even though she, too, disdains so feeble a Plan of Inaction as Watch & Wait. Watch and wait for what? Another murder, another attempted harvesting of a heart he deems worthless?

Both Speranza and I fear that the possession is perfect, for surely Caine and I gave Tumblety reason enough to solicit our help in his struggle against Set if, *if* he suffers a struggle within. Further proof of *perfection* is this victim's very femaleness, which bespeaks Tumblety's involvement; for Speranza reports—after close perusal in Budge's books and all the other funerary literature she can find—that nowhere is it stipulated that *a woman's heart* must be set upon the scales of Maat. Such—says Caine—would be Tumblety's take, for the man verily defines misogyny.

And so if this first woman was his—and I cannot doubt that butchery, those blade-borne horrors of the attempted harvesting were his clumsy work, clumsy because two entities engage the one body—... well, I fear that other women will follow, and doubtless they will be drawn from amongst the *worthless* of Whitechapel. So it is amongst them that I watch & wait.

Yes, the calls of *Sto-ker, Sto-ker* come as I wander those streets—but blessedly *not* the sensory confusion—and by them I know it is Whitechapel he haunts, Whitechapel he hunts. And yet I wonder: If it is not my sanity he wants—he has shown that it is his for the taking—nor my heart, why then does he suffer me to come amongst his quarry? *What does he want of me?*

And what do *I* want? Why do I go into the slums these nights as the summer sun sets? I cannot warn the women who stand about or saunter in groups of two or three—yes, ladies: Seek your safety in numbers!—or who sit on the stoops, chaffering good-naturedly about this or that though the alleys behind them recede to the very depths of Erebus.[24] Of course, as both night and their needs deepen—the need for mind-dulling drink and the need for 4p. to secure a night's bed—they turn in earnest to their time-dishonoured work. Oh, but the questions remain: What do I want & why do I go? I go, yes, to assess, if somehow I can, the type of Tumblety's possession. But I go, too, because I want to know these women. I go to learn how, *how* any Child of God can be ripped as that woman was in George Yard—may God rest her well, and relieve her soul of what horrors she witnessed her last moments on earth—... ripped and let to bleed to extinction, and *still* not have a name these ten days later? Was she not her mother's daughter, her father's, too? Was she not some woman's sister, friend, or confidante? Some man's helpmate or scourge? Some child's mother? I wonder. And I wish to learn. Already I know that the women are *not* worthless, and so each night as I walk Whitechapel, my ire rises: How dare he, and how dare his demon? And anger steels my step.

24. In Greek mythology, a place of pure darkness, passed through en route to Hades, i.e., Hell.

FROM THE METROPOLITAN POLICE FILES[25]

METROPOLITAN POLICE
H Division
24th day of August 1888

SUBJECT Murder, 7.8.88

I beg to report that Mr. George Collier, deputy Coroner for South East Middlesex, resumed the inquiry at the Working Lads' Institute, Whitechapel Road, at 2pm 23rd instant, respecting the death of Martha Tabram, alias Martha Turner, alias Emma, who was found dead in George Yard Buildings, Whitechapel, at 4.45am, 7th inst.

Mr. Henry Samuel Tabram, 6 River Terrace, East Greenwich, attended and identified the deceased as his wife who left him about 13 years ago, at which time the witness allowed her 12s. a week, but in consequence of her annoyance he stopped this allowance ten years ago.

Henry Turner, a carpenter staying at the Victoria Working Men's Home, Commercial Street East, Spitalfields, proved living with the deceased about 12 years, until about three weeks prior to her death when he left her. As a rule he was, he said, a man of sober habits, and when the deceased was sober they generally got on well together. Witness allows that he did not know deceased had lately retaken to the streets.

Mary Bousfield, wife of a wood cutter and resident at 4 Star Place, Commercial Road East, proved that the deceased and Turner rented a room at her house for about four months and left in debt 6 weeks ago without giving notice.

---

25. And copied out in a hand other than Stoker's: Swanson's, perhaps?

Mary Ann Connelly, alias Pearly Poll, a widow and an unfortunate, stated that she was drinking ale and rum with the deceased and two soldiers at several public houses in Whitechapel from 10 till 11.45 pm, 6th, Bank Holiday night, when they separated she (Connelly) going up Angel Alley with one of the soldiers whom she believes had stripes on his shoulder and a white band round his cap, and the deceased going up George Yard with the other soldier, and she saw nothing more of her till she saw her body in the dead house next day, since when the witness threatens to drown herself, but she only said it as a lark when I required that she remain available to the investigation, as careful inquiries are being continued.

[signed] Edmund Reid, Inspector

BRAM STOKER'S JOURNAL

31 August, Fri., 3 p.m.—Horrid night, last; horrid day, this.

Must tell all in its turn. *Must* write this Record for a reader. (*Q.:* Is *this*—of all my scribblings—destined to be my sole written legacy?) Have come to the theatre to do so, to record; for he has again fouled my house, has run me from it with blood.

The Record, *this* Record is all; and so I steady myself to record that:

I went into Whitechapel last night at dusk, undisguised. This has been my way of late; for, were I to encounter Abberline, I alone, without Caine, haven't fame enough to justify a disguise. Best to be Bram Stoker, and simply so. Best to let the Inspector think I slum. And a slummer I would have seemed—standing on the shadowed corner of Flower and Dean Street, watching the women and being watched in turn—when I heard the first of the fire bells.

I have seen things burn before. It humbles one. It puts one in mind of God, or leastways Nature; and, as a dose of Nature seemed prescriptive whilst I stood on that corner, attending the *un*natural, attending Tumblety's call—which had come two of the three nights prior—I set out to follow the fire bells to their cause. As I did so, my thoughts hied to H.I.; for, when he returns to-morrow to hear of Shadwell having burned, he will regret his late return to London, too late to see such a show, such *a study.*[26]

For Henry Irving never passes on the chance to study anything that may someday require re-creation upon the stage. So it is that I have walked at his side listening to the rain as it fell, first on slate, then stone, then wood, then tin, &c. So it was I once accompanied him to Bath to see that city in flood; though the floodwaters fast receded, and Henry came away disappointed. So it was we once sailed in a steamer from Southsea to the Isle of Wight to assess the roll of the sea, later adjusting *The Merchant*'s gondolas accordingly. And so it is that, here in the XO of the Lyceum, there sits a log in which, at Henry's direction, I have described the London light at this or that time of day, in this or that season: no more than a sentence or two, but which yet comprises the whole of my creative work of late. "What is *the effect?*" Henry asks of the rainfall, the sea, the light in its various states, &c.; for it is this—as realistic an effect as possible—that he wishes to impart to his audience, always. And so *the effect* of the fire was foremost in my mind as I approached as near as possible to the burning Shadwell docks.

The fire would not submit, neither to the men fighting it nor to the rain that now drove down on it; and drove down, too, on us several hundred spectators who stood watching the flames vie with lightning for supremacy in the sky. It seemed the fire and the storm fed each other; and just as the warmth of the one and the wet of the other conduced to send me home—or if not home, then elsewhere: back to the Lyceum to ready it for Henry's return, to work till tiredness overtook me and set me onto the office sofa—. . . just as I readied to turn from the fire, yes, I felt a hand clamp onto my shoulder.

"Are you well, Mr. Stoker?" It was Abberline. "Last I saw you, you seemed *un*well." And the silence that followed seemed somehow accusatory.

26. Shadwell Dry Dock blazed all through the night of Thursday, August 30, 1888.

"I am, sir; thank you." My heart was yet hammering, and thus I stupidly said, "So we meet again, Inspector." A trite line, this; one I would cut from any play script in which it appeared. I answered his next question, when finally he deigned to utter it, with more aplomb—the question, of course, concerned the health & well-being of Henry Irving—and then I queried him in turn, asking if the cause of the fire were known. His laconic response told me it was no concern of his, and neither did he suppose it should be one of mine. I took my leave as soon as I was able, all the while wondering if the warmth at my back were owing to the fire or to Inspector Abberline's too-steady regard.

With haste, with thirst, I betook myself fast to The Frying Pan public house, corner of Brick Lane and Thrawl Street. There I sat with a pint of stout, watching the browns and beiges of it swirl—as sad men will—and listening, yes, but avoiding converse of any kind.

It was whilst drinking—and wondering still who she might be, this unfortunate lately done to death in George Yard—that I heard his *Stoker, Sto-ker*, followed once again by laughter. The laughter came coincident with my seeing a woman stumble from The Frying Pan out into the fiery streets. She was much the worse for drink, and though she sought, quite vocally, 3p. for a pint of gin,[27] I might not have noticed her but for the design upon her brown ulster, that dirty, dripping-wet, brass-buttoned overcoat showing a woman astride a horse riding to the hunt. It seemed too apt a decoration, for the woman sporting it . . . , well, in her way, she was riding now to the hunt as well.

Sto-ker, Sto-ker. So, too, was the laughter repeated.

I spun about, looking this way and that. No-one. Nothing. Wondering, dare I say *hoping* he were outside on the street, I followed in the footsteps of the woman, coming so close behind her that I could smell the wet-dog scent of that woolen overcoat. Were those violets I smelt amidst the smoke, or was it the woman's perfume? I did not know. Out on the street, I heard again that sickening trill—"laughter" seems not the

---

27. Three pence was indeed the price for a pint of gin in 1888, but it was also the going rate for a "toss-off" in the streets. Stoker is here identifying the woman as a prostitute.

word for it. Though the rain had abated, still the sky was bright from both fire and lightning, and by a flash of the latter I saw . . . no-one. No-one and nothing. No-one but the woman, stumbling down Thrawl Street to disappear into the sulphurous dark.

By now it was past midnight, and when neither the call nor the laughter recurred—and I walked some while, listening—I thought it time to take my dampened self home, and so I would have done, save I'd no wish to go there alone. Here was a new fear, such that now I wonder if I didn't somehow know, somehow sense . . .

Regardless, instead I went by cab to the Lyceum, entering by the Burleigh Street door and proceeding to the XO by torchlight. I lit a lamp, locked the door behind me, and tasked myself with Henry's mail, lest he return to find it piled upon my desk, as then it was. I pored over the correspondence for three, nearly four, hours, leaving only as day broke over London. It was dawn, yes, when I headed for home.

Would that I never had.

Having first checked the front sills and stoop, I went down the left-side alley to enter by the scullery door. I found no footprints upon the path. Once inside the house, I knew with chilling clarity that no, he was not there at present, and yes, he had been there of late. Still, I could find no sign of it. No death-gift given. No note. And so: Might I be mistaken? I went room to room, checking every window and sill. I even looked twice in the letterbox. But I must have been fearful of what I might discover in the dining room; for I was late in going there, late in finding two bags of blood pendant from the gaselier.

Yes. . . . The lamp that overhangs the dining table is longer than it is wide, its brass arms reaching out towards the table's ends, and equidistant from the large light at its center there depended two bags of a thin, translucent sort, akin to wineskins. Dawn showed the bags' contents to be red, blood-red. As their bottoms had been pin-pricked, the blood dripped, dripped down to splash and spread upon the table. By the evident heft of the bags, by the slow dripping, by the still-pooling blood that had not yet spread to the table's sides, I concluded the bags could not have hung there over-long: an hour, no more.

From the scullery, I returned with a scissors to cut the cords by which the bags had been fastened, for the rude knots would not surrender to my shaking fingers. The knots were clumsily done, yes, and twice- or thrice-tied. Freeing the first bag set the second to slipping down the lamp's arm, and one of the lesser green-glass shades overbalanced, falling to shatter, to break into bits amidst the spilled blood. When finally I freed the second bag, I set both in a basin I'd brought in as well. Only when I lifted the basin—and it was the bags' weight that made me retch—only then did I realise I cried, nay had been crying and was crying still, crying and shaking so badly I was barely able to set the basin in the sink before I spilled the contents of my stomach beside it. There lay my spew beside the shivering bags of blood, bags which seemed like new-delivered . . . *things*.

I slit the bags with a butcher's knife and turned from the sight of the sluicing blood, turned, too, from the smell; but when finally I peered down into the scullery sink, I saw that the bags had contained bits of flesh, which now I had to pluck from the drain lest the blood back up. Whence the flesh came, I cannot say, but some of it I knew for skin.

When finally I'd raised a fierce enough fire, I burned both the bags and the rags by which I'd removed all the blood. Washing my hands, *scouring* them, I saw glittering on my skin, nay *in* my skin, green bits of the broken shade. I had cut myself in cleaning. I had married my own blood to that of the bags. One minute, five minutes, fifteen may have passed before I turned from the sink to stare into the fire. I confess to wondering, *to wanting* to send the whole house up, set it to burning like the Shadwell docks. I wondered, too, if I would run from such a fire or take to my bed and make of it a pyre, lying down upon it to die.

No more now. I cannot.

Later. Lately it has seemed he wants something of me. Now I know he does; and I suppose, too, that I know what it is. Oh, but first . . .

First let me say that I took hold of myself, or rather tried to—this shaking hand testifies that I have not yet succeeded;[28] and, seated on the

---

28. True: Stoker's penmanship—never neat—devolves to a scrawl upon these pages.

stairs, near the front door—which I'd found locked along with all the windows, such that the mystery of his in- and egress remains—I gathered up my scattered thoughts as earlier I'd gathered up the glittering shards of glass, and I found them no less sharp; specifically:

. . . Caine must come back. . . . Florence and Noel *cannot*. . . . Why does the fiend torment me so? What can he want? . . . Speranza has to be told of this. . . . Must hide the knives taken from the cabinets in Albert Mansions, for oughtn't I to expect Abberline here in the near future? . . . Is this silence in support of Caine wise? Would I be betraying him in telling *all & everything* to Abberline? Would his ruin follow, perforce? . . . &c. What to do? *What to do?* And recurrent was this more immediate question: Whence had all that blood come?

Now I know. To-day's *newspapers* all but tell me.

HORRIBLE MURDER IN WHITECHAPEL[29]

The Central News says;- Scarcely has the horror and sensation caused by the discovery of the murdered woman in Whitechapel some short time ago had time to abate, when another discovery is made, which, for the brutality exercised on the victim, is even more shocking, and will no doubt create a sensation in the vicinity of its predecessor. The affair up to the present is enveloped in complete mystery, and the police have as yet no evidence to trace the perpetrators of the horrible deeds, which they admit are likely the work of one individual.

The facts are these;- As Patrolling Constable John Neil was walking down Buck's-row, Whitechapel, about a quarter to four o'clock this morning, he discovered a woman lying at the side of the street with her throat cut right open from ear to ear. The site of the crime is said to be oddly bloodless.[30] Flashing his lantern, Constable Neil was answered by the lights from two other con-

---

29. Clipping—sources obscured, but dated 31 August 1888—pasted into Stoker's journal. Around this is drawn, or scratched, as if from repeated tracings, a box in blackest pencil-lead, marking both Stoker's mourning and, presumably, the long while he sat in consideration of these pages.

30. This last word circled in a hand presumably Stoker's. Marginalia: "How gathered, *how?*"

stables at either end of the street. These officers had seen no man leaving the spot to attract attention, and so the mystery is most complete.

Upon conveyance of the body to Whitechapel mortuary at half-past four this morning, when it was still warm, it was found that, besides the wound in the throat, the lower part of her person was completely ripped open. The wound extends nearly to her breast, and must have been effected with a large knife. As the corpse of the woman lies in the mortuary it presents a ghastly sight.

The woman has not yet been identified, and the only way the police can prosecute an enquiry at present is by finding someone who can identify the Deceased, and then, if possible, trace those in whose company she was last seen.

With this macabre tableau, Tumblety tells of not one murder but two: the one done in George Yard, certainly, but last night's as well; for the blood he brought me must be hers: that same unfortunate I watched disappear down Thrawl Street, both she and I wrong in thinking she walked alone.

Later, nearing nine. Still at the Lyceum, to which I returned after having set right the house; leastways having ranged it, for how can it ever be set right now? And in doing so, I discovered that his knives are already gone. Damn! He has reclaimed them from beneath my bed, where they were hid. And in searching the house, *searching* it—horrid, this!— he also discovered and stole the kukri knife given me by Burton. Its perch upon the mantel is empty. *Damn* him, indeed! And though surely it is better that my property be amongst his, rather than his mine, that'll be a small matter indeed in the mind of an Abberline: We two will be *allied* if all the knives are found together and the link forged! What to do? *What to do?*

. . . Alas, I am decided: I shall remain here till 10 p.m. o/c, whereupon I shall train and steam to Dublin with the night mails. I will be in family arms by dawn. (*Mem.:* Wire Thornley: *Matters most urgent. Arriving a.m. Must see you first, before Flo.*) Meanwhile, I shall render this Record current and write that what Tumblety wants from me. I was a long while wondering indeed; but now I know, though it fell to Lady Wilde to tell me:-

"Say again, Mr. Stoker, what it is you saw." We sat in her salon. I had told her the tale as written above. She had already seen *the newspapers.* "Repeat yourself."

I did so, prompting Speranza to muse, "The tableau. . . . Why, it is perfectly clear, Bram! He made with the bags and gaselier a balance. A scales. He wants you, *needs you* to be party to his plan." The instant she said the word "scales" I saw it all too clearly. A scales, of course!

Is he then ready to begin his weighing, that ritual by which Set seeks redemption? If so, he must surely have the heart of the Buck's Row woman. (*Mem.:* Solicit details of Scot. Yd., *at once.*) But however can the fiend think I will co-operate?

I took my leave of a worried Lady Wilde and headed here. She of course thinks it wise I go away. Indeed, she encourages me to stay away some while; but I shan't: a week at most. Meanwhile, to-night, I've much to do to ready the Lyceum for Henry's return to-morrow, the which I shall be glad to miss. By then I shall be in Dublin, blessedly too distant to hear him holler how *dare* I not be here to dance attendance on him?

BRAM STOKER'S JOURNAL

8 September, Ely Place, Dublin.[31]—It was indeed she in the coat, she whom I saw the night of the Shadwell fire.

Mrs. Mary Ann Nichols, by name. May her *worthy* soul rest. And may I someday absolve myself of having let her disappear into the laughing dark.

---

31. Thornley Stoker lived a Rochester-like life in an Ely Place mansion, his mad wife—schizophrenic, by to-day's diagnosis—requiring rooms of her own and constant care. Ironic, this, and sad: the reader of the *Dossier* is reminded that Thornley Stoker was preeminent amongst medical men treating madness.

FROM THE METROPOLITAN POLICE FILES[32]

METROPOLITAN POLICE

J Division

6th day of September 1888

SUBJECT Murder of M.A. Nichols at Whitechapel 31.8.88

P.C. 97J Neil reports that at 3.45 on the 31st August he found the dead body of a woman lying on her back with her clothes a little above her knees on a yard crossing at Bucks Row, Whitechapel. It is supposed in safety that the murder was committed where the body was found.

P.C. Neil obtained the assistance of P.C.s 55H Smizen and 96J Thain, the latter immediately leaving the site in pursuit of Dr. Llewellyn, No. 152, Whitechapel Road, who arrived quickly to pronounce life extinct but by minutes. He directed the body removed to the mortuary, stating that he would make a further examination there.

Upon said examination the Dr. stated that the throat had been cut from left to right, the windpipe and spinal cord being cut through. The abdomen had been opened from the centre of the bottom of the ribs along the right side, under pelvis to the left of the stomach, and there the wound was jagged. The stomach was also cut in several places, and two stabs on the private parts, apparently done with a strong bladed knife, were observed. The scarcity of blood at the scene remains unexplained.[33]

---

32. Copied out in a hand not Stoker's, this was presumably posted to Stoker in Dublin by his source within Scotland Yard and later laid into Stoker's journal behind the preceding entry.

33. Marginalia: "He bagged the blood even as it spurted! And so: *he plans*. Speranza writes to posit that the imperfectly possessed would not have the capacity to plan; they would merely act. And so it is as we supposed, and the Church will avail us naught. 'Pistols it must be,' closes Speranza. But does not the bagged blood bespeak an increased physical facility? If so, his body grows accustomed to its two tenants even though *he failed* in excising her heart."

Description of the Deceased is: Aged about 45, length 5 ft. 2. or 3., compx. Dark, hair dark brown (turning grey), eyes brown, slight laceration of tongue, deficient of one tooth upper jaw, two on left of lower jaw; dress: brown ulster with 7 large brass buttons (*w/ figure of a female riding a horse and a man at side thereon*),[34] brown linsey frock over grey woolen petticoat, white chest flannel, brown stays, white chemise, stained, black ribbed woolen stockings, man's side-spring boots, black straw bonnet trimmed w/ black velvet. It was later ascertained that the chemise bore the marks of Lambeth Workhouse and deceased, Mary Ann Nichols by name, was identified as an inmate of said house.

A husband, Wm. Nichols, is at present residing at 37 Coburg Row, Old Kent Road, and has employment as a machine printer, Messrs. Purkiss Bacon & Co., Whitefriars St. E.C. They separated nine years since in consequence of her drunken habits. For some time he allowed her 5/- per week, but in 1882, it having come to his knowledge that she was living the life of a prostitute, he discontinued the allowance, in consequence of which she became chargeable to the Guardians of the Parish of Lambeth, by whom the husband was Summoned to show cause why he should not be ordered to contribute towards her support. The facts of her dissolute life being proved, the Summons was dismissed. The husband has not heard anything of her since, and there are no grounds for suspecting him to be the guilty party.

Since 1882, the Deceased has at different periods been an inmate of Edmonton, The City of London, Holborn and Lambeth Workhouses. She left the latter institution on the 12th May last to take a situation at Ingleside, Rose Hill Road, Wandsworth, but absconded from there on the 12th July last, stealing the clothes she wore. Some days subsequent, she obtained lodgings at 18 Thrawl Street, Spitalfields, a common-lodging house, and remained there and at a similar establishment at 55 Flower and Dean Street close

---

34. Twice underlined; marginalia: "Damn him!"

by, living and working with others of that class known as unfortunate until the day she was found dead, 31st August inst.

The Deceased was seen walking the Whitechapel Road about
11 pm 30th, and at 12.30 pm 31st was seen to leave the Frying-pan
Public House, Spitalfields, and at 1.20 am 31st she was at her
common-lodging, 18 Thrawl Street, and at 2.30 am was seen again
at the corner of Osborne Street and Whitechapel Road. On each
occasion she was alone.[35] Fellow inmates of the Thrawl Street
doss house state that when Mrs. Nichols left there at 1.40 approx.
it was for the purpose of getting 4d. to pay for her bed (robbery
is thereby dismissed as motive for the murder). At 3.45 am 31st
she is found dead, and no person can be found at present who
saw her after 2.30 am 31st. Enquiries have been made amongst all
resident in the locality, watchmen who were employed in adjoining properties, P.C.'s on the adjoining beats and in every quarter
from which it has been thought any useful information might be
obtained, but at present not an atom of evidence is in hand connecting any person with the crime.

BRAM STOKER'S JOURNAL

Sunday, 9 September '88, 10 p.m., *aboard the* Magic *from Belfast to
Liverpool.*

"You quite try my rational mind, brother," said Thornley last evening; "and were it not *you* doing so, I confess it: I would dismiss all
you've said as bunkum, as balderdash, as what-have-you. The official
diagnosis would of course be 'dementia praecox,' or something similar,
and for it I'd have you set under scrutiny at an asylum. . . . But alas and
alack, it *is* you. *Damn!* Far easier it would be to disbelieve."

Thornley, his hand shaking, brought to his moustachioed lip his
glass of sherry. We sat in his library at the end of a long week that had

---

35. Marginalia: "No. He tracks her. He hunts. He *plans*."

just ended badly. "And besides," said he, "have I not learned that we cannot anticipate what it is life will deliver us? Is what you recount any more a mystery than . . . than . . . "; and my saddened sibling left the question unasked, though he tipped his chin towards the distant dining room lest I miss his reference to the humiliation that had passed there not two hours earlier:

We'd been eight at dinner: Thornley, myself, Florence, Noel, and two sets of spouses, the men co-medicos and colleagues of Thornley's. One of the latter was knighted, titled, and landed, and I liked him not at all, the less so when Thornley bade him take his seat at table's end, a mahogany mile of Sèvres and monogrammed silver separating the host from this, his most honoured guest. I was let to sit to the right of the second surgeon's wife, from whom I often turned aside, trying, trying and failing, to engage my own son in converse. Noel, however, was rather more concerned with the mint jelly a serving maid had lately ladled onto his plate, "hating it" and caring not that it might serve the coming lamb well. Florence commanded for the boy a new and un-jellied plate, and when he thanked her with a mumbled *merci,* I could but bemoan the distance between us, as broad as that sea that separates my wife & child from their adored France.

Alas. Dinner progressed. I partook as I was able; which is to say in-significantly, for too fresh in my mind were the things I've lately seen— viz., bags of blood dependent from our dining lamp, a lamp much like Thornley's only simpler: *all* we have is simpler, as Florence reminds me—and all I'd lately read, re: the particulars of Mrs. Nichols's murder, which had arrived with that day's post, the same that had brought three more letters from Henry, taking the week's total to ten.

It was as we sat over a vanilla pudding—rather too flesh-like in texture to suit my present tastes—that a secondary door to the dining room was thrown *blastingly* back onto its hinges by Emily, Mrs. Thornley Stoker, who thusly disclosed herself standing naked as a jay. Poor Thornley was the last to see the sight, and only when he turned in time to our slack-jawed stares did his wife announce, and screechingly so, "I, too, like a little intelligent conversation!" Whereupon, spurred by the fast approach of her two attendants, she tore into the room and rounded the table at full speed. Napery was put to concealing purpose, and when finally her attendants tamed the lady of the house, all three took their silent leave. Needless to say, our dinner soon disbanded with my brother begging discretion of his guests, who lied in saying they'd supply it.

Yes, a most ignominious end to the week it was; for I had arrived at Ely Place early Saturday last, September 1st, to join Florence & Noel, who'd been resident some while in two of Thornley's many splendid rooms. A whole week had passed in naught but pleasantries, even though the wire I'd sent had borne the word "urgent"; but those few times I'd found my brother alone, I found, too, that my nerve failed me. In truth, I feared just such a diagnosis—dementia—as he later delivered. But last evening, with my departure planned for the next day, Sunday, to-day, the time for truths had come.

Thornley and I had agreed to meet in the library for a much-deserved sherry once I had put Noel to bed. This I was keen to do; for, earlier that evening, after Emily's appearance, my bemused boy had asked me what madness was. Shamefully, I admit to sitting at his bedside a long while before asking if I mightn't tell him another time. "Perhaps by then I shall know," said I; and, having kissed onto his forehead the wish that his dreams would in no way resemble mine, I turned low the light and left him.

Finally, with all the rest of the household retired, I joined Thornley. Talk of dear, demented Emily was scant.[36] It pained him. What's more: The topic of Tumblety soon lay between us, for all the devilish details had come from me in a torrent. Perhaps it was my brother's own melancholy, or the fact that he listens and elicits such truths *professionally*, or . . . ; regardless, I spoke such that Speranza must now number Thornley amongst us Children of Light.

Thornley had heard of the Golden Dawn but knew little of the

---

36. And doubtlessly echoed later in *Dracula*, chapter 13, when Van Helsing—to whom Stoker would give a wife similarly afflicted—describes his own situation: ". . . me, with my poor wife dead to me, but alive by Church's law, though no wits, all gone—even I who am faithful husband to this now-no-wife. . . ."

Order. He knew even less of demonology and possession. Oh, but my brother knows much, *much* about madness and murderers. Too, as he may list amongst his many achievements pioneering work re: the processes of transfusion, I asked him—perhaps too pointedly—if the quantity of blood I'd discovered in the bags could have come from one body; for I'd wondered this since I'd watched it disappear down the drain. "Yes," said he, "a woman of standard size might hold within her six or more pints, nearly a gallon"; but he added that the ex-sanguination of said quantity would take some time, "particularly if efforts were being made to . . . to *bag* the blood, you say?"

I nodded; whereupon Thornley qualified his words, saying the speed of the bleeding was of course dependent upon how the blood was being drawn.

"Would so complete a blood-letting require a surgeon's skills?"

"Not necessarily," said he. "A slaughterer's might suffice." He sipped his sherry, once and again, before saying, slowly, "A vampire's would do nicely, too, I suppose."

"Do you mock me, Thornley?"

He thought a moment. "Yes," said he, "I suppose I do. . . . Forgive me, Bram. I shan't do it again." And he shan't. Poor Thornley is nothing if not devout: to Emily, descending ever deeper into her delusion, as to me yet wallowing in the shallows of mine. I fear I shall have reason to call upon his devotion, too; his devotion, his expertise, *and* his highly rational mind, which last was on display this morning when he led me from the terrace upon which we'd all partaken of a late breakfast. "Bram," said he, ". . . a moment, please?"

"What is it, Thornley?" We were playing at playing croquet so as to have some privacy. "Have you secured me a lunatic's room at Richmond?"[37]

"No, no," said he. "If ever it comes to that, brother, be assured"—and here he nodded to the mansion's distant wing, wherein his wife was resident—"you, too, shall be kept in comfort." As this talk of asylums—

37. Richmond Hospital, Dublin.

blithe on my part, oblique on his—reminded me of the visit to Stepney Latch, at the close of which I'd agreed to convey Dr. Stewart's regards to Thornley, I did so now; and these he happily heard, opining, "Ah, yes, a good man, that Dr. Tom Stewart. . . . But what I was wondering, Bram . . ."

"Go on," said I, thwacking a brightly-striped ball towards a distant picket.

"Correct me, brother, if I err in the following facts:

"This Abberline, of whom you speak none too fondly? You say he has had reason to question you previously? That is, previous to his having seen you at the burning docks?"

"Yes." And I recalled to Thornley the horrid incident of the hounds; told him, too, that Abberline had literally *dis*-covered Caine and me in Whitechapel, and later that same night had seen me sense-stricken upon the streets.

"And so he has reason to situate you in Whitechapel the night of the fire?"

"Yes."

"The night of the fire was also the night of this second murder, was it not?"

"It was." And with a wave of my mallet, I hurried my brother to his point, which was this:-

"Does it not dawn on you, Bram, that you were perhaps unwise to leave London when you did? I fear that you are so familiar with *the dots* of all this that you have failed to connect them. Inspector Abberline shall not fail similarly, count on that. And I shan't be surprised in the least if—upon your return to London—you find he has been making enquiries."

"As to my whereabouts?"

He nodded, and solemnly so.

"But I have been with you, Thornley, *here,* and tens of people can attest to it. And mightn't a man go about his business as it pleases him?"

"Indeed a man might; but that same man—when he has been proximate to murders recently committed— . . . that same man, I say, had best have an alibi ready to hand. And Bram, understand: At issue is not *that* you left London when you did but rather *why*. Abberline is an Inspector, Scotland Yard, man! His renown reaches us here. He shan't dismiss your trip as coincidence. He shall, indeed, wonder: *Why?* Have an answer at the ready, is all I am saying. That, and leave at once: The sooner you return to London, the better."

Thornley was right, of course. I really must endeavour to see things with Abberline's eyes if I am to act as an inspector myself. Oh, but could I possibly be *a suspect?* Nonsense. Rather it is through me that Abberline searches still for Tumblety, who left his hounds unmourned, who disappeared the day of their death and . . . And, Good God, if only Abberline knew the half of it! (*Mem.:* He can *never* know, not now; for we have already gone too far in our dissembling so as to spare Caine.)

In Dublin, I bade my wife and child adieu and trained to Belfast to board this faster boat. Florence had readily agreed to lengthen their stay indefinitely, Thornley's house being fine and lacking, too, its lady—a role Ellen Terry could not play half as well as my wife now does. And perhaps Noel can borrow a bit of a brogue and roughen his tongue whilst in Ireland. But be that as it may, in Dublin, with Thornley, I know wife & child are safe. I cannot say the same of London.

London. To what do I return? I cannot consider the question at present. Instead I shall heed the sea's lullaby and sleep my way to Liverpool, whence to London and who-knows-what.

Later, training from Liverpool to London.—We watched, we waited too long; and now there is naught to do but pray over the soul of a third murdered woman and say in our defence, *We knew not what else we could do.* But I know now. And I shall re-take to the hunt with purpose.

Hadn't debarked the *Magic* before I heard a newsboy call up from dockside: *Another Whitechapel Outrage!* Had to hurry lest I miss the 6.20 a.m. London train, but first—and fie!—I found this grisly bit in a *Pall Mall Gazette.*[38]

---

38. The newspaper Stoker found in the Liverpool train station was the prior day's *Pall Mall Gazette*—that is, the issue of Saturday evening, 8 September 1888. Clipping the relevant pages, he slipped them into the *Dossier* without further commentary of any kind. Surely none was needed.

ANOTHER MURDER—AND MORE TO FOLLOW?

SOMETHING like a panic will be occasioned in London to-day by the announcement that another horrible murder has taken place in densely populated Whitechapel. This makes the third murder of the same kind, the perpetrator of which has succeeded in escaping the vigilance of the police.

Three poor women, miserable and wretched, have been murdered in the heart of a densely-populated quarter, and not only murdered but mutilated in a peculiarly brutal fashion, and so far the police do not seem to have discovered a single clue to the perpetrator of the crimes.

There is some reason to hope that the latest in this grim and gory series of outrages will supply some evidence as to the identity of the murderer. A leather apron was, it is said, found by the corpse. If so, this is the only trace left by this mysterious criminal. The fact that the police have been freely talking for a week past about a man nicknamed Leather Apron may have led the criminal to leave a leather apron near his victim in order to mislead. He certainly seems to have been capable of such an act of deliberate preparation. The murder perpetrated this morning shows no indication of hurry or of alarm. He seems to have first killed the woman by cutting her throat so deeply as almost to sever her head from her shoulders, then to have disembowelled her, then to have removed certain internal organs, and then to have disposed of the viscera in a fashion recalling stories of Red Indian savagery. A man who was cool enough to do this, and who had time enough to do it, was not likely to leave his leather apron behind him apparently for no purpose but to serve as a clue. But be this as it may, if the police know of a ruffian who wears a leather apron in Whitechapel whom they have suspected of previous crimes, no time should be lost in ascertaining whether this leather apron, if it really exists, can be identified as his.

This renewed reminder of the potentialities of revolting

barbarity which lie latent in man will administer a salutary shock
to the complacent optimism which assumes that the progress of
civilisation has rendered unnecessary the bolts and bars, social,
moral, and legal, which keep the Mr. Hyde of humanity from
assuming visible shape among us. There certainly seems to be a
tolerably realistic impersonification of Mr. Hyde at large in
Whitechapel. The Savage of Civilisation whom we are raising by
the hundred thousand in our slums is quite as capable of bathing
his hands in blood as any Sioux who ever scalped a foe. But we
should not be surprised if the murderer in the present case
should not turn out to be slum bred. The nature of the outrages
and the calling of the victims suggests that we have to look out
for a man who is animated by that mania of bloodthirsty cruelty
which sometimes springs from the unbridled indulgence of the
worst passions. We may have a plebeian Marquis De Sade at
large in Whitechapel. If so, and if he is not promptly apprehended, we shall not have long to wait for another addition to the
ghastly catalogue of murder.

There is some reason to hope that the sentiment of horror
which the peculiar atrocity of the present crime excites even in
the most callous will spur the police into a display of vigorous
and intelligent activity. At present the disaffection in the force is
so widespread that, unless we are strangely misinformed, the
police are thinking more of the possibility of striking against a
system which has become intolerable than of overexerting themselves in the detection of crime. As for the community at large,
the panic will probably be confined to the area within which this
midnight murderer confines his operations. If, however, a similar
crime were now to be committed in the West-end, there would
be a panic, the like of which we have not seen in our time. From
that, however, we shall probably be spared; but the public will be
more or less uneasy as long as the Whitechapel murderer is left
at large.

Later.[39]—He has not been here.

From Euston, I took a hansom home, handing up half a sovereign for speed. At the station, gathered all papers possible. Details, or rather *the* detail—has he taken her heart?—yet unanswered; but word should come from within the Yard by to-morrow a.m.

Thornley supposed aright: Abberline has been round to the Lyceum enquiring. (*Q.:* Ought I to initiate contact to-morrow to forestall his return?) Of course, he cannot possibly suspect me now, as this last out-rage occurred whilst I was out of London. And so he only comes to me seeking Tumblety. (*Q.:* Must be of *no use* to Abberline in his search, but cannot he aid us in ours? *How?* Think on it. Ask Caine. Ask Speranza. We three must convene. *Mem.:* Write Caine: *Come!*)

Henry Irving is a bloody fool! He has been "inspired" by all this "hubbub," such that now we are to speed the season's opening & go up *again* with *Jekyll & Hyde* on 1 October. (*Mem.:* Wire word to Stevenson & have Harker retrieve scenery from storage.)[40] Leastways it shall be cheaper to re-mount *J & K* than *Faust*—*Faust* @ £200 per perf.—and doubtless far more profitable; which point I made to Henry, who, like a hound on the money-scent, is presently too distracted to pout & punish me over my Dublin absence.

Meanwhile the *Mach.* planning goes on apace as well. H.I. *insistent* now upon the E'burgh trip. (*Mem.:* Must draught a research agenda, w/ dates. When? Who will go?)

1 a.m. No sleep: out of laudanum: mind awhirl. Shall walk walk walk the riverside, briskly so: rather late for it, but *mens sana in corpore sano.*[41] Oh, but how *sana* shall my mind be if he calls to me, if he comes to me?

---

39. Still Sunday, 9 August 1888.

40. Robert Louis Stevenson, author of both *Dr. Jekyll and Mr. Hyde* and its adapted play, which already the Lyceum had mounted with much success with Richard Mansfield—*not* Henry Irving—in the title role(s).

41. *Mens sana in corpore sano:* Latin: "a sound mind in a sound body."

FROM THE METROPOLITAN POLICE FILES[42]

METROPOLITAN POLICE
H Division
8th September 1888

I beg to report that at 6.10 am 8th inst. while on duty in Commercial Street, Spitalfields, I received information that a woman had been murdered. I at once proceeded to No. 29 Hanbury Street, and in the back yard found a woman lying on her back, dead. I at once sent for Dr. Phillips Div. Surgeon and to the Station for the ambulance and assistance. The Doctor pronounced life extinct and stated the woman had been dead at least two hours. Examination of the body showed that the throat was severed deeply, incision jagged. Removed from but attached to body, & placed above right shoulder were a flap of the wall of belly, the whole of the small intestines & attachments. Two other portions of wall of belly & "Pubes" were placed above left shoulder in a large quantity of blood. The following parts were missing: part of belly wall including navel; the womb, the upper part of vagina & greater part of bladder.[43] The Dr. gives it as his opinion that the murderer is possessed of anatomical knowledge from the manner of removal of viscera, & that the knife used was not an ordinary knife, but such as a small amputating knife, or a well ground slaughterman's knife, narrow & thin, sharp & blade of six to eight inches in length.[44] The body was then removed on the Police Ambulance to the Whitechapel Mortuary.

The woman has lately been identified by Timothy Donovan,

42. Handwriting matches previous reports.
43. Marginalia: "Heart then present?"
44. Marginalia: "The kukri? *My* kukri?"

"Deputy," Crossinghams Lodging House, 35 Dorset Street, Spitalfields, who states he has known her about 16 months, as a prostitute, and for past 4 months she had lodged at above house and at 1.45 am 8th inst. she was in the kitchen, the worse for liquor, and eating potatoes, when he Donovan sent to her for the money for her bed, which she said she had not got and asked him to trust her, which he declined to do, she then left stating that she would not be long gone and would return with the 4d. for her bed. The Deputy said he would save the bed for her. He saw no man as her company.

Description, Annie Chapman, age 45, length 5ft, complexion fair, hair (wavy) dark brown, eyes blue, two teeth deficient in lower jaw, large thick nose; dress, black figured jacket, brown bodice, black skirt, lace boots, all old and dirty.

The Deceased was the widow of a coachman named Chapman who died at Windsor some 18 months since, from whom she had been separated several years previously through her drunken habits, and who up to the time of his death made her an allowance of 10/- per week. For some years past she has been a frequenter of common doss houses in the neighbourhood of Spitalfields, and for sometime previous had resided at Crossinghams, where she was last seen alive at 2 am the morning of the murder. From then until her body was found in Hanbury Street no reliable information has been obtained as to her movements.

A description of the woman has been circulated by wire to All Stations and a special enquiry called for at Lodging Houses &c. to ascertain if any men of a suspicious character or having blood on their clothing entered after 2 am 8th inst.

Every possible enquiry will be made with a view of tracing the murderer and no effort will be spared to elucidate the mysteries. Several persons have been detained already at various stations on suspicion, and their movements are being enquired into, numerous statements have also been made in the hours since discovery of the Deceased, and letters bearing on the subject have begun to be received, yet no useful result has been obtained. I would respectfully suggest that Inspr. Abberline, who is well acquainted with H Division, Whitechapel, be deputed to take up this enquiry as I believe he is already engaged in the case of the George Yard and Buck's Row murders which would appear to have been committed by the same person as this last in Hanbury Street.

[signed] JL. Chandler Inspr.

TELEGRAM, BRAM STOKER TO LADY JANE WILDE

10 Sept. 1888.—Heart present. Still it must be he. Thornley in. Caine coming.

Sto.

LETTER, BRAM STOKER TO HALL CAINE[45]

10 September [1888]

Friend Caine,

You had best consider coming to town. Apologies; but red events—viz., this third occurrence re: Mrs. Chapman—render your presence *imperative.*

Heart was not taken this last time—sought, it seems, but not taken. The womb *was* absent, however. Is he collecting again, as in days of old? More likely he failed at harvesting the heart and took what he could. Perhaps he cannot control himself, *literally* not: How else to explain the hash of it all, the horror? But his facility grows: They write now of his having "anatomical knowledge," of his bearing the blade with purpose; and so it seems he grows ever more accustomed

---

45. Written in cipher.

to his double-self. This bodes *most* ill, Caine. And at present our only hope—separate from our own ACTION—is that he be interrupted at his infernal work. Perhaps he cannot wholly & successfully dissemble, perhaps he can & will be seen, & so caught. That said, it seems Abberline pursues Tumblety mostly through me; but I give him nothing. Ought I to? Many such questions for our next convention— see that it happens soon, Caine. *Come!*

Thornley in, consulting from Dublin. Will come if called. Had to tell him *all*, of course, but fear not: He is Trust itself. Florence & Noel are in his care at present. Suggest you secure Mary & Ralph in the castle. Again I say fear not: It is me he wants. This I do not doubt. I have not disclosed all to you, Caine, not wanting to worry you. I shall do so henceforth, and I begin by saying that he came to No. 17 the morning of the Nichols murder and left a message: He, *they,* want the weighing ritual. It is why he hunts their hearts. Speranza certain more lives will be lost unless we indulge him, . . . *but how?*

9.45 a.m. L'pool train to town to-morrow. Wire if you *cannot* board. Otherwise seek me on the platform, whence we shall hie to Park Street *at speed.*

Stoker.

BRAM STOKER'S JOURNAL

Wednesday, 12 September.—We three convened yesterday afternoon at Park Street; so:-

"Omnia Romae venalia sunt," said Speranza.

"Juvenal," said Caine. "Satires. 'Everything in Rome was for sale.' . . . But pray, Lady Wilde, explain yourself."

We had been sitting some while in Speranza's salon, and we all three had fallen to arguing the virtues of our Watching & Waiting, Caine arguing *for* the latter plan's continuance, Speranza and I *against.*

"What I mean to say, Mr. Caine, is simply this: There are prices at-tached to everything, including both action and inaction; and it seems to me the price of the latter course has become rather too clear, rather too dear."

"But, Speranza, surely—"

"Surely, Mr. Caine," said Speranza, ". . . surely the price to be paid by waiting will be the life of a *fourth* woman. Do you wish to hazard that?"

"You impugn me with the very question, Lady Wilde."

"I do no such thing, Mr. Caine. I simply state—for it is plain as a pikestaff—that—"

My turn had come to interrupt:-

"Please," said I, emphatically, ". . . please;" and with the silence that ensued, I counseled calm. Only when it was achieved did I speak on:-

"I fear, Caine, that Lady Wilde is right: To watch and wait any longer is to risk more blood being shed." And I had yet, indeed *have* yet, to tell Caine what measure of message was left for me after Mrs. Nichols's murder. I had, however, told him of my missing kukri (*Q.:* the murder weapon?!) and how it could incriminate me, *us.* "We must act, Tommy. . . . Are you agreed?"

Too scared to speak his response, Caine could only nod. And if he wondered *how* we would act, and *what* we would do, and *when* precisely, &c., so, too, did I. The answer, when it came, was Lady Wilde's:-

"We must appeal to his demon."

Caine sprang from his chair. "Indeed! And in so doing, we shall surrender the last of our good sense! . . . Might I suggest a spiritist *conversazione* Saturday next, Speranza? One to which we might invite *all* our friends, terrestrial and celestial, infernal and astral?"

"Caine," said I, "now, now." Again I counseled calm, but as I failed to show it myself, Speranza may have felt free to reply to Caine, with feigned surprise:-

"Why, Mr. Caine, I *do* believe it is humour you essay. . . . I must admit: Having read your latest, I would not have thought you capable."

Fighting words, these. "'Capable,' do you say? *Capable!*. . . I remind you, my lady, that *my* latest book has moved some three hundred thousand copies these last six months, and that even as we speak, it passes into Finnish translation."

"Indeed? Well, may that be the finish of *all* translations, sir. . . . I should think the world has a surfeit of Caine at present."

"What then does the world need more of? More tame words from a Wilde?"

"No words of mine were ever tame, Mr. Caine. And if you mean to reference the work of my As-car, well . . ."

"I do not reference your *As-car,* Lady Wilde, neither here in private nor ever in public."

Whereupon Speranza slowly stood and timbered towards Caine. He rose as well, and there they stood, center-all in her salon, nose to . . . navel.

"Stand down, both of you! . . . *Absurd,* this. I beg you both to remove yourselves from the present moment and reflect upon what has just passed. See yourselves!" In time they each re-took their chairs, Caine doing so quickly whilst Speranza moved as if through water.

Returned to his corner, as it were, Caine clasped his hand to his mouth. I could see, verily see him wondering whence his words had come. "Lady Wilde," said he, seeming to breathe rather than speak his apology, "will you . . . *can* you forgive me?"

"I can indeed, Mr. Caine," said Speranza; "but I believe I shan't . . . not for some minutes more. Meanwhile, I proffer civility, civility only." And, as evidence of same, she rang a bell to summon the Betty; who eventually brought in the dreaded Park Street tea, the service of which was hampered by her holding in her left hand a long-stemmed lily. Too, she reeked of *eau de quelque chose.* So it was I knew we'd once again arrived at Park Street in the wake of Mr. Oscar Wilde.

Caine turned to me during this strange, spilling service and whispered, "I am ruined, *ruined,* Bram! My nerves . . . My fears . . . I cannot master myself!" No: Best not to tell him about the bags of blood. Finally, the cold tea and stale cakes served, and the perfumed maid departed, Caine turned to our hostess to say, "Speranza, I am sorry, most heartily sorry. And of course you both are right: We must act. . . . Speak, please."

With those eagle eyes of hers, Speranza stared over the chipped rim of her teacup, sipping still. Slowly, showily, she returned cup to saucer and said, "I meant only to suggest, sirs, that if we cannot communicate with Tumblety—and indeed we cannot even find him—then perhaps we should consider calling to his possessor. Perhaps *he* will come. It is he, after all, who wants this weighing. The American is but the means . . . as are you, Mr. Stoker."

"Set," I said. " . . . Set?" The idea was some while sinking in.

"The same," said Speranza. "For I think we may assume that, even were we to succeed in finding Tumblety, well . . . I very much doubt we would succeed in reasoning with him, in dissuading him. He is *murdering,* after all, not playing at cards or horses. He is beholden to a demon. And the possessing relationship would appear to be perfect, yes?" Caine and I agreed; for we have had no proof of imperfection. "Then my proposal is this: Let us summon the demon himself, let us appeal to Set, and in so doing sow a seed of discord."

Suddenly I understood. "And by sowing discord we will render the possession *im*perfect."

"Precisely," said a satisfied Speranza.

"And then hand them both off to a priest?" This from a hopeful Caine.

"I'm afraid we are rather past that point," said Speranza. "Not even my Roman would exorcise such a man as Tumblety, and another priest might alert the authorities."

"No authorities," said Caine, unnecessarily so.

Speranza continued, saying that in compromising the possession, we might make for ourselves an opening, some Avenue of Action. "But if they—human and demon—remain allied as they are at present, I fear that no plan shall avail. If, however, we *im*perfect the pairing, perhaps. . . ."

"Surely it is worth the effort," said I, enthused; but then the *How?* of it hit me.

"I shall tell you how," said Speranza, taking up a book from the table beside her; but just as she readied to read aloud, Caine questioned her source.

"My source, Mr. Caine, is myself." And so it was: Speranza had her own recent *Legends, Charms & Superstitions* in hand. "Though I have yet 'to move' as many copies as you, sir, I have dedicated and careful readers of my own."

"I do not doubt that in the least, Speranza. And I say again: I apologise for—"

"And such readers"—here she opened the book and readied to read; however, in fumbling about her bosom and high-piled hair, she failed to find her spectacles, and so shut the book and spoke from memory— ". . . such readers, I say, will discover that I have married Sir William's research into the East to my own regarding Eire; and in the course of doing so, I have come to conclude that the Irish lamentation of *Ul-lu-lu!* surely, *surely* derives from the Egyptian *Hi-loo-loo!*" Whereupon she proceeded to compare the two calls at such a pitch and at such length that even the deaf Betty returned, poking her head into the salon to say:-

"Mum? . . . Dropped the bell, did ye?"

"Pardon me, dear," said Speranza. "I was calling the gods, not you." Which explanation was sufficient to send the Betty wordlessly away; but as my interest was rather more piqued than the maid's, I asked:-

"That Irish call is a funerary one, is it not?"

"Indeed. So, too, the Egyptian."

"But it is not a god we mean to summon," said Caine; "it is a demon."

"Understood," said Speranza; who further explained, "We need only practise the lament *as prohibited*. Understand:

"It has been known from time immemorial that funerary chants— keening, as we Irish call them—are *not* to be raised in the hours following hard upon a funeral, lest they confuse the gods and render them deaf to the cries of the deceased's soul."

"Yes? . . . Continue, please." I was eager to keep with Speranza's reasoning.

"To do so," said she, "is to risk summoning a demon rather than a god."

"Do you mean to suggest," asked Caine, "that this *Hi-loo-loo!* will summon Set?"

"I mean to suggest, Mr. Caine, that we try *something* before your American succeeds in removing the heart of another woman of Whitechapel—as surely he will—and carries it to our Mr. Stoker here for weighing." Best to forestall *that* eventuality, yes.

"Let us try it," said I. Caine, too, acceded. And soon we heard the précis of Speranza's plan:

Picking up the topmost newspaper of a pile at her heels, Speranza squinted at its masthead and said, "We are the eleventh at present. Mrs. Chapman's committal to a plot at Manor Park Cemetery is planned for this Friday, the fourteenth. I propose we three attend. And when the last of the mourners have left, I shall call to Set."

"And," queried Caine, "say what, precisely, if he appears?"

"That, gentlemen, is a question we have four days to consider." And so we do.

BRAM STOKER'S JOURNAL

Friday, 14 Sept.—I steal these few minutes for the Record whilst yet at the theatre; and soon I shall go down to the stage to gather Caine and take a fast cab home from here, the hour being advanced—midnight nears—and the day having been a long one.

Much to consider of late; amongst which: How to respond to Henry Irving when he asked—as indeed he did—why I felt more beholden to a dead harlot than to him? My place this afternoon was at the Lyceum for the load-in of *J&H, not* amongst the masses mourning the murdered Mrs. Chapman. I answered him in advance, as it were, by soliciting Stevenson to come to the theatre to-day; for H.I. is like a tempestuous puppy, and to him I would simply throw a brighter, bouncier ball than myself. Occupied in fetching for the esteemed Author (*Mem.:* Send Stevenson round a bottle of whisky, well aged), Henry gave over berating me. Thusly was I able to slip away to meet up with Caine and Speranza at Mrs. Chapman's obsequy, as previously planned.

Rather, our rendezvous occurred later than planned; for last night Caine got word from a former peer of his in the press that the interment was being put off some hours: from the scheduled 10 a.m. to nearer noon, so as to allow for the photographing of her eyeballs.[46] I had sent word of the change round to Speranza, knowing that news of a later rendezvous would be welcome to her. But still she met us on the Strand this forenoon wondering why she'd bothered to sleep at all and raising her hand to shield the sun—of which there was but little—from her face, which already was occluded by the black lace veil of her mourning dress. "This noonday light is a trial. I suffer it not well, not well at all. Let us be about this business, gentlemen." And so we three set off, Speranza moving like a somnambulist whilst Caine self-fortified from a silver flask.

As previously Mrs. Nichols's funeral had become quite the show, precautions had been taken in Mrs. Chapman's case. There was no procession of mourning coaches to clog the streets, and her kin and acquaintances had all agreed to meet at Manor Park. False notice of time & place had been planted in the newspapers. Foul weather conspired in the lie as well: We three slipped into the cemetery under low skies and a spitting rain to stand behind twenty, thirty mourners. When finally the last of these had left, along with the sexton and shovel-men, Speranza said it was time.

She held that she had to raise the call no later than three hours after Mrs. Chapman's committal to the consecrated earth. This she did, humbly at first; but when no response came—we knew not what that response might be, of course, but told ourselves we'd know it if and when it came—Speranza began to bray, verily bray, such that we all three felt

---

46. This was fairly standard practice in cases of murder, it being held that the last image the victim saw remained on his retina. Earlier in 1888, a man had been convicted in France on the evidence of eyeball photography. Meanwhile, of course, fingerprinting and the use of bloodhounds had yet to find favour amongst criminologists.

the fool. Still nothing. Nothing save a greater fall of rain and Caine once crying out, swearing that a nearby shadow had borne uncommon depth the instant before; which observation had him fumbling in his pocket for his flask, the contents of which, when imbibed, emboldened him to ask mightn't we leave, and *immediately.*

We did. What point was there in staying? We'd called, and no demon had come. Our solid-seeming idea was naught but an embarrassment now.

Outside the cemetery gates, we waited some while in silence for an omnibus to come; having helped Lady Wilde clamber aboard, we, Caine and I, went up after her. Nearer Trafalgar Square, we descended. Lady Wilde, as chagrined as ever I've seen her, headed home in a hansom whilst Caine and I set off afoot for the theatre; and here we have remained all afternoon and evening, there being much business pursuant to Henry's change of bill. Into said business I threw myself; for I was surprised to gauge my disappointment and find it so profound. I'd wanted to summon the demon, though still I wonder what we might have said or done if he'd come; for, though writers all, we'd not arrived at a script seeming suited to demonic intercourse. More: I'd badly wanted to rile Tumblety. I'd wanted him and Set to split, *to imperfect,* and thusly afford us some means of laying a trap we'd later spring.

Alas. Nothing. And now I close, wondering, *What next?*

Later, 3 a.m.—We were wrong: He *did* hear the call. For he came. Here. *Here!* And oh, his message is a mean one indeed.

No more now. Cannot. There is . . . *this* to somehow dispose of. Pray that action will help calm Caine. And pray, too, that . . .

No time now for prayer, or words. *Action* instead.

BRAM STOKER'S JOURNAL

Sat., 15 Sept., 5.30 a.m.—Good God, the gruesomeness of it!

I sit here in my bedroom. Though dawn approaches, I dare not descend. Can I calm myself with pen & ink, with this Record?

Caine—much medicated—sleeps across the hall. We will see Speranza shortly. Will she be heartened to learn he heeded her call? Only if I forbear telling her of the corpse; and of course I cannot: our pact is predicated upon Truth. And it is truth I shall commit to these pages, perhaps passing them to her; for to speak all this could only sully the tongue and further compromise the mind.

Caine and I came home in the small hours—rather, we returned to this place which no longer seems a home only to find that the fiend had fouled it again and . . . Oh, where are the words for this, *all this?*

Alas, it was Caine who found the corpse, and Caine whose scream drew me to the dining room. I ought to have known to search there first, and I can only wonder why I did not. Was I eager to enlist Caine further via *the possibility* of his seeing a sight such as the blood-balance? Or was I merely more afraid than he? Horrid of me; but again, candour is all, and so I must ask & answer such questions truthfully. In truth lies sanity. Oh, but he has hung my sanity on tenterhooks, has Tumblety; and I fear the same for Caine. Speranza alone is *sure*. But she has not seen what we have seen. Pray may she never.

Caine's scream was no scream at all, but rather a plaintive lowing that rose and rose and rose like steam off a kettle. At first, I—having checked the sills and doorsteps, and being still in the scullery— . . . I did not associate the sound with Caine. Was it wind through the flue? A coal-choked boat down upon the Thames? But then the sound broke into a most insistent *Bram,* . . . *Bram,* which at first I mistook for Tumblety's call. But no: His *Sto-ker, Sto-ker* has ever been the same. And so: Caine, of course! It must be Caine. Which revelation chilled me and brought me fast to the dining room, and to a second tableau the likes of which . . .

This one was more . . . *telling* than the last: I knew immediately the message, if not the means; for, coming up on the headless corpse from behind, and seeing it as it sat in my writing seat, *mine,* I mistook the meat & bone of its neck for a log. A log sitting upright in my chair. I cannot account for this delusion. I can only say that I was disabused of it by Caine, who stood staring slack-jawed and shivering and about to let fall his lamp onto the carpet. Only as I rushed round to relieve Caine of his lamp did I see the corpse as he had discovered it.

Firstly I tried to send Caine to the scullery, or simply *elsewhere*. He would not go. He clove to my side, staring at the torso—to call it a corpse is incorrect: hacked from it were its legs and left arm as well as its head, and it showed, too, a cavity atop & betwixt the pendulous breasts: *the heart had been harvested*, yes. . . . There it sat, in my seat. Or should I say there *she* sat? No: There *it* sat; for I cannot countenance the fact of the torso's having lately been a living woman. And so there *it* sat, yes, just as I have sat innumerable hours whilst writing; and lest I lose said fact, he, *he* had laid the torso's stiffening right arm atop my writing slant, where it weighted down a note.

Secondly I had to see to Caine. Although I feared he might fall into nervous collapse, the horror seemed somehow to fortify him: I was taken aback by hearing him ask not *Who?* nor *What?* nor *Why?* but rather *How?* How were we to rid ourselves of this latest . . . message? Ever the writer, is Caine; for we writers often distance ourselves from life *as it passes* and watch from a remove, as if we write the very scenes we witness, asking only, *What next?* This, Caine did. The collapse would come later.

So, too, did I survive the sight by springing into Action. Clues! There must be clues. Certainly we knew the *who* of it all, but as for the rest . . .

The flesh was yet fresh: the victim had only lately been done to death. The disseverance of its limbs was artless and showed more a savage's hand than a savant's. Blood had soaked through the chair's cushion to the carpet. The blood upon the table was scant: no splay, no blood-show, this. And by the risen light of the lamp, I trailed blood to the window sill, where I discovered mud and so supposed the means of his ingress. Throwing up the sash, I shone the lamp onto the yard beyond: nothing. Later I would look upon the leaves of the bushes for blood: again, none; and so it would seem he had only unbagged or unbundled the torso in my home. Cold comfort, this, but comfort nonetheless. If no blood led to my home, there'd be no trail for an amateur Abberline or for the Inspector himself. This tells me, too, that Tumblety does not seek to pin his crimes upon me but rather seeks my collusion, my co-operation in their commission and in the completion of his plan. And all of this confirmed his ability *to plan*. It was as we'd supposed, and worrisomely so.

Minutes later—and not four hours ago—Caine urged me into further action. Soon the two of us slipped from No. 17, enacting a most rudimentary plan. In a disused pram of Noel's, drawn down from the attic, we trundled the torso down to and into the Thames. Caine proffered words of rest unto the woman we sent to sea; I, revenge. Revenge unto he who'd done the deed. (*Q.:* Why, *why* did we not weight the remains and thereby spare another the discovery, the sight?) Returning, we spoke not a word; for I was listening for a call that did not come.

We cleansed the dining room as best we could, but our best will not suffice. I shall see the dining set turned to tinder. As for its replacement and the rest—the rugs, &c.—a newly resolute Caine promises to see to it all. (*Mem.:* Write Florence of *a surprise,* and with the promise of same put off her & Noel's return some while longer.) To-day we shall apprise Speranza of events, though Caine and I both suppose she will suggest calling to Set again, riling Tumblety again in the hope he'll spring that trap we've yet to set. That, surely, will be our plan. That, surely, will be our penance.

I ascend now to lie at Caine's side.[47]

Messieurs Stoker & Caine,
 Did you mean to tease him from me with the lady's ululating? Fools.
Your derring-do finds another whore ripped, nothing more. I did this one for
you, Mr. Stoker, as Tommy is too easy to scare. Are you scared, Mr. Sto.ker?
Does your hand rise to the level of your own heart, unbidden? Fear not, Mr.
Sto.ker; I will leave you your heart if you prove its worth. So too yours,
Tommy. And Lady Wilde's as well. Nor am I to visit Dublin or Keswick.[48]

47. And so we may presume he did; but first he slipped the discovered note into the *Dossier,* where it appears on parchment-like paper, same as the scroll, its red "ink" traced over in lead.

48. Location of Hawthorns, Caine's home sitting outside of London; habitual residence of Mary and Ralph Caine.

So Set commands. And I am having far too much fun in London at present,
watching you & awaiting your next move, & ripping hores at will. You
can stopp it Sto.ker like you started it with the majic that rose me up to
slay and be savd Do you want to stop it Sto.ker if so call me to the Scales
of Maat I shall bring the hearts to Balnce but call me for OTHER
reasons & I shall rip rip rip & do not presume, gentlemen, that your
safety is assured. Yours hearts, too, may yet be wrested away for weighing
if Set commands or allows it. Trifle with me at your peril. NO the men
are needed take the OTHER or have another hore But I will do as I
am told. It is he, not I, who saves you; but, should you set yourselves
between us again, I will slice & rip you both I promised HIM he could
Set says I may. And I will use your knife, Mr. Sto.ker, as the blade of
it sits so well in our hand.

Call again to ME for the ONE reason ONLY The Weighing otherwise
we shall slay rip & rip & rip and Set will accede to my wish, and let me
take in hand your three worthless hearts as well as [49]

LETTER, BRAM STOKER TO THORNLEY STOKER

Mon., 17 Sep't. '88

CONFIDENTIAL

Dearest Brother,

Firstly, do not let Florence know I have written. I do so to apprise
you of developments here, and as you learn of same, you will
understand and no doubt honour my request. No-one save C., Sp., &
myself knows what I am about to confide in you, Thornley, the fourth
member of our stygian band, *and no-one can.*

Do, though, send word of Noel, pls. Send word of Emily as well.
Better still: Ready yourself to bring word in person. Truly, Thornley,

---

49. The letter ends, mid-page, without signature.

set your bag at the door; for you may soon be needed here, as all has devolved to *a veritable hell.*

The American man, the possessed—Tumblety, you will recall: Francis J. Tumblety—has shown himself again, and shown, too, his hellish handiwork; indeed, he has rendered our home a shambles. For, Friday last, he brought a woman's body (duly disposed of) to No. 17, though to call it a body does not bespeak the atrocities he'd committed unto it. As I told you in Dublin, he has brought death here before, but lately he has done so intending to leave me messages. He has even left me two notes of the strangest sort, the gist of which is that he wishes us—*me* in particular, doubtless because I was present at the ritual via which his possessing demon rose—to assist him in another ritual, one to be done along Egyptian lines, and for a fuller comprehension of which I can only, at present, refer you to the Papyrus of Ani and those chapters speaking to the Weighing of the Heart. (Will explain more & better in person, Thorn.) Suffice it to say that requisite to said ritual are hearts, *human hearts,* and this accounts for the Wh'chapel horrors of which you, of which *all the world,* lately reads.

Make no mistake, Thornley: A brutal business, this, and bloody; and the blood is being drawn, I fear, with a blade of my own. (Again, I will explain.) . . . Thornley, brother, do you recall how, as a child, I hated blood? Well, now that I am verily awash in it, I find that the feeling has persisted into adulthood. I don't know how you & the other Bros. Stoker do it, truly I don't.[50] Indeed, can you not hear me screaming, still, like a Banshee, as Uncle Willy comes round my sickbed with his lancet and leeches, eager to bleed me?[51] Dreadful, that; and the stuff of many a nightmare since. Indeed, the night mare runs roughshod over my days at present, if not my nights; for *I cannot*

---

50. Bram Stoker was alone amongst his brothers in not becoming a surgeon.

51. Referenced here is Wm. Stoker, long associated with Dublin's Fever Hospital and House of Recovery; who, like other doctors of the day, frequently practised bleeding via the application of leeches or the opening of the temporal artery. It may be supposed that young Bram, being sickly, was subjected to these practices more than most.

sleep, not at all, leastways not without the help of those addictive aids against which you have long warned me. I do take care, brother. I take care as best I can.

Alas. The horrors of Friday last seem to have been occasioned by a plan of Lady Wilde's, which at first we'd deemed ineffectual. Brief: Speranza had struck upon a means of summoning the demon, and summon him we did; rather I should write summon *them,* the double-entity. Our hope was to dissever possessor from possessed and set them to struggling; in the course of which, we would throw-in with one or the other, depending, doing whatever might stop the atrocities. Although you may deem us over-ambitious or deluded, or worse, let me say that we did succeed in summoning the demon (madness, this!); but in so doing we taunted Tumblety, who took terrible action in consequence: the torso.

Still, Speranza is convinced that we ought to do the same again, reasoning thus: If we set the villain into action, perhaps we can predict his *re*action. Our only goal is to stop the slaughter, though now Caine insists we ought to somehow steer Tumblety towards the Yard, towards Inspector Abberline as well. This *must* be done, says Caine, even if those ruinous letters of his come to light. I disagree. He is doing his best to be brave, is Caine; but I fear for him, Thornley, truly I do. And I refer not only to his name but his health as well—another reason we may need you near.

More: We are agreed that the only way to turn Abberline from my door—yes, he persists, and lately knocked at No. 17 when yet the dining room was in disarray, the bloodied carpet still rolled in the corner, but blessedly Caine put him off, explaining that the draperies covering the dining set, &c., were owing to a gift I am about to make my wife: a renovation; the now *fact* of which is a welcome distraction for Caine, yes, but also serves to explain both Florence's extended absence and my Dublin week, about which, as you supposed, the Inspector was quite curious— . . . I say that the only way to turn Abberline from my door is to stop Tumblety. But we have yet to locate the door, be it a metaphorical one, viz., the means of entrapment, or a literal door—in Batty Street or elsewhere—behind which he hides. And so what more can we do but call again to Set, and hope Tumblety shows? If you find fault in this, Thornley, if our reasoning seems to you spurious, wire at once. I am not at all certain we are thinking straight; rather, I know Caine is not, and I have suspicions re: Speranza and myself.

Yours,
Bram

P.S. Will write Flo. under separate cover to apprise her of a decorative surprise, done in collusion w/ Caine, that necessitates her staying at Ely Place some while longer. Wire at once if this does not suit; and bless you, brother, if it does. B.

P.P.S Pls retain or return this letter; will explain.

BRAM STOKER'S JOURNAL

Wednesday, 19 Sept.—Caine is crazed indeed, but now it is with catalogues ordered over from this and that manufactory. I am told we Stokers shall soon dine in a room the lower walls of which will be colored *café-au-lait*; and that the new crimson carpet coming from Peter Robinson's is still *au courant* "despite the opinions proffered by Mrs. Panton," whoever she might be. ("Green—and green alone—is to be avoided," says Caine, contrarily.) It would seem that an over-mantel and larger mirror are to factor in the re-done room as well. My role—other than being measured, as though for a suit, by a man from Maples in the Tottenham Court Road, from which place will come a customised escritoire, Caine being determined to end my habit of writing at my slant at the dining table: a habit that I, too, am ready to surrender, considering— ... my only role in this redecorating is to choose a pattern of china that will please Florence. Service of same, for twenty, is to be ordered and paid for by Mr. Hall Caine himself. That fact will perforce render whatever china I choose *most* appealing to my wife. So, too, will she enjoy telling her callers that the *papier peint* upon our walls was chosen from samples sent over for Caine's consideration by none other than Mr. William Morris. (*Q.:* Do people do Caine's bidding because he writes or because he has grown rich from it? I confess I cannot tell.)

And so it seems we will maintain ourselves at No. 17 some while longer, though I wonder as to the wisdom of Caine's doing all this now. Oughtn't we to wait upon . . . whatever may come? Caine says no. Caine says he cannot wait. He must busy himself with things other than this red-business and cares not a whit for cost; and so I consent, opining only that a crimson rug seems to me a wise as well as a tasteful choice, considering. Too, I sat this morning poring over china patterns. Only when I realised that a quarter-hour had passed without thoughts of Whitechapel, &c. . . . well, only then did I understand the motivation of my dear Hommy-Beg. And he is right: Blessed be *distraction* nowadays, no matter the means.

BRAM STOKER'S JOURNAL

Sun., 23 September 1888.—The week being quiet, & still, & with no calls or corpses coming, we three determined to convene after Speranza's Saturday at-home, for she has resumed her *conversazioni* so as to preserve her name and self, says she.

We were late in arriving yesterday, Caine and I, and purposefully so: social converse seems rather beside the point at present. Alas, we were not late enough, for we ran smack into a departing Inspector Abberline.

"Inspector," said I, quite surprised, when we met him on the Park Street steps.

"Mr. Stoker," said he. "Mr. Caine. . . . I thought it likely I might find you here."

"But how *un*likely that we would find you," said Caine. "Have you been to Lady Wilde's before?"

"I have not had the pleasure previously," said he.

"To what, then," queried Caine, "is the pleasure owing *at present?*" Rather arch, that. And the Inspector agreed, for he verily spat what next he said, which was:-

"A cloak, Mr. Caine.... A torn and bloody cloak has lately been discovered in the vicinity of Westminster, near about Parliament Street and the St. Stephen's Club."

Caine and I shared a glance, but it was I who asked, "Is that not near—"

"It is indeed," answered Abberline, peremptorily. "Very near the site of what is to be the new headquarters of the Metropolitan Police."

Caine and I shared a second glance. "Inspector," said he, "I know nearly as well as you that London is chockablock with . . . with bloody cloaks."

"Not quite, Mr. Caine. Not quite. Take care not to confuse your romances with the real world."

Before Caine could take the Inspector's bait, I said, "Regardless, Inspector, what has this cloak to do with us? For I suspect you came here to-day to convey this news to us."

"The news I came to convey to you, Mr. Stoker, is not that a bloody cloak has been found but rather that said cloak bears a label sewn into its liner reading *Property of the Lyceum Theatre.*"

"Are you . . . are you certain, Inspector?" It was Caine who asked the question. I was struck silent.

Said Abberline—with a derisive snort? a half-snort and a shallow sigh?—"As it is the writer's job, Mr. Caine, to be clear, concise, and clever, so it is an Inspector's to be certain.... Yes, Mr. Caine, I am certain." He turned now to me, continuing with, "However, I am not at all certain what you, Mr. Stoker, may know about the costume in question."

"A *man's* cloak, was it?" Had Caine lost the cloak from *The Merch.* marked *Jessica,* the one he'd worn the night my senses had riled me so? Abberline affirmed he had not, saying:-

"A man's cloak, yes. Black, worsted wool," adding, somewhat snidely, "with silk at the collar and sleeves." Henry, then? Was this his spit-stained

Shylock cloak? The one he'd worn the night I'd first seen Tumblety in Batty Street?

"I . . . I shall have to check with Henry. He does sometimes venture out in costume, and borrows from the Lyceum at will, of course."

"Please do check with Mr. Irving," said he. "I shall await word from you."

"And you shall have it," said I, adding, as Abberline stepped onto the sidewalk proper, "Inspector? The press . . . ? Surely there is no need to . . . ?"

"No need at all, Mr. Stoker," said he. "Hounds, they are. Hounds with no sense of smell."

"Indeed," said I, my smile forced. And just as I pushed open the Park Street door, I heard his call behind me:-

"Oh, and Mr. Stoker . . . ?"

"Sir?" said I, turning round.

"As it relates to the Lyceum's own"—here he dropped his voice, as if we two were co-conspirators—"*hounds*, was not there a question of some articles of clothing having gone missing from your store about that same time?"

He knew the answer full well. "Unfortunately, Inspector, our store is such that its mistress was unable to say definitively if that were the case."

"I see," said he, and I quite feared he did, *does*. "And I assume you've heard nothing from Mr. Tumblety?"

I shook my head. So, too, did Caine.

"Strange, that," said Abberline, "*most* strange. Rarely have I known a man of means to vanish like . . . like that," and he snapped his fingers before using them to run the brim of his bowler and thereby bid us good-day.

"What do you make of this latest?" asked Speranza some half-hour later, her salon clear now of all save two fawning Frenchmen intent on meeting her second, absent son.

"I . . . I don't know," said I, and I did not. "Except—"

"Wait please, Mr. Stoker," said she; and, gesturing to the Frenchmen, beckoning them nearer, she sent them away in their own language. This—to judge by their collective sneer—they were not at all happy to hear. "If they hope to see As-car," said Speranza, "then they ought to search their own capital city. I am *merely* the man's mother, and as such I have surrendered all expectation of filial kindness; oh, but still, Mr. Stoker, are two or three words in a telegram asking too much?"

I shook my head in sympathy, in solidarity.

"Go on, Mr. Stoker," said Speranza with a sigh. "About the cloak . . ."

"As I told the Inspector, I know nothing of it, nothing certain. Except, well . . . it is quite feasible that Henry let it fall in the streets of Whitechapel."

"Or *he* may have stolen it." Caine meant, of course, Tumblety, but he has fallen so far from calling the fiend Francis that now he is unable to name him at all.

"I shall check with Henry and Mrs. Pinch post-haste," said I. And, feeling quite the cabalist, I added, "If the cloak is not at the Lyceum, and if Henry cannot recall losing it, well, then, I will simply convince him of the possibility of same; for I am the man's memory, after all, am I not? And then Henry Irving shall send word, *signed* word, of same to Inspector Abberline."

"That will be well done, Mr. Stoker," said Speranza. "Well done indeed. . . . I do not favor this Abberline at all, and can only hope that none present at to-day's *conversazione* knew him from the Yard."

"Even if they did," said Caine, "no-one could think he'd come on *official* business."

"You miss my point entirely, Mr. Caine." Whereupon Speranza put it in plainer terms: "If the police are known to be present at my salons, then the criminal element will not come. And with whom, Mr. Caine, would *you* rather consort of a Saturday?"

I steered my peers back to more immediate concerns, and Speranza—just as we'd supposed she would—spoke persuasively of calling again to Set so as to rile his vessel, Tumblety, into action.

"But when he takes action," said Caine, "blood is shed."

"True; and of that we have had excess of proof," said Speranza. "But I believe we shan't see the same again."

"How can you be sure?" I asked.

"I cannot be sure, of course; and to be wrong is to see another . . . another of that sad sorority done to death. This I understand too well, I do. But I beg you to consider:

"One: He will not harm *you,* Mr. Stoker; for he needs you, or rather believes he does."

"What about me?" This from Caine.

"Of your security, Mr. Caine, I am less certain. . . . Two: As he believes he needs you, Bram, so, too, does he believe he needs you *now;* for he has his human heart, does he not, drawn from the cadaver set down at your dining table?"

"So we may assume."

"Indeed," said Speranza. "Now we have only to goad his . . . his Devourer into action at a time and place best suited to our purpose."

"Our purpose being what, precisely?" I asked. "Are we to apprehend him somehow? Train our pistols upon him?" Speranza confessed she did not know.

Caine, however, supposed he did. "It is clear: We surrender him to Abberline. I no longer care about the cost to myself. I cannot. What I might suffer is naught, *naught* compared to . . ." To what the torso, to what *she* whom we'd lately committed to the Thames had suffered; she and however many others done to death before her. And *after* her as well, for if we . . . Oh, but it is too horrid to consider what may come if we fail.

"You are courageous, Mr. Caine," said Speranza. "But understand: I jested about the salutary benefits of scandal, quite; and a man like yourself, sir . . . Well, let me simply say that the odds of your surviving forced labour in jail would *not* be good."

"Agreed," said I. "No Abberline, leastways not till we take fuller measure of Tumblety. . . . Perhaps he has no letters. Perhaps he has them and will hand them over to us in exchange for this ritual of his."

"You are kind, my friends. Too kind." Caine hung his head, cha-grined. I feared tears, and so was heartened to hear, "We speak *lunacy* here: summoning demons, arranging to rendezvous with a ripping murderer..."

"We *live* lunacy at present, Mr. Caine," said Speranza, "and the only way to survive it is to forge through it. Agreed?" It seemed so, to judge by our silence.

"Our impediments, then, are these," said Speranza. "Will we be able to summon Set a second time if we keen over a corpse that concerns him not at all? Will the anonymous dead do?" I was not in the least sure the anonymous dead *would* do, but still I acceded to Speranza's suggestion that we all three return to the Manor Park Cemetery, and I convinced Caine to do the same. But before we left her salon, Speranza arranged a word with me in private, sending Caine into her study to sign her copy of *The Deemster*—my copy, in point of fact, which she had lately borrowed; but no matter. And when we were alone, she wasted no time in whisper-ing to me, "Steel yourself, Bram. And arm yourself as well. For I recall to you that—in the rare case, and indeed this is that—my Roman coun-sels murder. And I don't suppose the deed will fall to Mr. Hall Caine."

"Speranza," said I, "I cannot!"

"No, you cannot," said she. "Yet it may come to pass that you must, in which case you *will*." And if so—Heaven help me!—I shall hark back to Burton's words for strength: *The explorer in savage places holds, day and night, his life in his hand; and if he is not prepared for every emergency, he should not attempt such adventures.*

LETTER, THORNLEY STOKER TO BRAM STOKER

Friday, 21 September 1888

Bram, dearest brother,

Let my delay in responding to your letter of the 17th indicate nothing more than that I have had some deviltry of my own here in

Dublin, dealing with Emily, who worsens. Your Florence, may I say, has been a balm throughout, and the light of your Noel a benediction. Be assured, they are welcome here at Ely Place for as long as it suits your situation. Indeed, their company is most welcome to me at present, as my poor wife— But alas, I steal this time to address your troubles and not my own.

Were I you, I would worry about the American and Abberline *in that order*. I mean not to state the obvious, Bram, but rather to warn: Do not underestimate the Inspector! Surely he watches you three if he knew enough to search you out at Lady Wilde's with this business of the bloody cloak. But do you suppose he—Tumblety—is behind that? If so, beware. He may be seeking to set the Inspector onto you with the purloined property. In any case, you have not heard the last regarding that cloak, surely.

As regards your imminent actions—Call out to the demon *with extreme of care*. I cannot say I am wholly in accord with Lady Wilde's suggestion, yet that is a personal and not a professional opinion. I know the mad well, yes, and have met many a murderer amongst their number, but never have I been party to such insanity as this! Indeed, this species of beast is as new to me as it is you. It is, in a word, otherworldly; and so to pull the possessor onto the worldly plane, as Speranza suggests, is a risk, a risk indeed. One that may eventuate in either the wished-for "dialogue"—is it to be supposed that the possessed can be *reasoned* with?—or, yes, more bloodshed.

And of course I will come when called. I shall simply tell Florence that I am called away on consultation and ask her to manage my house and wife. She, by the way, received your letter well and is content to stay here in Dublin till all the work be done, and indeed she wonders—aloud and at length—what Caine's decorators will do; and so it may behoove you, Bram, to redo your dining room as *grandly* as Caine's coin allows. Thusly you will both buy yourself time and rid the room of its associated horrors as well.

Meanwhile, till such time as you call me to your side, do keep me apprised by whatever means. And if it be but a communiqué of few words, pray let those words be *All is well.* Somehow all will be well, though would that I knew how! Would, too, that I had sounder advice than *Take care!* If only you Children of Light could write your way clear of this Tumblety—pursued by your three pens, he would stand no chance of escape. Oh, but he is real, too real, and these present truths are indeed stranger than any fiction.

With blessings on you,
and a brother's love,
TH. Sto.

BRAM STOKER'S JOURNAL

Mon., 24 Sept., mid-night.—How dared we to gamble when the stakes were lives other than our own? What penance can cleanse us? For we have called, and now he has come promising to rip anew.

Yesterday we three fools retraced our steps of Friday the 14th and returned to the site of Mrs. Chapman's interment, Manor Park Cemetery; for we'd deemed Sunday *the day of death.* It was again drear, with rain drizzling down. The hour was noon. Speranza had risen early and had done herself down in blackest mourning; and though Caine and I hadn't benefit of a like veil, so, too, did we dissemble lest we be seen falsely mourning the stranger we'd yet to select.

We had to wait some while for a funeral to come and conclude; whereupon Speranza would keen over the anonymous soul whilst hoping, *hoping* it would be as suited to the summoning as Mrs. Chapman's had been. And then, supposing Set heeded the summons and sent Tumblety to us, I would agree to the Weighing—whatever shape *that* might take—if he, Tumblety, would stop the slaying. And if the struggle within rendered him rational, for wont of a better word, we would reason with him further, perhaps even securing Caine's letters or the promise of their disposal in exchange for we-knew-not-what. Only then, with Caine's name in surety, would we go further: If an avenue opened to us, we would draw Tumblety down it, nearer to Inspector Abberline. We would drive the demon/Devourer to bay in some place where the catching and the destroying would be sure. It was, in sum, an arrogant plan. Pathetic-seeming, too, now that it shall never come to pass.

Alas. Lady Wilde took it as luck when we learned that an Irishman had been interred at noontide, as, said she, no-one would look askance at a widow keening over her departed Paddy. And she seemed just that: a widow in her weeds, going slowly down onto her knees beside the fresh gravesite. Caine and I watched from a distance. We'd gone to Manor Park the long way round, watching for men from the Yard. We'd seen none, and saw none now. Finally, Speranza's death-song was sung, was done. She was some while in righting herself, but then she sailed back towards us like a pirate ship on a stilled sea, her black veil billowing on the risen breeze.

There we stood in the cemetery, attendant. Did we think Tumblety would suddenly show? Did we think the weather would worsen, and Set would speak as thunder? It shames and embarrasses me to wonder what it was we thought; so I shall record only that we waited, and waited, and waited some more, till finally I grew fearful of going home. Surely it was there he'd show himself again—I shuddered at wondering how—if he'd heard the summons.

And hear it he had. So, too, did he show. Though this time it was in word only, but oh, what horrid words they were, or rather are; for a letter, *this* letter, arrived in to-day's post.[52]

> *You disobey. You mock. WE said call when the WEIGHING was ready.*
> *Now watch for more whores. 2 more yes yes For mighty SET Almighty SET*
> *frees me to do as I please, and your blade being so sharp at present STO.*
> *KER I will put off the rite & instead say LETS PLAY 2 more to rip rip*
> *one for STO.KER one for CAINE. Watch the post for proof Jolly Jolly &*

---

52. Stoker pasted said letter into his journal at this point—best of luck, Ms. Durand, should your lawyers seek to cull the *Dossier* for DNA. Like the others, this letter is on parchment-like paper, and the medium would seem to be blood. (Nota bene: no envelope extant.)

STOP ME STOP ME does Saturday suit for slaughter ha ha Tell Boss all about it & catch me if you can STOP ME please Will be a rip & a clip & TO HELL with the hearts FJT

BRAM STOKER'S JOURNAL (CONTINUED)

"Francis *J*. Tumblety, yes, I believe so," said Caine in response to my query. "John, perhaps . . . or maybe James. But what of it, Bram?"

"Yes," seconded Speranza, who'd come round in a cab at my call, "what of it? The sender's middle initial seems hardly the salient point of such correspondence as this."

Perhaps not; but I'd struck upon an idea.

"This letter threatens the lives of two women, yes? Lives to be taken Saturday next, in five days' time." On this we were agreed. The threat was plain. "What, then, are we to do in the—"

"Yes," blurted out Caine, "what *are* we do? To watch and wait does not work."

"And look what's come now of our taking action," said Speranza. "Oh, dear . . . oh, dear"; and we barely got a chair beneath her before she fell into a half-swoon. "I . . . I . . ."

"We all have grounds for self-recrimination, Speranza," said I, "but I suggest we desist in practising it. Instead let us take heart"—a most unfortunate phrase, this— ". . . I mean to say we should be encouraged that for the first time we are forewarned. We have five days; five days in which to work."

"To work at *what?*" asked Caine.

"To work at saving two lives," said I.

"Oh, but *how,* Mr. Stoker? Pray tell us."

"By doing what it is we do best. By writing." Silence, silence till Speranza said:-

"Do you propose that we prowl through Whitechapel and its surrounds, me keening and you stepping out of the shadows to bash the murderer down with a weighty book bearing the name of our Mr. Caine?"

Caine took up the game. "Or perhaps we might incite emotional paresis with bits of Lady Wilde's poesy?"

"Well, then, league up, friends! What do *you* propose? That you, Caine, tuck your tail and hie back to your castle keep? And you, Lady Wilde? Do you mean to delve deeper into the surreal in search of more and better ways to frenzy the fiend?"

"Well," said Lady Wilde as I stood there staring, steaming, "... 'by *writing*,' eh? It must be said: It *is* the sole thing we all do well. ... Explain, please, Mr. Stoker."

"It was Thornley who put me in mind of it. In a recent letter, he lamented that we three could not pursue the murderer with our pens. Said he, 'No criminal could escape you then.' And so I fell to wondering: Mightn't we write?"

"Write of what?" asked Speranza.

"Write to whom?" asked Caine.

"Yes! *To* whom is the question, Caine. And the answer is Abberline, of course, in care of Scotland Yard." I reasoned it out thusly:

We have five days before the promised murders occur—and we are all three agreed: They *will* occur. If, in those five days, we have Abberline on our tails and not Tumblety's, then we are constrained whilst he is free. The women of Whitechapel require the reverse: we free, and he hindered. And so we ought to write to Abberline, letting him put all the Yard on lookout for Saturday next as well as the days precedent to it.

Said Caine, "But all along we have told the Inspector we know nothing of Tumblety. How do we recant now?"

"*We* are not going to write Abberline," said I. "He is. ... Tumblety is."

"Impersonate him, do you mean?" I nodded to Caine and waved the villain's latest letter.

"Well," mused Speranza, "it *is* an idea. And if all Whitechapel is acrawl with the authorities Saturday next—"

"Will he not simply desist?" interrupted Caine. "Wait to strike another time?"

"No," said Speranza and I simultaneously, though it was she who continued:-

"Remember, Mr. Caine, our enemy is driven by a demon, and no demon will demur before humanity. Was Lucifer not arrogance itself? So, too, will Tumblety proceed: *arrogantly.* But arrogance has been the bane of many a murderer, and by it they betray themselves."

"And what if he succeeds at murder first?" asked Caine. "What then?"

No-one cared to consider the question. Instead Speranza said, simply, "Let's begin"; and further asked if I had any red ink to hand.

"Blood-red, do you mean? Brilliant! Yes, yes, I have some upstairs: Henry insists that I log all debits in red."

"Fetch it down, Mr. Stoker. And choose the pen of your preference, as I think it best you write the letter, my penmanship being execrable even by the standards of the criminally insane, and as for Mr. Caine's shaking hands. . . . As said, Mr. Stoker, I think this falls to you." And so it did.

I sat down to christen the newly-delivered escritoire. My friends overhung my shoulders, commenting on each writing style I tried. Too wild. Too left-slanting, &c. It was Speranza who spurred me to a suitable style in saying, "Remember, Bram: You are a madman."

"So I am," said I. "So I am." And soon we set about composing.

The salutation came from Caine: "'Dear Boss,'" he quoted, and I wrote it; for thusly had Tumblety referred to Abberline.

"He is an American, remember," said Speranza.

"I shall bear it in mind," said I. "But are we to hint at Tumblety in this? With Americanisms? With anatomical references such as a doctor might make?"

"I think so, yes," said Speranza. "It is, after all, Tumblety they must be on the lookout for."

"True," said Caine. "And we must hint, too,—or *more than hint*—at his madness."

"Yes, but make no mention of the demon," said Speranza. "Rather much, that, for the men of Scotland Yard. A *mere* madman, a *mere* murderer must suffice."

"All of which is well and good," said I, sitting back; for my co-authors had come too near, each slavering for the pen as a dog does a bone. "But it is words we want now." I gestured down at the still-blank sheet. "*Words,* if you please."

Caine began to pace: to compose, in other words. Lady Wilde slowly lowered herself to recline upon the new crimson carpet, hoping her stays would not do to her words what they were doing to her once-waist. She worried needlessly; for when she next spoke, it was to proffer the first usable line, viz. a line on which two of us three were agreed. It was a reference to the many men whom the police have in custody at present:-

"'I keep on hearing the police have caught me, but they won't fix me just yet.'"

"Oh, yes," enthused Caine, "quite good, that; especially the 'fix me yet.' But make special mention of the Jew they have in hand—or have they already let him go?"

"Leather Apron, do you mean?"[53] And I fanned my fingers, lest my hand tighten and the writing seem . . . what? Sane?

"Leather Apron, yes," said Caine. "How about this: 'I have laughed when they look so clever and talk about being on the right track.'" I underlined in red the word "right," as Tumblety had his *ha ha.* "'That joke about Leather Apron gave me real fits.'"

"Good," enthused Speranza from the floor. "Are you misspelling at all, Mr. Stoker?"

"I have not as yet."

"Do so; but not badly," said Caine. "Subtlety will see the job done. . . . What's wanted now is something American? Something . . . boastful of all the blood. Bram?"

And so the next line was mine: "I am down on whores and I shant

---

53. Suspicion briefly fell on a Jewish Pole, an émigré named Kaminsky, also known as Leather Apron (owing to his work as a cobbler). Kaminsky was soon exonerated, but the rumour of his involvement threatened the large Jewish population of Whitechapel, many of whose members had lately fled pogroms in their home countries.

quit ripping them till I do get buckled." It was at Speranza's suggestion that I let fall the apostrophe on "shan't."

So it went, we three composing in uncommon accord till the letter read:

... "Grand work the last job was. I gave the lady no time to squeal How can they catch me now, I love my work and want to start again. you will soon hear of me with my funny little games. I saved some of the proper red stuff in a ginger beer bottle over the last job to write with but it went thick like glue and I cant use it. Red ink is fit enough I hope *ha, ha.*"

This last line was owing to my observation that the drying ink resembled blood not at all; and if I knew as much, so, too, would the police, surely.

I continued: "The next job I do I shall clip the ladys ears off and send to the police officers just for jolly wouldn't you."

Caine objected that "shall" was not sufficiently American, and when I disagreed with him, it fell to Speranza, who threw the quorum toward "shall," as it were, saying, "We have already used 'shan't.' Simply avoid a second usage, Mr. Stoker, and we will spare ourselves having to recommence. I dislike multiple draughts.... Continue, please." And we did, taking up the timing of it all and agreeing that we'd write & post it for receipt by Abberline on Friday next:

"Keep this letter back till I do a bit more work then give it out straight. My knife's so nice and sharp I want to get to work right away if I get a chance. Good luck."

And though I balked at any mention of a knife, lest my kukri ever come to light, I was outnumbered, and the mention remains. Now there was naught to do but sign the letter, and so I did, writing, before I knew it, "Yours truly"; and as that seemed so placid, so pale, I followed it up fast with "Jack the Ripper."

"Capital, that," said Caine. "Jack for Tumblety's J., do you mean?"

I shrugged my shoulders. I supposed so, I said.

"But we made no mention of his being a medical man," said Caine, coming to peer over my shoulder at the second page, and adding, "Plus, it's far too neat. Soil it somehow, Bram." And so I did, with ink spills and such, before adding:

". . . wasn't good enough to post this before I got all the red ink off my hands curse it.

"No luck yet. They say I'm a doctor now *ha ha*," and that is how I closed, relieved to set aside the pen and the persona, both.

"Are we done, then?" asked Speranza. It took Caine and me both to raise her up from her recumbency on the rug. "Is it ready for a Friday posting to Abberline?"

"I don't know," said I, rethinking my original idea. "Do you think sending it to Abberline is perhaps too . . . too pat, too predictable?"

"Who then?" asked Caine.

I did not need to think long, for had I not just sent facsimiles to 400 members of the press announcing our season-opening *Jekyll and Hyde?* Indeed I had, and so it was I said, "The Central News Agency."

"For dissemination?" asked Caine. "I hardly think—"

"Not at all. We shall send it to Abberline *in care of* the Central News Agency."

"Well, it *does* seem to me something a madman, a murderer might do," said Speranza. "Rather risky, after all, dealing directly with Scotland Yard. . . . But what if—Heaven forfend—the pressmen publish it?"

"They will not," said I. "I know the men of the press, and they are as honourable a lot as one finds in any other profession. If the letter is, or rather seems, addressed to Inspector Abberline—and I will address the envelope to 'The Boss' as well—then they will see that he receives it. As concerns the Whitechapel outrages, who else might the boss be? No-one but Abberline, surely."

Caine sighed and said, "Bram, having been a member of the press, I cannot say I share your high opinion of its personnel. That said, I see by Lady Wilde's wagging chin that she is like-minded with you in the matter: I am outnumbered, and so I desist. . . . Let us send it to the Central News Agency Friday next, a.m. Let us send it, and hope to Heaven—

Heaven and Hell, both—that it finds its mark and *all* constabularies are called out Saturday next and that he, Tumblety, is apprehended at, nay before, pray let it be *before* he sees his threat through."

And there the matter stands at present: The letter is written and waiting.[54]

LETTER, BRAM STOKER TO THORNLEY STOKER

25 September 1888[55]

Dear Thornley,

Do do *do* thank Noel for his note of last week. I have written doing so, of course, but a tap atop the head from his Uncle Thornley— along with a few words of what his note meant to his Ol' Da, if you please—would be man-making to the boy, I'm sure. And Florence? I miss them much at present; but they must stay in Dublin, and these letters must do till this business be done.

Letters. Of letters *other* than those from loved ones, I've had quite enough of late. I cannot explain upon this page, but I shall do so as soon as we meet. Suffice it to say, now, that your last letter put a plan into action, and indeed we three have written. Look for *a review* to appear in the papers soon.

Bram.

P.S. Pray, Thornley, that our letter not be misdelivered. Pray that its purpose be achieved. For if he is not stopped, we are to see 2 more Saturday next.

---

54. In point of fact, the infamous "Dear Boss" letter was posted on Thursday, 27 September 1888, not Friday the 28th, as agreed upon by its writers. Did Stoker worry that if he waited, the letter might not find its way to Abberline in time? We cannot know.

55. A Tuesday; one day after the composition of the "Dear Boss" letter.

TELEGRAM, BRAM STOKER TO LADY JANE WILDE

29 September, 1888.—Word from w/in the Yard. The letter has arrived 1 day later than wanted. They think it a hoax. Horrors to-night. C. & I to Wh.ch. at nightfall. News to you as it is known.

BRAM STOKER'S JOURNAL

29 Sept. '88.—Fools! A hoax, indeed. Caine & I compose again: T-A-K-E H-E-E-D. Can only pray that they will. A card this time, and into the post with speed.[56]

BRAM STOKER'S JOURNAL

30 Sept.; 5 a.m.—He has taken us to Hell.

CLIPPING FROM *LLOYD'S WEEKLY NEWSPAPER,* SUNDAY, 30 SEPTEMBER 1888

MORE EAST-END TRAGEDIES
THIS (SUNDAY) MORNING.
ATROCIOUS MURDER OF A WOMAN IN ALDGATE.
THE VICTIM DISEMBOWELLED AND MUTILATED.
2ND HORRIBLE MURDER IN COMMERCIAL ROAD EAST.
About 25 minutes to two o'clock this (Sunday) morning a murder
of a most atrocious character, in which the revolting details of

---

56. This entry seems to indicate that Stoker and Caine also wrote what is known as the "Saucy Jacky" note, a postcard showing the same handwriting and written in the same red ink as the "Dear Boss" letter. Its contents:

the recent tragedies in Whitechapel have been intensified, was discovered by a City policeman on duty in Mitre-square, Aldgate, a thoroughfare at the junction of Leadenhall and Fenchurch streets. A woman, who appeared to be between 35 and 40 years of age, was found lying in the right-hand (south-east) corner of the square, completely disembowelled. Her clothes were thrown over the head, and this revealed the fact that a gash extending right up the body to the breast had been inflicted. There were, in addition, other gashes on both sides of the face, and the nose had been completely severed.

The woman is said to have been respectably dressed, and her figure well developed. The sound of a policeman's whistle attracted attention to the square, and the first spectators who arrived were despatched for medical and other aid. A most sickening spectacle presented itself. The whole of the inside of the murdered woman, with the heart and lungs, appeared to have been wrenched from the body, and lay, in ghastly prominence, scattered about the head and neck, and on the pavement near.

The police and detectives speedily mustered in force, and blocked the thoroughfares leading to the awful scene, around which the most intense excitement prevailed.

Between 12 and 1 this (Sunday) morning a second woman, with her throat gashed and torn, was found in the back yard of 40, Berner-street, Commercial-road E., a few minutes' walk from Hanbury-street. The premises belong to the International Working Men's club. Mr. Demship, the steward of the club, went to the yard, and in a corner he discovered the woman. He at once communicated with the police on duty, and assistance was sent

---

"I was not codding dear old Boss when I gave you the tip, you'll hear about Saucy Jacky's work to-morrow double event this time number one squealed a bit couldn't finish straight off. ha not the time to get ears for police. thanks for keeping last letter back till I got to work again." And again it was signed "Jack the Ripper."

As the card referenced "the double event"—as it would henceforth be called—*before* it occurred, it succeeded in rousing the authorities upon its receipt, 1 October 1888. Of course, by then it was too late.

for from the Leman-street police-station, from whence officers were despatched with an ambulance. Dr. Phillips was sent for, who came at 1.30 in a cab. Other medical gentlemen subsequently arrived. In comparison with the horrible mutilation of the Mitre-square victim, this was said to be "an ordinary murder," though reasons exist for believing that the assassin was disturbed, and thus his savage intention unfulfilled.

LATEST PARTICULARS.
NO CLUE.

On making inquiries at Shoreditch police station, at eleven o'clock to-day (Sunday), we were informed that the police were still without the slightest clue to the mystery. There is a growing belief that the two crimes were committed by one man, as the two bodies were found within a distance of each other which can be easily walked in ten minutes—one shortly after half-past twelve, and the other an hour later.

LETTER, BRAM STOKER TO THORNLEY STOKER

2 Oct. '88

Thornley,

The news reaches you.

We are not well. We know not what to do. Caine is prostrated, and, loaded with laudanum, he sleeps with a pistol beneath his pillow. Lady Wilde persists at wit's end, repeating ad nauseam the motto of Paris.[57] All the while I seek distraction—and the preservation of sanity—in the new season; for these bloodlusting Londoners flock to our *Jekyll*.

B.

---

57. Strange, this; but the motto is *Fluctuat nec mergitur:* "It is tossed by the waves but does not sink."

BRAM STOKER'S JOURNAL

3 October, 8 a.m. o/c.—I sit here at home, attendant upon Abberline; for this latest news from W'minster tells me he will come calling.

Firstly, I record that we were there, Caine and I, in Wh'chapel Sat. last; but we witnessed nothing—no call came—and so we were helpless. The police were scant; or rather, no more a presence than they typically are. When finally a constable's whistle rose so shrilly up from the scene in Mitre Square, we hastened home, helpless indeed and thinking it best we not be espied thereabouts by Abberline, by anyone. We summoned Speranza to No. 17; and, sitting silently through the small hours, we all three awaited word, viz., the newspapers. When finally word was had, our regret at having left Wh'chapel redoubled; for it hadn't occurred to us that the victims would not be taken in tandem. Had we stayed, mightn't we have spared the 2nd victim, a Mrs. Eddowes?

Naught to do these last days but watch the press and wait for word from w/in the Yard or from the Adversary himself. Or Abberline; to whom, we have agreed, innocence/ignorance will be pled regarding these late developments in W'minster:[58]

ANOTHER GHASTLY DISCOVERY IN LONDON.
A MUTILATED BODY AT WESTMINSTER.

About twenty minutes past three o'clock yesterday afternoon Frederick Wildborn, a carpenter employed by Messrs. J. Grover and Sons, builders of Pimlico, who are the contractors for the new Metropolitan Police headquarters on the Thames Embankment, was working on the foundation, when he came across a neatly done up parcel in one of the cellars. It was opened, and the body of a woman, very much decomposed, was found carefully wrapped

---

58. Into the journal, at this point, a partial clipping—traceable to the *Pall Mall Gazette* of 3 October 1888—has been pasted.

in a piece of what is supposed to be a black petticoat.[59] The trunk was without head, arms, or legs, and presented a horrible spectacle. Dr. Bond, the divisional surgeon, and several other medical gentlemen were communicated with, and from what can be ascertained the conclusion has been arrived at by them that these remains are those of a woman whose arms have recently been discovered in different parts of the metropolis. Dr. Nevill, who examined the arm of a woman found a few weeks ago in the Thames, off Ebury Bridge, said on that occasion that he did not think that it had been skilfully taken from the body. This fact would appear to favour the theory that that arm, together with the one found in the grounds of the Blind Asylum in the Lambeth-road last week, belong to the trunk discovered yesterday, for it is stated that the limbs appear to have been taken from it in anything but a skilful manner. . . .

BRAM STOKER'S JOURNAL (CONTINUED)

I sent word to Abberline, as I'd promised I would when we stood before Speranza's: Henry cannot aver that he did *not* drop the cloak somewhere, at some point in time; and so . . .

The door. It is he.

Later.—Indeed it was he: Abberline; come and now gone.

Caine came down at the Inspector's insistence, and as we three sat in the parlour, I grew thankful for the many hours I have spent watching fine actors at work; for I had not only to dissemble, to feign a greater ignorance than I own at present, but I had also to time my responses to Abberline's questions so as to preclude Caine's offering his own, as, the laudanum lingering, my friend's faculties were yet compromised. Brief: As I could neither step on Abberline's lines nor cede the stage to Caine, timing was all; and I am exhausted.

59. The word "petticoat" has been circled by Stoker. Marginalia: "Cloak?"

Abberline informed us of what we had already supposed: The cloth in which the body parts found at Whitehall were wrapped was not a petticoat, as reported, but rather was a match, in size and fabric, to the torn and blood-stained Lyceum cloak found earlier in the vicinity. The two fit together puzzle-like. I feigned surprise. And I repeated Henry's claim, adding to it a bit of stage business: I shrugged and presented my open palms as if to say, *See, Inspector: I've nothing to hide.* Alas, I am not an actor, and Abberline seemed . . . unsatisfied. He put more muscle into what next he said:

He had learned that the "ubiquitous Mr. Stoker" was not present at the Lyceum last Saturday evening. Was that not unusual?

"Quite;" said I, "but life does sometimes intervene in one's work, Inspector. Mr. Caine and I—"

"Mr. Caine, you say?" And, turning to him, Abberline asked, "You were with Mr. Stoker on Saturday evening, sir?"

"He was," said I; whereupon the Inspector stared at Caine till confirmation came in the form of a deep, deep nod.

Of me, Abberline then asked, "Is Mr. Caine not feeling well?"

"Indeed he is not," said I, adding, my voice fallen to conspiring tones, "The creative temperament, sir. . . . You understand, surely. And so, too, was Lady Wilde laid low Saturday last. Indeed we were both—Mr. Caine and myself—at the bedside of our Lady Wilde, to which fact she will happily attest."

"Both your friends similarly afflicted? Quite coincidental, is it not, Mr. Stoker? . . . Well, Lady Wilde must have been quite sickly Saturday last; for I am told by various persons in the Lyceum employ that you are rarely, *rarely* absent from that place the night of a performance."

"Lady Wilde was unwell, sir, as I have said."

"I trust her illness was short-lived, and that she has recovered completely."

"So she has."

"Indeed." Whereupon we arrived at an impasse, in the course of which I saw Caine's hands atremble in his lap. Abberline must have remarked the same; for he turned to Caine with a pressuring question:-

"Sir, to what do we attribute your lengthy stay in London? I learn from Her Majesty's tax inspectorate that you are often away from our fair city for long stretches and—"

"Do you know, Inspector," said I, suddenly and seemingly apropos of naught, "that *I* am a writer as well?"

Abberline nodded, but still he stared at Caine.

"I only ask, sir, in order to say that I am struggling at present with a project; and my friend—the accomplished Mr. Caine—has come to my aid. Hence his residence here."

"A project, do you say?"

"That is what I say, sir, yes; and if you insist on specificity, I will name it as a novel-in-progress."

"A novel? May I ask the topic?"

Astounding, the cheek! "You may ask whatever you wish, Inspector. Likewise I take some liberty myself in informing you that, firstly, only inferior novels may be said to have topics. Secondly, I am disinclined to speak about my work prior to its completion, as *to talk* is not *to write*. Indeed, the two acts can be called contradictory, as *talked* novels rarely evolve into *written* ones."

"I see," said Abberline, his cheeks rouging at my impertinence. "How very . . . *kind* of you to educate me, Mr. Stoker."

"Yes, well; enough about that." And then I changed tack, for Abberline as baited boded ill. "Tell me, Inspector: What does the Yard make of these most recent outrages?"

Silence ensued; a staring silence which ended only when Abberline rose and betook himself—*un*invited—into the half-done dining room. "A gift to my wife," said I, "as Mr. Caine has explained previously. It is a surprise, and the reason she and my son stay in Dublin over-long." Abberline seemed to me to be staring at the spot where the torso had lately been arrayed, as if he saw there the companion of the corpse lately found at Whitehall. (*Q:* How many more might the American have murdered? *How many?*) In time, Abberline returned to the parlour, yet seemed too agitated to sit. Indeed, he all but barked in reply when I repeated my earlier question re: the W'minster victim.

"Your work, Mr. Stoker," said he, "... play-acting, ... writing"— words spoken with a denigrating emphasis—"may be in the public province. Not so my work. What is more, sirs: It is always best to leave police work to the police, ... yes?"

"My apologies, Inspector. It is simply that we, Mr. Caine and I, are as curious as all Londoners are. We want nothing more than the ready apprehension of this ... this fiend."

"Then I can count on your full co-operation?"

Caine nodded. I said, "You may indeed." By now we all three stood in my foyer. My relief was profound as Abberline set that hat of his in place. *Leave,* I willed; but he did not, instead blindsiding us both with:-

"Tell me then, gentlemen: Where is Francis Tumblety?"

Caine sidled nearer to me. I could only hope he'd not betray himself further by taking my arm, or dropping in a dead faint. And if he meant to speak, he produced naught but a groan; the which I over-spoke, saying, with no little heat:-

"By the mere question, sir, it would seem you accuse us of ... of complicity in these crimes! I shall not stand for such—"

"Sirs," said Abberline, matching my heat with his own, "did you not leave me to discover Mr. Caine's close, *very* close, relationship with Mr. Tumblety? You did. And so I *have* discovered it. Further, I have word from the Americans that he, Tumblety, is a man of deeply shaded, indeed *suspect* character, someone whose association with men such as yourselves is most curious to me."

"Do you mean to say, Inspector, that the Doctor is a suspect in these crimes?"

"He is, Mr. Stoker, someone whom I seek in earnest, someone whom I would *very* much like to question."

"No more a suspect, though, than the several hundred *other* men currently in police custody? For the newspapers report—"

"I do not read the newspapers, Mr. Stoker."

"It would appear not. *Were* you of the habit, Inspector, then surely you'd have given greater consideration to the recent correspondence—

seemingly come from the killer himself—which has now been so widely reported; the same in which he forewarned you of—"

"I will tell you this much, Mr. Stoker: The correspondence to which you refer is currently being considered with the greatest care; so, too, the many false and misleading letters to which it has already given rise. Indeed, I have wired to America in search of samples of Dr. Tumblety's handwriting."

"Do you . . . do you foresee a match?" managed Caine.

"Ought I to, Mr. Caine? Spare me some bit of trouble, sir, if you are able. In so doing, you may perhaps spare another life as well."

Caine looked to me, to Abberline, and back to me before saying, "I . . . I . . ."

"Tommy," said I, pityingly, "the Inspector is too busy to stay, surely; but I could very much do with a spot of tea. Would you be so kind?" And I set my chin in the direction of the kitchen.

"No wife," observed Abberline. "No maids either?"

I left the man to his suppositions, his insinuations, and once Caine was out of earshot, I said instead, "Inspector, if you'll allow me . . . Mr. Caine has a history with the American, yes, one he wishes to conceal not so much from the law—in the person of yourself—as from his wife. I trust you take my meaning?"

"Well," said he.

"May we then, as gentlemen, strike the following bargain: In exchange for your discretion in this matter, Mr. Caine and I will inform you if, or rather *when*, we hear from Mr. Tumblety again? For I have reason to believe we may." And I quite meant my words. We three, we failed Children of Light, are agreed: *We cannot continue in this alone;* but still we need more time, time to entrap Tumblety, to solicit from him security of Caine's name, and to lure him towards the Yard. Time, too, to manipulate the truth; for if our story, as it stands at present, were to be learned by anyone, anyone at all, it would rain down ridicule upon Speranza and myself in addition to causing Caine's ruin.

"'Again,' you say, Mr. Stoker? '. . . hear from him *again*'? Do not set yourself, sir, betwixt myself and justice." And with that threat, twinned to the handshake that tacitly sealed our deal, Inspector Abberline took his leave and . . .

Poor Caine. Here he finally comes: I hear the clack and jangle of the tea service he's been tasking himself with all this while.

BRAM STOKER'S JOURNAL

Mon., 8 October '88, midnight nearing.—Surely another language would seem requisite to describing a *tête-à-tête* with the devil himself, but of we two, only Tumblety attends the Scholomance wherein such things are taught.[60] I have only English; the which I now apply with purpose:

We three went to-day to the interment of Catherine Eddowes, as we went two days ago to that of Mrs. Stride, Elizabeth Stride. Not for Speranza to keen, of course. That lesson has been learned. Rather we went to mourn two lives hard-lived and horribly lost, lost owing to our . . .

I shan't. I shall simply record:

Mrs. Stride had made her way to a pauper's grave in the East London Cemetery Saturday last, the 6th. Mrs. Eddowes did the same to-day, on what seemed a state occasion. Indeed, it may well have been one; for when Caine enquired and quietly offered to meet the costs of both burials, he was told these had already been absorbed by certain authorities of the Church & City. (*Q*: What have we wrought? ALL THE WORLD talks of Jack the Ripper.)

Precisely at the announced hour of 1.30 p.m., a cortège rolled from the mortuary in Golden Lane. An open hearse was followed hard by a mourning coach in which rode the main mourners, all so nattily attired it seemed Black Peter Robinson's had done them up in advert.[61] In a brougham at the rear of the cortège were members of the national, nay national and *inter*national, press. And whilst the propertied peoples of

60. In eastern folkore—and in *Dracula*—the Scholomance is the school in which the devil teaches his secrets to the chosen few, claiming the soul of every tenth scholar as his due.

61. And well they may have. Peter Robinson's was a department store, while Black Peter Robinson's was an offshoot of same specialising in mourning attire.

London are using that same press to show themselves sympathetic to the slain—their correspondence clogs the press with calls ranging from modest social reforms to the razing of the rookery that is Whitechapel, &c.—the lesser inhabitants of London came to mourn Mrs. Eddowes in person: bevies of bedraggled women—some of whom I recognised as ravens of the aforesaid rookery—came behind the cortège like a human broom, their babes in their arms and their older children told to hold tightly to their sweeping skirts.

Golden Lane itself was flanked by spectators standing five deep. No window was faceless. People had scampered onto roofs to stare down at the show, yet even they doffed their hats as the procession moved onto Old, Great Eastern, and Commercial streets before turning into Whitechapel High Street, where another close crowd attended. The show of sympathy before St. Mary's Church was most sincere, and even the roughest-looking labouring men bared and bent their heads as the body passed.

It was not until 3.30 that Mrs. Eddowes achieved her place of rest, the City of London Cemetery at Ilford. We were late arriving there, owing to the fact that Lady Wilde is something less than locomotive in her progress; and indeed once, when she stumbled over some impediment in the street, it was a Yard-man who offered his arm—one knows them by their billycock hats and thick-soled boots—so closely did they trail and surveil us. And all the while that we were watched, we watched for Tumblety in turn.

In time we joined the many mourners graveside, bidding Mrs. Eddowes a literal adieu and praying our apologies.

Before splitting and taking our separate leaves of the cemetery—so as to shake the Yard-men—we three had agreed to rendezvous in Covent Garden, whence, once it was known we were alone, we would progress to The Skunk & Trumpet, a pub whose name belies its decorous calm. This we were some two hours in achieving—I had two tails to lose, Caine one, & Speranza none—but eventually we reconvened.

In a corner of The Skunk, amidst its ferns, low lamps, and etched-glass panels—all of which offered the promise of privacy, if not privacy itself—we whispered re: *What next?* More pointedly: Were we in present need of my brother Thornley's coming to London? For we three were agreed: We had descended into a rather tremulous torpor, the upshot of which was that our Jack, our Saucy Jacky, our jackanapes, held sway. Perhaps Thornley, as our fourth Child of Light, might . . .

It was then they came concomitantly: I heard his *Sto-ker, Sto-ker* just as a red-cheeked boy no older than Noel appeared at our table. "What is it, child?" asked Lady Wilde, alerted by the look upon my face. "Speak!"

But the boy could barely do so, stammering, ". . . a man. He . . ."

Caine sat the child down and calmed him; or perhaps it was the proffering of coin that did the trick. Regardless:-

"I . . . I cannit even swear 'e was a man proper. But there 'e stood. . . . " And when the child raised a filthy finger toward the nearest window, Caine's lurching up set my pint to spilling; but there was no sign of Tumblety in the darkening street beyond, and the boy spoke on. "And when I walked near 'im, 'e whispered me over and said in a voice like two rocks rubbin', 'See there,'—meanin' you all, course. 'Go in there, boy, and tell that man—the big 'un—to meet me in St. James's.'"

"The palace?" queried Caine.

"The park, sir," said the boy. "St. James's Park. . . . My memory of it is runnin' away like water, even now, but sure I am that 'e said St. James's Park."

"When?" asked Lady Wilde.

" 'E said it wasn't no matter, ma'am, as . . . as 'e wanted me to tell ye 'e's always watchin', and 'e'll know when you show. . . . Scared me into streakin' me skivvies, 'e did."

Still I had to ask, "What did he look like, son? Can you recall?"

"That's the thing of it, sir—I cannit recall 'im, though there 'e stood not two minutes past."

"You've done well, son," said I, patting his cap as I stood.

"One more thing, sir," said the boy. " 'E said, 'Tell 'im to keep to the trees.'"

In a trice we were back upon the street, looking this way and that: no sign of Tumblety, no call. Through that same window, I saw the boy where we'd lately sat, drinking down the dregs of what liquor we'd left.

Tumblety had summoned me and me alone. Scared though I was, I knew it to be for the best: Caine could not go, simply could not, despite his protestations to the contrary, for now he was wound tighter than an eight-day clock and seemed ready to spring. Nor could Speranza go, of course. So it was I insisted that Caine accompany Lady Wilde home in a calèche, thusly rendering my friend both *of use* and relieved. If I did not make contact with either of them by midnight, they were to hasten to Abberline with *all & everything*. Good-byes were said, and in the course of same, Caine dropped his pearl-handled pistol into my pocket.

The lamplighters were already at their work. Hoping to encounter Tumblety before night fell fully, I hired a fly and directed its driver towards St. James's Park. Soon I was hopping down from the still-rolling fly before Buckingham Palace, handing up my fare and hurrying east-wards into the park.

As directed, I kept to the ever-lengthening shadows cast by the plane trees parallelling Birdcage Walk. Few feet-folk were about.[62] But he was there.

Sto-ker, Sto-ker. Each approaching tree was a test, each passed tree a triumph. The too-animate shadows made me wish now for darkness, darkness absolute.

Sto-ker, Sto-ker. Here came the violet stench: He was near; but I knew naught would avail of my looking for him. I had to wait for him to show. I had to walk, walk, walk . . . and wait for him to show.

Suddenly a bird cried in blue tones, and the breeze blew like a ham-mering nail, and . . . Here went my senses. And so I turned. *This* tree. *Here.* I stepped nearer, and nearer still, holding now to the tree for sup-port; but . . . nothing.

Nothing but the first of the moonlight shafting down through the last of the leaves and shining, shining on the tree's scaly, scabrous bark. But when bits of light came crawling round the bole of the tree, I saw them for the scorpions they were. Then a piece of the bark fell away,

---

62. Pedestrians, literally, or tourists.

and . . . No bark, this: rather a hood, a hood shrugged away now to show Tumblety's left eye as it rolled back from white to black-pupiled sight.

"Sto-ker," said he. I heard both the word and its echoed *Sto-ker*.

I weakened. All five senses were one. Lest I fall, I found myself clinging the more to the same tree behind which he stood. I was so near him now I could taste his speech, taste it as violets laid Communion-like upon my tongue. And the boy had been right: His voice *was* like two rocks rubbing; for within him his two voices contended. "Sto-ker," said he in the one. "I want the weighing," came the other. And when the two voices came as one—"We want the weighing. We are ready."—I saw his face tauten and his scar split to loose blackness into his stained moustache. His saliva, too, was black. And the muscles of the face moved in imitation of a smile as he, as *they* said again, "We want the weighing. We are ready."

"Tell . . . tell me my part."

Laughter now, though their mouth did not move till they said, "You know it. You rose us up as one."

"A mistake," said I.

Again they laughed. "The weighing. We want the weighing."

"Have you . . . have you the hearts?"

"We want the weighing. Upon the Scales of Anubis."

"I shall . . . I shall do it. On condition that—" But my speech was arrested by the hook of their left hand rising fast to my throat. They stepped out now to show their whole face, drawing me nearer, so near I smelt their repeated, "We want the weighing." Indeed, I gasped when they let go of my throat, and in gasping I drew deep their scents, their stench: the violets, yes, but also turned earth, waste, and the staleness of unbathed skin. I bent double and retched. They laughed as I did so.

Four lovers passing in parade saw naught of Tumblety and sped past me, dismissively.

"You shall have it," said I. "The weighing."

"We shall."

"When? Where?"

"For you to know. For us to show." And oh, that laughter, that infernal laughter! Will it ever cease to peal for me? Perhaps not; for just then, in taking firm hold of my senses, in abusing and braiding the five into one, they laid me low with the laughter. And the last I recall is the wind whistling through the trees like strung diamonds, and the moonlight letting go with a low, low tune before the packed dirt of the path hit me hard.

It was perhaps a quarter-hour later that I woke, dirtied and dumbstruck. What had happened? Soon, sickening, I recalled his every word. I rose from the base of that same tree. Rather, I *tried* to rise, but in the act was again arrested: He'd staked my coat to the ground with my knife, my kukri. I pulled myself free. I stood with the knife in hand, and, raising it to the moonlight, saw its blade brown with dried blood. I felt frantically all over my person, but of course it was not my blood. It was theirs. *Theirs.* The blood of the Whitechapel women, the torsos, and the untold others.

Quickly I slipped the kukri into my pocket and moved towards the Duck Pond. I meant to toss the knife away; but the moon upon the pond gave me pause: I might well be espied casting the knife out into the deeper waters at the pond's middle. How then to dispose of the knife? But as I stood in consideration of same, I decided to keep the kukri. I cleansed it in the waters of the pond and slipped it back into my pocket; for the fiend was right: It *does* fit well the hand that holds it.

Arriving home, I found Caine crouched in a corner of the darkened parlour. He heartened at my safe return, and even gathered himself sufficiently to send word round to Speranza: *He is home.* And so I am, feeling stronger, and purposed; for I have now the weapon, and naught remains but to set and spring the trap.

LETTER, BRAM STOKER TO THORNLEY STOKER

11 October 1888

Dearest Thornley,
Much to apprise you of in person. Finally I say, *Come!* Come at your earliest convenience, & bring with you my much-missed Stokers.

I have reason to think London safe, leastways for us. Again, I will explain.

Abberline? Absent; though his men trail us betimes. It seems we busied the Inspector by our letter. As Lady Wilde says, "All the world fancies they can write."[63]

Advise of your *imminent* arrival.

B.

TELEGRAM, THORNLEY STOKER TO BRAM STOKER

13 October 1888.—All four arriving Tuesday next, 16th. Thorn.[64]

FROM THE METROPOLITAN POLICE FILES [65]

METROPOLITAN POLICE
Criminal Investigation Department,
Scotland Yard.
19th day of October, 1888

SUBJECT: Murder of Elizabeth Stride

At Duffields yard,[66] Berner Street
Body found at 1 am
30th Sept. 1888

I beg to report that the following are the particulars respecting the murder of Elizabeth Stride on the morning of 30th Sept. 1888.—

---

63. Referencing, surely, the several hundred hoax letters sent to the authorities that autumn of 1888 in the wake of the two written by the *Dossier*'s self-styled "Children of Light."

64. Thornley, Florence, and Noel Stoker, along with the governess, Mlle Dupont.

65. Matching in all particulars the previous reports, save that before pasting this one into his journal, Stoker first cut away what he must have considered its extraneous contents. (Ellipses in this transcription are mine, coincident with Stoker's cuts.)

66. Should be "Dutfield's" throughout.

1 a.m. 30th Sept.—A body of a woman was found with the throat cut, but not otherwise mutilated, by Louis Diemshitz (Secretary to the Socialist Club) inside the gates of Duffield's Yard in Berner St., Commercial Road East, who gave information to the police. P.C. 252H Lamb proceeded with them to the spot & sent for Drs. Blackwell & Phillips.

1.10 a.m.—Body examined by the Doctors mentioned who pronounced life extinct, the position of the body was as follows:- lying on left side, left arm extended from elbow, cachous[67] lying in right, right arm over stomach back offhand & inner surface of wrist dotted with blood, legs drawn up with knees fixed feet close to wall, body still warm, silk handkerchief round throat, slightly torn corresponding to the angle of right jaw, throat deeply gashed and below the right angle apparent abrasion of skin about an inch and a quarter in diameter.

From enquiries made it was found that at:-

12.35 a.m. 30th—P.C. 452H Smith saw a man and woman, the latter with a red rose talking in Berner Street, this P.C. on seeing the body identified it as being that of the woman whom he had seen & he thus describes the man as about age 28. ht. 5ft. 7in: comp. dark, small dark moustache, dress black diagonal coat, hard felt hat, white collar & tie.

12.45 a.m. 30th—Israel Schwartz of 22 Helen Street,[68] Backchurch Lane stated that at that hour on turning into Berner St. from Commercial Road & had got as far as the gateway where the murder was committed he saw a man stop & speak to a woman,

67. Webster's: a cachou is "a pill or pastille used to sweeten the breath."
68. Should be "Ellen Street."

who was standing in the gateway. The man tried to pull the woman into the street, but he turned her round & threw her down on the footway & the woman screamed three times, but not very loudly. On crossing to the opposite side of the street, he saw a second man standing lighting his pipe. . . . Schwartz cannot say whether the two men were together or known to each other. Upon being taken to the mortuary Schwartz identified the body as that of the woman he had seen & he thus describes the first man who threw the woman down:- age 30. ht. 5ft. 5in. comp. fair hair dark, small brown moustache, full face, broad shouldered, dress dark jacket & trousers black cap with peak, had nothing in his hands. Second man age 35. ht. 5ft. 11in. comp. fresh, hair light brown, moustache brown, dress dark overcoat, old black hard felt hat wide brim, had a clay pipe in hand. . . .

The description of the man seen by the P.C. was circulated amongst the Police by wire, & by authority of Commissioner it was also given to the press. On the evening of the 30th the man Schwartz gave the description of the man he had seen ten minutes later than the P.C. and it was circulated by wire. It will be observed that allowing for differences of opinion between the P.C. and Schwartz as to apparent age & height of the man each saw with the woman whose body they both identified there are serious differences in the description of dress:- thus the P.C. describes the dress of the man whom he saw as black diagonal coat, hard felt hat, while Schwartz describes the dress of the man he saw as dark jacket, black cap with peak, so that it is at least rendered doubtful whether they are describing the same man. . . . Before concluding in dealing with the descriptions of these two men I venture to insert here for the purpose of comparison with these two descriptions, the description of a man seen with a woman in Church Passage close to Mitre Square at 1.35 a.m. 30th by two men coming out of a club close by;- age 30. ht. 5ft. 7 or 8in. comp. fair, fair moustache, medium build, dress pepper & salt colour loose jacket, grey cloth cap with peak of same colour, reddish handkerchief tied in a knot round neck, appearance of a sailor. In this case I understand from City Police that only one of the men identified the clothes of the murdered woman ..., which is a serious drawback to the value of the description of the man.[69]

The body was identified as that of Elizabeth Stride, a Prostitute, & it may be shortly stated that the enquiry into her history did not disclose the slightest pretext for a motive on behalf of friends or associates or anybody who had known her. The action of police, besides being continued in the directions mentioned in the report respecting the murder of Annie Chapman, was as follows:

a. Immediately after the police were on the spot the whole of the members who were in the Socialist Club were searched, their clothes examined and their statements taken.
b. Extended enquiries were made in Berner Street to ascertain if any person was seen with the woman.
c. Leaflets were printed & distributed in H Division asking the occupiers of houses to give information to police of any suspicious persons lodging in their houses.
d. The numerous statements made to police were enquired into and the persons (of whom there were many) were required to account for their presence at the time of the murders & every care taken as far as possible to verify the statements.

Concurrently with enquiry under head a. the yard where the body was found was searched but no instrument was found.

Arising out of head b. a Mr. Packer, a fruiterer, of Berner St. stated that at 11 p.m. 29th Sept. he saw a young man age 25 to 30

69. Marginalia: "See me not/nor understand."

about 5ft. 7in. dress long black coat, buttoned up, soft felt hat (Kind of Yankee hat), rather broad shoulders, rough voice, rather quick speaking, with a woman wearing a geranium like flower, white outside, red inside, & he sold him ½lb of grapes. The man & woman went to the other side of road & stood talking till 11.30 p.m. then they went toward the Club (Socialist) apparently listening to the music. Mr. Packer when asked by the police stated that he did not see any suspicious person about, and it was not until after the publication in the newspapers of the description of man seen by the P.C. that Mr. Packer gave the foregoing particulars to two private enquiry men acting conjointly with the Vigilance Comtee. and the press, who upon searching a drain in the yard found a grape stem which was amongst the other matter swept from the yard after its examination by the police & then calling upon Mr. Packer whom they took to the mortuary where he identified the body of Elizabeth Stride as that of the woman. Packer, who is an elderly man, has unfortunately made different statements so that apart from the fact of the hour at which he saw the woman (and she was seen afterwards by the P.C. & Schwartz as stated) any statement he made would be rendered almost valueless as evidence.

Under head c. 80,000 pamphlets to occupier were issued and a house to house enquiry made not only involving the result of enquiries from the occupiers but also a search by police & with a few exceptions—but not such as to convey suspicion—covered the area bounded by the City Police boundary on the one hand, Lamb St. Commercial St. Great Eastern Railway & Buxton St. then by Albert St. Dunk St. Chicksand St. & Great Garden St. to Whitechapel Rd. and then to the City boundary, under this head also Common Lodging Houses were visited & over 2000 lodgers were examined.

Enquiry was also made by Thames Police as to sailors on board ships in Docks or river & extended enquiry as to asiatics present in London, about 80 persons have been detained at the different police stations in the Metropolis & their statements taken and verified by police & enquiry has been made into the movements of a number of persons estimated at upwards of 300 respecting whom communications were received by police & such enquiries are being continued.

Seventy six butchers & slaughterers have been visited & the characters of the men employed enquired into, this embraces all servants who had been employed for the past six months.

Enquiries have also been made as to the alleged presence in London of Greek Gipsies, but it was found that they had not been in London during the times of the previous murders.

Three of the persons calling themselves Cowboys who belonged to the American Exhibition were traced & satisfactorily accounted for themselves.[70]

Up to date although the number of letters daily is considerably lessened, the other enquiries respecting alleged suspicious persons continues as numerous.

There are now 994 Dockets besides police reports.[71]

[signature obscured][72]

BRAM STOKER'S JOURNAL

23 Oct., '88.—Have tried to keep my head above this hullabaloo: the letters, the rewards, & the bit with the bloodhounds.[73]

But now I have word from w/in the Yard that the letter sent to

---

70. Marginalia: "!"

71. Marginalia: "Chaos!"

72. Research has shown this to be Chief Inspector Donald S. Swanson's report, yet Stoker's copy in the *Dossier* has the signature struck through multiple times, rendering it illegible.

73. On October 9th and 10th, 1888, the bloodhounds Barnaby and Burgho were tested in, respectively, Regent's and Hyde parks. The first test was successful, but the second—in which Police Commissioner Charles Warren ordered that the dogs seek *him*—was not, and it brought such embarrassment upon the police that soon both the dogs and the Commissioner were retired.

Lusk,[74] or rather the kidney accompanying same, may indeed be real, viz., human; in which case it was almost certainly sent by Tumblety; for the organ—its state, means of removal, &c.—matches the mutilations done unto poor Mrs. Eddowes.

Does he mean to taunt us with this last message? Does he want us to know that *he* knows of *our* letters?

His letter has caused the police to progress in their suspicions from the Jews to the Irish, owing to its "prasarved" and "tother," &c.—fools!— and doubtless this was Tumblety's intent: To stir the pot some more. Oh, it *is* Tumblety this time, of that I'm sure; if not, why mention the knife so . . . pointedly? He means to remind me that he did his last deeds with the kukri; but he wants to tell me, too, that he can take the knife back *at will.* "I may send you the bloody knif . . . ," &c. Is it a threat, then? I think not, but the CoL[75] are less certain, even though I remind them that he needs me, and has said so. Still, scant assurance, that; for what is the value of a murderer's word?

Meanwhile, here we sit gathered in safety at No. 17: Florence, eager to host a dinner in her new dining room, and put off at present with pleas re: too much business at the Lyceum; Noel; Caine; Thornley, who has left his poor Emily with her nurses; and even Lady Wilde, who has deigned to take an upstairs room alongside the Frenchwoman and the maids, for Ada and Mary have been recalled to tend to us all. We have reinstituted the watch as well, with Caine, Thornley, and me sharing its duties with subtlety, viz. claims of insomnia, late-night hearkening to the Muses, manuscript-tending, &c.

For Florence & the others have been led to believe that we work at

---

74. On 16 October 1888, Geo. Lusk, head of the East End Vigilance Committee, received the infamous "From Hell" letter, posted in a cardboard box three inches square along with a human kidney preserved in wine. The text of the letter reads as follows:

"From Hell.

"Mr Lusk

"Sir,

"I send you half the Kidne I took from one woman prasarved it for you. Tother piece I fried and ate it was very nise. I may send you the bloody knif that took it out if you only wate a whil longer"

And it is signed, "Catch me when/ you can/ Mishter Lusk."

75. Children of Light, presumably, i.e., Hall Caine, Lady Jane Wilde, and Thornley Stoker.

our writing *ensemble:* a play, we say, with which we hope to surprise Henry. "But what," wondered Florence, who is sometimes sharp and more than *socially* lucid, ". . . what has Thornley to do with playwriting?" To which I replied, "He assists us with the character of a medical man, my dear. He loans knowledge as Lady Wilde loans wit"; and there the matter rests. And so Flo. is unsuspicious of us Children repairing to the parlour *to plot,* and plot we do; but I dare not commit the particulars to paper. Privacy is what's wanted till our play, our most perilous play, goes-up in two days' time.

BRAM STOKER'S JOURNAL

Thurs., 25 Oct. '88., 4 a.m.—No calls, no signs of his being near. Still we keep watch in turns. It is mine now; and so I write.

Thornley has seen to the details and returns to Dublin to-morrow for as few days as his doctoring dictates, returning here *post-haste.* It falls now to Caine to play *his* part. "Would that Oscar were here," says he, though he means it not at all; "for with this foul business he could surely be of help." It was well Lady Wilde had already retired. (*Q.:* What *does* she know of her As-car's wanton ways?)

To-morrow I step onto the stage, as it were, presenting the *Macb.* calendar to Henry. He must assent to cast & crew travelling to E'burgh the 2nd week of November, *no later.* As Mansfield is pulling them into *J&H,* and coin clanks into the Lyceum coffers, a happy Henry will accede to my calendar, surely. Meanwhile, Peck secures for us the castle.[76]

6 a.m. now.—I am relieved by Caine. Sleep? Unlikely; as it is too late for laudanum.

---

76. Richard Peck, City Astronomer of Edinburgh; present at the Isis-Urania Temple for "the Setian event," and apparently recruited by Stoker for its sequel. The castle in question is Edinburgh Castle.

BRAM STOKER'S JOURNAL

Tues., 30th Oct.—I watch the blessedly bloodless press; for we worry re: his patience. Will he wait? Has he hearts enough?

No Whitechapel. The CoL forbid me to go.

I wonder: Whence does he watch?

Thornley returns to-morrow from Dublin via Purfleet with the last of our dramatis personae; and so it will soon eventuate. The play, the plan: *Imposture.*[77]

BRAM STOKER'S JOURNAL

Friday 2nd November, p.m., post-perf.—He certainly *seems* sane, does P. No-one meeting him in the larger world would suspect otherwise. Still Thornley stays with him at the Carfax Arms,[78] near Fenchurch Street Station, lest Abberline espy him before it is time. Thornley reports that Mr. P. is most amenable to our deal, and walked from Stepney Latch "a malcontented man," viz. happy in his unhappiness. As per our conditions, he submits to sedation, seclusion & supervision. His time, *his life,* will soon enough be his own, whereupon he will be free to . . . to do what his will dictates; but not for three days more; for:

On Monday at sunrise, we shall sneak P. into the day-dark Lyceum and with our trickery make of him a right Tumblety.

Caine wants the week-end to secure our boy accomplices. He is about the business even now. *Must* have them by Tuesday next, the 6th. For on the 7th, our *faux* T. goes to Abberline.

Word is already out—out so that Tumblety may hear it—that we *all*

---

77. Thrice underlined by Stoker.

78. Dracula's London estate will be named Carfax.

of us shall away to E'burgh for Henry's Shakespeare Summit, the long-insisted-upon *Macb.* sojourn, on Sunday the 11th. We are to meet upon the quay of King's Cross in time for the 11.15 a.m. train, and woe betide any who do not show. No time now for trifling, for this is Life & Death. Would that all concerned could know it, but no no *no.*

(*Mem.:* Sent a request round to Constance at Tite Street: We want & need the artwork from the Temple. She will secure it if no questions are asked *of her,* & no information given *to her;* for, as Speranza says, "Ignorance is her preferred state at present, no matter the topic." If she fails, Harker & Hawes Craven will have to create comparable canvases on-site. *Q.:* If this last, how to explain away the Egyptian themes? They are artists, after all, and *dis*inclined to obedience. *Do it!* does not suffice. Oh, never have I had to dissemble so! But neither has so much depended on anything I've ever done.)

BRAM STOKER'S JOURNAL

5 November 1888.—To-day at noon, Mr. Terrence M. Penfold rose from the bowels of the Lyceum Theatre looking the twin to Francis J. Tumblety. Caine and I conspired in the transformation, Caine knowing Tumblety and I having seen him altogether too often since his return to London. Physically, P. is well suited to the imposture: age, strength, stature, &c. All that was wanted were the bottle-brush moustaches, some reddening hair-dye, and those voice lessons from Caine and me, by which we succeeded—*please* may we have done so—in converting the Englishman's accent into the American's affectation.

And though we have imparted to P. all we know of Tumblety's mannerisms, &c., we have taken care not to tell him *all* we know of the man. A measure of ignorance will aid the impostor in fending off Abberline's questions. (*Mem.:* Remind P. that, in playing T., he knows only that his hounds were lost, and has heard nothing of their fiery fate; for, having been offended—how???—by Henry Irving, he took long leave of the Lyceum. Tell P., as T., to refuse to say where it was he went in the interim, as he mustn't have an alibi.) We have also dissimulated somewhat in saying that yes, Tumblety is wanted for questioning re: the Whitechapel outrages, but "so, too, are a hundred other men," as Caine off-handedly put it. And when P. questioned us as to what we were about, I left Caine to explain and proceeded to pick through the costumery for clothes of the requisite . . . flash. (*Mem.:* Confirm that I cut away *all* labels reading *Lyceum Property.*)

Mr. Penfold then repaired to the Carfax Arms with Thornley. There the two were to rehearse P.'s lines from *Macb.;* for we will justify his presence in E'burgh. by saying he is an acquaintance of Caine's—name of Godalming[79]—who wishes to play the Thane of Ross (& the Porter, of course) in our read-through. Another toff wanting indulgence, nothing more; although to gain Henry's agreement to this, our Godalming has had to gift the Lyceum Co. money enough to refurbish our lobby. It was Caine's money, of course; but he gave it contentedly. Far easier to contribute cash than do what it was he did last week-end, viz. troll the depths in search of four Mary Anns both purchasable & amenable to our plans; but this he bravely did, and our Ganymedes were gained, such that now all the supporting roles of our play have been cast. *We go-up to-morrow!* With *T. & his boys,* we shall lure Inspector Abberline onto the stage, and by curtain-fall he shall have his Tumblety; or rather *ours.*

The only regrettable part of the plan is that Mr. Penfold shall have to sit some days in prison. "I don't mind at all, gentlemen," said he upon hearing this; "but let no man tell you that incarceration builds character. It simply *ingrains* it." Rather lucid, that, from a man wholly devoted to his own death.

---

79. Readers of *Dracula* will recall that book's Arthur Holmwood, AKA Lord Godalming. It is likely the name came to Stoker at the time of the *Dossier* owing to the fact that the city of Godalming had recently become the first in England to usher electric lighting into wide use, including in its theatres: a fact surely not lost upon Henry Irving and, therefore, all the people in his employ.

BRAM STOKER'S JOURNAL

7 Nov. '88., 8 p.m.—Down into the hole goes Abberline the hound, following hard the fox, the *faux* Tumblety!

A sullying business, this last bit; but it must be recorded; so:

Some days past, Caine made contact—under a name not his own, assuredly—with a Mr. Hammond, now resident at No. 19 Cleveland Street, a nondescript street situated between Regent's Park and Oxford Street. Mr. Hammond's house is one to which Uranians[80] are wont to go when searching out telegraph boys, street types, &c., willing to do . . . *anything* at four shillings a go. Caine chose and paid four boys for their compliance earlier to-day, having first ascertained that they were *not* unknown to the police and that another run-in with same wouldn't do them excess of harm. That done, naught remained but to create that Dionysian tableau featuring our false Tumblety and his newfound friends. This Caine and Penfold saw to whilst, simultaneously, I carried word to Abberline in person, as promised: *The American has shown, and can be caught out to-day at 4 p.m. in the precincts of Cleveland Street—No. 19 in particular—using the name Frank Townsend.*

And so it is that Mr. Penfold, AKA Frank Townsend, AKA Francis Tumblety, sits at present in the Marlborough Street Police Court, charged with four counts of gross indecency, one per playmate.[81] Misdemeanors, these; and so Abberline will have but one day in which to question T., whereupon he will either have to remand him into custody, charging him with concern and/or complicity in the Whitechapel murders, *or* grant him bail for seven days and try to better his case against him, whereupon . . . Well, we shall deal with that if & when it eventuates.

---

80. Uranian is a contemporary term adapted from the German *Urning*, first used by Karl Heinrich Ulrichs in a series of writings collectively known, in their English translation, as "The Riddle of Man-Manly Love," and adopted by those Victorians just beginning to discourse on same-sex issues.

81. John Doughty, Arthur Brice, Albert Fisher, and James Crowley, as history has it.

Meanwhile, here we sit nervously by in the Carfax suite, this business being rather too hot to conduct from home. Caine counts again and again his store of bailable cash. Speranza sits with her Aeschylus, satisfied at having secured from Constance the scenery prerequisite to our play's final act. Thornley, for his part, has just confided to us his faith in Mr. Penfold, he on whom all our plans depend, he who does our bidding only because we have sprung him, as it were, from Stepney Latch. & now this just-delivered; Peck wires from Edinburgh that all sits in readiness.

Edinburgh! The hours betwixt here and there—between these Friday fears and our setting-out on Sunday—number 51 in sum. Pray may they pass as scripted!

BRAM STOKER'S JOURNAL

9 Nov. '88.—Success! Thornley and Caine have just left the hotel and head toward Marlborough Street, bail in hand. This they will convey to two men whom they have yet to select—strangers; men unknown to Abberline—who will agree to post bail for profit of their own. Bail was set at £300. What can such a considerable sum mean? It can only mean Abberline would prefer to keep hold of T., of course; and this is good, as it further means he will continue to trail T. when the time comes, *as he must.*

Surely Tumblety knows what we have done, as news of his own capture appears in to-day's papers and he has sworn to watch us from . . . well, I care not to think from where. From Hell, let it be! And for once, I fear, he shall not hearten to see his name in type. What will he do? Pray naught but pack his already-harvested hearts and follow us to Edinburgh, pray pray *pray* may he do nothing more.

Meanwhile, Mr. Penfold poses more questions than he provides answers, as he has had a rough two days returned to detention; but it seems he played his part well: He is remanded on bail for seven days' time, in the course of which Abberline & his men will strive to arrive at charges they can cause to stick. . . . Seven days hence. What will our situation be seven long days hence?

BRAM STOKER'S JOURNAL[82]

Is our arrogance unbounded? Prior references to all this as *a play* now unsettle my stomach, and Mr. Penfold the would-be suicide must be the sanest of us all.

My knees all but buckled when I heard the cry of the newsboy on the street. In truth, I heard naught but *Whitechapel . . . !* and fell onto the first bench I found. As I was nearer the Lyceum than home, I continued to that place; but on the way I went into the post to wire Speranza at St. Leonard's and the others at the Carfax Arms. At the Lyceum, I went wordlessly into the XO and sent a flyboy in search of Harker, whom I dispatched to Miller's Court, directing him to get as near the scene as possible and report back to me w/ details, as details are yet scant in the newspapers. Then I locked the door and curled up on the couch, crying like a child till Harker re-came.

What news he brought, he could hardly impart. Instead here we two sat sharing a bottle of Henry's best, Harker drinking away what he has lately seen, I drinking away what we have done. Or rather failed to do. *Why?* wondered Harker. Why had I sent him to that slaughterhouse? I would not have, had I known what a shambles Tumblety has made of Miller's Court. I apologised; and I took Harker into my arms before taking him into my confidence. Rather, I took the man as far into my confidence as I could, viz., I forbore all talk of the super-natural and said it was a *mere* murderer we contended with. And though Speranza will chide me for converting this fifth Child of Light, we have now Harker's co-operation, and this will stand us in good stead; for, hailing from there, the man knows Edinburgh well.

---

82. Though undated, this entry must have been made Saturday, 10 November 1888, in the hours after the discovery of murdered Mary Kelly.

Details came from a calmed Harker in time. All Whitechapel is wild, says he.

Oh, would that we had let Penfold sit another day in prison! Then our false Tumblety would have been freed of all suspicion, and we'd have shaken Abberline once and for all; but no, the fiend would never have let that happen. And now Speranza speaks true. "We were as arrogant as he," says she to me, confidentially, "but now all discourse, all dealings are done. The devil must die."

And so he shall: I will see to it, even if I die in the doing.

FROM THE METROPOLITAN POLICE FILES[83]

the draught report of Dr. Bond

Result of Post Mortem examination of body of woman found murdered & mutilated in Dorset St., Miller's Court, to-day 10.11.88; thus:

Position of the body when found:

Deceased was lying naked in the middle of the bed, the shoulders flat, but the axis of the body inclined to the left side of the bed. The head was turned on the left cheek. The lt arm was close to the body with the forearm flexed at a rt angle & lying across the abdomen. The rt arm was slightly abducted from the body & rested on the mattress, the elbow bent & the forearm supine with the fingers clenched. The legs were wide apart, the lt thigh at rt angles to the trunk & the rt forming an obtuse angle with the pubes.

The whole of the surface of the abdomen & thighs was removed & the abdominal cavity emptied of its viscera. The breasts were cut off. The arms were mutilated w/ several jagged

---

83. Like prior reports, this was copied out—in evident haste—in a hand not Stoker's and pasted into the *Dossier*.

wounds. The face was hacked beyond recognition of its features. Tissues of the neck were severed all round down to the bone.

The viscera were found in various parts viz; the uterus & kidneys with one breast under the head, the other breast by the rt foot, the liver btw the feet, the intestines by the rt side & the spleen by the lt side of the body.

The flaps cut from the abdomen & thighs were on a nearby table.

The bed clothing at the rt corner was saturated with blood, & on the floor beneath was a pool of blood covering about 2 ft sq. The wall by the rt side of the bed & in a line with the neck was marked by blood which had struck it in a number of separate splashes.

Postmortem Examination:

The face was gashed in all directions, the nose, cheeks, eyebrows & ears being partly removed. The lips were blanched & cut by several incisions running obliquely down to the chin. Numerous other cuts extending across all the features.

The neck was cut through the skin & other tissue right down to the vertebrae the 5th & 6th being deeply notched. The skin cuts in the front of the neck showed distinct ecchymosis.[84]

The air passage was cut through at the lower part of the larynx through the cricoid artery.

Both breasts were removed by more or less circular incisions, the muscles down to the ribs being attached at the breasts. The intercostals btw the 4th 5th & 6th ribs were cut through & the contents of the thorax visible through the openings.

The skin & tissues of the abdomen from the costal arch to the pubes were removed in three large flaps. The rt thigh was denuded in front to the bone, the flap of skin, including the external organs

---

84. Ecchymosis: the leeching of blood into tissue due to the rupture of blood vessels.

of generation & part of the rt buttock. The lt thigh was stripped of skin, fascia & muscles as far as the knee.

The lt calf showed a long gash through skin & tissues to the deep muscles & reaching past the knee to 5 ins. above the ankle.

Both arms & forearms had extensive & jagged wounds.

On opening the thorax it was found that the rt lung was minimally adherent by old firm adhesions. The lower part of the lung was broken & torn away.

The left lung was intact. It was adherent at the apex & there were a few adhesions over the side. In the substances of the lung were several nodules of consolidation.

In the abdominal cavity was some partly digested food of fish & potatoes & similar food was found in the remains of the stomach attached to the intestines.

The Pericardium was open below & the Heart absent.[85]

MEMORANDUM TO THE *DOSSIER*[86]

The 13th day of December, 1888.

It has been more than a month since I last took up this Record. I return to it now to tell of all, *all* that passed in the interim.

The day after the discovery of murdered, mutilated Mary Kelly, the Home Office offered full pardon to anyone "other than the murderer," and our poor Caine had to be restrained, restrained and later sedated, so determined was he to go to Abberline with *all & everything*. Now it seemed that it was Caine, not I, who had *eaten on the insane root that takes the reason prisoner.*[87] Indeed, such was Caine's state that we feared he would not be able to accompany us to Edinburgh the next day, Sunday,

---

85. Marginalia: "Her name was Mary Kelly."
86. In the hand of Bram Stoker.
87. *Macbeth*, Act I, Scene III.

11 November, as planned. Thornley advised against it, in fact; but two factors conspired to overturn my brother's professional opinion: the first was Caine's utter refusal to stay behind in London, and the second was the lack of a warder to watch over him if we insisted he do so, viz., someone to keep him from confessing. So it was that in the end Hall Caine accompanied us from the Carfax Arms to King's Cross, where our party boarded a train due to steam northwards towards the Scottish capital.

We were ten. We Children of Light were of course myself, Hall Caine, Lady Wilde, Thornley, Joseph Harker, and Mr. Penfold; who, along with his three pseudonyms of Godalming, Tumblety, and Townsend, had traveled to Edinburgh the night prior with Thornley, and circuitously, too, lest any men of the Yard be trailing them. The rest of our party was comprised of Henry Irving, Ellen Terry, and two ancillaries, viz. actors, recruited to read the parts of Banquo and Macduff, with all lesser parts to be accorded us amateurs. It was, after all, research and ambience Henry was after, not acting excellence; not yet. As those actors factor not at all in what follows, I shan't here commit their names to this summarising Record. Nor am I at liberty to say who else it was had travelled ahead of us—at Speranza's urging, nay *insistence*—to meet up with Mr. Peck and see to arrangements re: the castle, the creation of a Temple, & the pseudo-rites we would later read and by which the bloody business would be done.[88]

Ironic indeed that we the Children were the truer actors whilst keeping the company of Henry Irving and Ellen Terry; but we dissembled well, taking our cue from the Bard: . . . *to beguile the time, look like the time.*[89] So it was we partook of chatter upon the train, &c. Caine, of course, was yet somewhat sedated, and upon our arrival would have retired to the hotel as *unwell* had we let him; but we did not: He needed

---

88. It is my supposition—and a supposition only—that Stoker here refers to Constance Wilde and Wm. Butler Yeats, both of whom were 1. informed, 2. involved, and 3. beholden to Lady Wilde. Again, this is a bit of historical swashbuckling on my part; but though the historical record does not confirm their presence in Edinburgh, neither does it contradict it.

89. *Macbeth*, Act I, Scene V.

watching. For her part, Speranza was never so demure. She did not even contend for the floor at luncheon, but freely ceded it to Henry, who toasted us with Macbeth's "to the general joy o' th' whole table," before proceeding to hold forth re: the staging of Banquo's ghost and other such business. Thornley and Godalming alone had reason for their reticence at luncheon, they both being in beyond their ken—mere "aficionados," as Henry had it. I? I busied myself as always I do, seeing to the details of both our read-through & research as well as those pertaining to our truer purpose, slipping away from the table once, twice, to hear privately from Mr. Peck that everything sat in readiness in our chosen corner of the castle.

As Henry had insisted all our Edinburgh business be done in a day, we proceeded from luncheon to a short conference with the Edinburgh press. This I'd arranged to please Henry, yes, but also as an alibi: newspapers would report that we were all out of London and therefore heedless of whatever the bailed—and of course absented, searched-for—false Tumblety was up to. Finally, we repaired to our hotel for naps and what-not, in the quiet course of which we Children, sans Harker, convened in Caine's room to see to the last details. It was late afternoon before I introduced Mr. Peck to our party, whereupon he led the slow way up, up, up the sloping Royal Mile toward Edinburgh Castle.

There we took our tour, a still-blanched Harker stopping to sketch this or that at Henry's direction; for, as ever, it was the Guv'nor's goal to carry the castle's *effect* onto the Lyceum stage, to impress it upon his public when finally *Macb.* opens some weeks hence, at year's end. [90] And whilst Henry pointed out to Harker the battlements, the stones' various shades of beige, &c., so, too, did he drop crumb-like comments for me to record— . . . *Macbeth ought to see Birnham Wood moving through crenellations identical to these; . . . let us be sure the limelight doesn't reflect off Ellen's beetle-wing dress so as to render her silver daggers bronze; . . . more vermilion*

---

90. The Lyceum Company would indeed premier "the Scottish play" on 29 December 1888, going on to play 151 performances—still the tragedy's longest run.

than blue in the dying light, &c.—and this I did, listening all the while for the call; and when finally it came, *Sto-ker, Sto-ker,* my sudden inhalation caused Henry to turn and ask if I were well. I was not. Tumblety had come. Tumblety was in the castle. Doubtless, too, he had with him the heart of Miss Mary Kelly.

"Yes, yes, Henry," said I, "I am well. Rather *close* in here, though, don't you find?" But then I turned my complaint to compliment so as to assuage Henry and stop his questions from coming. "Don't you *feel* it, Henry? . . . The air here seems the very breath of the Bard! Would that we could bottle it and bring it back to the theatre. . . . Oh, right you were, Henry, in having us all come; right you were indeed." Whereupon he smiled and was smugly silent some while, some blessed while, whilst I listened for it again:

Sto-ker, Sto-ker.

By torchlight, Peck led us to the room he had arranged. One of the rooms, rather. And there, amidst the spirits of untold Scotsmen, we circled ourselves and read through the tale of the usurping, mad-becoming king and queen; but, as neither Henry nor Ellen deigned *to play* their parts at present, leastways not to the full, our focus fell upon the group scenes, and in the course of these, Mr. Penfold acquitted himself surprisingly well. So, too, did it amuse to hear Thornley read the role of Lennox. My amusement was short-lived, however. Throughout our reading there came the call *Sto-ker, Sto-ker,* and at times scent verged on sight, sight touch, touch taste, &c., such that I knew he was near and nearing still.

It was well nigh midnight before our circle broke, but by the application of the names Irving, Terry, and Caine, I had earlier convinced a restaurateur to remain open into the small hours; and it was there, in the shadow of the castle, that we all supped.

His call came now with insistence, such that I hurried the supper as best I could, though now, with some ale in him, Henry thought it time to soliloquise. But eventually we all repaired to our hotel midway down the Mile, bade one another good night, and betook ourselves to bed; or such was the ruse. A half-hour on, we Children convened again in

Caine's room, whence we slipped out into the Edinburgh night and made our way back to the castle behind Peck, naught but moonlight brightening the stones of the street. *Come like shadows, so depart!*[91] Such was our plan. Such was our hope.

Sto-ker, Sto-ker. It seemed he might slip out from every wynd, from every close we passed on our ascent. Or was it the disquieted dead I sensed? For Edinburgh is a sepulchral city; and if once its tenements rose fourteen stories high—so they did in medieval times, such that none living at street-level knew the light—in the centuries since, those same tenements have sunken somehow, nay the streets have been raised up to render the tenements' lower stories tomb-like. Sepulchral indeed; for down there lay the bones of the plaguey dead: Once—when word of a plague was but a whisper—the city fathers decreed the effectual death of all those resident in Mary King's Close, and in the night all means of egress from that place were stoppered, were forever sealed. Elsewhere, earlier in this very century, the body-snatchers Burke & Hare plied their trade in the subterranean city as well, and in its abandoned vaults did their brisk business in bodies, murdering for the monies the Medical College paid per corpse. Oh, indeed, best to tread lightly the streets of Edinburgh lest one wake its dead.

Nor does the city bear the name Auld Reekie for naught. It is redolent of many things, not all of them pleasant; but it was the sea's salt and sulphur, blowing in from the Firth of Forth, that were prominent upon the air the night of our shadowed ascent. I was relieved to smell these scents, *simply* smell them: better by far that my senses not be disordered on this of all nights.

We climbed and we climbed and we climbed towards the castle, sitting there high upon its rock these thousand-odd years. Our destination: its dungeons; namely, those rooms far beneath the Half Moon Battery, built upon the remains of what was once a ten-story keep called David's Tower, battered down in the sixteenth century when Kirkcaldy of Grange failed to defend it on behalf of Queen Mary, who'd borne

91. *Macbeth*, Act IV, Scene I.

behind its walls the future James VI of Scotland—our James I, of course—successor to Elizabeth. Secret rooms were later carved from the ruins, rooms into which the King could escape if ever the castle came under siege again. The floor before his door was built to be false: by the removal of rods laid under it, it would collapse beneath the weight of any enemies daring to descend in search of the King. Said enemies would then find themselves fallen into the den of a ravenous lion. Rather a short stay would ensue, I suppose. But true, all this, according to Peck. And it was into that erstwhile lion's den that we descended by ladder.

Sto-ker, Sto-ker. He had followed. He would soon show. With a nod, I told the others so, and said aloud that we had better hurry.

Peck and a blessedly unquestioning Harker had done their parts indeed: the rounded walls of the den were adorned with the repaired canvases secured by Constance, the same I'd last seen in the Isis-Urania Temple; and a dais featuring three places of prominence had been set before a table-cum-altar atop which sundry tools of ritual & rite had been laid, chief amongst these a golden scales, each of its trays bearing the shape of two cupped hands—the same that have been seen by so many upon the Lyceum stage when Shylock insists on having his pound of flesh cut from near the heart of the hated Antonio.

Soon all was in array. We had only to don our robes and hoods and assume our assigned roles.

Recent events had tired Lady Wilde terribly, and the ladder down into the den had nearly undone her; so it was that she was accorded the dress of the Imperatrix and let to sit center-all at the dais. At her left sat Caine as Cancellarius, whilst to her right was Thornley, progressing in the day's play from Lennox to the Praemonstratur. That left but Peck, Penfold, Harker, X, Y, and myself to fill out the Order. We fell, then, one short of the Order's full complement; but it was doubted that Tumblety or his demon would count.

Peck, dressed as the Hegemon, stood to the east of the altar. Penfold was the Keryx standing southwest, and so steadfast or stunned was he that the light of his red lamp wavered not at all. Harker, dear Harker, stood to the north as the Stolistes. X stood to the south as the Dadouche, and Y, the eye of Horus on his hood, stood to the southwest, beside the Keryx.

I stood center-all in the white robe and hood of the Hierophant.

Now we'd naught to do but wait, and this we did some while in silence, nearly sick with suspense, as if attending some dread bell soon to peal out powerfully. All present were watching me, whilst I in my turn looked up at the ladder and listened.

Sto-ker, Sto-ker. Torchlight lit the high den door.

Down he came, climbing slowly backwards. His bare feet were filthy, scarred and scabbed. He wore a cloak the color of night. His body showed its crookedness as he descended rung by rung—his hands like claws, a bagged heart in his left hand—till suddenly, mid-ladder, he leapt down to the ground, landing in a crouch. Cat-like, he scampered fast to the canvas showing Osiris. His hood was deep, his face hidden; but when I walked towards the altar and summoned him nearer, he came. He came slowly, slowly, as if to let his scent subsume us: . . . the violets yes, but also his own void, turned dirt and bladed, bloodied flesh. And though I'd told all present what it was he looked like, and how it was he would change as his two selves vied for supremacy within, and how his voices would sound as he spoke, still there could be heard the ill-stifled intake of air from all the cast as Tumblety tossed back his hood and showed himself, saying—wordlessly, or so it seemed to me— *Weigh it,* and drew up from deep within his bag the freshly harvested heart of Mary Kelly, poor Mary Kelly.

By the lamplight, her heart seemed verily to burn, and its smell—for he held it high and forwards, as if he were a fruiterer proffering an apple—came to me as iron laid onto my tongue. *Weigh it,* said he voicelessly, whilst with the second voice, and simultaneously, he said for all to hear, "It wants ritual. It wants rite."

Now Tumblety held, nay *shook,* the heart at the scales, such that it seemed he might toss it into one of the sets of cupped hands. Oh, but what then? What would I weigh in opposition to Mary Kelly's heart? Or would Set somehow see to this, somehow place himself, his essence, his metaphoric *self* upon this, the Scales of Anubis? Might he somehow cause to fall onto it the feather of Maat? Or might Tumblety draw out from his bloodied bag more . . . more of his *worthless*, harvested hearts. I knew not. I knew only that I had to act, and so I commanded Tumblety to "Kneel. *Kneel!*"

This he did, holding to the heart whilst letting fall the bag, the blessedly empty bag. I saw his long, dirtied fingernails digging into the dead red of the heart-flesh. Now he was arm's length from the table, the altar atop which sat the scales and atop which lay other *things*, things prerequisite to our performance.

What to do? *What to do?* I had assumed he would let us lead a rite, but no: Tumblety wanted the weighing now, *now*. *What to do?* I did not know. There I stood, staring through the holes of my hood at Tumblety; and it *was* he alone who knelt before me now: I knew by the slackened skin of his face that Set was in abeyance.

As if on cue, Speranza spoke, reading from the nonsensical rite we'd written. Tumblety seemed to recoil from her voice as Set re-took him. He snarled like a cur now, and his face went suddenly taut, and the still-livid scar upon his cheek split anew, and that treacle, that black blood, seeped into, nay *through* his moustaches and into his mouth, where he licked it from his lips with his thickened tongue. Two light-bright scorpions came to crawl down the length of his bare calf onto his cracked and horn-hard heel. Two more scampered up his forearm towards the heart he held. It was Set, yes, who spoke now to the Imperatrix, asking, "Who speaketh so? Are you Uatchet, the Lady of Flames, resident in the Eye of Ra?"

His words resounded through the den despite the dampening canvas.

There seemed to be but one right answer; and so:-

"She is," said I, adding, "Heed the Lady of Flames."

Tumblety's face slackened. Once again Set receded.

"Weigh it." And again he proffered the heart. *Weigh it!*

And somehow I found myself holding the heart of Mary Kelly.

Whereupon Lady Wilde knew it was high time she intone from the book secured by X. Caine's tremulous voice could be heard as well. So, too, Thornley's. All others present set to humming in those dissonant, horridly dissonant, tones by which we'd hoped to distract the fiend; and it seemed to work; for, as I turned bloody-handed from the still-tipping scales onto which I'd set the heart, and from beside which I'd taken up the kukri, Tumblety knelt still as a supplicant and moved not at all as I stepped behind him, bent to say, *Blood will have blood,* and, reaching round him, slid fast the knife into his neck at the left of his jaw and ripped it, ripped it to the right with all my might.

The spurt of it, the spray of it, spattered onto the white robes of those on the dais. Caine fell back. Speranza rose and went to X, who'd fallen as both her nerves and knees failed her. Thornley sat resolute. So, too, did Penfold and Harker hold their nerves as I withdrew the kukri and, coming up from beneath Tumblety now, drove it deep into his own heart, and . . . alas, it was butcher-work, and *To know my deed, 'twere best not know myself.*[92]

Indeed, these weeks later, still my hand shakes as I write the tale. These weeks later, still I feel his resisting flesh, still hear the suck and spurt of that red rending, that cut by which I killed him. And though I had often toyed with stage knives and their retractable blades, and had told myself again and again, had *resolved* to consider the kukri nothing but, still this was wholly different. The force of the blow did not double-back into my hand as it does upon the stage, but rather it went forward into Tumblety's heart, such that I felt the split of flesh and the heart's shock, the heart's seizing, the heart's slowly ceasing to beat, and from my hand through my own heart and to my brain was conveyed death, *death,* such that I knew what I had done: I had succeeded.

My robe was red and wet. So, too, were my hands, such that they slipped their grip on the hilt of the kukri. I held it no longer. Blood rushed blackly down its blade, buried deeply in Tumblety. His hands were fists upon the knife's hilt now. He shuddered. He stilled. And there

---

92. *Macbeth,* Act II, Scene II. Similarly, Stoker's last words to Tumblety—"blood will have blood"—come from Act III, Scene IV.

I stood as the fiend tipped forward, toward the altar. Fallen now, his back bowed; for, landing on the kukri, he'd driven it deeper in. He was dead, dead indeed. But what of his demon? What of Set, thusly un-housed?

The ensuing silence was as deep as it was short-lived.

The first of the canvases to rip, *to shred,* was that of the False Door, which split now along its repaired seams; oh, but Set would not take his leave as easily as that, no, and soon all the other canvases followed suit. It was as though unseen persons stood before them drawing knives this way and that, helter-skelter. The sound seemed that of the ghosted lion roaring once again in its den. Soon the canvases were naught but colored ribbon. And as I turned Tumblety over onto his back, *Turn, hellhound, turn!*[93] so as to see his face—and it was *his* face that I saw now, though scorpions came light-like from his wide-open mouth to dissolve in the near-dark— . . . alas, it was then that our lamps guttered and the oddly weighty shadows they cast upon the floor seemed a thousand, nay a million, serpents. And upon a wind swirling violets round the stony room, Set descended, unredeemed, whilst at my feet lay Francis Tumblety, rightly slain.

It was over. We—*bloody, bold, and resolute*[94]—had done the deed; and now there remained but this: *How to let the world know Jack the Ripper was no more?*

And too: the body: *What would we do with the body?*

This last, of course, was a problem we had hoped to have; and so Thornley had carried down into the den two large syringes plumbed with I-know-not-what. I know only that the solution was meant to speed the *dis*solution of Tumblety's remains; which, wrapped in sackcloth, will seem naught but anonymous bones if ever they are found buried deep, deep in the lion's den, in the ruins of David's Tower, far beneath the Half Moon Battery of Edinburgh Castle. And if any place can contain such remains, can still a soul as foul as Tumblety's was, surely it is that place, in that city. Rather, pray let it be.

93. Act V, Scene VIII.
94. Act IV, Scene I.

Up from the den we all climbed. Peck came last and brought the ladder up behind him. With the help of Harker, he gathered our scenery, as it were, and replaced the den's door whilst I washed using a skin of water which Peck, in his prescience, had brought. Our robes and hoods we handed to Peck as well, to be rendered down to ash that very night, along with the shredded canvas. Caine, last amongst us, came from the site backwards, brushing away the footprints of our procession with a bundle of rushes.

Peck led us out by torchlight, each of us stooping, silent, shivering still from all we'd seen and done. Too, there was the cold of the earth to contend with; for we were a good while taking our leave of the castle precincts via a long, low-roofed tunnel that wound down and down before finally giving out onto a street far below the Half Moon Battery. There a lone lamplighter went about his snuffing work. For it was dawn now. It was light.

We trained to London on Monday at noon, not a one of us having slept. Neither did any Child sleep on the train, as doubtless we were all afraid of what dreams might come. Newspapers were had at the station, and so it was my companions read all about the murder of Mary Kelly. I, for my part, refused the news; and there I sat instead, staring out the window, mourning the murdered woman whose heart I'd held not eight hours past.

CLIPPING FROM *THE TIMES,* 13 NOVEMBER 1888[95]

Middlesex, TO WIT.
The Informations of Witnesses severally taken and acknowledged on behalf of our Sovereign Lady the Queen, touching the

---

95. Here Stoker has interleaved into his Memorandum a folded page of *The Times* dated Monday, 13 November 1888: the day after his return trip to London.

death of *Marie Jeannette Kelly*, at the House known by the sign of the Town Hall in the Parish of *Shoreditch* in the County of Middlesex, on the *12 day of November*, in the year of our Lord One thousand eight hundred and *eighty eight* before me, RODERICK MACDONALD, Esquire, one of Her Majesty's Coroners for the said County, on an Inquisition then and there taken on View of the body of the said *Marie J Kelly* then and there lying dead.

Joseph Barnett, having been sworn upon the day and year and at the place above mentioned, deposed as follows:-

I reside at 24 and 25 New Street, Bishopsgate, which is a common lodging house. I am a labourer & have been a fish porter. I now live at my sister's, 21 Portpool Lane, Grays Inn Road. I have lived with the deceased one year and eight months, her name was Marie Jeannette Kelly. Kelly was her maiden name and the name she always went by. I have seen the body. I identify her by the ear and the eyes. I am positive it is the same woman. I have lived with her at No. 13 room, Miller's Court, eight months or longer. I separated from her on the 30th of October. Deceased has often told me as to her parents, she said she was born in Limerick— that she was 25 years of age—& from there went to Wales when very young. She told me she came to London about 4 years ago. Her father's name was John Kelly, he was a Gauger at some iron works in Carnarvonshire. She told me she had one sister, who was a traveller with materials from market place to market place. She also said she had 6 brothers at home and one in the army, Henry Kelly. I never spoke to any of them. She told me she had been married when very young in Wales. She was married to a Collier, she told me the name was Davis or Davies, I think Davies. She told me she was lawfully married to him until he died in an explosion. She said she lived with him 2 or 3 years up to his death. She told me she was married at the age of 16 years. She came to London about 4 years ago, after her husband's death. She said she first went to Cardiff and was in an infirmary there 8 or 9 months and followed a bad life with a cousin whilst in Cardiff. When she left Cardiff she said she came to London. In London she was first in a gay house in the West End of the Town. A gentleman there asked her to go to France. She described to me she went to France. As she told me she did not like the part she did not stay there long, she lived there about a fortnight. She did not like it and returned. She came back and was living near the Gas Works. Morganstone was the man she lived with there. She did not tell me how long she lived there. Then she lived with a Flemming, she was very fond of him. He was a mason's plasterer. He lived in Bethnal Green Rd. She told me all this, and Flemming used to visit her. I picked up with her in Commercial Street, Spital-fields. The first night we had a drink together and I arranged to see her the next day, and then on the Saturday we agreed to remain together and I took lodgings in Miller's Court where I was known. I lived with her from then till I left her the other day. She had on several occasions asked me to read about the murders to her and she seemed afraid of some one, but she did not express fear of any particular individual except when she rowed with me but we always came to terms quickly.

I left her because she had a person who was a prostitute whom she took in and I objected to her doing so, that was the only rea-son. I left her on the 30th October between 5 & 6 pm. I last saw her alive on Thursday morning the 8th about half past eight am, as she was then standing on the corner of Miller's Court in Dor-set Street. I said to her, what brings you up so early, and she said, I have the horrors of drink upon me Joe. I could see she had been drinking for some days past, though she was as long as she was with me of sober habits. I said why don't you go to Mrs. Ringers, meaning the public house, corner Dorset Street, called the Bri-tannia, and have a ½ pint of beer. She said I have been there and had it but I have brought it all up again, at the same time pointing to some vomit on the roadway. I then passed on. I told her when I left her I had no work and had nothing to give her of which I was very sorry.

By the jury no questions.

MEMORANDUM TO THE *DOSSIER* (CONTINUED)

Once back in London, we disbanded. Caine rejoined his Mary and Ralph at Greeba Castle. Speranza returned to Park Street. Thornley and Mr. Penfold spent the night at the rooms we had retained at the Carfax Arms, whence they went to Dublin together, remaining there till the next part of our plan could be put into practice. I forbore against Henry and went home rather than head directly to the Lyceum, and though I made the case that Mr. Harker had earned his rest as well, Henry insisted that our scenarist, shaken still, join the rest of the party in cabs hired at King's Cross and directed to head to the theatre. Poor Joseph Harker. I quite owe the man.

Florence and Noel have been as a balm, and with Tumblety *seen to,* No. 17 St. Leonard's Terrace was rather more liveable than previously it had seemed. Though I was woken from my first dreamless, unaided sleep that Sunday afternoon by none other than Inspector Abberline, wondering who the two men were who'd bailed Tumblety only to disappear. So, too, had his Tumblety disappeared, of course; and though he, having been bailed, was not required by law to return to the Police Courts before 16 November, still the Inspector wanted very much to know where he was *at present.*

"Would that I could help you, Inspector," was all I said, with a shrug; and my words were truth: Would that I *could* have helped him, but what was I to say? *Why, sir, I have lately murdered the true Tumblety whilst you have sought the false; . . . yes, yes, you are most welcome; . . . and you may reclaim the former's corpse, if you are so inclined, from the riven rock some seven storeys below Edinburgh Castle.* And then bid the Inspector good day and adieu? Hardly.

I had to desist, had to dissemble some days more, till such time as we would hand him, once again, our *faux* Tumblety.

The Inspector must have bided his time with lessening patience as the 16th approached; for the 17th was yet young when he came to me again, this time angering Florence with his fast refusal of tea. "Who is that man?" she asked. "He is *most* cold." To which opinion I assented, adding only that he was from Scotland Yard and didn't she agree that he would do better to task himself with this Whitechapel business rather than bother citing the Lyceum Co. for its *J&H* lines, which, said he, were complicating the nightly traffic upon Wellington Street and its surrounds, &c.? For indeed he'd done so: He'd brought me a citation! "Indeed," said Florence apropos of Abberline, and there the business ended.

On that morning of the 17th—pre-citation, mind—I told Abberline, yet again, that I'd not heard from Tumblety and neither had Mr. Caine; and I promised, again, to alert him if and when either of us did have word of the man. This, of course, I could not do for some days more; for Thornley—owing to some dolorous dealings with Emily and her doctors—had wired that he would be unable to accompany Mr. Penfold to France before the 23rd instant. And so it was on the 24th that I wired Inspector Abberline:

Word of the man. Come at once to the Lyceum. Stoker.

I knew my mistake only when, in short order, Abberline showed at the Lyceum with seven men of the Yard and I had both he and Henry to contend with. "What business is this?" asked the Guv'nor. "More about those blasted hounds?"

"Indeed so, Henry," said I, suggesting he let his Stoker see to it. So he did. And I was able to turn my attention to Abberline, whom I ushered alone into E.T.'s dressing room, vacated by her refusal to play in our *Jekyll*.

"Sir," said I.

"Sir," said he; and therewith went all pleasantries.

"Mr. Caine has had word from an acquaintance of his that the American is headed home."

"Not so fast, he isn't," said Abberline. "What more do you know, Mr. Stoker? And who is this acquaintance of Mr. Caine's?"

"I am afraid I cannot tell you that, Inspector, as—"

"Tumblety," said he, fairly livid. "Where is Tumbelty *now?*"

"He sailed to-day from Le Havre, aboard a boat of the Transatlantic Line. *La Bretagne,* by name."

"To-day? *Tarnation!* Destination, Stoker! Where is he headed, *man?*"

"New York, it would seem," and I'd barely spoken the words before Abberline blew from the room, throwing the door back upon its hinges so hard that Ellen's star fell to the floor. I followed him out into the hallway, meaning to call after him the last information I'd meant to impart—that Tumblety had sailed under his Townsend alias—but Abberline was already gone. So be it: Better, perhaps, that he detect that much on his own.

Two days later, Thornley, returned to Dublin, wrote that all had gone well; that, in his opinion, Mr. Penfold could be counted on to uphold his end of our bargain. Which is to say that he would not cast himself into the sea, though he was—now and for the first time—alone and free, free as he had not been since Thornley had arranged with Dr. Stewart for the patient's removal to Richmond Hospital, in Dublin; where, said Thornley, he would be studied as a self-murderer. Of course, in Thornley's opinion Mr. Penfold is not insane; rather, he simply wants to die. And I suppose now he means to do so, for I have here some newly-arrived copies of the New York *World,* dated 4th & 6th December, in which I read, with great relief, that our plan has now eventuated to its end:

CLIPPING, THE NEW YORK *WORLD,* 4 DECEMBER 1888

TUMBLETY IS IN THIS CITY HE ARRIVED SUNDAY UNDER A FALSE NAME FROM FRANCE

A Big English Detective Is Watching Him Closely, and a Crowd of Curious People Gaze at the House He Lives In—Inspector Byrnes's Men Have Been on His Track Since He Landed.

Francis Tumblety, or Twomblety, who was sought in London for supposed complicity in the Whitechapel crimes and held under bail for other offenses, arrived in this city Sunday, and is now stopping in East Tenth Street. Two of Inspector Byrnes's men are watching him, and so is an English detective who is making himself the laughing stock of the entire neighborhood.

When the French line steamer *La Bretagne,* from Havre, came to her dock at 1:30 Sunday afternoon two keen-looking men pushed through the crowd and stood on either side of the gangplank. They glanced impatiently at the passengers until a big, fine-looking man hurried across the deck and began to descend. He had a heavy, fierce-looking mustache, waxed at the ends; his face was pale and he looked hurried and excited. He wore a dark blue ulster, with belt buttoned. He carried under his arm two canes and an umbrella fastened together with a strap. He must have kept himself very quiet on the *La Bretagne,* for a number of passengers who were interviewed could not remember having seen any one answering his description. It will be remembered that he fled from London to Paris to escape being prosecuted under the new "Fall of Babylon" act.

He hurriedly engaged a cab, gave the directions in a low voice and was driven away. The two keen-looking men jumped into another cab and followed him. The fine-looking man was the notorious Dr. Francis Twomblety or Tumblety, and his pursuers were two of Inspector Byrnes's best men, Crowley and Hickey.

Dr. Twomblety's cab stopped at Fourth Avenue and Tenth Street, where the doctor got out, paid the driver and stepped briskly up the steps of No. 75 East Tenth Street, the Arnold House. He pulled the bell, and, as no-one came, he grew impatient and walked a little further down the street to No. 81. Here there was another delay in responding to his summons, and he became so impatient that he tried the next house No. 79. This time there was a prompt answer to his ring and he entered. It was just 2:20 when the door closed on Dr. Twomblety and he has not been seen since.

Many people were searching for the doctor yesterday and the bell of No. 79 was kept merrily jingling all day long. The owner of the house is Mrs. McNamara who rents out apartments to gentlemen. She is a fat, good-natured, old lady. Mrs. McNamara at first said the doctor was stopping there. He had spent the night in his room, she said, and in the morning he had gone downtown to get his baggage. He would be back at 2 o'clock. The next statement was that she had heard some of those awful stories about him, but bless his heart, he would not hurt a chicken! The revised story, to which Mrs. McNamara stuck tenaciously at last, was that she had no idea who Dr. Twomblety was. She didn't know anything about him, didn't want to know anything about him, and could not understand why she was bothered so much, but every body in the neighborhood seems to have heard of Dr. Twomblety's arrival, and he is spoken of everywhere with loathing and contempt.

It was just as this story was being furnished to the press that a new character appeared on the scene, and it was not long before he completely absorbed the attention of every one.

He was a little man with enormous red side whiskers and a smoothly shaven chin. He was dressed in an English tweed suit and wore an enormous pair of boots with soles an inch thick. He could not be mistaken in his mission. Everything about him told of his business. He was a typical English detective. If he had been put on a stage just as he paraded up and down Fourth Avenue and Tenth Street yesterday he would have been called a caricature. First he would assume his heavy villain appearance. Then his hat would be pulled down over his eyes and he would walk up and down in front of No. 79 staring intently into the windows as he passed, to the intense dismay of Mrs. McNamara, who was peering out behind the blinds at him with ever-increasing alarm.

Then his mood changed. His hat was pushed back in a devil-may-care way and he marched to No. 79 with a swagger, whistling gaily, convinced that his disguise was complete and that no one could possibly recognize him.

When night came the English detective became more and more enterprising. At one time he stood for fifteen minutes with his coat collar turned up and his hat pulled down, behind the lamp-post on the corner, staring fixedly at No. 79. Then he changed his base of operations to the stoop of No. 81 and looked sharply into the faces of every one who passed. He almost went into a spasm of excitement when a man went into the basement of No. 79 and when a lame servant girl limped out of No. 81 he followed her a block, regarding her most suspiciously.

His headquarters was a saloon on the corner, where he held long and mysterious conversations with the barkeeper always ending in both of them drinking together. The barkeeper epitomized the conversations by saying: "He wanted to know about a feller named Tumblety, and I sez I didn't know nothink at all about him; and he says he wuz an English detective and he told me all about them Whitechapel murders, and how he came over to get the chap that did it."

"Do you think he is Jack the Ripper?" Inspector Byrnes was asked. "I don't know anything about it, and therefore I don't care to be quoted. But I simply wanted to put a tag on him so that if they think in London that they may need him, and he turns out to be guilty, our men will probably have a good idea where he can be found. Of course, he cannot be arrested, for there is no proof of his complicity in the Whitechapel murders, and the crime for which he was under bond in London is not extraditable."[96]

---

96. Marginalia: "*Not* extraditable." Stoker and company must have known as much, and breathed a collective sigh of relief upon learning that their Tumblety was safely out of England.

CLIPPING, THE NEW YORK *WORLD*, 6 DECEMBER 1888

DR. TUMBLETY HAS FLOWN
He Gives His Watchers the Slip and Has
Probably Gone Out of Town

It is now certain that Dr. Thomas F. Tumblety, the notorious Whitechapel suspect, who has been stopping at 79 East Tenth Street since last Sunday afternoon, is no longer an inmate of the house. It is not known exactly when the doctor eluded his watchers, but a workman named Jas. Rush, living directly opposite No. 79, says that he saw a man answering the doctor's well-known description standing on the stoop of No. 79, early yesterday morning, and he noticed that he showed a great deal of nervousness, glancing over his shoulder constantly. He finally walked to Fourth Avenue and took an uptown car.

A WORLD reporter last night managed to elude the vigilant Mrs. McNally, the landlady, and visited the room formerly occupied by the doctor. No response being given to several knocks, the door was opened and the room was found to be empty. The bed had not been touched and there was no evidence that the room had been entered since early morning. A half-open valise on a chair near the window and a big pair of boots of the English cavalry regulation pattern were all that remained to tell the story of Dr. Tumblety's flight. Those who knew him best think he has left New York for some quiet country town, where he expects to live until the excitement dies down.

MEMORANDUM TO THE *DOSSIER (CONTINUED)*

Pray may Mr. Penfold elude life as easefully as he has these American and English detectives. I believe now that it is his right to do so.

Pray, too, may this "excitement" die down soon, and this Ripper business be forgotten for all time.

And so: It is done. And if I have not yet signed God's name to the letter of my life, I have leastways erased from it the devil's.

Note to *The Dossier*

Saturday, 25 May 1895

Seven years ago, we all of us went through the flames; and the happiness of some of us since then is, we think, well worth the pains endured. Others among us fare less well at present. And to-day of all days, that contrast is stark, so stark as to send me back to this *Dossier* which I long ago foreswore; for I could hardly ask any one—even did I wish to—to accept these pages as proof of so improbable, so impossible, a story. Indeed, it is only owing to Caine that I did not destroy it, but rather secreted it away; as I shall again once recent events are added; so:

Late yesterday afternoon, I received a telegram from Henry Irving asking, "Could you look in at quarter to six. Something important." Doing so, I discovered the Guv'nor sitting in his rooms, staring quite contentedly, and alternately, at the two letters he held in his hands. The first was from the Prime Minister, the Earl of Roseberry, and informed the actor that the Queen wished to confer on him the honour of knighthood in recognition of his services to art. The second letter, from the Prince of Wales, congratulated Henry on the contents of the first. This of course pleased Henry *no end*, as no actor *qua* actor has ever been recognised so, and he asked that I join him in driving to Ellen Terry's home in Longridge Road to convey the news personally to the Lady of the Lyceum.[97] This we happily did.

---

97. Ellen Terry herself became a Dame Grand Cross of the Order of the British Empire in 1925. She died three years later at the age of 81.

Upon my late-night return to the Lyceum, I found that the news had spread: already the congratulatory cables had begun to come from the four corners of the world. One telegram of the many was, however, meant for me; and in same I discovered that the name, the *dear* name, of my brother, Thornley Stoker, M.D., is on the same Honours List as Irving's.[98] Henry and Thornley both are to be knighted at Windsor Castle on 18 July; and it is to be hoped that on that occasion I will know less of the sadness I suffer at present; for more news—this of the opposite sort—came to-day from the Old Bailey, where the harshest of sentences was handed down against Oscar Wilde:

He has been found guilty of gross indecency and sentenced to two years' hard labour. Already his denigrators do their work: His name upon the posters at the theatres running his *Husband* and his *Earnest* have been papered over in black. Surely Oscar shan't survive so harsh, so *unduly* harsh, a sentence.[99] Neither, I fear, will his mother.[100]

As for another Child of Light, Thomas Henry Hall Caine gets on well at Greeba Castle in the company of his Mary and their sons, Ralph and Derwent. In her scrapbooks, Mary keeps her record of Caine's continuing successes; for still the world hangs upon his every word.[101]

---

98. Sir Thornley Stoker, d. 1912. Having survived his wife, Emily, by two years, Thornley found contentment with her nurse, Florence Dugdale, who, upon Thornley's death, became the typist for and eventually the wife of Thomas Hardy.

99. He did, albeit barely. Oscar Wilde died in Paris, 30 November 1900.

100. Lady Wilde took to her bed the day of her As-car's sentencing and never rose from it again.

Upon her death, Willie Wilde had black-banded mourning cards made. They read, "In Memoriam JANE FRANCESCA AGNES SPERANZA WILDE, Widow of Sir William Wilde, MD, Surgeon Oculist to the Queen in Ireland, Knight of the Order of the North Star in Sweden. Died at her residence. London. Feb 3rd 1896." And though Lady Wilde was buried in plot number 127 in Kensal Green Cemetery, Willie never bought a headstone nor paid for permanent sepulture; and so Speranza's remains were removed after the standard seven years. Nothing marks the final resting place of she who was once Speranza of the Nation.

101. Thomas Henry Hall Caine, later Sir, d. 31 August 1931. Part of his considerable estate was bequeathed to the West London Mission "for the aid and reformation of fallen women."

Caine and Stoker were friends to the end; and Caine's dedication of his *Cap'n Davey's Honeymoon* (1893) to Stoker both establishes that fact and shows why Hall Caine—in his day ranked amongst such writers as Harriet Beecher Stowe, George Eliot, Charles Dickens, and Wm. Makepeace Thackeray as novelists of the highest import—is to-day amongst the most deservedly forgotten of all forgotten writers:

"When in dark hours and evil humours my bad angel has sometimes made me think that friendship as it used to be of old, friendship as we read of it in books, that friendship which is not a jilt sure

Me? I continue to work for Henry Irving.[102] Florence and Noel get on well.[103] I write.[104] But I have yet to write *my best*. I have, though, an idea—its *Grip & Go*, as Caine would call it—and I am most eager to pursue it. It is the story of a man who—though not a hero, per se—finds himself suffering, nay *surviving*, heroic circumstances. What will become of it, I, of course, cannot say; but I *do* have an idea.[105]

to desert us, but a brother born to adversity as well as success, is not a lost quality, a forgotten virtue, a high partnership in fate degraded to a low traffic in self-interest, a mere league of pleasure and business, then my good angel for admonition or reproof has whispered the names of a little band of friends, whose friendship is a deep stream that buoys me up and makes no noise; and first among these names has been your own."

102. Sir Henry Irving, d. 1905, Friday the 13th, aged 67. Owing to the influence of his powerful friends, he was interred in Poets' Corner, Westminster Abbey.

103. Florence Stoker, d. 1937, aged 78. As her husband's literary executor, Florence fought till the end against those who she thought had misappropriated Stoker's work, all the while referring to *Dracula* as "The Second Bathroom Book," as all she'd been able to buy with the scant proceeds from its publication was a powder room set beneath her stairs. Her dogged efforts included a lawsuit the settlement of which stipulated the destruction of all existing prints of F. W. Murnau's *Nosferatu* (1922). However, in 1931, Universal Pictures paid $400 for a still-extant print of the film and acquired the rights to a second film based on the book, this one starring an unknown Hungarian actor named Bela Lugosi.

Irving Thornley Noel Stoker, d. 1961, moved to France upon his maturity and later sued to have the first of his given names removed, saying he had no wish to pay homage to the man who'd taken his father from him.

104. Increasingly so: Stoker's output would, in the end, be prodigious. Novels, stories, lectures, plays, and, of course, his monumental, two-volume *Personal Reminiscences of Henry Irving* (1906).

105. *Dracula* (1897), by Bram Stoker, b. 8 November 1847, d. 20 April 1912, aged 64.

AUTHOR'S NOTE

In the writing of his novel *The Name of the Rose,* Umberto Eco referred to the genre of fiction known as the "swashbuckler" novel: novels that not only use historical backgrounds, but also incorporate historical figures. This is sometimes done as a pretext, one intended to add authenticity to the narrative and thereby facilitate that "suspension of disbelief" so key to a reader's enjoyment. In *The Dracula Dossier,* I have attempted to take the notion of "swashbuckling" fiction further, neither merely co-opting "real" history nor proposing an alternative to it, but rather writing a "shadow" history. In so doing, I have held fast to one of Eco's tenets of swashbuckling fiction; and therefore I can assure the reader that nothing—rather, *nearly* nothing—in *The Dracula Dossier* contradicts the historical record. In other words: This *could* have happened as written.

In response to the reader who wonders, perhaps impatiently, what, *precisely,* is true, I offer the following notes, which are by no means exhaustive.

All main characters in *The Dracula Dossier* are historical personages, excepting Mr. Penfold (analogous to *Dracula*'s Renfield) and those characters who come onstage in supporting roles, such as the Lyceum's pricking seamstress, Mrs. Pinch. Further, these historical figures did indeed know one another. Bram Stoker and Oscar Wilde were allied by their dual courtship of Florence Balcombe, which, though it ended badly for Wilde, did not see Stoker banished from the good graces—and salon—of Lady Jane Wilde. Further, Stoker *did* worship Walt Whitman, and their relationship was in fact closer than the present fiction allowed. Hall Caine *did* know Francis Tumblety, intimately, and the excerpts from Tumblety's letters to Caine presented in the *Dossier* are more or less factual, as are Stoker's to Whitman. So, too, is the balance of the fiction pertaining to Hall Caine supported by fact, from the illegality of his marriage to his relationship to Rossetti (who, yes, *did* hope to train an elephant to wash the windows of Tudor House). Ditto the Wildes, the first family of flamboyance, upon whom no fiction could hope to improve.

Stoker *did* work for Henry Irving, and though he of course knew the Lyceum's leading lady, Ellen Terry—who *did* research sundry roles in London asylums, Stoker accompanying her on occasion—their visit to Stepney Latch is as fictitious as the place itself. So too is the novel-ending trip to Edinburgh imagined, though Irving & Co. *did* go there to research their much anticipated *Macbeth*.

Though some famous creatives have been synesthetes—such as Chopin—Stoker, as far as is known, was not one. (Readers wishing to read more about this neurological phenomenon can turn, as I did, to Richard E. Cytowic's *The Man Who Tasted Shapes*.) Stoker *did*, however, lead an unhappy home life, and died mere days after the sinking of the *Titanic*. We can only wonder what the great ship must have heralded for the dying author as it set out from Southampton; for Stoker was always drawn to the sea and the ship's sinking is said to have hastened his end.

Upon his death, Stoker's papers were dispersed via auction, and though the "miscellaneous lot 128" *did* exist, my supposition that Stoker's journal of 1888 was among the auctioned miscellany is just that: a sup-position, for which I claim a fictioneer's prerogative.

The Golden Dawn is represented here as truthfully as fact and fiction allowed, though the location and decoration of the Isis-Urania

No. 3 temple is my own doing. Likewise, all persons mentioned as members of the Golden Dawn are either known, supposed, or reputed to have been members.

The "real" Francis J. Tumblety died in May of 1903 at age seventy-three, in St. Louis. His remains were transported to Rochester, where he was interred in the family tomb. Supposedly.

In researching *The Dracula Dossier,* I have turned to many sources, among which: Leonard Wolf's *Annotated Dracula; Bram Stoker and the Man Who Was Dracula* by Barbara Belford; *From the Shadow of Dracula: A Life of Bram Stoker* by Paul Murray; Stoker's own *Personal Reminiscences of Henry Irving; The Secret Life of Oscar Wilde* by Neil McKenna; *Oscar Wilde* by Richard Ellmann; *Mother of Oscar* by Joy Melville; and *Hall Caine: Portrait of a Victorian Romancer* by Vivien Allen. Regarding the rites and rituals of the Golden Dawn, I am indebted, primarily, to *The Golden Dawn* by Israel Regardie and *The Essential Golden Dawn* by Chic and Sandra Tabatha Cicero.

As regards Jack the Ripper, I owe a special debt to the authors of *Jack the Ripper: First American Serial Killer,* Stewart Evans and Paul Gainey, as well as Philip Sugden, whose *Complete History of Jack the Ripper* is indeed that. And I acknowledge a debt to www.casebook.org, which is, as of this writing, the premier online clearinghouse of Ripperana.

I thank the authors and contributors to all those sources listed above—as well as others too numerous to cite here—and ask, too, that they forgive me for any mistakes made or liberties taken in the crafting of this fiction, the former owing to ignorance, the latter imagination.

I remind the legion of Ripperologists that my aim in writing *The Dracula Dossier* was not to indict Francis J. Tumblety, but rather to explore the life of Bram Stoker. And though Jack the Ripper has evolved into myth, his victims have not. Time has proved them all too mortal, and so it is they and not their murderer—whoever he may have been—who are deserving of remembrance here: Mary Ann Nichols. Annie Chapman. Elizabeth Stride. Catherine Eddowes. Mary Jane Kelly.

A sincere *thank-you* to my editor, Sarah Durand—the same to whom the "Comte de Ville" addresses his letter at the outset of this novel—and my agent, Suzanne Gluck.

And finally, I'd like to thank my own Children of Light, whose love and support sustain me: JER, MMR, PML, MMR, AJL, and MCF.

ABOUT THE TYPE

This book was set in Janson, a typeface long thought to have been made by the Dutchman Anton Janson, who was a practicing typefounder in Leipzig during the years 1668–1687. However, it has been conclusively demonstrated that these types are actually the work of Nicholas Kis (1650–1702), a Hungarian, who most probably learned his trade from the master Dutch typefounder Dirk Voskens. The type is an excellent example of the influential and sturdy Dutch types that prevailed in England up to the time William Caslon (1692–1766) developed his own incomparable designs from them.